Praise for the Dales D...

'Great fun!' – CAROL DRINKWATER

'Chapman delivers on every level in this intriguing
murder mystery' – *Lancashire Evening Post*

'A delightful Dales tale to warm the cockles!'
– *Peterborough Telegraph*

'A rollicking read' – *Craven Herald*

'For above all else, there is warmth and heart to her novels'
– *Yorkshire Times*

'Bags of Yorkshire charm and wit' – *Northern Echo*

'A delightful read' – *Dalesman*

'A classic whodunit set in the spectacular landscape
of the Yorkshire Dales, written with affection for
the area and its people' – CATH STAINCLIFFE

'Charming . . . full of dry wit and clever plotting . . . will
delight and entertain the reader' – *Countryside*

'Nicely told and rather charming, so it should give
traditionalists hours of innocent delight' – *Literary Review*

'An engaging twist on the lonely-hearts killer motif . . .
should leave readers eager for the sequel' –
Publishers Weekly

'An engaging cast of characters and a cleverly clued
puzzle move Chapman's debut to the top of the English
village murder list' – *Kirkus*

Date with Evil

Julia Chapman is the pseudonym of Julia Stagg, who has had five novels, the Fogas Chronicles set in the French Pyrenees, published by Hodder. *Date with Evil* is the eighth in the Dales Detective series, following on from *Date with Betrayal*.

Julia Chapman

DATE WITH EVIL

PAN BOOKS

First published 2023 by Pan Books
an imprint of Pan Macmillan
The Smithson, 6 Briset Street, London EC1M 5NR
EU representative: Macmillan Publishers Ireland Ltd, 1st Floor,
The Liffey Trust Centre, 117–126 Sheriff Street Upper,
Dublin 1, D01 YC43
Associated companies throughout the world
www.panmacmillan.com

ISBN 978-1-5290-9540-1

1 3 5 7 9 8 6 4 2

A CIP catalogue record for this book is available from the British Library.

Map artwork by Hemesh Alles

Typeset by Palimpsest Book Production Limited, Falkirk, Stirlingshire
Printed and bound by CPI Group (UK) Ltd, Croydon, CR0 4YY

Visit **www.panmacmillan.com** to read more about all our books
and to buy them. You will also find features, author interviews and
news of any author events, and you can sign up for e-newsletters
so that you're always first to hear about our new releases.

*For all those
who at some point have found themselves
exiled to a foreign land.*

HORTON →
(MIRE END FARM)

(CR & TWIS

RAINSRIGG QUARRY

HIGH MILL

HORTON ROAD

QUARRY HOUSE

GUNNERSTANG BROW

HARDACRE FARM

HILL TOP CAFE (FORMER HARRISON FARM)

ALLOTMENTS

HAWBER WOODS

THE CROWN

INDUSTRIAL ESTATE & DAIRY

A 65

CRICKET CLUB

LOW MILL

BRUNCLIFFE OLD STATION

RIVER

- HEMESH ALLES -

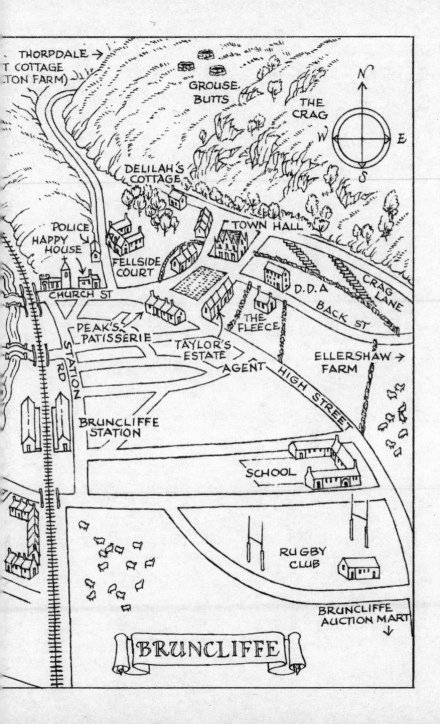

Prologue

The dog was gaining on them. Paws scrabbling across the land as the light faded, taking with it their chances of escape.

'Faster!' A voice guttural with effort and fear came from the man in front.

A grunt, nothing more, from the second man. He was weakening. Legs stumbling. Face stricken with terror. Behind him, the Rottweiler a black mass, two further figures some way beyond it.

There would be no mercy if they were caught. Not least from the beast on their tails, a coil of lethal energy working efficiently, its sole task to hunt them down. A task it was currently doing very well, the distance reducing with every bound of muscle. No bark. Just that heavy panting. And those teeth, stark against the growing gloom.

A short cry as the second man stumbled over the uneven terrain, staggering forward, exhaustion showing as he struggled to recover his balance. 'I can't make it,' he gasped. 'Go on without me.'

'No!' The rebuke from the older man sharper than intended, even though their flight was useless. They were dead. Nothing ahead to offer shelter. No one around. Just the isolated hills that loomed over them, hemming them in as the dusk slipped further into night.

A last desperate glance over his shoulder, the dog even closer. It would only be a few minutes before the animal leaped. Taking the weaker of the two.

'Please, Grigore, just leave me.' It came out as a plea. 'For Mama's sake.'

Grigore didn't reply. The thought of going back without Pavel worse than neither of them making it home. Instead, he grabbed his brother's elbow, bone prominent beneath his fingers as he dragged him on. And he found himself praying. Hopelessly.

But still that relentless pursuit from the dog. A shout carrying from the chasing party. Would they shoot? Take the risk? From what he'd seen of them, Grigore didn't think they'd care. They were ruthless.

'Grigore! I can't . . .'

His brother slipping from his grasp, one foot sliding out from under him, his full weight – what was left of it – falling onto Grigore and then they were both sinking, the soil sucking at them, dragging at their shoes.

Sinking!

The miracle he'd been praying for.

With a superhuman effort, Grigore hauled Pavel back to his feet and onto a clump of reeds. They were at the edge of a wide expanse of bog, the bleak brown land stretching in all directions, the ground underfoot no longer firm. No longer safe. Impossible to cross, which meant turning back and facing their pursuers.

Unless you were born to it, raised in an area where such terrain was second nature . . .

It was risky. One wrong step and it would be fatal. But it was their only chance.

'We can do this!' Grigore said. 'Just follow me the way we used to follow Papa.'

Pavel nodded, a spark of hope as he looked back once more at the Rottweiler and then at the land ahead, moss gleaming wetly, the white heads of cotton grass bobbing in the wind.

With a leap of faith, Grigore started striding, feet landing on tufts, confident in his footing as he pushed thickets of reeds over underneath him. His brother the same, both of them fuelled by sudden optimism. Four strides, four more. Zigzagging haphazardly further and further across the uncertain terrain, their direction dictated only by the solidity of the land beneath their feet. Two more long leaps and he looked back.

The dog had faltered, a whine of confusion as his paws hit the moist ground. He retreated, turned an unsure circle. A vexed shout met its hesitation, commanding it on. It was trained to obey. And so it jumped, a huge leap, covering most of the distance the brothers' erratic progress had put between them.

'Grigore!' Pavel screamed, as the dog lunged.

The Rottweiler landed just short of him, front paws hitting the ground with all its weight, preparing to spring again. Pavel froze, Grigore awash with terror.

Then that sound. The squelch of wet land. The dog clearly puzzled as its legs started to sink. Panic set in, the Rottweiler beginning to thrash around. Doing exactly what it shouldn't as the mire began to claim it.

The men behind were gaining, still yelling at the dog,

ordering it to attack, oblivious to what was happening. They were close enough that Grigore could make out the glint of guns in their hands.

'Hurry!' he shouted, urging Pavel after him as he resumed his negotiation of the treacherous land. It might have stopped the dog, but it wouldn't stop the bullets the men would soon be firing. And if they made it to the other side, what then for the brothers? In his weakened state, Pavel wouldn't be able to run for much longer.

Curses now, carrying over the darkening landscape. The men had reached the edge of the bog. Had realised the double impediments to their pursuit, their first means of attack yelping in pain. In normal circumstances, Grigore would have turned back to help, never one to ignore animals in distress. But these weren't normal circumstances.

A loud splash. More curses. The men trying to reach the distraught Rottweiler.

Grigore kept striding, his brother's shadow in his peripheral vision, until his feet hit solid ground. Or what passed for solid ground in this sodden wilderness. Only then did he turn, helping Pavel to his side and staring back across the morass. The men had managed to reach the Rottweiler and were hauling it to safety. It wouldn't be long before they circumvented this obstacle and were back on the hunt again.

The ragged breaths from his brother told Grigore all he needed to know. Running was out of the question. They needed to find somewhere to hide. And quickly.

He scanned the hills encircling them on three sides. He was well acquainted with this terrain even though he'd never been here before. The crag-topped fells, the spectacular

4

limestone pavement. He'd been born in mountains such as these and knew the wealth of opportunities to hide up there – a cave perhaps, some hollow in the limestone that could offer them sanctuary until the hunters gave up?

A harsh cough from Pavel, who was leaning against his brother, one hand clasped to his side. Broken ribs, Grigore suspected. The man was in no shape to make it up the steep slopes. And besides, the dog would track them easily up there.

'What now?' Pavel asked wearily.

What indeed. In an ideal world, treatment, food and warmth. And a guardian angel to keep them safe.

Even as he thought it, Grigore felt the wind change, as though he'd conjured up a divine messenger which was now whispering to him from behind. He turned, feeling the breeze on his cheek, seeing the hunters across the bog. Hunters who were no longer able to rely on scenting their prey. No longer able to rely on the light either.

'This way,' said Grigore, pointing away from the safety of the hills, to where the valley narrowed into a bottleneck.

Trying to look more confident than he felt, he led his brother into the dark.

1

Barbara Hargreaves wasn't one for losing her temper. A working life lived serving the good folk of Bruncliffe their weekly rations of meat across the counter of her husband's shop had smoothed away any of the irascible edges she'd once had. But if there was one thing that was likely to rise her ire in these her middle ages, it was having her time wasted. And so as she sat in the office of the Dales Detective Agency on that Monday morning, late spring sunshine shining down on the narrow street outside, she was doing her best to bite her tongue.

Because her time was most certainly being wasted.

She didn't in any way suspect it was personal or malicious. It was just that the place was in meltdown.

The desk before her was littered with paperwork, pages spilling out of folders, post-it notes stuck haphazardly on whatever bits of the surface could be seen, and three abandoned mugs were perched perilously close to the edge, dull, milky residues of undrunk tea in the bottom. The multiple circles staining the metal suggested the mugs had been there for some days, if not weeks. In the corner of the room, the ancient filing cabinet had two drawers hanging open, a pile of suspension files dumped on the floor as though someone had been interrupted in the process of trying to impose order on the chaos, but had only added to the disarray. And the dust balls collecting on the peeling lino were doing nothing to alleviate Barbara's sense that things were falling apart. Not to mention she'd been in the office more than ten minutes and hadn't even been offered a cuppa.

As to how her issue was being dealt with? Well, it wasn't what Barbara had come to expect from Bruncliffe's detective agency.

'Two weeks ago I asked you to look into this,' she stated, arms folded across her substantial front. 'I've yet to hear a word on how you're progressing.'

'We've been a bit busy,' came the terse reply. 'Just remind me what went missing—'

'Stolen!' said Barbara sharply. 'It was stolen. Two pairs of Ken's jeans, a couple of T-shirts, a Bruncliffe rugby top and a hoodie, taken off the washing line the day everything kicked off.'

She had no need to elaborate as to which particular day she was referring to. The entire town was still reeling from the events that Saturday a fortnight ago, when a hitman had come to Bruncliffe to target Samson O'Brien, the man behind the very agency she was now calling on.

'As I said the following Monday when I stopped by to report it, I don't normally leave washing out overnight, but things got a bit out of hand across the road.' She tipped her head towards the Fleece, its sullen front visible through the window. 'Happen I wasn't best sorted for dealing with it when I got home.'

Staggered home, her and Ken, his arm around her as she sang her way back to the butcher's shop and their apartment over it, her good mood oiled by more than a couple of glasses of prosecco in the post-hitman celebrations. So oiled in fact that she hadn't been able to rise from her bed the next day until the morning was well advanced. And hadn't in fact realised her washing had been stolen until late afternoon when she'd finally remembered it was still out on the line.

'And they haven't turned up?'

Barbara snorted. 'A fortnight on and that's all you've got to offer me?'

'Like I said, we've been busy!' The tone was sharper, a defiant jaw sticking out like a pugilist intent on fighting. But the sudden burst of a phone ringing broke the brittle tension, prompting a flurry of searching on the desk before the mobile was located under what looked like a packet of dog biscuits. 'Dales Detective Agency?'

The curt greeting prompted a torrent of language on the other end, Barbara hearing only muted squawks. Judging by the heavy sigh they triggered, she was guessing it was yet another dissatisfied customer.

She waited while the call was dealt with, using the time to gather in the loose ends of her fraying patience, while another phone rang unanswered somewhere in the building.

'Right!' The mobile was slapped back onto the desk, a glare cast in its direction, before Barbara became the centre of attention once more. 'Where were we? The missing laundry—'

'What you need,' said Barbara Hargreaves, her mood swinging to one of compassion for this fellow townsperson who was unravelling so spectacularly before her eyes, 'is some help.'

Ida Capstick lowered the pen she'd been holding, rubbed a hand across her weary face and nodded. 'Tha's not wrong there,' she said.

On the floor above, James 'Herriot' Ellison was in a meeting in a room in a similar state of dishevelment, and was similarly ill at ease. But unlike Mrs Hargreaves, his discomfort didn't arise from the air of neglect being fostered by the unwashed mugs, the messy desk, the piles of paperwork on the nearby sofa and the slightly stale air that smelled of damp dog and running shoes. His discomfort was all of his own making.

He wasn't the most outgoing of folk anyway, apart from when it came to sheep or cows or the pets of Bruncliffe. Then he was confident in his knowledge, providing an exceptional level of veterinary care that had earned him both the respect of the town and, given that this was the Yorkshire Dales, his nickname. But this?

He was in a whole new world. One that made him squirm and pull at the collar of his checked shirt, which seemed to have shrunk around his Adam's apple in the last few minutes. The constant ringing of the mobile on the desk in front of him wasn't helping any.

'Are you going to get that?' he finally asked.

The woman opposite glanced up from her laptop screen, looked at the phone and shook her head. 'Too busy,' she said. 'Last thing I need is more clients.'

'Not a bad way to be,' said Herriot, with a lopsided smile.

Delilah Metcalfe grimaced. 'Time was I'd have agreed with you. But now . . .' She exhaled, a sigh far older than her years, the frown on her forehead making her look like she was carrying the world on her shoulders. 'So, Speedy Date night, is it?'

The tone was devoid of nuance but still Herriot blushed. 'Yes. Please. I mean, you know, thought I'd give it a try. I mean, what harm could it do?'

The words of encouragement he'd been hoping for from the owner of the Dales Dating Agency, something to calm his nerves, didn't materialise. Instead Delilah had her head tipped to one side, pen resting against her bottom lip as though she was giving his question serious thought. Deciding he didn't want to hear whatever answer she might conjure up, he changed the topic.

'How's the arm?'

She shrugged, her right hand going to her left shoulder. 'A bit stiff. But healing.'

A bit stiff. An innocuous way to describe the after-effects of being shot, Delilah having been one of several walking wounded following the shocking events of two weeks ago.

'Does it hurt still?'

Delilah shook her head. 'Not so much,' she said. 'Just as well, as I haven't had time to rest it seeing as we're a man down.'

'Have you had any word from Samson? Do you know when he's coming back?'

In the corner of the room, a grey head lifted off crossed paws, Delilah's Weimaraner Tolpuddle suddenly looking alert at the name. Delilah, however, winced, her hand dropping to her heart, as though that was where the worst pain resided.

'He's busy.' Her words were clipped, inviting no more

enquiries. 'Right, you're booked in for three weeks from now, Tuesday twenty-first.' She clicked a few more keys and then looked at him expectantly. All business. 'Anything else?'

There *was* something else, but somehow he couldn't force the words past his lips. So instead he heard himself saying something completely different.

'Actually, just an oddity I thought I'd run past you and Samson. Someone dropped a dog off at the surgery last week. Left it outside on the doorstep, rang the bell, and did a runner. By the time I opened the door, they'd gone.'

'You don't know who they are?'

'Not a clue.'

'How bizarre.' But despite her acknowledgement that this was indeed strange, Delilah's eyes flicked to her watch, her attention being pulled back to her mountain of work.

'Anyway,' Herriot continued, speaking faster, 'the dog had a bad cut to its leg which was infected and needed urgent treatment. But what was more interesting was that whoever brought it to me had sedated it before dropping it off. With ketamine.'

Her focus sharpened back onto the vet, an eyebrow going up. 'Ketamine?'

It was a drug which had unfortunately become common parlance in Bruncliffe over the last seven months, showing up most recently in the lurchers left behind by Pete Ferris when he'd taken his own life, the poacher having presumably intended to bring them with him to the afterlife. Luckily for the dogs, the dose had been non-fatal.

'Thought that might interest you.'

But Delilah was merely nodding, turning back to her

laptop, her mind moving onto the next task. 'I'll make a note,' she was saying, and Herriot found himself standing and walking towards the door.

He was almost there when he turned around, trying so hard to be casual. 'Oh, I meant to ask, is anyone else going to the date night? I mean, anyone I know?'

The mobile started ringing again and this time Delilah reached for it, answering him distractedly.

'Off the top of my head, Elaine Bullock, Frank Thistlethwaite, Hannah Wilson . . . Oh, and Lucy. She signed up on Friday.'

Delilah's widowed sister-in-law, Lucy Metcalfe, would be at the Speedy Date night. Which, of course, Herriot already knew. Which, of course, was why Herriot was here.

'Thanks,' he said, feeling the sense of reassurance he'd been seeking; a sensation that was swiftly followed by terror.

Delilah smiled, nodded, but was already talking on the phone. He'd reached the door when she called his name.

'Herriot, just a sec,' she said, covering the mobile with her hand, her gaze finally curious. 'Why did they need to anaesthetise the dog?'

'Because it was a Rottweiler.'

Her eyes widened. Then she turned back to the call, leaving Herriot to depart the building in a turmoil of emotions.

Grigore woke with a start, torn from a dream where Pavel was being dragged to the ground by the strong jaws of the Rottweiler. Heart thumping, he lay there, listening. Wondering if he'd shouted. If he'd given them away.

The sound of hens clucking and scratching unconcernedly came from the other side of the closed door, a crack of light filtering through, telling of a fine day outside. Of a warm sun, which Grigore suddenly had an overwhelming desire to feel on his face after so long confined to the chill air of their hiding place. Beside him came the uneven rasp of Pavel's breath. He was asleep. A combination of pain and hunger having finally worn him out.

It wasn't ideal, this situation they were in. But Grigore couldn't see any way out of it. To keep running was impossible with Pavel's condition as it was, yet every day they waited was a day closer to being discovered. A day closer to being found and forced back into the hell they had fled from. Something he would do anything to avoid, even kill again if necessary.

Another few days, and then they might be able to resume their escape. But even as Grigore tried to convince himself of this, his brother's breath caught and he woke with a sharp cough which made him groan in pain.

'Shush!' Grigore clamped a hand over Pavel's mouth, the panic that had subsided flooding back as the hens fell silent. He could imagine them, heads raised, looking round for the source of the unexpected noise.

One second passed, another, countless more, as the brothers lay there, Pavel's face damp under Grigore's touch. And then the sound that Grigore had been dreading. The loud screech of the door being pulled open below. Sunlight flooding the interior and bringing with it men's voices.

Pavel whimpered and tucked himself even tighter into Grigore's side in the confines of their hiding place.

2

'Tha needs to call him. Tell him to come back.'

Delilah shook her head with a strength of feeling that belied her exhaustion. 'It's not happening.'

'Aye, well, it's either that or we throw in the towel,' Ida muttered, thumping her mug onto the small table in the upstairs kitchen where the two women had sat to share the details of their respective mornings, neither of which could have been termed successful. 'Because there's no way we can keep going as we are, lass.'

The shrill demand of unanswered phones emanating from the two empty offices punctuated Ida's weary words, underlining her point. They were overworked and understaffed.

Lying in front of the cooker, Tolpuddle was watching the women with an anxious gaze. Not only was he mourning the abrupt termination of the treats he'd become accustomed to, Ida no longer having time to clean, let alone rustle up bacon butties first thing, but the Weimaraner also hadn't taken particularly well to the recent changes in personnel. Or to be more precise, the recent loss of a certain person. Already ridden with anxiety, Delilah's dog looked on the verge of lapsing back into the stress-induced behaviour that had once been his hallmark.

He wasn't the only one.

Two weeks they'd been staggering under the weight of trying to keep the Dales Detective Agency going while also managing the ridiculously successful Dales Dating Agency as well as Delilah's website design business, not to mention Ida keeping up her various cleaning commitments. And while Delilah had to give Ida Capstick the credit she deserved, the cleaner having turned herself into an admirable admin assistant in the last few months, the brusque Daleswoman was no detective.

Delilah wasn't even sure she deserved the mantle herself, come to think of it.

'He'd come if tha called him. Tha knows he would,' Ida persisted. 'Like a shot.'

It was true. But it didn't mean Delilah was going to succumb and make the call. Because if there was one trait she'd inherited from the Metcalfe side of the family – her fiery temper and strong right hook having always been attributed to her mother's folk – it was stubbornness. And over this particular issue, she felt very stubborn.

She would not be begging Samson O'Brien to come home any time soon.

For a start, the memory of waking fully clothed and alone in his bed on the top storey of the office building a fortnight ago, full of expectation for the start of their new relationship, was still too raw. The expectation had held until she'd padded out onto the landing and realised how quiet the place was. No sound coming from the kitchen on the floor below. No affectionate reply to her shout of good morning. Arm in a sling, she'd made her way down to the ground floor and found Tolpuddle, lying outside Samson's office, head on his paws, a note tucked into his collar.

Samson was gone. To London. No kiss goodbye – not one she was awake for, at any rate. No idea of how long he'd be away. His previous life had come calling and he hadn't been able to leave quickly enough.

The hurt had been intense. Almost as bad as being shot. But Delilah Metcalfe was nothing if not pragmatic, every bit as durable as the stone walls that criss-crossed the fields and fells beyond the town. So she'd set about running things until such times as Samson returned, Ida volunteering to help out.

Thus stubbornness was one obstacle in the way of her making the first move. The other factor was even harder to overcome: Delilah wasn't sure that Bruncliffe was home for Samson any longer. Events in the last month had granted him the opportunity to resume his former profession, and although at present he was only helping out with enquiries into his corrupt former boss, DI Warren, it wouldn't be long before he was fully reinstated and offered the chance to pick up where he'd left off. To resume his life as an undercover officer with the National Crime Agency.

Which was where the problem lay. Because while Delilah loved Samson with a passion that befitted her temperament, she wasn't prepared to stand between him and his career. Deciding to come back to Bruncliffe had to be his choice. And his alone.

'Not like I can get hold of him anyway,' she muttered, gesturing over her shoulder towards the incessant ringing from downstairs, where Samson's mobile lay on what was now Ida's desk. Helpfully left behind by its owner so that

Julia Chapman

the running of the Dales Detective Agency could carry on uninterrupted in his absence, its continued presence in the office had effectively severed communication between Bruncliffe and its black sheep. Samson had disappeared as suddenly and as totally as he had fifteen years ago, and had shown no inclination in the last fortnight to make contact.

If Delilah had needed any further impetus to withhold communication, this was it.

'I don't have a number for him,' she concluded churlishly.

Ida snorted before reaching in the pocket of her apron and slapping a business card on the table like an ace out of her sleeve. 'That DC Green lass gave me this before she left. She'll be able to get a message to him.' A stern finger jabbed at the number of the woman who'd been Samson's support officer while he'd been suspended, and a key part of the investigation into Warren. 'If tha doesn't make the call, I will!' She grunted, rubbing her knees with a bony hand. 'Not sure as I can take much more of this sitting behind a desk lark. Not something I'm cut out for. Besides, I've got enough on my plate.'

There was something in the grumble, a quaver of worry beneath the gruff tone, sufficient to make Delilah put down her own mug and focus on this woman who had become such a large part of her life.

'Is everything okay?'

Ida pursed her lips, as though deciding how much to divulge. Then she shrugged. 'It's George. He keeps on saying that there's something paranormal going on up at the house, like he thinks the place is riddled with ghosts.'

Anyone else uttering those words, Delilah would have laughed. But this was Ida, a no-nonsense woman who didn't make light of life. Especially not when it came to her brother.

'He's stressed,' Ida continued. 'Even more than usual.'

'Have you tried talking to him?'

'Aye, but all I get is some witterings about supernatural activities and then he starts back up with those blasted tractor statistics.' Ida sighed. 'Reckon I'll know more about the Fordson Model N than anyone at this rate.'

Delilah didn't say anything, thinking about the man in question and the way he anchored himself through life by reciting random information about whichever vintage tractor he was working on at the time. She was also thinking about the remote cottage at the start of Thorpdale, the brother and sister living there alone since their parents had passed away. With its ramshackle outbuildings and the wild land around it, it was a property that would inspire talk of the paranormal in the most orthodox of minds. And George's mind was far from orthodox.

'Have you had a look around? I mean, checked to see if—'

'If there's a ghoul lurking in the barn?' The look Ida gave Delilah was as withering as an easterly wind blowing over the Crag that loomed above Bruncliffe. 'Happen tha's getting as addled as George. Must be all this work. Talking of which, these cases won't solve themselves.' She got to her feet, a red marker pen in her hand, and turned to the whiteboard which she'd insisted on being installed above the table the week before, in an effort to bring order to their chaos.

'Right then, lass, where do we start?'

Delilah looked at the items listed in Ida's neat,

unpretentious handwriting, and her heart plummeted. While her colleague's idea to provide a place where all of the agency's cases – plus the business generated by Delilah's own enterprises – could be seen at one time had been a good one, in the current situation, seeing the sheer volume of projects they'd agreed to take on felt overwhelming. It was tempting to just pull down the privacy cover that had come with the board, and hide it all from sight.

Even Ida seemed to blanch as she stared at her creation.

'What you need to do,' said a voice from the landing, 'is triage!'

Delilah and Ida turned to see young Nina Hussain standing there, holding up Samson's mobile and Ida's notebook in her right hand.

'I heard you needed help,' she said. 'So I took the liberty of answering the phone on my way up. And I've brought some treats from the restaurant.' She held up a brown bag in her other hand, smells wonderful enough to have Tolpuddle lifting his head in anticipation issuing from within.

With the light from Delilah's office spilling over her shoulders and the wide chiffon sleeves of her summer top hanging down from her slender arms, the teenager looked the closest to an angel the beleaguered Dales Detective Agency team had ever seen.

While Delilah and Ida were seeing angels, up above Bruncliffe, in the shadow of the abandoned quarry on Gunnerstang Brow, PC Danny Bradley had a feeling that whatever was behind the back door of the unoccupied foreman's cottage, it was going to be far from divine.

He looked at the broken pane of glass, a jagged hole punched just above the handle. Large enough for an arm to fit through and turn the key protruding from the lock on the inside. A classic method of breaking and entering.

Trying not to let his nerves show, the stark landscape of Rainsrigg Quarry always giving him the jitters, he turned the handle and pushed the door open. A loud screech of oil-starved hinges made him jump.

As did the voice from behind.

'Probably summat and nothing,' Jimmy Thornton was saying, a farmer who'd been raised at Quarry House and whose mother had been its last tenant. Since her death at the beginning of the year, the cottage had lain empty. 'Just thought I'd best call it in. You know, after all the goings on up here the other week.' He gestured over his shoulder at the crime-scene tape flapping in the slight breeze over by one of the Portakabins.

'You did right,' said Danny, managing to steady his voice as he stepped over the broken glass and into the kitchen.

Jimmy made no move to follow him, remaining at the back door, the scarred wall of the quarried fellside rearing up behind him.

'Did you notice anything missing when you arrived?' Danny asked, casting a glance around the room. No longer the heart of the Thornton family home, it had adopted the same aura of desolation as the worksite it had once presided over. Cupboard doors hanging open revealing bare shelves. A chipped cup and a handleless saucepan left on the dusty worktop. And that smell – the damp, lonely scent of a place unloved and unlived in.

'Not as such. Thing is, I was only popping into the barn

to pick up the last of Mother's stuff as I've just been informed the owners are putting the quarry on the market. Rumour is Rick Procter'll snap it up – turn it round like he's apparently going doing with the Harrisons' old place.' Jimmy nodded in the direction of the road and the abandoned cafe that sat at the top of Gunnerstang Brow, a hint of derision entering his voice. 'Because more chic flats are just what the town needs.'

Not in a position to question the farmer's theorising where Bruncliffe's most successful property developer was concerned, Danny gently steered the conversation back onto topic.

'So you didn't come in the house at all?' he asked.

The answering shrug was accompanied by an embarrassed grin. 'No. To be honest, I got a bit spooked.'

Danny didn't blame him. The oppressive rockface looming over the place, the rusting machinery and the melancholy moan of the wind were enough to give anyone the creeps, notwithstanding the fact that there'd been two major incidents up here in the last four months. The young constable had been involved in both and was still having nightmares about the latest, waking up sweating in the small hours, haunted by the image of Delilah Metcalfe lying in a pool of blood on the dusty ground.

'Do you think it's connected, like? To that nasty business Samson was caught up in?' Jimmy's questions had mirrored Danny's thoughts.

'Possibly. Although I'm surprised the detectives didn't notice this when they were up here processing the crime scene.'

The kidnap and shooting which had transpired two weeks

ago had been serious enough to warrant a major police presence in its aftermath, the quarry a centre of activity in the following days in a way it hadn't been in years. And yet, no one – including Danny himself, who had shadowed the investigators, eager to add knowledge to that gained so far in his fledgling career – had noticed the broken door.

Jimmy scratched his head. 'To be fair, I almost didn't spot it. It was only as I was carrying the boxes to the car that I saw the light glinting on one of the broken shards and walked over to see what it was.'

'So I'm guessing there was nothing much in here to steal?'

'Bugger all. Livvy and I cleared it out before she went back to Australia. We left the bedroom curtains and a few bits of furniture that came with the place, but they're so old, no one in their right mind would take them.' He looked at his watch and pulled a face. 'Sorry, Danny, but I've got to go. Got a feed delivery coming and I don't want Gemma trying to lift those bags because I'm not there – baby's due soon.'

'No worries.' Danny waved away the apology. 'Tell her I was asking after her.'

With one last nod, Jimmy turned and left, the sound of his Land Rover rattling into the distance until it disappeared, an eerie stillness falling once more on Quarry House.

Danny's unease came stealing back, too. 'It's just a routine break in,' he muttered as he took another long look around the kitchen. 'Just kids larking about—'

He paused. Something wasn't right. He'd sensed it when he walked in but hadn't been able to put a finger on it. Now, in the ghostly silence, it seemed obvious.

Dust. A thick layer of it over pretty much everything. But not in the sink or on the taps.

He crossed the slate floor and examined the saucepan, picking it up with the sleeve of his jumper. Clean inside, a few drops of water in the bottom. Same with the cup.

They'd both been used recently. And if he was sticking to his kids-having-fun theory, they'd had their fun while sitting at the table, one end of it and a couple of chairs also free of dust. Which didn't seem remotely realistic.

He turned to the old Rayburn that dominated one wall, no longer confident he was investigating something as simple as bored locals. A quick glance at the hotplate cover on the left showed recent use, unlike its dusty counterpart on the right. He lifted it, saw a smear of something yellow on the cooking surface beneath. Egg?

Knowing Jimmy's mother had been extremely house-proud, he doubted it was a remnant from her time, so what on earth . . . ?

Someone had broken into the house to eat their breakfast? And stayed a while. Until something had made them move on.

Danny stooped down and checked the fuel control valve at the side of the range. It was switched on, and yet the stove was cold. There was no way Jimmy would have left the Rayburn running after he'd finished clearing out the house, which suggested that whoever had broken in had turned it on, and then run out of oil.

Perhaps that was what had made them leave? While it was almost the end of May and the daytime temperatures were hitting the high teens, the nights were still capable of dropping down to low single figures. Especially up here in the bleakest of spots. The house wouldn't have been the warmest of havens once the Rayburn stopped working.

Better than sleeping under a hedgerow, though. Especially as hedgerows were few and far between in this part of the Dales, where stone walls lined the fields.

The fluttering blue-and-white tape outside caught Danny's eye. He stared out of the window, revising his theory. Maybe it was heat problems of a different sort that had caused the departure? Perhaps all the commotion when the police descended on the quarry in the wake of the shooting had been enough to scare the squatter off?

A sound from overhead made Danny startle.

Or perhaps, he reassessed nervously, whoever it was hadn't been scared off at all?

Feeling far from brave, he eased open the door into the hallway and began to inch his way towards the stairs.

It was the Devil. Grigore was sure of it. That voice. He'd only heard a few muffled words through the floor but it had been enough to make his insides twist with terror.

Next to him, Pavel had gone unnaturally still, the statue-like stance of a rabbit cornered by a stoat, he too sensing the danger.

They'd lain there while the men murmured below, Grigore having to fight the instinct to steal a glance down, knowing that any movement at all would give them away. Finally there'd been the sound of a car departing. But the relief had been short-lived.

A period of silence and then small noises, someone pottering around, prying into things, as though looking for something. Someone.

And now, footsteps, coming closer.

Grigore could feel Pavel beginning to shake. If they were

discovered, it was all over. There'd be no second chances. Just a bullet each in the head, bodies disposed of somewhere remote. Because Grigore had seen the Devil's work first-hand and knew to expect no mercy.

Of all the places they could have hidden, somehow they'd ended right back in the same trap.

He cursed himself for not having taken a chance on the limestone hills, which would have at least provided a last glimpse of the blue sky and the warmth of the May sunshine on his face before death came calling. Better than this grim hideout where they'd been holed up in the dark for eight days.

Another sound below.

Grigore softly got to his feet, reached out his hand and curled his fingers around cold metal. The closest thing he had to a weapon. Stupidly he'd left behind the one he'd made. The one that had proved so useful. He picked up the substitute, knowing he'd have no qualms in using it to protect himself and his brother if anyone appeared up here. He'd killed before. Condemned a second man to certain death through his actions. A third time would be easier.

Taking up his stance by the only exit, he was fervently hoping it wouldn't come to that.

But then Pavel coughed again.

3

'*Triage?*' Out of Ida's mouth, the word sounded like something fancy on a menu she had no intention of ordering.

Having shocked the Dales Detective team into silence, Nina had entered the kitchen, found some plates in a cupboard, served up the samosas – earning Tolpuddle's eternal devotion by popping one in his bowl – and then leaned up against the counter, arms folded across her chest, a challenge Delilah recognised from the repertoire of her teenage nephew, Nathan.

'So, can I work here or what?' she'd demanded.

'How did tha hear we needed help?' Ida had been first to find her voice.

'I was in Peaks Patisserie with some friends and heard Mrs Hargreaves telling Elaine Bullock that she thought you were understaffed, and seeing as I'm on half-term this week, I thought I'd offer my services. But if you're not interested—'

'What makes thee think tha's qualified, lass?'

A shrug. Less confident now. 'I know how to answer a phone. And take notes.' Nina looked at Delilah. 'I'm a hard worker. You can ask Dad.'

Delilah didn't need to ask Kamal Hussain about the work

ethic of his oldest child. She'd seen if for herself at Rice N Spice, the teenager helping run front of house in her father's restaurant three nights a week. 'What does your dad think about you working here?' she asked instead. 'Haven't you got your GCSEs coming up this summer?'

'He's fine with it.' Nina grinned. 'He thinks you and Samson are good role models.'

'Huh!' muttered Ida, reaching for her second samosa.

'But why here?' Delilah had continued. 'Why this line of work?'

Nina's face had become serious. 'Actually, I was already planning on asking if I could work the summer with you, as an intern or something. See, thing is,' her head dipped, her bravado dropping with it until she became almost shy, 'I want to join the police. And I was thinking this would be good experience.'

'None better,' said Ida. 'But tha'll need to have an interview.'

Delilah glanced at her colleague, wondering how this criteria had suddenly become mandatory when Ida had added herself to the team without so much as an informal chat. As had Delilah, come to think of it.

But Nina had nodded, as though she'd expected nothing less.

'In the meantime, get the kettle on, lass, and tell us what tha meant by . . . what was that expression tha used?'

'Triage,' Nina had offered, pouring warm water into the teapot and swilling it round while the kettle boiled.

Which was when Ida repeated the word with her own unique inflection.

Nina wasn't put off. 'It's a medical term,' she continued, scooping three teaspoons of tea into the pot. She added the boiling water, pulled on the tea cosy and turned back to her audience. 'My cousin is a doctor in A&E. She uses it all the time. Basically we sort out which of these cases deserve urgent attention and which can wait. Then we target our focus where it's needed most.'

Ida looked from the newcomer to the whiteboard and back again, this time granting a small nod in Nina's direction.

'Sounds like a brilliant idea,' said Delilah.

Nina's grin re-emerged, her arms folding across her chest once more. 'Reckon I'll be good at this detecting lark.'

'Lark?' Ida's face fell back into its customary scowl, her tone harsh enough to make Tolpuddle pick up his ears. 'This is no game, lass. Happen as Samson and Delilah have had enough brushes with death in the past seven months to make Lazarus seem like an amateur. If it's larks tha's looking for, tha's in the wrong place.'

'I didn't mean . . . I wasn't . . .' Nina stammered, her cheeks darkening.

'It's okay,' said Delilah. 'No one is suggesting you're taking this lightly. But Ida is right. This job has its dangers. It's important you understand that.'

Nina nodded, turning to pour the tea in an attempt to hide her upset. When she turned back, it was to place a mug each in front of the two women.

'Thanks,' said Delilah.

Ida said nothing. Just stared at the liquid, its milky colour, the strong odour of well-brewed tea rising from it. She raised the mug to her lips, took a sip, and grunted, a look akin to bliss passing over her granite features.

'Go grab a chair from Delilah's office, lass,' she said to Nina. 'Tha's hired.'

Danny Bradley's heart was rattling as he paused on the dog-leg of the stairs of Quarry House. He'd been climbing slowly, back against the wall, feet placed right on the inside of each step in an attempt to avoid squeaky boards. But as his pulse reached levels he wasn't sure were safe, he found himself debating the wisdom of this approach, wondering if a fast run up to the landing wouldn't have been better, offering the element of surprise.

Then he heard the cough.

A hacking sound. Definitely from above. From the room on the right of the small hallway, where the door was ajar.

Baton in hand, he flung caution to the wind and took the remaining steps two at a time, hurling himself towards the door. Through it. Shouting 'Police!' as he burst into the room to be confronted by . . .

A feral cat standing on a pile of material, hissing back at him, a hairball in front of it on the threadbare carpet.

They stood there for a few seconds, staring at each other, both almost dead with fright. Then the cat shot out between Danny's legs and thumped down the stairs, leaving the constable to sag against the old dressing table inside the door.

A cat. Bringing up a hairball. Danny was already making the decision that this incident wouldn't be finding its way into his report. It would be all over town and he'd hear nothing but cat-burglar wisecracks for the rest of his career.

Deciding he might as well do a thorough inspection of the property while he was there, he crossed the room for a closer look at what the cat had been using as a bed. The bedroom curtains Jimmy had mentioned, he surmised, glancing at the bare window as he pulled the material up off the floor. But not just one set, judging by the six lengths of varied cloth in his hands.

Someone had taken down the curtains and dumped them all on the floor in this one room. Jimmy and his sister, Livvy, when they were clearing out the place? Danny doubted it. Why would they have done that?

The policeman stared at the faded fabric, aware of the weight of it. Aware it would have provided warmth for someone sleeping rough. A makeshift bed which had since been usurped by the cat.

He gave the curtains a speculative shake, something falling from their folds to the carpet. Not sure what it was at first, he prodded it with his boot, the light catching the sharp edges and making it clearer.

A knife, crudely fashioned from a spoon, the handle honed to form a blade, twine wrapped around the other end. Basic but effective, judging by the dark smear encrusted on the metal.

Deciding this definitely hadn't been left by the Thorntons, Danny reached into his pocket for one of the plastic bags he always carried in case he happened upon evidence – much to Sergeant Clayton's amusement – and placed the knife inside it. He'd been right to be cautious when he'd begun searching the premises – here was an indicator of yet more violence at Quarry House, a property that seemed to be seeped in it.

Spurred on by his find, he began conducting a more thorough inspection of the remaining rooms. Which is how, when he went back down to the kitchen, he spotted something else. Something under the table. He bent down, looked at it, and felt his memory stirring.

Unable to forge any connection between his two discoveries, Danny realised he needed help. Luckily, he knew just who to call.

At about the same time as Danny had arrived at Quarry House, across town and up over the fells to the north, at the start of the isolated Thorpdale, George Capstick's morning had begun to get interesting. And in George's world, interesting was not something to aspire to.

Having spent an hour replacing a tap in the kitchen that had finally died after a long life of servitude, he'd crossed the yard, ready to continue work on the troublesome carburettor from a Fordson Model N he was restoring. He'd been in the process of opening the barn door when he heard two unwelcome sounds. One was like the tortured moan of the wind through the porch when an easterly blew down the dale. The other was a vehicle in the distance, coming up the track from the direction of Bruncliffe.

The vehicle took prior claim on his attention, making him pause, the barn door half open behind him. Because George recognised the engine.

A Range Rover.

He stood facing the road, waiting for the 4x4 to come into sight, hoping it would drive straight past and on to Twistleton Farm, the only other dwelling in this remote dale. But it didn't. It pulled into the yard and the driver got out.

'Where's Ida?' the man demanded.

'Three-speed gearbox hand-cranked not here,' George muttered back, the tractor statistics his buffer against the jangle of agitation which had set up in his finely wired brain at this intrusion into his ordered world.

He shifted from one leg to the other, focus fixed on the ground because he found communication with other people difficult. Looking them in the eyes just added to the trauma.

'Right. Well, I need to check your barn.'

George blinked several times, trying to process the statement. The barn was his space. His alone. Even Ida never went in it without asking him first. It was the one place on the planet where he didn't have to try to fit in with the rest of humanity. He was still striving to formulate a reply to this impossible situation when, to his consternation, the man started striding towards him. George snapped his gaze up from the concrete and took a step backwards, blocking the door.

'Four-cylinder gasoline no entry!'

'Don't be stupid, George,' snapped the man, still walking forwards. An arm reaching out to push him aside. 'This is really important—'

The sentence ended abruptly as George found himself brandishing the tool he'd been using that morning.

'Twenty-four-inch forged-steel adjustable extra-large wrench no entry!' he shouted, reciting the merits of the weapon he was now wielding in a manner that needed no further explanation.

There was a long pause, during which George stared at the man, huge spanner held aloft, making himself maintain eye contact as he overcame the white noise in his head by murmuring to himself. More tractor stats.

'Christ!' The man took a step back, watching him warily. 'You should be locked up! You're a bloody nutter!'

The words didn't hurt. George had heard them and worse before. But the wrench was getting heavy, his wrist starting to shake with the effort of holding it. Then the man walked away, the loud slam of the car door making George flinch. It was followed by the rapid acceleration of the Range Rover, scattering the hens as it tore onto the rough track that led out of Thorpdale.

George remained standing there, arm up, weapon ready. Long enough for silence to descend back on the dale. Long enough to remember that he'd heard something else just before his unpleasant visitor had arrived.

That unearthly moan.

He lowered the spanner, let it drop to the ground as he contemplated an uncomfortable truth. Because if George was honest – which he always was, not possessing the devious wiring that duplicity demanded – the anguished wail couldn't have been caused by the wind. Not when it was blowing so gently, and from the west.

It had to have been the ghost.

That's what Ida had called it. Only it couldn't be a ghost, because George didn't accept the existence of anything so irrational. Except . . .

What else could it be?

For the last week he'd had the sense that something wasn't right. A low buzzing disquiet vibrating his hypersensitive antennae, bringing disruption to the tranquillity he liked to surround himself with and leaving a ridge of anxiety in his chest. An anxiety that was getting in the way of his work, diminishing the pleasure he usually took from the methodical restoration process, his progress on his current project even slower than usual thanks to these supernatural occurrences.

Supernatural, in that, to George's scientific mind, they were unexplainable.

Like the odd smell one morning when he opened the barn doors, as though a fox had stolen in during the night. He'd conducted a search of the cavernous space, but found nothing. Then there was the old kitchen chair with the missing spindle which Ida had given him to use. Twice he'd entered the barn first thing and it had been moved from its night-time resting place. Not so much as anyone else would have noticed, but for George, who calculated everything in his life to the nearest inch, the slight shift out of position had been as obvious as if someone had painted it bright pink.

And the egg shells? Were they part of it, too?

A few flakes of beige on his oil-stained workbench the other morning, which had crunched under his touch. At the time, he'd worked through the options and decided that a weasel or a wild ferret must have been to blame, sneaking into the barn to eat its plunder via the fist-sized gap at the bottom of one of the doors where the wood was rotting. Wanting to calm the static the discrepancy had caused, he'd allowed his theory to hold sway, notwithstanding the obvious contradiction the contented hens pecking away outside posed.

Because every county person knew that if a weasel or ferret had somehow managed to get inside a chicken coop to steal an egg, there would have been nothing but a pile of dead hens and bloody feathers left behind.

Following this latest unexplained noise, however, George was having to confront the fact that his egg-theft theory was lacking in substance.

Already agitated from his encounter out in the yard, he entered the barn and cocked his head. First one way. Then the other. Listening for the groan, which had definitely come from inside the building.

Nothing. Or rather, lots of noises but all part of the normal daily cycle of life at Croft Cottage. The contented clucking of the hens, the call of a lapwing from the fells, the buzz of a hopeful bee, attracted by the faded red cover of George's Evil Knievel lunch box, which was on the floor where he'd left it while he opened the barn.

He gazed around. At the workbench and the precisely arranged pieces of the old carburettor he'd been struggling to fix for the last couple of days. At the Fordson Model N parked to the right. Then he raised his eyes to the baulks, the old hayloft that covered half of the overhead space and which currently served as storage for the bits and pieces of machinery he no longer had use for but couldn't bear to throw out.

Not having the best of tolerances for heights, George hardly ever went up there. In fact, Ida had forbidden him from going up the ladder unless she was present after she'd once found him clinging precariously to its rungs, his head so dizzy he couldn't think how to get down. He'd had no idea how long he'd been there. Couldn't even remember what he'd been going up into the baulks for. All he knew was that by the time Ida entered the barn when she got home from work, his legs had started to go numb and his fingers were cramping.

So from that day on, as a permanent reminder of Ida's injunction, the ladder had lain along the ground, leaning against the opposite wall of the barn. A physical barrier to George accessing the loft. Not that he would deliberately disobey her – he wasn't one for breaking rules. But when consumed by the passion of a restoration project, he was capable of forgetting such strictures if there was something he really needed up there.

Right now, staring up at the rough boards that formed the loft floor, he was aware of Ida's warning. Aware too that his sister was out at work, as she had been pretty much every day of late. So he wouldn't be using the ladder to investigate the mysterious sound. But he could use his chair, conveniently positioned in its night-time resting place under the outer edge of the baulks. That hadn't been included in Ida's ban.

'Four-point-four litre hand-cranked not breaking the rules,' he murmured, attempting to quell the panic as he strapped on his head torch, switching the illumination to its highest setting. Holding on to the back of the chair, he stood up on it, one foot at a time, and slowly straightened, the supporting beam of the baulks still some distance above him, his fingertips just grazing its underneath. 'Liquid-cooled standard-tread more height needed.'

He stepped back down and surveyed his workshop for something suitable, rejecting his toolbox and the large cardboard box stuffed full of gaskets, his gaze settling instead on the two plastic crates used to house bottles of dirty engine oil. Emptying the contents of one onto the floor, he turned the crate upside down and placed it on the seat of the chair.

'Twenty-six brake horsepower be careful,' he muttered as he climbed back onto the chair and then up onto the crate, arms outstretched to grab the edge of the loft.

Still he was too short, his fingers able to wrap around the railings that rose from the loft floor to form a protective barrier from the deadly drop below, but his eyes unable to see over the edge. He glanced down at his workspace and everything dipped and swayed, so he snapped his vision back onto the railings, mooring himself by concentrating on the wood beneath his grasp, holding him steady.

Then he heard it. The sound. A harsh cry. Like a cough. Definitely coming from the space above him.

Heart racing now, he pulled on the railings and hauled himself up off his tiptoes until his chin was level with the loft floor and the light from his torch was shining into the dark void, spotlighting the distorted humps and bumps of the tarpaulin draped across boxes and bits of old tractors. He was turning his head, trying to inspect the entire space before his arms gave way, when it flew out at him with a shriek. A flutter of wings, something warm and soft brushing his hand.

A bat. In close-up. Enough to make George let go of the railings and lurch backwards. Only there was nothing to lurch back against. Just the emptiness of the air above the crate that was balanced on the chair, neither of which had been designed with their current employment in mind.

He felt his arms windmill uselessly, struggling to regain his equilibrium, and then he was falling, the chair and crate kicked out from underneath him. It was a short fall. One mercifully cushioned by something that yielded to his weight but still knocked the breath from him.

He lay there, aware of pain in his left arm, aware of the rubber gaskets he'd landed on sticking to his face. Aware that someone – or something – was standing over him.

George Capstick didn't believe in ghosts. And yet, as he blinked his eyes fully open, he was staring at one right now. A pale, emaciated figure looming over him, holding a corroded David Brown 850 exhaust pipe at an angle that suggested violent intent.

'Two-point-five litre thirty-five horsepower diesel,' recited George in panic as he waited for the fatal blow to fall.

4

'Mrs Hargreaves' stolen washing,' said Ida, tapping the line at the top of the whiteboard beneath the heading *Dales Detective Agency*. With Nina offering to take notes, Ida had resumed her position in front of the board, red pen in hand. 'Happen as she's getting her knickers in a twist that we've done bugger all about it, so I'll take that. I've got time to call in later this morning before I start at Taylor's.'

'Agreed,' said Delilah, accepting the pragmatic suggestion, the Hargreaves' shop directly across the market square from the estate agent's where Ida cleaned. 'But,' she added, pointing at the second line, 'I'd best deal with trying to trace the money Nancy Taylor found in Bernard's wardrobe. She's called me twice about it this week. Now his funeral's over, she wants its legality established before the will is read.'

Ida snorted. 'A hundred and twenty-five thousand in banknotes stuffed in a holdall belonging to her dead husband? Doubt we need a detective to work out whether that's above board or not.'

Nina's head snapped up from the notes she'd been taking, eyes wide. 'That's a lot of cash!'

'Aye,' came a sharp retort. 'And like owt connected with

tha work here, it's not to be talked about beyond these walls.'

A solemn nod from Nina, the teenager not in the least cowed by Ida's tone. 'Probably tax-dodging,' she said. 'Or money laundering. Either way, definitely not kosher.'

Delilah had to agree with her colleagues. Whatever persona the deceased mayor and estate agent Bernard Taylor had presented to the town of Bruncliffe, the presence of a substantial sum squirrelled away which even his wife hadn't known about suggested there must have been more to the man than met the eye. More than Delilah had seen in her entire life living there, or in her brief stint as his daughter-in-law.

As to how she was going to go about establishing the origin of the money now the man himself was dead and buried, Delilah didn't have a clue. But Ida had already written her name alongside the case in careful letters.

'Next up, the request from Turpin's solicitors to establish Pete Ferris as the rightful owner of the caravan and land he left in his will,' continued Ida, in a tone straight out of a TV courtroom. 'And if said assets are proven to be rightfully his, to also establish whether his decision to leave such assets to his neighbour Clive Knowles will provoke any dispute within the deceased's family.'

Delilah had to take a swig of her cold tea to stop herself from laughing, Nina flashing her a sideways grin. Not that it was a laughing matter, there being something incredibly poignant in the thought of poor Pete having made sure his meagre belongings were rightfully assigned before he took his own life.

'I'll take the family,' said Ida, adding her name in red

on the board as she lapsed back into the broad accent of Bruncliffe. 'Happen as Pete's uncle is married to a cousin of mine. She'll know if there's owt being said about contesting the will.'

'Do you think you could do the groundwork on checking the caravan and land were actually Pete's as well?' asked Delilah. 'It's mostly a matter of looking it up on the land registry online.'

'I could do that,' said Nina, raising her hand like she was in class.

Ida paused, looking like she was about to spurn the offer, but then she simply nodded, and wrote Nina's name on the board, getting a huge smile from the teenager in return.

'Great,' said Delilah. 'That should at least get Matty Thistlethwaite off our backs.' Eager to have the will sorted, the solicitor had called into the office several times over the last couple of weeks and was growing impatient at the slow progress. Along with all their clients. 'Which brings us to Mr Hussain's cousin and the insurance work he offered Samson.'

'Cousin Zak wants to hire us?' asked Nina, excited. 'Does this mean we'll be tailing fraudsters and the like? He's always moaning about people trying to pull a fast one.'

Ida raised an eyebrow at Delilah. 'Bit out of my league.'

'Mine too,' muttered Delilah. Checking up on customers to verify their claims wasn't something she really wanted to take on. From the little Samson had told her before, it was time-consuming and sometimes led to confrontation. But if the Dales Detective Agency was to keep its doors open, this could prove to be a lucrative line of work.

Delilah didn't allow herself to dwell on the magnitude of the word *if*.

'Perhaps we can just establish contact to begin with?' she said. 'Get your cousin's details and go from there?'

'Consider it done,' said Nina, positively glowing now as Ida added her name to the whiteboard for a second time.

'Onto *Other Business*.' Ida tapped her pen at the next section, which contained two entries. 'First up, the Dales Dating Agency.' She looked at Delilah in expectation.

'Twenty new clients last week, all needing inputting on the system. A fully booked Speedy Date night for the twenty-first, the inaugural Silver Solos event next week and already filling up for the Summer Speedy in July. Plus numerous enquiries to respond to . . .' Delilah couldn't help the sigh that passed her lips, even while instantly berating herself for bemoaning a success she'd have given everything for a few months ago. Now, with her loan and mortgage payments being met and more than enough left over to keep her hound in Dog-gestives, it seemed churlish to be begrudging the amount of work coming in.

'Admin, Nina and I can do,' said Ida, putting their names next to yet another task. 'So that just leaves Taylor's IT system overhaul—' She broke off, a look of panic on her face that made Delilah laugh.

'Don't worry, that's all mine,' she said. 'Although I wish I could share the load. I've had both Nancy and Neil on my case about it. They want it finished as soon as possible now that things are on a bit more of an even keel.'

Ida's forehead puckered into a frown. 'Perhaps if that good-for-nothing stopped calling in so often to ask how tha's progressing, tha'd get more done!'

'Neil Taylor,' Delilah explained, seeing the bewildered look on Nina's face at this sudden outburst. 'We used to be—'

'Married,' said Nina, nodding, reminding Delilah that this was Bruncliffe, a place where the 'private' had yet to be put next to the word 'life'.

'Ida's not a fan,' she added dryly.

Which was an understatement. Ida had made clear her disapproval of 'that Taylor lad' – as she was wont to refer to Delilah's ex-husband in her kinder moments – and his frequent visits to the office since he'd arrived back in Bruncliffe for his father's funeral. Despite the legitimacy of his presence, the son having taken on the role of overseeing the IT upgrade of the family business, no offer of tea had been forthcoming from Delilah's colleague. Not once. Which, for a woman who prided herself on her Bruncliffe manners and whose currency of affection was strong, milky brews, was rather telling.

Ida was nothing if not loyal. And the fact that Neil Taylor had cheated on Delilah during their ill-fated marriage, his philandering finally causing their union to collapse, was unforgiveable in the Capstick civil code.

But while Delilah understood the origins of this condemnation, she wasn't made from the same granite. Time had done a lot to heal her wounds. As had the company of Tolpuddle, Neil's last present to his wife before they split up. And she'd be a liar if she didn't admit that having Samson O'Brien in her life had changed her outlook on love. Combined with the appalling tragedy which had struck the Taylor family recently, robbing Neil of his father, circumstances had conspired to render Delilah a lot more amenable to spending time in his company. Besides, it was only work.

Which didn't explain why she felt the telltale warmth of

a blush stealing up her cheeks as Ida kept her formidable gaze resting on her.

'Are we done?' asked Delilah, determined to change the topic.

'What about the call I took when I came in. A Mrs Lister?' said Nina, reading her notes. 'Said she wanted to speak to Delilah.'

Delilah groaned and Ida shook her head. 'Tha's going to have to call her back, lass. That must be the hundredth time she's called.'

'What's it about?' asked Nina.

'We don't know. She wouldn't tell me,' said Ida with a sniff, arms folding, the right to be added to the white-board clearly being denied this Mrs Lister until more was known.

'I'll give her a call this afternoon. Anything else?' Delilah asked, preparing to stand.

'Aye. A Mr Marsden from Yorkshire Lockers called earlier. Wanted to speak to Samson. I explained he wasn't here but the bloke wouldn't leave a message. Thought tha might know which case it's connected to?'

'Mr Marsden?' Delilah couldn't place the name. Or the context in which Samson would have had recourse to someone who made lockers. 'Not a clue,' she said, as her mobile started to ring. She'd barely got it to her ear before a familiar voice was speaking.

'Delilah?' PC Danny Bradley sounded hassled, a car horn blaring in the background, followed by frantic bleating. 'I've been trying all morning to get hold of you. Got a bit of a puzzle going on. Any chance you could meet me up at Quarry House at some point today?'

At the mention of the quarry, Delilah tensed, as though she was back there with Samson, facing imminent death.

'Is it connected to the Warren case?' she asked warily. Ida's head snapped round, Nina's too, all attention now on her.

'Not that I know of,' said Danny. 'More likely connected to the work you were doing for Seth Thistlethwaite. But it might be nothing. I'd just appreciate your take on— You little bugger!'

'Excuse me?'

'Sorry, that wasn't aimed at you! It's these blasted lambs. I'm out on the Horton Road trying to round up a couple that have escaped.' Another curse, followed by the sound of heavy breathing and hard running.

'Let me know when you're done sheep wrestling and I'll meet you up at Gunnerstang Brow,' said Delilah, laughing now at the sounds of the policeman trying to catch the errant animals.

'Will do. Damn it, you buggers!' A crash, followed by muffled swearing and then the call ended abruptly.

'More work?' asked Ida, glaring at the mobile and then at her whiteboard, on which the words *Yorkshire Lockers* had been squeezed in at the bottom of the first section, a question mark allocated instead of a name. A question mark that only Ida could make appear angular, its solid shape almost removing any sense of uncertainty and adding instead a sharp statement which made her final entry stand out.

'Possibly,' said Delilah tentatively, sensing that Ida didn't want anything else to mess up her pristine overview. 'Danny thinks he may have something that ties in with the break-ins at the allotments.'

'Thought as tha'd solved that case for Seth?'

Delilah shrugged. 'Depends what you mean by solved.'

Five nights of stake-outs, sitting in Seth Thistlethwaite's shed on the allotments on the outskirts of town in an attempt to catch the thieves who'd been stealing vegetables, had yielded nothing, apart from a lack of sleep and an aching lower back. With Samson having already left for London, there hadn't even been the added spice of sharing the night-time hours alone with him as they kept watch. Instead, it had been Delilah and Tolpuddle, and much as she loved her dog, having him fall asleep with his head on her lap while she struggled to stay awake by drinking endless coffee wasn't quite the same. In the end, with no culprits showing up to purloin more eggs from the henhouse or tea and biscuits from the shed, it had been Seth who'd called it a day and cancelled the operation, claiming that it was costing him as much in Hobnobs as when the thief had been active. Wiping crumbs from her coat, Delilah hadn't been able to disagree with his verdict.

So her first solo effort for the Dales Detective Agency had been a failure, the perpetrators still at large. Unless Danny had discovered something . . .

'Tha wants me to include that too, no doubt,' grumbled Ida, reaching forward with her pen to insert *Allotment thefts* into the small space left on her not-so-tidy-any-more board. She added Delilah's name next to it without any discussion, as though the case were somehow unworthy of her own attentions. Then she clicked the lid back on the pen and gave a satisfied nod. 'There,' she said, regarding her handywork. 'That's better.'

Nina was nodding, too, but looking at the full board,

Delilah didn't feel anything was better at all. Nor was it about to improve, for all at once there was a frantic ringing of the doorbell, followed by impatient hammering of the knocker before the front door crashed open.

While the rest of the team were slow to react to this intrusion, Tolpuddle was already tearing across the landing and heading for the stairs, his deep booming bark accompanying his stride as from below came a woman's voice.

'Delilah Metcalfe? I need to speak to Delilah Metcalfe at once! It's concerning—'

But whatever it was concerning was drowned out as Tolpuddle started wailing. A strident, ear-splitting howl of the kind that had the three colleagues of the Dales Detective Agency on their feet and hurrying for the stairs.

'Kill him,' whispered Pavel from up above, voice quivering with fear. 'Or he'll tell them where we are.'

Grigore stood over their intended victim, arm raised, weapon in it, calculating his options. His brother was right. The man currently cowering on the barn floor was in cahoots with the Devil, because despite not having seen who it was who'd come calling that morning, Grigore would recognise that voice anywhere.

But if he complied with Pavel's suggestion, they were going to have to go back on the run, with yet another murder to their name. If he didn't, however, they were done for. Because this man had seen them and was sure to report their presence to the very people they were fleeing from. To the Devil, who'd already been here, no doubt looking for them.

There was really only one choice to make. Kill or be killed.

Date with Evil

When the brothers had stumbled across the barn a week ago, exhausted and terrified, legs and lungs giving out after being chased, dusk had yielded to night. But even by the light of the half-moon in the clear sky, Grigore had been confident they'd found a safe haven. Skirting around the small cottage, careful not to trample on the neatly tended vegetable patch or to go too close to the chicken coop and alarm the hens, he'd led Pavel across the yard. With huge stones making up its walls, the barn was nothing like the wooden equivalents in his village, but even so, it had reminded him of home. As had the unlocked doors, a complete contrast to the dangerous world Grigore had been inhabiting for the best part of the past four months.

Once inside, with the doors closed, Grigore had felt bold enough to turn on the torch he'd taken from his last hideout. With the air scented with the familiar smell of oil, he'd not been surprised when the yellow light had revealed an old tractor parked on the right – the very same model he'd kept running for a wealthy neighbour as a teenager in what now seemed like a distant memory – or the workbench along the back wall, tools lined up precisely on the pegboard above it, parts of a dismantled carburettor laid out on its surface. The sense of homecoming had been even stronger.

'There's nowhere to hide,' Pavel had groaned, sinking onto a chair, clutching his side. 'We'll have to be out of here by dawn.' His head dropped into his hands, his voice breaking. 'I'm so sorry, Grigore. This is all my fault.'

Desperately looking around the barn, Grigore had begun to share his brother's despair, but then he'd let the beam travel upwards. A hayloft, covering half of the floor, its outer edge directly above where Pavel was sitting. No ladder coming down from it, which suggested it wasn't used much. If they could find a way to get up there . . .

He'd swung the light back down, casting it all over the barn until he saw something sticking out from behind the tractor. A ladder.

They'd somehow managed to get Pavel into the loft, no easy feat with his ribs aching and his limbs barely functioning. But getting Grigore up there had been even trickier as they couldn't afford to leave the ladder out of place. They'd finally found a coil of thick rope shoved under a tarpaulin, tied it around the balustrade that formed a guard at the open end of the loft, and once Grigore had descended the ladder and put it back in its rightful place, he'd stood on the chair and used the rope to haul himself up and over the railings, drawing the rope after him.

Eight days the two brothers managed to stay hidden. Lying under the tarpaulin on a bed of mildewing blankets they'd discovered in a box, they'd spent the daylight hours waiting for the terrifying bark of the Rottweiler or for the doors to crash open and their pursuers to appear. Yet somehow they'd remained undetected, despite the unnerving mutterings which sometimes drifted up from the floor below. When night fell, Grigore would lower himself down the rope onto the chair and sneak out into the yard to forage for whatever food he could find. Some carrots from the vegetable patch. A lettuce. A couple of spring onions and some radishes. Cautious not to take too much or it would be noticed. He'd supplemented this pitiful diet with whatever he could find in the bins – although there was never much thrown out, whoever lived in the cottage not the type to waste anything. The saving grace was the chicken coop, the brothers having been raised looking after hens and Grigore knowing well how to sneak in and take a couple of eggs without sending the birds into panic.

With the water he took from the outside tap, a rinsed-out old milk bottle used to hold it, he'd managed to keep them from starving. But it wasn't enough. So he'd already been planning their next move, in a day or two perhaps, when Pavel had recovered more of his strength. Then a coughing fit had given them away.

'Go on, Grigore,' urged Pavel hoarsely, staring down from between the railings like the condemned man he was. 'Do it!'

When the blinding light had appeared over the edge of the loft, Grigore had been waiting with the exhaust pipe, intending to strike. But the bat had flown out of the eaves and straight at the man, sending him sprawling. Grigore had reacted on instinct, throwing the rope over the railings and scrabbling down into the barn, intent on killing him. But now . . . ?

There was something innocent about this man on the floor. A childlike quality, evident even through the language barrier, a stream of staccato English issuing from his mouth.

Angel or devil? Kill or be killed?

'Do it!' Pavel said again, sensing his brother's hesitation.

Desperation lifted Grigore's arm higher. He tried not to look at the face of his victim. Tried not to heed what were no doubt words of supplication, not having more than a spattering of the language.

Except . . . he recognised some of it.

Horsepower ... cylinder ... diesel ... David Brown ...

Grigore paused. Aware of the exhaust pipe in his hand, knowing it was from a tractor. A David Brown. Knowing this because of his work in a place where these machines weren't museum pieces but functioning essentials.

It was as though he was hearing the man afresh, the incantation sounding like Mama saying her prayers, her thick fingers working the beads on her prayer rope, the repeated words giving her solace. But this man wasn't praying to any deity for mercy. This man was reciting tractor statistics.

'What are you doing?' hissed Pavel as the exhaust dropped to the floor, making the man flinch, the mutterings abruptly halted.

In the silence, Grigore turned to his brother. 'This isn't us,' he said, feeling a weariness in his soul from the deeds he'd already committed. 'Mama didn't raise us to be violent men.'

'But he'll call them! Even if we run now, they'll catch us! And then what?'

Grigore shook his head. He was out of ideas. He was out of energy. He'd been living on his wits for what felt like a lifetime, trying to find Pavel. And now ...

He held out a hand to the man on the floor, who shied away like a stray dog beaten too many times.

'Don't worry,' said Grigore. 'We won't hurt you.'

Still the man stared at him in terror, the muttering starting up once more. Grigore smiled. Gestured at the tractor in the corner of the barn, and started speaking the few English words he knew.

'*Fordson N,*' he said, and then held up four fingers. '*Cylinder.*'

The man looked from him to the tractor and began nodding.

'*Horsepower,*' continued Grigore, showing two fingers and then six.

'*Zenith carburettor,*' replied the man, getting to his feet, grinning now, pointing at the parts on the bench.

Grigore scratched his head, trying to recall what he could of the first tractor he'd ever worked on. But he was out of statistics and out of English. 'Sorry,' he said, smiling at the man as he reverted to his own language. 'I don't know any more.'

The man stared at him in incomprehension, until Grigore's stomach rumbled loudly.

A giggle from their host. '*Standard-tread liquid-cooled food?*'

Grigore didn't have a clue what his new friend was saying but he watched him cross the barn in rapid steps.

'He's going for his phone!' warned Pavel. 'You have to kill him!'

But before Grigore could even think about picking his discarded weapon back up, the man was returning, holding out a box with a picture of a motorbike jumping over a line of cars on the front. He opened it and gestured at the two brothers.

Grigore looked up at Pavel and smiled for the first time in months.

'He's an angel,' he said, as he reached for a ham-and-cheese sandwich.

*

It was bedlam. Tolpuddle was halfway down the stairs, in full air-raid-siren mode, wailing his head off while being held at bay by a snappy West Highland terrier a fraction of his size. Nina was trying unsuccessfully to placate both dogs, and Ida, who'd managed to squeeze past them, had closed the front door on the onlookers from the pub and was doing her best to guide their visitor into the ground-floor office.

But the woman – a middle-aged lady Delilah had never set eyes on before – had sat down on one of the chairs in the hall, placed there as an ad hoc waiting room to deal with the recent overflow of clients, and was showing no sign of budging. She was gripping the edges of her seat while making the same demand in a voice forced louder and louder by the cacophony of the dogs.

'I insist on speaking to Delilah Metcalfe!' she was exclaiming. 'I'm not going anywhere until I do!'

'I'm here!' Delilah said, from her boxed-in position on the stairs, one anxious eye on her Weimaraner and the other on this woman as the noise swelled even higher, Tolpuddle now reaching a pitch reserved for maximum anxiety levels. Not for the first time in the last fortnight, she found herself raining down silent curses and the odd death threat on the owner of the detective agency, who'd absconded and left her to deal with this mayhem. 'But can you please call off your dog, Ms . . . ?'

'Lister!' shouted the woman. 'I'm Mrs Lister and you've been ignoring my calls.'

Ida shot Delilah a glower. At which point the doorbell went, sending the dogs into an even louder frenzy, Ida hollering over them, 'We're closed!'

But the door was flung open anyway, to reveal Samson

Date with Evil

O'Brien, rucksack in one hand and a Peaks Patisserie box in the other.

That mane of black hair. The piercing blue gaze, locking on her. That hint of a roguish smile.

In a whirl of emotions, Delilah didn't take time to think. She just lunged.

5

Samson O'Brien had made a rookie mistake.

Standing there on the doorstep, witnessing what looked like a minor riot in the hallway – Tolpuddle and a Westie going full throttle, Nina from Rice N Spice trying to calm them, Ida being shouted at by a woman sitting outside his office who was gripping onto a chair and declaring she wouldn't be moved, while Delilah was partway up the stairs, looking frazzled – in that split second Samson realised the error he'd made.

The manner in which he'd departed, leaving town the morning after they'd finally come some way towards starting a relationship, Delilah still asleep in his bed as he stole out of the door. His lack of communication during the subsequent, hectic two weeks when he'd been helping the Met gather more evidence against his old boss. The fact he'd left her to cope with the business he'd created while she was trying to juggle her own work too. All of that he'd done, knowing it might provoke her famous temper.

But they weren't the mistakes. No. His mistake was opening the door to the office building with both of his hands full and no way to fend off a greeting from an irate Metcalfe. Because he happened to have had experience of how that clan tended to welcome folk they were annoyed with, his jaw still carrying the memory of Delilah's right hook on his first day back in town last October.

So there he was, on the doorstep, totally vulnerable. He saw her register his arrival. The widening of the eyes. Delight suffusing her face, followed by a frown, her fists clenching. Then she was moving, lunging down the stairs past Nina and the dogs, heading straight for him. He had the foresight to drop the rucksack and the Peaks Patisserie box and then everything seemed to slow down . . .

The box hitting the floor, cakes spilling out onto the tiles. The dogs turning, sensing treats. Nina open-mouthed, staring at him. Ida and the woman falling into stunned silence. And then it was just Delilah. Filling his vision. Coming straight at him. He braced himself for the punch—

'You're back!' she exclaimed.

And she jumped up, into his empty arms, sending him staggering against the doorjamb, her lips on his.

One second. Five minutes. A lifetime.

He emerged from the kiss as she drew back, the world reforming around him. Aware of the women in the hallway watching, Ida almost smiling. Aware of the two dogs contentedly eating what was meant to have been an apology. Aware of a wry voice from out on the street.

'Get a bloody room, you two!' Troy Murgatroyd standing in the doorway of the pub, a crowd of regulars with him, all of them watching and laughing.

Samson was more than ready to take the landlord up on the suggestion, acutely aware that the one time he'd shared a bed with Delilah, she'd been asleep for the entire night – thanks to a combination of a bullet wound and pain medication. But she was already dropping out of his arms, a shy grin on her face.

'Welcome home to Bruncliffe,' she said. 'Now get inside. We've got work to do.'

They persuaded Mrs Lister to go to Peaks Patisserie and have something to eat – on the Dales Detective Agency's account – while they held a staff meeting in the kitchen, Nina accompanying their client to collect food for their working lunch, and more cakes to replace the ones Tolpuddle and the Westie had consumed. Having already demolished two slices of an exquisite mushroom-and-leek tart, Samson was now devoting his attention to a large piece of chocolate-and-pear cake and marvelling, as he always did, at the culinary skills of Delilah's sister-in-law Lucy, who ran the cafe. Her amazing array of cakes and tarts was just one of the many things he'd missed in his two weeks away.

Unlike the local brew, the cup of tea Ida had made for him sitting relatively untouched at his elbow.

'So that's where we are,' Delilah was concluding, having run through the agency's workload using a whiteboard positioned above the table. 'Probably the only thing we really need your input on right now, Samson, is this item.' She pointed at a line halfway down. 'Someone from there called wanting to speak to you—'

'A Mr Marsden,' said Ida, managing to make the name sound suspicious.

'Anyway, we weren't sure if it was an ongoing case or not, so we included it. Not like we were already overloaded or anything,' Delilah added with a dry laugh.

Samson stared at where she was pointing. *Yorkshire Lockers?*

The words triggered a wave of guilt, even without the accusatory question mark completing them. It certainly was an ongoing case. An enquiry into who had tried to frame Lucy Metcalfe's son – and Samson's godson – Nathan Metcalfe, by stuffing his school locker full of ketamine. But although Samson had made progress several weeks ago, establishing the supplier of the lockers – the same Yorkshire Lockers now featuring on the agency's new whiteboard – and that Bruncliffe's very own Procter Properties had installed them, in the wake of the attempt on his life and Delilah getting shot, not to mention the frantic couple of weeks down in London, the case had completely slipped his mind.

What hadn't slipped his mind, however, was that this was an investigation he didn't want Delilah playing any part in. Not until he had more proof as to who had set up the lad, placing the teenager in a position where he could have been facing a ruined future, marred forever as a drug dealer. For Delilah and her oldest brother Will, neither of them the most cool-headed in normal times and certainly not when it came to what had happened to their nephew, that burden of proof would be set at a much lower bar. If they were aware Samson had discovered a link – no matter how tenuous – to Rick Procter, they would confront the property developer straight away and ruin any chances of building a proper case against him. If it was indeed Rick who was behind it all.

So, barely an hour back in Bruncliffe, Samson found himself lying.

Julia Chapman

'Sorry to have wasted your time,' he said, a grin covering his duplicity. 'I called some folk about getting storage for downstairs before I left. I guess they must be as busy as we are if they're only just getting back to me.'

Delilah was already wiping the board with a damp tissue, the name of the locker suppliers reduced to no more than a faint outline between more pressing matters. Making a mental note to return Mr Marsden's call as soon as he got a chance, Samson promised himself that he would put some energy into the investigation now he was back.

While he was back . . .

'One less case to deal with,' Delilah was saying with a smile. 'And last but not least, as you've probably figured out by now, we have a new member on the team.'

Samson smiled at Nina. 'Welcome on board,' he said.

The teenager grinned at him. 'If it's anything like this morning's been, it's going to be a blast!'

'Aye, happen as there's very few dull moments,' muttered Ida, standing up and placing her mug and plate in the sink. 'Right, I'm off to Hargreaves' to get a statement about that missing laundry before going to Taylor's to clean.'

'And I've got to meet Danny up at Quarry House,' said Delilah, rising also. 'So I'm sorry, but catching up on your London adventures is going to have to wait until later.'

She blushed slightly as she said it, Samson sensing there was more than just a recap of his two weeks in the capital she was wanting to catch up on. Which suited him, as he wasn't ready to tell her his news just yet. Not until it was officially confirmed.

'No rush,' he said, as the two women began to move for the door, leaving Nina and Samson at the table. 'But what

60

about this Mrs Lister? How does she fit into all this?' He gestured at the board.

'Oh, she doesn't,' said Delilah, a grin forming that he recognised and had missed. 'Not yet. She's a whole new investigation you can have all to yourself. Presuming you're going to be around long enough to solve it, that is?'

It was said casually, but he wasn't fooled. Neither was Ida, her sharp focus on him, waiting for the answer.

'Shouldn't be an issue,' he said, just as casually.

Ida humphed and Delilah merely nodded, then they were both gone down the stairs, while Nina wrote *Mrs Lister* on the board, adding a question mark and Samson's name.

'I'll leave you to it,' she said with a cheeky smile, before she too left the kitchen.

He heard her enter Delilah's office and then the rapid tap of fingers dancing across a keyboard. Samson stared at the whiteboard and the list of names assigned to tasks, even Nina making the cut despite her recent arrival. While he'd been down in London, caught up in tracing evidence that might assist in bringing his former boss's accomplices to trial in what was turning into a major corruption case, he'd imagined Delilah counting the hours to his return. Yet this very board was proof that she'd been too busy to miss him. So busy in fact, she'd just gone out without him, on a case he knew nothing about.

The sense of alienation he'd experienced when he'd arrived home last autumn crept back over him. Two weeks away and he was like a stranger again.

A heavy weight cut through his self-pity – Tolpuddle, head on Samson's lap, let out a long sigh, as though the world had finally fallen back into place.

'At least you missed me, eh, boy?' Samson said, rubbing the dog's ears.

Then the front door opened and a woman's voice called up the stairs, accompanied by a sharp yap. The Weimaraner looked up at Samson with a martyred expression, accurately reflecting the detective's own sentiments.

Somehow he had the feeling this wasn't going to go smoothly.

Tolpuddle on his heels, he descended the stairs, hand outstretched to welcome the woman who'd been at the centre of the maelstrom on his return.

'Mrs Lister, sorry about the wait,' he said, as the two dogs watched each other warily. 'Come on through to my office.'

He pushed open the office door and got an appreciation of how overwhelmed the women he'd left running the agency had been. The dirty mugs, the piles of paperwork, the balls of dust on the lino were like a tidemark of frenzied activity. Ida Capstick, the demon cleaner, hadn't even had time to clean!

With a pang of guilt, he moved aside a packet of dog biscuits and a couple of folders to clear a space on his desk as Mrs Lister took a seat opposite him, her dog on her lap. Tolpuddle opted to curl up in his bed to the side, one eye still on the Westie.

'So,' said Samson, finally ready to get to business, 'what can we do to help?'

'It's my son, Stuart,' she said.

Stuart Lister. The name brought to mind the gangly lettings agent who'd worked for Taylor's until recently, when he'd given up work to see the world.

'Ah, how is he?' asked Samson. 'Enjoying his travels?'

To his great consternation, his client burst into tears, which wasn't the first time this had happened. And Samson O'Brien found himself wondering what exactly it was about Bruncliffe and his detective agency he'd missed after all.

The intense joy Delilah had felt upon seeing Samson on the doorstep of the office building lasted until she hit the outskirts of town. But as she nursed her Micra up the steep climb past the allotments, the inane grin she'd been sporting dissolved into a frown of concern. There was something wrong with her car. It had struggled to start, belching out thick clouds of black smoke as it set off from Back Street, and now there was a strange clicking noise coming from the engine.

It really didn't sound good.

Making a note to drop by the garage on her way back to the office, she was relieved to finally crest Gunnerstang Brow, where Danny's police car was already turning off the road and into the quarry. She headed down the dusty track after him, her throat tightening as the stark rockface came into sight.

It was too soon. Only a couple of weeks since she'd faced death here. Wishing she'd stayed in the office and delegated Samson to this task, she parked up and got out of the car.

'I hear Samson's home,' the constable said by way of greeting as he walked towards her, his huge grin showing his delight at the news. 'And I hear you gave him quite the welcome!'

'Bloody Bruncliffe!' She managed a smile, tension at the edges of it.

'From all reports, Mrs Pettiford nearly choked on a cheese scone when she heard the details.'

'Ha!' Delilah wasn't surprised at the idea of the local gossip being outraged by her behaviour. 'I'd have gone even further if I'd known she'd have that reaction. Killed two birds with one scone.'

Danny grinned. 'You'd have done us all a favour.' Then he touched her arm. 'You okay. Being back up here? I didn't think about it until after I'd called you.'

'I'm fine,' she lied, keeping her back towards the Portakabins and the patch of ground which had been stained with both her and Samson's blood. It didn't stop the memory of that moment though. Samson's arms around her. The shock of the bullet hitting her. Fearing the worst as she fell—

'Delilah?' Danny was looking at her with concern. 'Are you sure you're okay?'

'Yeah. Just . . . you know . . . this place is creepy at the best of times but now, even more so.'

Danny nodded. 'It's not exactly in my top ten of Bruncliffe's hot spots.'

'You have a top ten?' Delilah asked, amused at the revelation.

'Doesn't everyone?' The constable's grin was infectious. 'And before you ask, number one isn't Peaks Patisserie. I'll leave that to Sarge.'

Delilah found herself smiling, the town's sergeant known for his fondness for Lucy Metcalfe's cakes. 'So, what is it then? Your number one?'

There was no hesitation, Danny having obviously given this some thought. 'The Fleece on darts night,' he announced. 'But only if we're winning!'

At the idea of the pub's lamentable darts team leading Danny's chart, a burst of laughter sprang from Delilah and echoed around the quarry, chasing away the shadows that had been lingering.

'Right,' said Danny, giving a satisfied nod at her lighter demeanour, 'let's get this done with. It won't take long.'

Rick Procter had thought his day couldn't get any worse. He'd already had his fill of bumbling idiots, trying as he had been to sort out what seemed to be a never-ending succession of bad luck that was befalling his enterprise. But now this.

The police were back at Rainsrigg Quarry.

As he'd crested the top of Gunnerstang Brow, fretting over the latest screw-up involving what he liked to term 'staffing' issues – or mislaid staff, to be precise – he'd caught a glimpse of an insignificant red car turning right into the quarry up ahead. Only it hadn't been insignificant. It had been the decrepit Micra owned by none other than Delilah Metcalfe.

Whereas the prospect of an encounter with the youngest Metcalfe – a woman he'd held hopes of starting a relationship with – would once have brought him pleasure, of late she'd become a thorn in his side. He blamed that bloody Samson O'Brien and his damn detective agency, embroiling Delilah in his investigations, turning her into someone Rick now had to be wary of.

So instead of following her, taking the opportunity for a chat and perhaps even setting up a date, he'd braked, waiting until she was down the track before he took a sharp left at Hill Top Cafe, his intended destination. Situated at the top of the brow across from the quarry entrance, in what had once been the Harrisons' farmhouse, it had lain empty for some months until acquired recently by Procter Properties. Officially, it remained unoccupied, awaiting planning permissions. Unofficially, it was a place Rick couldn't afford to be seen at. Not yet.

Sod's law, then, that Delilah Metcalfe would be hanging around when he had cause to visit his latest venture.

Curious as to the reason for her presence in the area, he'd left his Range Rover hidden in the horseshoe courtyard round the back of the cafe and, binoculars in hand, hurried across the deserted road to scramble up the fellside that overlooked the quarry. Lying down behind an outcrop of limestone, he was currently training his binoculars on the two people stood in front of the old foreman's cottage. And the police car parked there.

They were supposed to be done processing the crime scene. He'd watched the last of the detectives leave only two days ago. Yet here they still were. Poking around.

Rick, like the law-abiding citizens of Bruncliffe, should have been content to know the police were carrying out a thorough investigation into the shooting. To know that his taxes were being put to good use to protect his community. But Rick Procter wasn't law-abiding. Hadn't been for a long time. And this renewed interest in the quarry from law-enforcement officials was nothing but a cause for concern for him. Even if it was just the Bradley lad in his oversize uniform. The Bradley lad *and* Delilah Metcalfe, an added worry in itself. Because where she was involved, you could bet your life O'Brien wouldn't be far behind.

Which was what was really making Rick Procter nervous.

He'd thought he was shot of the former Met officer for good, the lure of the capital and his old job too hard to resist, no matter Ms Metcalfe's undeniable charms. Yet, hot off the town's grapevine was the news that O'Brien had arrived back from London that morning.

It wasn't the first time Rick had been wrong about the imminent disappearance of the man. It didn't make his renewed presence in the area any more palatable. Or less stressful.

Down below, he watched the two figures walk around the rear of the building and out of sight. Inside the house.

What where they doing in there when the crime scene was over by the Portakabins? He turned his binoculars onto the blue-and-white tape marking out the exact spot where O'Brien was supposed to have met his demise. No one there.

So was this something new entirely? Or just a further development in the original investigation? Either way, was it going to demand more officers? More of a police presence? All of which would mean that Rick's business still wouldn't be able to resume.

Two weeks he'd already lost in production, his workforce temporarily relocated, a couple of security guards all that remained, guarding an empty premises. In any line of trade, that would need explaining to associates relying on your product. When those associates were of the calibre he was dealing with, a simple email of apology wasn't going to do the trick. In fact, Rick couldn't think of one piece of advice from all the business books he'd read when starting out which would be useful in this unique situation.

Problem was, his latest operation, the one established to take up the slack after the enforced – and rapid – abandonment of one of his other premises, was now directly opposite a crime scene. And that was a problem because what was actually behind the blank windows of the empty cafe was a cannabis farm. One of many Rick operated in a business that had seem him grow rich. But which was now going pear-shaped.

Basically, if he didn't get production back underway soon, he was a dead man.

Danny led Delilah around the back of Quarry House, explaining on the way how Jimmy Thornton's call had brought him up there that morning. And this being Delilah, not someone known for gossiping and a woman the young constable held quite a torch for, he even told her about the cat. She was still laughing as they entered the kitchen, stepping over the broken glass on the way in.

'So apart from the smashed pane in the back door, there was no damage done?' she asked, as she took in the room.

'Nope. Everything suggests whoever was in here was looking for a place to hide out. There's the makings of a bed upstairs and the Rayburn had been used, until the oil ran out. I called Jimmy just before you got here and he's adamant he left it switched off, so our mystery person must have turned it back on.'

'Do you think that's what made them leave? The lack of heating?'

'That was my initial thought. But it's not exactly Baltic in here and it still has to be better than sleeping outside.' He gestured towards the Portakabin and the police tape.

'There's been a lot of commotion up here lately. I reckon that had more of an impact.'

Delilah looked out across what had been Mrs Thornton's vegetable garden but was now just a wild tangle of weeds, to the quarry in the background. Danny was right. Anyone who'd broken into a cottage and was living there illegally probably wouldn't react too well to a sudden influx of police. Not to mention the shooting which had preceded their arrival.

'So what makes you think this could be connected to the thefts at the allotments?' she asked, turning back to the constable.

He simply crossed to the range and lifted the cover of the left-hand hotplate. A yellow blotch clung to the edge of the cooking surface.

'Egg?' Delilah asked, puzzled. 'You brought me up here to see a bit of yolk left on a cooker?'

'Not just that. Those, too.' Danny pointed beneath the table.

Delilah leaned down and saw a couple of green leaves; rough and dark, they weren't from any tree.

'Cauliflower leaves!' she exclaimed, suddenly getting it.

Danny was nodding vigorously. 'The egg didn't trigger it at first but when I saw them, I remembered Samson saying something about finding some in the woods between here and the allotments when he was investigating the break-ins at Seth's shed. Didn't he have a theory that someone was stealing eggs and cauliflowers and coming back up this way with them?'

Delilah had a sudden memory of standing in the trees above the allotments, the bluebells forming an inviting carpet, listening to Samson explain who he thought was behind the crime Seth Thistlethwaite wanted solving, while pointing at eggshells on the ground. He'd been wrong, thinking whoever it was had a connection to the danger that was coming for him. She also remembered that even as she'd been taking in the import of what he was saying, knowing the peril they were facing, she'd been contemplating kissing him, lying down with him in that sea of blue flowers and—

'Delilah?'

'Sorry, yes,' she muttered, straightening up and praying Danny would think her scarlet face was simply a result of bending over. 'Samson was pretty sure it was someone living rough who was taking food from the allotments. It all seemed a bit too regular and lacking in wanton destruction to be kids larking around. And these leaves would suggest a possible connection to whoever was staying up here, but . . .'

'You're not convinced?

'Whoever was using Seth's shed was also using his kettle to boil the eggs they stole. I just can't see why they would have taken the added risk of lingering down there, where they were more likely to be caught, when they had access to electricity and an oil range where they were squatting.'

Danny leaned across to the doorway and flipped the light switch on and off, to no effect. 'Leccy's off. Jimmy cancelled the account when he'd finished clearing everything out. And as for the Rayburn,' he shrugged, 'perhaps when the oil ran out up here, they made the most of the kettle down at Seth's to cook their eggs?'

It was plausible. Delilah had to grant him that.

'So what are we looking at then?' she mused. 'Someone homeless, making the most of an empty house and sourcing food nearby?'

'That's what I thought. Until I found this upstairs beneath the curtains they were sleeping on.' Danny reached into his back pocket and pulled out a plastic bag. Inside was what looked like a spoon, sharpened to a lethal point. 'It's what folk in prison would call a shiv,' he explained.

'A homemade knife?' Delilah looked even closer. At the rusty stain on the makeshift blade. 'Is that blood?'

The constable nodded. 'Pretty sure it is. Which suggests —'

'We're looking for someone dangerous. Someone who might have already committed a crime far worse than breaking and entering . . .'

'Aye. And if that's the case, I reckon you had a lucky escape that they didn't come back while you were doing your stakeouts in Seth's shed.'

Delilah stared at the brutal weapon in Danny's hand and felt the shiver of someone walking over her grave.

6

It took Samson a while to locate a box of tissues, the one he normally kept on top of his desk having been left empty and unreplaced. He finally struck lucky in Delilah's office – Nina handing him one from a desk drawer in a room in the same state of dishevelment as his own, he noted with yet more guilt – and returned to Mrs Lister. He brought a cup of tea with him as well.

'Thanks,' she said, wiping her eyes and reaching for the mug. 'You're a good lad. Stuart thinks highly of you.'

Her voice wobbled at the mention of her son. Samson, beginning to be an old hand at warding off clients' distress, jumped in.

'You were saying that's why you're here. About Stuart. Is he in some kind of trouble abroad?'

He was envisaging the worst. Stuart wasn't the worldliest of souls, the young man easily the type to naively help out a fellow tourist by carrying their bags through customs, only to end up as an unwitting drugs mule. So it was a surprise when Mrs Lister shook her head and said 'He's not abroad.'

'Pardon?'

'Stuart. He didn't go travelling.'

Date with Evil

'But I thought . . . he gave up his job . . .'

Mrs Lister sniffed. 'That's all rubbish. There's no way he would have left Taylor's like that. He was making something of himself. Making me proud.'

'So what do you think—'

'Not think! Know!' Her indignant exclamation startled the Westie, which had been on the verge of sleep on her lap. 'Sorry, Snowy,' she murmured, stroking the dog before resuming with a more measured tone. 'Look, I just know he didn't go travelling. I know he wouldn't have left in such a hurry that he had no time to speak to his mother. I know my boy.'

'He didn't tell you he was thinking of going?'

'Not a word. All I got was a text the night before he supposedly set off. A text!' Her voice rose again, this time Snowy simply jumping from her lap and crossing the floor to curl up next to Tolpuddle in the bed, a development the Weimaraner accepted without murmur.

Mrs Lister sighed. 'Sorry, I'm not handling this very well but it's the little things that are making me sure something's not right. That text, for instance. He never texted me about important stuff. He'd come home and we'd talk it through.'

'And home is where?'

'Skipton. Not exactly a long way to come.'

Samson didn't refute the claim, even though he knew plenty of folk in Bruncliffe who regarded the town fifteen miles to the south as one on a distant continent.

'But he didn't come home this time?' he asked. 'He didn't run his plans past you?'

'No. Just a few lines saying he was heading off. No itinerary. Nothing.'

'Had he ever been this impulsive before?'

'Never. Stuart isn't one of life's risk-takers.' She gave a soft laugh. 'When he was a kid, on the rare occasion I had enough money to treat him to a cake on the way home from school, he'd take an age deciding which one to have, worried he'd make the wrong choice. He certainly wasn't someone to throw over his career and take off on a whim.'

'Okay, so if he hasn't gone backpacking, where is he?'

The look Mrs Lister gave was one of exasperation. 'That's why I'm here! I want you to find him. Because I can't help feeling that something bad has happened to him.'

Despite the conviction in his client's voice, Samson was struggling not to let his scepticism show.

'I can see you don't believe me,' she continued, proving that his powers of deception were a bit rusty. 'But I won't be put off. Not when my Stuart's life is at stake. That's why I came down here in person when your colleagues didn't return my calls.'

Mrs Lister's statement clarified the scene he'd walked in on that morning. The mayhem in the hallway. The concerned mother refusing to budge until she was heard.

'To be honest, Mrs Lister, if you are right, then this is probably a matter for—'

'Don't go fobbing me off and telling me to go to the police!' she interrupted him, anticipating his advice. 'All they'll say is that he's an adult and capable of making his own way in the world and if he wants to stay out of touch, then that's up to him. But they don't know him. Every Friday night he calls without fail. And at least once a month he's over for a Sunday roast.' She smiled fondly. 'He can't get enough of my Yorkshires.'

'What about his friends? Or a partner? Is he in a relationship, do you know?'

A mournful shake of the head was the reply. 'He's always been a bit slow to mix. Even as a nipper he didn't have many friends round. And as for a girlfriend . . . ' Mrs Lister gave a wry smile, 'it's been a while. Although he did tell me he'd signed up with the local dating agency.'

'The Dales Dating Agency?'

'That's the one. Now why would he have gone to the expense of doing that if he wasn't planning on being around?'

It was a valid question. One Samson made a note of to follow up with Delilah when she got back.

'And Stuart's father?' he continued. 'Does he share your concern?'

Mrs Lister's nose wrinkled in distaste. 'Happen as he's not around. He skipped town when Stuart wasn't even weaned and we haven't seen hide nor hair of him since.'

'Could Stuart have tracked him down? Maybe gone to see him and not told you. Hence the elaborate stories about going abroad?'

'Not a chance. He'd have said. We've never had any secrets between us. Couldn't afford to seeing as we spent most of his childhood barely getting by. My wages as a cleaner at the hospital aren't much and we've no family to fall back on.' She shrugged. 'Somehow, that hardship just made us closer. So no, Stuart wouldn't have gone behind my back like that.'

'Well, in that case,' Samson concluded, 'without any concrete evidence to contradict Stuart's story, I maintain that your best course of action is to go to the police—'

His words were silenced by the thump of Mrs Lister's hand on the table, loud enough to rouse the two dogs asleep in the corner.

'What about this for evidence, then? It came this morning.' She raised her hand to reveal a postcard.

The photo on the front was enough to make anyone ditch their job and go globetrotting. A beach at dawn, lined with palm trees and looking out over a tranquil bay, green hills curving around the azure sea with a small bar enticingly captured in the background. It was stunning. The kind of shot that won awards. Underneath, the words 'Patong Beach, Phuket' gave the first indication as to Stuart Lister's destination.

'Thailand?' said Samson. The lad really had gone all out.

'Go on, read it,' said Mrs Lister, pushing the postcard towards him.

He picked it up and turned it over, surprised to see the text was typewritten.

> *Got here safely. Having a great time.*
> *Not sure when I'll be home.*
> *Love*
> *Stuart*

The brief message seemed pretty standard fare for a young man, in Samson's experience. Not that he was an expert on how sons and parents communicated, seeing as he'd managed fourteen years without so much as a phone call to his father. But either way, it wasn't what he'd expected given Mrs Lister's triumphant tone.

He looked up at his client nonplussed. 'Is it the fact

Stuart used an online service that's thrown you?' he asked, pointing at the small print on the back. 'This "Postcard4Me" company? Because I'd say that's fairly standard these days—'

'I'm not a compete dinosaur,' she snapped. 'Happen I'm well aware this is how young folk do things.' She took back the postcard and pointed at the computer-generated writing. 'Here, this is what has me worried,' she said, her finger on the bottom line. 'What do you make of that?'

Samson stared at Stuart's name. And back at Mrs Lister. 'I'm sorry, I'm not following you.'

'Kisses!' she declared. 'There's none on there. There's not a chance in hell Stuart wouldn't have added kisses.' She leaned back in her chair and gave Samson a defiant look. 'This postcard isn't from him.'

A familiar feeling of despair welled up in Samson. A feeling he would forever associate with his time as a detective in the town of Bruncliffe.

Standing in the back garden of the butcher's shop, Bruncliffe's newest detective was feeling out of her depth.

'The washing was there.' Barbara Hargreaves pointed to a line strung across the surprisingly generous space. It was currently hosting a set of bedsheets, snapping in the healthy breeze that was blowing from the west.

Ida nodded, not really sure what she should be making of all this. She was still taking in the size of the garden. Large enough for a well-kept lawn, a compact vegetable patch and a cosy terrace, complete with two chairs and a small table. Surrounded by high stone walls on all three sides, it offered a privacy she hadn't anticipated, seeing as the property was smack bang in the middle of town on the cobbled marketplace. And with the sun leaning into the west post-lunch, it was a positive suntrap.

'Does tha keep that locked?' she asked, pointing at the arched gate set snugly into the bottom wall, beyond which there was a ginnel, curving around the back of the shops on the square, from the optician's at the top of Church Street to the Spar at the bottom of Crag Hill.

'Aye. Not sure as we need to but there's some folk as think we might have a fortune sitting in the till overnight.' Mrs Hargreaves gave a dry laugh. 'Shows what they know about the current state of the meat trade.'

Ida made a note in her notebook, labouring over the words while she frantically tried to think of what to ask next. When she lifted her head, voices from the other side of the right-hand wall offered her an opportunity.

'Is that the back of the bank?' she asked.

But Barbara Hargreaves was shaking her head. 'Not that bit. The bank's yard only comes this far.' She indicated a portion of the wall nearer her own back door, about a quarter of the length of her own garden. 'The rest belongs to the Taylors.'

'The Taylors?' Ida couldn't keep the confusion out of her voice. The imposing Georgian property which had been the residence of the recently deceased mayor – his widow now rattling around it on her own – sat at the top end of the marketplace, angled in such a way that it looked as though it was shunning the commercial properties which surrounded it. 'I didn't realise they owned all that.'

'First thing Bernard Taylor did when he bought it was negotiate with the bank for their unused land at the rear.

He got it for a song,' confided Mrs Hargreaves, leaning towards Ida and lowering her voice. 'Persuaded them it was better for their security to have his premises surround them at the back. Knowing that bugger, I wouldn't be surprised if he persuaded them to stump up some of the cash for the security lights he had installed either.'

'They've got security lights on that side?'

'Yep. Super sensitive too. Our lounge looks out this way and we see them flash on and off a fair bit in the winter evenings. We sleep facing the front so it's not a problem.'

'Hmm,' said Ida, making more notes. 'And the other side, behind the chemist's?'

'Just an open parking space. Although it's not much used. Do you want to have a look?'

Mrs Hargreaves was already walking down the garden, fishing her keys out of her pocket and unlocking the gate, so Ida followed. They stepped out into the ginnel, Mrs Hargreaves remaining in the gateway while Ida prowled around, not sure what, if anything, she was looking for. After all, the incident had happened two weeks ago.

Deciding taking photos would help persuade her client she knew what she was up to, Ida took a few snaps of the empty parking lot next door, an unenclosed space that offered no cover for someone seeking to commit a crime. Between that and the tight security on the Taylors' side, it was looking like there could only have been one way in for the miscreant she was chasing. But how had they got through a locked gate? Or over a wall that was too high for scaling?

Keeping up the pretence of being a legitimate detective, Ida took a photo of the ginnel. At the very least, she could run all of this past Delilah and Samson when she got back to the office. But as she lowered her mobile, she noticed the wheelie bin left haphazardly against the wall.

'Today's bin day here, isn't it?' she asked, knowing it was from the numerous times she'd had to drag the bin round the back of the estate agent's when she was cleaning there on a Monday. 'So this wouldn't normally be out here at the weekend?'

'Aye, but that's the Taylors'. They always put theirs out on a Saturday. Happen as they're away on a Sunday, they don't have to think about it if they get back late.'

Ida was already at the bin, an idea germinating. An idea which sprouted leaves when she noticed the dent in the lid. She ran her hand over it, a sizeable hollow, took another photo and then, stuffing her phone in a pocket, began clambering up onto the bin.

'Ida Capstick,' exclaimed Mrs Hargreaves, 'what on earth are you doing? You'll break summat doing that at your age!'

Ida wasn't listening. She was too busy concentrating on standing up, palming her way up the wall as she straightened to her full height, heart pounding. Hands both on top of the wall now, she was able to lean over and look down into the Hargreaves' garden.

'Go and stand there,' she commanded, pointing to the inside.

Still looking shocked, Mrs Hargreaves did as she was ordered, taking up position on the other side of the wall opposite Ida.

Which was just as well, as Ida Capstick wouldn't have wanted anyone to witness her undignified descent from her improvised platform, ruining a good pair of tights in the process. Slightly flustered and rosy of cheeks from her exertions, she joined Barbara Hargreaves in the garden, peering at the flower bed directly below the wall where herbs had been planted. Some of which had recently suffered the full impact of something, judging by the crushed leaves.

'There!' she said, feeling a shot of satisfaction. 'Look at that sage! It's been trampled on.'

She whipped out her phone and took some photos while Mrs Hargreaves murmured her appreciation.

'So that's how they got in,' Ida said, adding more notes to her book. She paused. Another idea striking her. 'Tha said it were Ken's clothes as was taken?'

'Aye. Trousers, T-shirts and tops. Two of everything.'

'Nowt else? Tha smalls, for instance?'

Barbara Hargreaves let out a loud laugh, placing her hands on her apron where it stretched over her ample hips. 'Smalls? I'd hardly call them that. But no, my underwear was left untouched, so it wasn't some bloke with a penchant for large knickers!'

Ida nodded. She'd already figured that out. The wall and that bin – it had taken effort to discover the washing, meaning this wasn't the work of someone who happened to see it hanging out and felt drawn to take some. The items taken also suggested this wasn't a prank carried out by youngsters the worse for wear after a night in the Fleece. This was premeditated. Someone had been looking for specific clothing. Two complete outfits, in fact.

'Happen as this was someone homeless,' she said, a tingling in her veins at how much she'd managed to discover. 'A bloke most likely. Perhaps even two.'

'Great,' said Mrs Hargreaves, nodding in approval. 'Now all you have to do is find the buggers and get Ken's clothes back.'

Ida felt her bubble of optimism burst. Mrs Hargreaves was right. It was all good and well knowing how the criminals had got in. Even narrowing down the type of person it could have been. But that put her no closer to finding them.

Deciding this detective business had a lot more to it than met the eye, she flipped her notebook closed, said her farewells and crossed the marketplace to resume her real job. As she entered the estate agent's, said hello to Julie behind the desk at reception and headed for the cupboard where she kept her supplies, Ida Capstick was sure of two things.

Cleaning didn't make her feel as alive as being a detective did. And, as she wheeled out the vacuum cleaner and noted her snagged tights yet again, if she was going to continue in this snooping around lark, she was going to need a whole new wardrobe.

Crouched behind the limestone outcrop at the abandoned quarry, Rick lowered the binoculars and wiped a hand over his face, feeling the beads of sweat along his hairline. Fear. That's what was driving him now. Fear of being caught balanced against the fear of screwing things up so badly that his partners felt the need to step in. Which is why he'd spent the last few weeks devising an escape plan. A plan so final there would be no coming back from it . . .

It had all been so easy at first. When Procter Properties had hit a liquidity problem while trying to raise the funds

to develop Fellside Court – the retirement apartments iron-
ically just up from the police station in town – the situation
had been eased by the offer of help from an associate of
an associate down in London. Slightly on the shady side,
but nothing which concerned the ambitious young developer from Bruncliffe. Some time later, when the interest
on that loan became difficult to meet thanks to an unfore-
seen dip in the property market, a suggestion had been
made. An alternative way of paying back what was owed
and, to be honest, a way for Rick to make even more money.

He'd gone into it with his eyes open and his wallet empty.
He'd even persuaded Bernard Taylor to join him, the perfect
combination. An estate agency with rental property out in
the middle of nowhere on its books, owned by folk who
lived far enough away that they were satisfied to leave
Taylor's to deal with all the paperwork and the inspections,
combined with a developer able to turn those properties
around into fully functioning cannabis farms. Starting out
small, they'd tested the waters with a couple of rentals but
the rewards had been so great and the work so easy, they'd
soon scaled up until they had a thriving criminal operation
on their hands. Spending no more than eighteen months to
two years in each property before restoring it to its original
state and placing it back on the rental market, they were
making more money than they'd ever imagined. And then
the offer came to make more. To branch out, adding other
facets to their business, getting ever and ever more complicated. Ever and ever more entangled within the web of
organised crime.

All the while, they'd maintained a flawless front, no one
in Bruncliffe suspecting that hidden behind the spotless

facade of the town's mayor and the up-and-coming property developer was a very lucrative drugs trade. They simply didn't have the imagination, too willing to believe the good-looking, blond-haired Rick Procter was the man they wanted him to be. A local lad who'd worked his way up from nothing. The owner of a property empire and generous benefactor to the town.

Wasn't it Rick who'd donated large sums of money to the school? Wasn't it also him who'd been the first to dip his hands in his pockets when the rugby club was burned to the ground? Plus, he always insisted on standing a round in the pub.

Rick Procter, in the eyes of those he lived amongst, could do no wrong.

But that facade was now developing cracks, and it was getting harder to plaster over them. And what had begun as a way to make a fast profit had become a lethal quagmire from which Rick couldn't escape.

How did you tell the likes of Niko Karamanski and his brother, Andrey, part of the Bulgarian mafia and the real power behind those initial investors from the shady London firm, that you wanted to retire?

A nervous laugh escaped Rick's lips. Retire? There was too much water under the bridge. Too many things he could be done for, not least murder.

The binoculars shook in his grasp, the memory of that night, Pete Ferris' dogs, the small hovel of a caravan, the feeling of Pete struggling—

There'd been no other option. And no one to ask to do his dirty work. Because Rick knew that if his associates had got wind of the blackmail plot the poacher had hatched, it wouldn't have been just Pete who'd have been wiped off the slate. He was also painfully aware that if Niko or Andrey found out he'd screwed up in his panic, leaving behind Pete's mobile and the incriminating photos of activities out at Henside Road, they'd give him a retirement of a different sort.

So here he was. Struggling to see a way through this latest mess, just as he'd thought the sudden death of Bernard Taylor had been a turning point for the better. That the chaos of the last few months – the attempted blackmail, Taylor getting cold feet, and then the disastrous visit from the Karamanski brothers and their thuggish entourage, who'd insisted on taking part in a shoot up at Bruncliffe Manor which had quickly spiralled out of control – was finally behind him.

But when he'd seen the demise of Taylor as a blessing from above, Rick hadn't been counting on the fact that he'd be left frantically trying to erase key evidence his idiot partner hadn't seen fit to conceal. Days spent at Taylor's desk in the supposed role of a concerned friend, helping the mayor's widow keep the estate agent's ticking over while secretly deleting files and monitoring the operation.

It was becoming more and more difficult to juggle, and his brilliant idea of buying the business from the grieving – and clueless – Nancy Taylor, was so far meeting with unexpected resistance. He'd thought she'd snap his hand off at the proposition. But instead, when he'd broached the notion last week, having allowed a respectful few days to pass after the funeral, Nancy had asked for more time to consider her options.

Her options! He felt like telling her that if she insisted

on taking over the estate agent's herself, she'd wind up with an enterprise that made far less than appeared in the official books.

But of course he couldn't say that. All he could do was smile sympathetically while fuming inside. And now her equally clueless son, Neil, was back in town, strutting around like a reincarnation of his father, sticking his nose into the business before Rick had had a chance to complete his deep clean. It was heaping on even more pressure, leading to sleepless nights and a sense that he wasn't just up to his neck in this, but that the waters were beginning to close in over his head.

Voices from down below had Rick raising the binoculars back up. Delilah Metcalfe and the Bradley lad had re-appeared, expressions serious. Whatever they'd found in the cottage, it wasn't a laughing matter. They spoke for a few minutes, Delilah saying something that had the pair of them staring round, scouring the area as though searching for something, someone. Rick dropped down behind the limestone, waiting a few heartbeats before once more peering cautiously around the rock. The pair were saying goodbye, Delilah getting into the Micra, the closing of the door sounding unnaturally loud. He watched her trying to start the car. Watched her slamming her hands against the steering wheel in exasperation as the motor remained silent. And then watched her resignedly get out, Danny waving at her to join him, offering her a lift.

Together they left the quarry in the police car, the engine fading into the distance to leave Rick staring at the red Micra, stark against the white backdrop of the exposed rockface.

His thoughts were every bit as bleak.

Stick or twist?

Glancing at the date on his watch, he was aware he needed to make a decision. Because in three days' time, when Thursday came around, the decision would no longer be his to make.

But the thought of what he had planned, of what it would mean . . . A scorched-earth policy that would see nothing survive.

Forty-eight hours, he concluded. He would give himself forty-eight hours to assess the situation before taking the drastic steps he'd devised. Meanwhile, however, there were plenty of loose ends which needed to be tied up before one of them unravelled enough to strangle him. And if that meant getting blood on his hands yet again, it was a risk he was going to have to take.

In a ruthless frame of mind, Rick Procter rose to his feet and headed for his 4x4.

7

All the way back down into Bruncliffe, Delilah hadn't been able to shake the notion of being watched, a sense of something malevolent stalking her that always seemed to accompany her visits to Rainsrigg Quarry. But then, given she'd been shot at on two occasions up there – once with an air rifle, which had taken out her car window, and another time with a pistol, which had taken out her shoulder – perhaps it wasn't so much a premonition as a flashback, the residue of her previous encounters washing up against her consciousness.

Whatever it was, the creepy feeling had been bad enough inside Quarry House, its disturbing atmosphere only made worse by the barbaric homemade knife Danny had discovered. But when they'd stepped outside to leave, the skin on Delilah's neck had rippled, like someone had actually taken up residence on her burial site, not just walked over it. A ghostlike encounter of something brushing past her unseen.

She'd mentioned it to Danny, who'd confessed he felt the same, and she sensed he'd been just as glad to have her company on the drive down as she'd been to have his.

Although she'd have preferred her defunct Micra not to

have been the cause of their enforced companionship. Having been dropped off at French's garage in the industrial estate on the outskirts of Bruncliffe, she was currently surrounded by vehicles in various stages of repair, the blaring local radio station cutting through air thick with the odour of oil and engine fumes, an environment where the only possible malignancy was the imminent threat to her bank account.

Delilah could tell from Baggy's questions that the prognosis for her little car wasn't good.

'So it made no sound at all when you tried the ignition?' Tony French, whose exceptional height and thinness had earned him the nickname Baguette many moons ago – a nickname since shortened to 'Baggy', which rolled off a Bruncliffe tongue far easier – was looming over Delilah, scratching the stubble on his chin, a worried look on his long face.

'Not a peep,' she said.

'What about on the way up there? Any problems?'

'A lot of black smoke when I set off and a bit of a clicking noise.'

Baggy sucked air through his teeth and shook his head and Delilah's hopes sank even further. She started mentally assessing her savings, wondering if the small amount she'd managed to eke away over the past month was about to be swallowed up.

'I can't tell without having a proper inspection,' Baggy finally pronounced in the tones of an undertaker, 'but I'm thinking it'll be the cambelt. I did warn you it was due a change.'

He had. Back at the beginning of the year, when Delilah

could barely afford to buy fuel, let alone pay out for an expensive repair. Now it seemed her cost-cutting might have backfired, because she knew enough about cars to realise this was serious.

'How soon can you get up there and have a look?'

'I'll head up later and let you know what I find. But if it is what I think it is . . .' Baggy drew a long finger across his scrawny throat.

'Thanks for the warning,' she said, turning to go.

'Look on the bright side,' the mechanic called after her with a grin. 'If I'm right, you'll have the perfect excuse for hopping up behind O'Brien on that Royal Enfield of his. I'm sure he won't mind giving you the odd lift seeing as you gave him such a warm welcome home this morning.'

'Bloody Bruncliffe,' Delilah shot back over her shoulder with a laugh.

She walked off up Church Street, still laughing, and it struck her that she wasn't feeling the usual resentment about her personal life being public property. Samson was only just back and already her romantic involvement with him had twice been alluded to, yet she hadn't bristled. Why was that? While still in its infancy, was her relationship with him making her feel more secure?

She turned off the cobbled square to head down Back Street and saw a familiar figure standing on the doorstep of the office building, about to ring the bell. Her sense of security evaporated into thin air.

Neil Taylor, her ex-husband.

She'd completely forgotten she had an appointment with him. And she hadn't yet had a chance to tell Samson she'd been seeing him. Purely professionally, of course. Because she didn't need to explain her actions. But then again, what would he make of it . . . ?

Flustered in the extreme, she started running towards the office, just as Samson opened the door.

Rick Procter was in a foul mood. He wasn't a man high up in Ida Capstick's estimation anyway, but right now he was getting perilously close to getting a piece of her mind.

She'd just finished at Taylor's and was about to put the vacuum back in its cupboard along with her bucket of cleaning supplies – a new bucket, courtesy of Samson after her old one was stolen in a theft Mr Procter had dismissed as 'trivial nonsense' when she'd reported it! – when he'd stormed in. Letting the glass doors slam in his wake, he'd marched across the reception area and into Mr Taylor's office without so much as a hello to Ida or Julie. The door had closed firmly behind him.

Bad manners were enough to raise Ida's ire. But the trail of mud he'd tracked across the carpet she'd just cleaned really made her cross.

'Sorry, Ida,' Julie murmured, the receptionist shooting Ida a sympathetic glance. 'He's been like a bear with a sore backside for the last couple of weeks. I think the stress of running two businesses is getting to him.'

Ida bit her tongue, thinking that Delilah still managed to be civil with all the work she was currently carrying out. Starting up the vacuum, she ran it along the carpet but no sooner approached the small office at the back than the door swung open.

'Can you stop that infernal racket!' Mr Procter snapped, looking at his watch. 'And what are you doing cleaning at this time anyway? I thought we paid you to clean first thing.'

Against the noise of the running vacuum, Ida held a cupped hand to her ear. She waited for him to raise his voice before flicking the machine off.

'I SAID STOP—!' In the sudden silence, Mr Procter found himself shouting at his cleaner, Julie looking shocked in the background.

'Did tha say tha wants tea?' asked Ida. Face blank.

'Jesus. Yes. Tea.' He went back into the office.

Ida turned towards the kitchenette, catching Julie's grin as she did so. Then she set about making tea. She put the kettle on, ran the teapot under a cold tap, put one teabag in it and poured on the hot water before it had boiled. A few quick dips of the bag, barely enough to add colour, then she yanked it out, poured the liquid into a mug and added a generous amount of milk from the bottle that was on the turn.

Mr Procter was focused on the computer screen in front of him when she walked in. But as she placed the tea on the coaster and turned to go, he glanced up.

'I need you to go over to the flat on Church Street tomorrow and give it a clean, please, Ida. Julie will give you the keys.'

Ida paused in the doorway. 'Tha means the one above the takeaway?'

'Yes. We've got new tenants and it needs a thorough going over. A Capstick clean.' He smiled, that winning smile which had eased his path through life and won so many people over.

Ida didn't smile back. 'As tha wishes.'

'Great. Excellent. I'll make sure you get paid extra.'

She didn't enlighten him to the fact that every single penny he paid her went in the middle drawer of the dresser in her kitchen. A contingency fund for when he decided to try and steal Croft Cottage the way he'd stolen the O'Brien farm just up the dale from the Capsticks. Because Ida didn't share the view most folk in Bruncliffe had of this man. She knew him for the devil he was. The way he'd hounded poor Joseph O'Brien, manipulating a man in the grip of an addiction to alcohol, paying him well under the odds for Twistleton Farm and then further stinging him by persuading him to lease an apartment in Procter Property's Fellside Court. All done with that same white-toothed smile.

So Ida happily took the devil's money. But one day she was going to use it to get back at him.

Unaware of his subordinate's treacherous thoughts – she was a mere cleaner, after all – Rick Procter reached for his tea, dismissing her with a flick of his head. As the office door closed behind her, Ida was satisfied to just catch the muffled expletive as he tasted the foul brew she'd concocted.

'Did I hear Mr Procter say something about reletting Stuart's place?' asked Julie, looking up from her desk.

It was only then Ida made the connection. She'd been so caught up in meting out her own peculiar kind of justice that she'd not really been paying attention as to where it was she'd been ordered the following morning.

The apartment over the Chinese takeaway was where young Stuart Lister, the lad who'd worked for Taylor's as their lettings agent, had lived before his abrupt departure earlier in the month. His desk across the office from Julie's remained unoccupied.

'Aye, lass. Mr Procter says as tha has the keys?'

Julie was already reaching into a drawer, pulling out a key ring holding two keys. 'I guess that means he's not coming back in a hurry,' she said sadly as she handed them over. 'I mean, if he's given up the lease on his flat.'

There was something in the mournful look on the lovely receptionist's face that made Ida think she was missing her colleague more than merely in a work sense.

'Tha's not heard from him?'

Julie shook her head. 'I thought maybe he'd be in touch, a text or something, but no.' She gave a bright smile, the wattage of which didn't blind Ida. 'Can't blame him for forgetting us lot though. Who'd want to be thinking about Bruncliffe when you're sunning yourself on an exotic beach somewhere.'

It wasn't a scenario Ida had ever considered, never having been on what could be termed an exotic beach. She was pretty sure Morecambe with its shifting sands didn't count.

'I'm sure he won't have forgotten thee, lass,' she found herself saying as she took the keys. 'Happen as he's just stretching his wings a bit.'

'Thanks, Ida.' Julie gave her a grateful look.

'And just so tha knows, I've set aside some milk in the fridge for Mr Procter's tea. It's on the turn.'

Julie burst out laughing, immediately stifling it with a hand, eyes darting to the closed office door.

Pleased to have brought a smile to the face of the hard-working lass, Ida left the building, stepping out into late-afternoon sunshine on the cobbled square. As she walked to her next job, up at the retirement apartments at

Fellside Court, she mused over the odd demand Mr Procter had made. In all her time working for Taylor's, not once had she been asked to clean a rental flat at the end of a lease. Nor had she heard of anyone else being contracted to do so.

Which was odd.

But what struck Ida Capstick as even more out of character was the fact that, when making his demand, Mr Procter had used the word 'please'.

'O'Brien! I heard you were back in town. Staying long?'

Samson took in the razor-sharp cheekbones, the tawny hair flopping over the forehead and the effortless confidence that came from good looks and an upbringing sheltered by wealth. Neil Taylor had been the last person he'd expected on the doorstep.

He stared at the outstretched hand for a split second, tempted not to shake it. But Bruncliffe manners had a way of rubbing off on people and he found himself accepting the greeting, unsurprised by the extra pressure Delilah's ex-husband put into his grip.

'Longer than you, I'd imagine,' he retorted, before throwing in a jibe of his own. 'You here for the rest of your stuff?'

Neil smiled easily, dismissing the notion with a lazy flick of his hand as though the boxes and furniture stored on the top floor were something insignificant, rather than the manifestation of a failed relationship.

'Actually, I'm here to see Delilah. We're working on a project.'

The way he said it. *Project.* Something private. Something that had been going on a while.

About to succumb to his inner teen and rise to the bait, Samson felt a gentle pressure on his leg. Tolpuddle, the hound having come down the stairs at the sound of voices, was now leaning against him.

'Hello, boy!' Neil held out a hand. Tolpuddle sniffed it warily in a way that suggested it wasn't just elephants that had long memories.

Samson's gloating was interrupted by a voice hailing them from outside. Coming down Back Street at a canter was Delilah, cheeks rosy, a smile on her face.

'Sorry, Neil,' she was exclaiming. 'I got held up and then I clean forgot our meeting.'

'Actually, that's why I'm here,' said Neil, straightening up from trying to seduce Tolpuddle to lean forward and kiss her on both cheeks. Like they were in Paris or some-where. 'I need to reschedule and wondered if I could take you out for a meal tonight at the Coach and Horses instead? We could combine work and pleasure like we did last time?'

His hand was still on her shoulder. Samson was processing that. Along with the phrase 'last time'. And the Coach and Horses? Bruncliffe's attempt at an upscale pub with its fancy menu and candles on tables. What on earth was wrong with the Fleece for a business meeting? If that's what it was . . .

'Erm, not tonight, I'm afraid,' Delilah said, ushering Neil into the hall past Samson, who was still standing there, guarding the entry. In the window of the pub opposite, several faces had already gathered. 'It's been a long day and to compound things, my car's just blown up. Or rather, died quietly.'

Before Samson could comment, Neil jumped in. 'Oh no! What's happened to the Micra?'

'Baggy reckons it could be the cambelt.' Delilah ran a hand over her face, suddenly looking weary. 'So, like I said, I just want to take it easy this evening. Perhaps we could get together tomorrow morning? Ten o'clock here?'

Leaving the front door open, as big a hint as he could manage, Samson moved over towards his office and leaned against the doorframe. He had no intention of giving them privacy.

'Ten it is.' If Neil was disappointed, he didn't let it show, his smile full strength as he turned to go. But then he paused. 'Oh, I almost forgot. Can you write down the name of the software package you recommended for the business the other day? My mobile is on the blink and I don't seem to be able to retrieve emails.'

'Sure.' Delilah was heading for Samson's office. Only for him to put an arm out, blocking the way.

'Sorry,' he muttered, heart thudding, feeling stupid. 'I haven't got any pens. Ida's taken them all.'

She stared at him, head tilting to one side, eyes wide. 'Pencils?'

He shook his head, aware of Neil watching him. Aware of how petulant he must seem.

'Right. Well I'll just nip up to my office,' said Delilah, tone clipped.

She jogged up the stairs, Tolpuddle following her, leaving the two men in a strained silence.

'How's your girlfriend?' The words seemed to leap out of Samson's mouth and into the hallway of their own accord. 'Abbie, isn't it?'

'We split up.' Neil smiled again. This time a hint of challenge in the look. 'Her behaviour over Tolpuddle was the last straw.'

'Sorry to hear that,' said Samson. Thinking about how Delilah had nearly lost the Weimaraner because her ex-husband had been determined to satisfy his girlfriend's whim to own a dog. Delilah's dog.

'It's for the best,' Neil said, looking up the stairs where Delilah had reappeared at the top. 'Made me realise what I was missing up here.'

'Did I hear you saying you were missing Bruncliffe?' she asked as she joined them in the hall, handing Neil a post-it note with a grin. 'Don't tell me London's attractions are wearing thin, even for an artistic soul like yourself?'

'A man can only take so much caviar before he starts yearning for a decent pie and pea supper,' he retorted, making her laugh.

And in that split second, Samson saw it. The chemistry that had bound them together. Two Bruncliffe locals, a heritage shared that spanned the generations. Throw in a spark of attraction and it was a recipe for love.

Still could be.

'All joking aside,' Neil continued, 'I'm in no rush to head back down there. In fact, I've been thinking about relocating. The attractions of Bruncliffe have been winning me over.' The smile accompanying this comment was dazzling. And aimed solely at Delilah. Whose expression was hard to read.

'Didn't you have a go at being a graphic designer up here once before?' muttered Samson. 'I hear that didn't turn out too well.'

Neil's smile turned rigid. 'Luckily we're not all one-trick ponies, O'Brien. As it happens I'm considering other business opportunities.' He turned towards the door. 'Right, I'd best be off.' Yet again, however, he irritatingly paused in the open doorway. 'About your car, Delilah,' he said, 'how are you planning on getting around while it's out of action?'

'I don't know . . . I hadn't really thought . . .' Delilah stammered, glancing at Samson.

Samson, who was too slow on the uptake yet again, the Royal Enfield out in the yard not at the forefront of his mind right then. He was pipped at the post once more.

'Well, we've got a car sitting doing nothing since that Lister lad quit,' continued Neil. 'It's yours to use as you wish. As long as you don't mind driving around in an orange Mini with "Taylors" emblazoned down the side?'

'Oh!' Delilah's face lit up. 'That would be wonderful. Thank you so much!'

'I'll let Julie in the office know you'll be dropping by for the keys. And I'll see you tomorrow. I might even bring some cakes if you're lucky.' With one last grin, Neil Taylor finally left.

Delilah closed the door. The two of them alone in the hall now, which seemed even smaller than usual.

'So . . .' began Delilah, looking flustered. 'What was all that nonsense about the pens?'

'Cup of tea?' blurted out Samson in a diversion technique that was pure Bruncliffe. Which is how he found himself leading the woman he'd spent all afternoon planning on seducing up the stairs to the first-floor kitchen instead.

Because after that little visit from Delilah's ex-husband, Samson was no longer confident she would appreciate his efforts.

Neil Taylor's reason for rescheduling his appointment with Delilah took him up Back Street, onto the cobbles of the marketplace and along the square to the double-fronted estate agent's. His father's business. Although, as he monitored the young man's approach from the doorway of what had been Bernard Taylor's office, a perturbed Rick Procter was confident the name spanning the glass would soon be changing.

Even while he wasn't confident he would be around long enough to savour that particular victory.

The incident up at Quarry House and the return of Samson O'Brien had settled on Rick like a pint of bad bitter, souring his stomach and making him queasy. But he hadn't got where he was in life by buckling under pressure. So, for now, he had to maintain business as normal. And today's business was the purchase of his former partner's assets.

With Nancy unexpectedly digging in her heels when it came to the sale, Rick had decided to attack the weakest link. And the Taylor peacock was certainly that. He watched as Neil paused to check his appearance in the window before pulling open the door, his attention immediately going to the receptionist, a charming smile at the ready.

This was going to be like taking candy from a child.

'Afternoon, Julie,' Neil was purring. 'How's your mother?'

Julie gave a pained smile. 'She has good and bad days. But thanks for asking.'

Not knowing what ailed her parent, nor even caring – and suspecting that Neil Taylor wouldn't be caring either if Julie wasn't so attractive – Rick hid his impatience at the social niceties until the pair had exchanged a few more words. Then he stepped forward.

'Sorry, Neil, but we need to get on. I've got another meeting after this.'

'Right! Of course.' Neil gave the receptionist one last brilliant smile, and headed into the office. 'So, I'm guessing this is about you wanting to buy us out,' he said as he entered, his voice carrying back out into the main room, Julie's head swivelling round in shock.

Shutting the door on her wide-eyed stare, Rick reassessed his opinion. This was going to be like taking candy from a bloody idiot. One that would happily have his business dealings broadcast around town.

'Kind of,' he replied, taking his seat behind the desk, his smile every bit as charming as Neil's. 'There's something I need to discuss and I just thought we could have a chat about it man to man, without having to bother your mother. She's got so much on her plate at the moment. Plus, I suspect you might have a bit more of a grip on the details, given you've run your own businesses.'

The young man preened, sitting up straight, shoulders back, nodding along, as though the website design service and the dating agency Delilah Metcalfe was now running very successfully owed all their profitability to him. Whereas the truth was he'd run them into the ground before skipping town and leaving her with a crippling amount of debt.

'I appreciate your sensitivity,' said Neil. 'Mum isn't really herself at the moment. But I have to be honest, she's dead

set against selling. She seems to think she can run it herself.'
He gave a laugh, as though the idea was incredulous.

'That's what I suspected.' Rick steepled his fingers, allowing a pause to stretch as he gave the man opposite a frank gaze, enough to suggest he was contemplating whether or not to take him into his confidence. Then he nodded. 'Thing is, there are a few things I've uncovered while holding on to the reins for you and while I'm reluctant to drop this on Nancy right now, I suspect you're more capable of dealing with it.'

'What kind of things?'

'Financial improprieties.'

Neil blinked, sitting forward, his urbane demeanour more than ruffled. 'Right, I see, er . . . what kind of improprieties?'

'Erm, let's just say your father was being more than creative with the accounts. Lots of money coming in and going out without sufficient paperwork. In fact, I'd go so far as to say there was something very dodgy going on.'

'Christ!' Neil ran a hand through his hair, which flopped back onto his forehead, the brow beneath it furrowed in genuine concern. 'That could explain the holdall of cash Mum found in his wardrobe!'

Rick nodded in agreement, as if he didn't know the true origin of that money, the payoff for a blackmail never fulfilled. 'Nancy mentioned that to me after Bernard died and yes, I suspect it's tied up with what I'm seeing. And I have to be honest, it would be remiss of me as your father's closest friend to allow your mother to walk into this mess blindfolded. Especially when there's a very real risk she could end up going to prison.'

Another curse from across the desk, Neil's face ashen now. 'So what do we . . . how do we . . . ?' He stared down at the floor and back up at Rick. 'Can't we just . . . I don't know . . . clean it all up somehow?'

'It's not that easy. We're not talking a bit of unpaid tax here or something that can be simply swept under a carpet. This is going to take a lot of careful manoeuvring to keep the police out of it and your father's reputation intact.'

He saw the words hit their target, taking perverse delight in seeing someone else under pressure as Neil dropped his head into his hands before looking up with the air of a desperate man.

'I don't suppose there's any chance you're still interested in acquiring it?'

Spreading his arms wide, Rick grimaced. 'I can't say I'm as keen as I was. I'm a businessman, not an idiot. And I don't see anyone else taking it on either. It's too toxic.'

'Bloody hell, Dad,' Neil muttered. 'Why did you always have to sail so close to the wind?'

Rick gave a sympathetic murmur, while thinking the son had no idea that 'wind' didn't begin to cover the hurricane forces Bernard Taylor had been navigating for the last few years. Or rather, had been navigated through, because the inept mayor would have foundered a long time ago if it hadn't been for Rick.

The silence lengthened, and into it Rick fired his final shot. 'I can't imagine what will happen when this gets out around town. Your poor mother . . .'

A strangled oath. Then Neil cleared his throat and set his shoulders back. A businessman about to make a deal. 'What would it require for you to take it off our hands?'

'For me to buy out Taylor's in this state?' Rick shrugged. 'I wouldn't want to insult you.'

'You can't insult me. You'd be doing me a favour. So let's talk numbers.'

Half an hour later, Neil Taylor left the building in a much less jaunty manor than he'd entered. In fact, as Julie would remark later that evening to her mother, who was in a more lucid state than the Alzheimer's normally left her, he had the air of a man who'd found a fiver but lost a fortune.

By contrast, watching the young Taylor's departure, Rick Procter found himself in a much more optimistic mood. Perhaps his house of cards could survive the storm which was threatening it after all and there would be no need for that last-resort panic button. But however things turned out, he'd either just made a cunning bid for another take-over or he'd provided a bit of cover for what would be his final act in the town.

Samson was behaving oddly. That business with the pens, making her run up to her own office to get one when she knew there were plenty on his desk. Delilah couldn't imagine what was going on. Or rather, she could. Neil Taylor turning up at the office had clearly thrown him. As had the news that Neil was planning on moving back to town.

That particular nugget had thrown her, too. Not in the way it would have done a year ago, when her hurt over their broken relationship was still raw. It was more surprise than anything, that he hadn't mentioned his plans during their recent meetings. She could see how it might look from

Samson's perspective, however. He'd be presuming she'd known and not said anything.

But, she thought stubbornly, as she watched him pouring tea into two mugs, she was damned if she was going to take the time to explain. She wasn't the one who'd left town without a word and stayed away for two weeks without any contact, not even a text—

She broke off from her internal rant to sniff the air.

What was that smell? A citrusy scent. One she normally identified with Ida.

From her position in the doorway, she looked around the kitchen, taking in the gleaming sink, the washed dishes, the worktop free of crumbs. Even Tolpuddle's bowls were sparkling.

'You cleaned?' she said.

He nodded, shrugged, his smile contrite as he handed her a mug. 'Least I could do considering how busy you've all been.'

Delilah's indignation dissipated like the mist on Pen-y-ghent when the sun shone. 'It *has* been a bit manic,' she conceded. 'So, how was London?'

'Oh, you know . . . full on. Sorry I didn't get a chance to call.' He was leaning against the worktop, staring at her over his mug.

'No worries,' she heard herself say. The frustration and annoyance at his lack of communication no longer there. Instead, she was fighting the urge to just put her drink down, cross the small kitchen and kiss him. 'How's the case against Warren going?'

'Good, but there's still a way to go. Seems the corruption permeated his entire team. DC Green thinks I was the only one of the boss's crew that wasn't involved, which made me the perfect fall guy.' He grimaced and looked out of the window, leaving Delilah to contemplate how it must feel – to know that someone you'd placed such trust in could deceive you so badly. Could even try to kill you.

'What about here?' Samson asked, turning his gaze back on her with an intensity that made her senses skitter. 'How have you been? Is your shoulder healing?'

'It's getting there. Just a shame technology doesn't heal as well,' she said dryly as she held out her wrist, showing him the new smartwatch she'd had to buy after the last one was irreparably damaged in her fall following the shooting. 'That's two I've had to replace while working for the Dales Detective Agency. I'm going to have to start invoicing you!'

He laughed. 'Take it up with Ida. I think she's in charge of accounts now.' Then he nodded towards the whiteboard. 'What's going on at Quarry House that had you up there today?'

'Danny might have discovered a link to the thefts at the allotments. Someone's been squatting up there – someone with a nefarious past judging by the weapon Danny found. Kind of glad they didn't show up for the stake-out.'

Samson frowned. 'You did the stake-out? On your own?'

'No,' retorted Delilah with a flash of annoyance, wondering what he'd expected her to do when he'd buggered off. 'Tolpuddle was with me.'

Hearing his name, Tolpuddle wandered in, tail wagging when he saw them both there. No recrimination. Deciding to take her cue from the Weimaraner and move on, Delilah pointed at the postcard on the table. 'What's that?'

'Mrs Lister's evidence that her son, Stuart, is missing,' said Samson, his tone wry.

The name registered straight away. 'Stuart Lister from Taylor's? That was his mother this morning?'

'The very same.'

Confused, Delilah stared at the postcard, the palm trees and the beach a tempting proposition. 'He's in Thailand?'

'Not according to his mother. She thinks he's gone missing.'

'So what's this . . . ?' She picked up the card, turning it over to read the back, and looked at Samson. 'Isn't this proof that he's travelling?'

'Not according to her. She's adamant that the whole sudden departure is not in her son's nature. She's also convinced he would have told her before he left. But the clincher, apparently, is the lack of kisses on that postcard.'

Delilah laughed, then saw his expression. 'Seriously? That's what she's basing her suspicions on?'

He shrugged. 'That was my reaction at first. But there is something odd about it. I mean, it's not handwritten for a start – one of those websites that send it for you.'

'Nothing unusual in that. Saves the hassle of having to track down stamps or a postbox.'

'Would the photo even need to be Stuart's own, though?'

'Not necessarily. It could be a stock photo . . .' She paused, nodding. 'I see what you mean. Anyone could have sent it.' Pulling out her mobile, she navigated to the Postcard4Me website and began searching. It didn't take long. 'It's Stuart's. Has to be – there isn't a picture like that in their Thailand collection. Plus there's some graininess in this image – it's a good shot but it doesn't look professionally touched-up or anything.' She looked up at him. 'So, kisses or no kisses, I'd say you can be fairly certain Stuart sent this postcard.'

Samson laughed. 'Well, that case didn't take long to crack. It was barely worth putting up.' He glanced at the whiteboard in mock despair.

Delilah grinned. 'Happy to add your name to another one. We've got plenty for you to do.'

'Sounds like it.' He paused. 'Going back to Stuart, what about his subscription to the dating agency? Did he cancel that before he left?'

Visualising the list of participants for the upcoming Speedy Date night, she frowned. 'No,' she said. 'In fact, he's down for the next event.'

'Isn't that a bit odd? I can't imagine he earned a fortune at Taylor's, despite his grandiose title. Surely he'd have wanted to take every penny he could if he was setting off on the trip of a lifetime?'

It was a puzzle all right. It was also a pain in the backside, as Delilah now had a blank space in her schedule which would need to be filled by a suitable male. She was still processing this when Samson raised both hands in horror.

'No!' he exclaimed. 'Don't even think about it.'

'What?' she asked, trying for innocence.

'I'm not going to be a substitute for Stuart Lister. I've done enough of your date nights. And besides, Hannah Wilson is going to be there.'

'And? Are you afraid of her?' The look she gave him was full of flirtation.

He crossed the room, put his hands either side of her

on the wall, his smile melting her bones. 'Aren't you? What happens if she manages to seduce me?'

Delilah grinned up at him. 'I have it on good authority she only goes for men in unif—'

Her words were smothered by a kiss. A kiss that wasn't an accident. A kiss that wasn't interrupted by the need to catch a killer. A kiss that had Samson pulling her towards him and—

Tolpuddle watched them leave the kitchen. Heard the laughter as they negotiated the stairs, a tangle of two bodies, stumbling up the steps. He was still sitting there when the first item floated down over the bannister, landing on the floor just beyond him. A piece of cloth. He nuzzled it, feeling the warmth, the comforting scent of the man who'd come back and made everything better. More items drifted down. Then the sound of the bedroom door slamming shut.

Bemused, Tolpuddle stared at the discarded clothing. Glanced back up the stairs. And with a resigned sigh, crossed to his clean but empty bowl, and lay down next to it on the kitchen floor. It would be some time before he got fed. But the Weimaraner wasn't stressed. The bubble of anxiety which had been ballooning in his chest over the last couple of weeks had gone, leaving behind a sense of contentment and security. They were both here. His world was complete. Even if he was a bit hungry.

With May well advanced, the sun yielded its place slowly as day became evening, withdrawing reluctantly from the fields outside of town only to linger on the slate roofs, before setting the limestone crag above the marketplace ablaze in one final defiant act. By the time twilight stole in, prompting an evensong from the birds, most of the businesses in Bruncliffe had long since closed.

The three-storey building opposite the Fleece was no exception. Although a passer-by would have been forgiven for thinking there was still some commercial activity taking place inside. For through the downstairs window, there came a flicker of light. Dancing behind the gold letters that arched across the glass, it was enough to illuminate two figures, dressed but dishevelled, a large grey dog by their side.

'I wanted it to be a surprise,' Samson was saying as he led Delilah into his office, which no longer resembled a workspace.

The filing cabinet couldn't be seen, covered in a velvet curtain, a vase of flowers on its top. And the metal desk was now a bijou table, draped in a scarlet tablecloth and set for two. In the centre, three red candles in a silver candelabra provided the only light, casting a golden warmth that softened even the hideous red-flocked wallpaper and the peeling lino.

'When did you . . . is that why . . . the pens?' murmured Delilah in surprise.

'It was my seduction plan, which your ex-husband almost ruined.' Samson grinned as Delilah's cheeks matched the tablecloth. 'I realised we've never really had a first date, so I thought I'd rectify that.' He pulled out a chair and gestured for Delilah to sit. 'Dinner will be served in ten minutes.'

Leaving Delilah in a state of glorious emotion, and Tolpuddle sniffing around, inspecting the changes, Samson headed for the kitchen.

He wasn't the only one concerned with food. Out of town to the north, where twilight had got a stronger hold, already smothering the fields in pre-dark, sending the sheep silent and even beginning to steal the white from the stone walls, Croft Cottage was no more than a pinprick of light nestled against the looming fells.

Inside, Ida Capstick was clearing the table while George was putting his shoes back on, preparing to go and do some more work on his beloved tractors.

'Happen as tha's had a healthy appetite tonight,' she exclaimed, picking up the bowl that had contained the new potatoes. Not a single one remained.

George nodded, already reaching for the door, a plastic bag in one hand. He disappeared out into the yard and moments later she had a brief glimpse of the barn lights before the doors were closed and she was left staring at her own reflection in the kitchen window.

Ida Capstick, detective!

She allowed herself a grunt of amusement as she crossed to the fridge to make their sandwiches for the next day, a nice bit of ham and mustard being her intended filling. Only, there was no ham left.

Ida stared into her fridge in bemusement. There'd been four slices of Hargreaves' best Yorkshire there this morning. She was sure of it. Now the Tupperware box she kept it in was empty. It'd have to be cheese, then. But when she pulled out the chunk of cheddar, it was half the size it had been when she'd used it the previous evening.

'He's eating us out of house and home!' she muttered. For it could only be George who'd consumed it.

She set to making his sandwiches – cheese and pickle as

a necessary substitute – but when she came to place them in his Evil Knievel box, it was missing. As was his flask. He must have left them out in the barn – which was unheard of, George having a routine for everything, which included bringing his things in, rinsing them and stacking them on the drainer.

Tutting to herself, she turned to the fruit bowl on the worktop, knowing her brother liked at least a banana and an apple every day. But he was to be out of luck. The empty bowl sat there accusingly, not even the two ageing satsumas left.

Ida glanced back out of the window, across what was fast becoming a dark void to the silhouette of the barn, trying to reason why her brother was suddenly so hungry.

Was he ill? She thought not, knowing that most folk who took ill lost their desire for food. And he hadn't looked like he was ailing as he headed back to the barn. Pregnant then? She gave another grunt of amusement. Then she frowned. There was only one thing she could think of that would trigger this excess of eating.

Her brother had a tapeworm.

This thought preoccupied her for the next couple of hours as she tried to settle to her knitting. It was still with her by the time the last of the lingering light had been snuffed out in Thorpdale, enough to keep her awake as she lay in bed, staring out of the curtainless window at the stars. When she did finally drop off to sleep, her troubled dreams were accompanied by the wistful sound of a flute, playing low and plaintively.

The haunting melody didn't carry far. Certainly not over Simon's Fell or the black hump of Pen-y-ghent to Mire

End Farm, where a figure was leaning against a gate, looking up at the same stars Ida had been watching.

It was Ida's cousin, in fact. Insomnia had drawn Carol Kirby outside, hoping that a bit of fresh air might bring slumber on its heels. And that Clive Knowles, the man whose life – and bedroom – she now shared, might have stopped his infernal snoring by the time she got back under the duvet.

She stood there, marvelling at the pinpricks of light in the moonless sky with the wonder of a townie. She'd never seen stars like this in Bridlington. It was almost worth the interrupted sleep.

A soft bleat came from a nearby field, pulling her attention down across the horizon and . . .

What was that? A flicker of orange licking into the dark from the other side of the river which ran at the back of the farm. Curious, Carol opened the gate and moved down the sloping paddock towards it, glad she'd thought to take the torch off the hook at the back door, the land an unfathomable mass without it. When she reached the river-bank, she was close enough to realise what it was she'd seen.

Flames. Coming from the derelict caravan once owned by the poacher Pete Ferris.

No sooner had this dawned on her than she was running along the river to the footbridge, torchlight swinging wildly. Torchlight which became redundant as she got nearer, the fire offering more than enough illumination.

Enough to see the silhouette of someone sprinting away.

'Hey!' she shouted into the night. 'Stop!'

They didn't stop, the dark swallowing them up. But Carol did. Stopped and stared at the net curtains burning brightly in the windows. At the smoke beginning to curl out from under the roof.

Being of Capstick stock, Carol Kirby was a sensible woman. Normally. But this was a caravan which had been bequeathed to Clive by his friend Pete. A caravan she'd taken the time to clean, a herculean task only made bearable by the thought of the income they'd be able to generate from holiday lets. And so she found herself running towards it, planning on opening the door. Planning on at least turning on the taps, trying to douse the flames which looked like they had yet to get a real grip.

But the fire had other ideas. For while it was still in its infancy, it had found something. A squat metal cylinder, tucked inside one of the kitchen cupboards. Already it was wrapping itself around the rubber hose protruding from the top. Burning through it, releasing the gas inside . . .

Intent on rescuing her fiancé's property, Carol Kirby stepped up onto the rotting wooden porch at the front of the caravan just as it exploded.

8

Rain, hammering down from the sky, forming puddles in the yard and casting a veil over the Crag which rose above the back of the office building.

Normally it would be a sight to make her groan. But standing at the rear window on the top floor in just her T-shirt, Delilah let the curtain fall back into place and grinned.

'It's tipping down. Perhaps we should just take the day off?'

At the other end of the room, beyond the boxes of belongings she'd jettisoned here after her failed marriage, from the likewise-discarded double bed, Samson was watching her, a lazy smile on his lips, his dark hair falling onto bare broad shoulders.

'How do you suggest we pass the time, then?' he asked.

Her grin grew wider and she was about to elaborate when suddenly he lifted his nose, sniffed, and then leaped from the bed.

'Bacon! Shit! Ida!'

Like two teenagers discovered by unexpected parents, the pair of them started throwing on clothes.

*

In the kitchen on the floor below, Ida heard the sudden commotion of feet on floorboards. She could tell from the noise Samson wasn't alone up there.

'Happen tha didn't get much sleep, lad,' she commented to the Weimaraner waiting patiently by the cooker as she flipped the bacon.

Tolpuddle looked up at her, head tilted to one side, and let out a low whine. Whether at the nocturnal activities of his housemates or at the slow progress of the bacon, Ida couldn't tell. But she guessed both were appropriate.

When she'd entered the building and spotted the table-cloth and the candles in the downstairs office, she'd known straight away what they signified.

'Took their bloody time!' she'd muttered into the empty hallway.

And then she'd felt a shot of joy so powerful, for a second she'd thought she was about to drop down dead with a heart attack, like her cousin Carol's husband. Thinking Samson and Delilah could do with some quality time together, she'd been on the verge of creeping back out, when Tolpuddle padded down the stairs, tail wagging, expression hopeful. Deciding that a hearty breakfast was what the lovebirds – and their dog – needed more than anything, Ida had set to work.

Besides, she thought as she put the teapot and two mugs on the table and glanced at the whiteboard above it, there were investigations to see to. A heck of a lot of them.

'Good morning, Ida!' Samson was in the doorway, grinning, hair tousled, a spark of energy about him.

'Don't see what's so good about it,' she grunted, casting a glare at the grey skies and pouring rain outside the window before fixing her gaze on him. 'Happen tha knows summat I don't.'

She had the pleasure of seeing his cheeks redden. But still he grinned at her. And she was struck by the wish that his mother could see him like this, so happy with life and clearly in love.

'Morning.' Delilah slipped into the room and took a seat at the table, eyes not catching Ida's, a radiance about her Ida had never seen before. Certainly not during the years she was with that Taylor scoundrel. She had nothing to be sheepish about in Ida's book.

'Morning, lass.' Ida accompanied her greeting with a rare piece of affection, a pat on Delilah's arm as she placed a plate in front of her. That the pat was of the solid type, identical to the ones she gave Tolpuddle, didn't detract from the intention. 'Eat up,' she said.

'Crikey, Ida.' Samson was eyeing the two bacon sandwiches on his plate as he carried it to the table and sat next to Delilah. 'Are you trying to fatten me up?'

'I heard tha needs stamina,' she retorted.

Samson laughed while Delilah dipped her head, but not before Ida caught the grin.

Placing the last slice of bacon in Tolpuddle's bowl, the dog nudging her out of the way in his eagerness, she leaned back against the worktop, mug in hand, and watched them.

Delilah's foot, resting on Samson's. His knee touching hers.

'So,' she said into the silence, 'what are tha plans for the morning?'

They looked at each other, Delilah almost choking on her sandwich as she suppressed a laugh. Ida shook her head, turning to roll her eyes at Tolpuddle, who in turn was staring at the frying pan in hope.

It was going to be a long day.

'Morning!' From below came a cheery shout, closely followed by a scamper of youthful footsteps up the stairs, Nina appearing on the landing, breathless with news. 'Have you heard about the fire?'

Whatever levity had been in the kitchen was quelled by her serious expression.

'What fire?' asked Delilah.

'A caravan blew up last night over in Selside. I think it was the one we're supposed to be investigating.' She pointed at the whiteboard.

'Pete Ferris's caravan?' Samson asked. 'Are you sure?'

Nina nodded. 'I was helping Dad bring in the supplies this morning and one of the delivery guys is a volunteer fireman. It was all he could talk about. Seems someone was caught in the explosion. They've been taken to hospital but it doesn't sound good. He reckoned they were a goner.'

'Did he say who it was?'

The teenager shook her head. 'Not by name. He just said it was a woman from across the river. From that farm beneath Pen-y-ghent—'

There was a crash of ceramic hitting a hard surface and a bark from Tolpuddle, as Ida Capstick's mug shattered at her feet.

Samson had never seen Ida so shaken. Living at the other end of Thorpdale to the O'Brien farm, the woman had been a rock his entire childhood, all through his mother's illness, all through the initial trauma of her death, and in the years that followed when Samson's father lost himself in alcohol, leaving his pre-teen son trying to run the farm.

That rock was currently sitting at the kitchen table, grey with shock, a replacement mug of tea untouched in front of her.

Unable to get through to Clive Knowles at Mire End Farm, Delilah had finally verified Nina's account by calling Sergeant Clayton at the station. Pete Ferris's caravan had indeed been destroyed in a fire, which had culminated in the gas tank exploding. And yes, Carol Kirby had been badly injured in the blast.

'Do they think it was an accident?' Samson asked, the vague disquiet he'd felt when Nina had first blurted out her news having cemented into something more solid. Yet another accident with Pete Ferris and his property at its centre.

'The fire investigator's been there since first light,' said Delilah, 'so we'll have to wait for the official report. But Sergeant Clayton thinks it was probably just kids mucking around. I mean, who'd want to burn Pete's caravan down?'

'And Ida's cousin?' Nina's voice had lost some of its confidence since the news she'd carried in had turned out to have consequences closer to home. She was sitting next to Ida, eyes wide, following the conversation. 'If she lives across the river, how come she was there at that time of night?'

It was a valid question, one Samson had been asking himself.

'Bad timing?' Delilah shrugged. 'Until we've spoken to Clive we won't know more.'

'That's what we'll do, then,' he said, standing up. 'Let's

go over to the farm and see if we can find him. Have a look around the scene of the fire while we're there.'

Ida's gaze snapped back into focus and onto Samson. 'Tha suspects there was more to this than mere tomfoolery, then?'

'Possibly not. But it won't hurt to keep an open mind.'

She nodded, still holding him with a fierce regard. 'Tha'll find who did this,' she said, more of a demand than a question. 'For Carol's sake.'

'I'll do my best.'

'That's good enough for me, lad.'

Nina stood, pen in hand, and solemnly added the words *Caravan Fire* to the whiteboard, putting Samson's name next to it.

'It's a bit garish!' Half an hour later, in the car park behind the town hall with the rain still pelting down, Samson was staring at the orange Mini with exaggerated horror. 'Not quite the vehicle for undercover work.'

'Beggars can't be choosers,' retorted Delilah, letting Tolpuddle onto the back seat before getting behind the wheel and starting the engine. 'Are you coming or not?'

Having been responsible for bringing Clive and Carol together, Delilah had felt compelled to check up on the farmer, to make sure he was coping in the wake of the dreadful accident and to see if there was any more news from the hospital. She'd also been keen to accompany Samson to the burned-out caravan because she could tell he was brooding on something. The way he'd been brooding since they'd discovered poor Pete after he'd taken his own life.

While she acknowledged her partner's preoccupation could be attributed to unfounded guilt – Samson having missed several calls from the poacher in the hours leading up to the man's death – she'd learned to trust his amazing investigative instinct. If it was twitching, she wanted to be there.

So she'd called Neil Taylor to put back their meeting to the next day, leaving a message when her call went unanswered, and then jogged round to the estate agent's to collect the keys for the Mini. Because while she might be high on emotions after the incredible evening she'd just spent with Samson – evening, night and the early hours! – Delilah had no intention of riding pillion all the way out to Mire End Farm in the pouring rain.

Samson was clearly of the same opinion, finally opening the passenger door and getting in. Long legs folded uncomfortably in the small space, he was fiddling around, trying to adjust the seat as she pulled out of the car park and headed for the Horton Road. Having had no success by the time they left the town behind, he sat back, knees still jutting up awkwardly.

'Bloody seat's jammed,' he muttered. 'Perhaps the Enfield was a better option after all. Plus I'd somehow managed to forget about your rally-style driving.'

His comments came as Delilah increased the speed, the Mini surging forward in a way the Micra never had. Samson placed a hand on the dashboard.

She grinned. 'Relax. It's raining. I'm taking it easy.'

And she was, because the road was awash with water from the downpour, large puddles spanning across the tarmac, the fields behind the stone walls flooded in patches and the large hump of Pen-y-ghent hidden behind grey cloud. It was hard to believe summer was just around the corner.

'You can see why Stuart took off for Thailand,' said Samson, sharing her thoughts as the rain lashed the windscreen.

'Talking of Stuart, have you decided what you're going to tell Mrs Lister? Are you taking the case?'

'I don't know.' The statement was accompanied by a sigh. 'I'd feel like a fraud accepting her hard-earned cash when there's so little basis for an investigation. The postcard seems legit and no one else has raised any concerns. So all we have to go on is a few missing kisses.'

'And an uncancelled direct debit to the Dales Dating Agency.'

Samson looked at her in surprise. 'You think this is worth pursuing, then?'

Delilah shrugged. 'What harm would it do to carry out a few preliminary enquiries? Maybe talk to some people who knew him in Bruncliffe and see if they share his mother's unease. Then take it from there.'

Conscious he was still looking at her, she glanced at him and saw a wide grin on his face, and a glint in his eyes that made her cheeks burn.

'Hark at you, Delilah Metcalfe! You sound like a proper detective. Perhaps I should have left you running the business for longer.'

She glowered and he laughed. Then her attention was back on the road. Just in time, as they came round a corner to see a sheep and lambs on the tarmac, straddling the white line.

Delilah braked, the antilock kicking in, the car juddering but holding firm despite the surface water before it snapped to a halt, and sent Samson flying backwards as his seat finally came unstuck.

The ewe and her lambs stood for a few seconds, staring at them in shock, before running across the road and scrabbling over a portion of collapsed wall.

'You both okay?' Heart rattling, Delilah looked over her shoulder to Samson in his new position, Tolpuddle on the backseat giving a surprised bark in reply.

'Fine,' said Samson, hugging the Weimaraner. 'Just glad we weren't in the Micra. Not sure the outcome would have been as good.'

Dry-mouthed, Delilah just nodded, focused on getting the car moving before something came around the corner and slammed into them.

'On the plus side,' he continued, readjusting his seat as she pulled away, driving even more cautiously than before, 'at least my leg-room problem is sorted—'

He broke off at the sound of rustling paper coming from under his feet, and leaned into the footwell. When he sat back up, he was holding a buff-coloured folder in his hand. He flipped it open, leafing through the contents.

'Huh. That's ironic,' he murmured.

'What is it?'

'A file from Taylor's for a rental property. Stuart mustn't have noticed he'd left it in here. It's for Henside Road.'

'And?'

'Wasn't that where he had his near-death experience with the tractor last autumn? Maybe that's what pushed him over the edge. An inspection visit to the place where he almost died.' Samson gave a dry laugh, placing the file on the back seat. 'It'd be enough to make anyone yearn for something different.'

'That and this bloody rain,' agreed Delilah as she pulled off the road and onto the track at Mire End Farm.

Just as she said it, the rain stopped as suddenly as it had started, and it was into watery sunshine that the stooped figure of Clive Knowles emerged from the farmhouse. The farmer looked like he'd aged a decade overnight.

Not even waiting for Delilah to park, he flagged them down and bent to the open window, eyes red with fatigue and face lined with worry.

'I'm just heading back to the hospital,' he said.

'How is she?' asked Samson.

Clive shook his head, biting his bottom lip. 'Not good. Her condition deteriorated last night so they've taken her to Leeds. They said she's got a suspected bleed on the brain—' He broke off to stare up at the fells, fighting to maintain his composure.

Delilah put a hand on his arm. 'If there's anything we can do . . .'

He nodded, turning back to look at them, his expression now severe. 'Aye, there's something you pair can do. Find the bastard who did this. Because I'm damn sure this were no accident.'

Ida wasn't one for slacking. Even if she had just had a shock. So after Samson and Delilah left for Mire End Farm, she'd gathered her scattered wits and headed off to work. Cleaning bucket in one hand and umbrella in the other, she walked across town to Church Street and the Happy House takeaway, where she let herself into the shared hallway of the flats above.

Closing the door behind her, she was immediately aware of the damp. Over the aromatic scent of Chinese cooking was the heavier odour of washing put away wet, and on the wall to the side of the entrance was a telltale dark patch seeping up past the skirting board. Whoever the landlord was, they weren't keeping the place in good repair.

Ida made her way upstairs, the umbrella and bucket clanking against each. Two flats occupied the upper floor, one directly at the top of the stairs, and Stuart's at the other end of a dingy landing. As she turned the key in Stuart's door, she heard a baby's cry coming from the neighbouring flat. Glancing over her shoulder, she saw Mrs Lee, the takeaway owner's wife, peeking out into the hall, before the door was eased shut, the baby's cries more muffled now, but still audible.

Thinking that nothing much would get past Stuart's neighbour, Ida let herself into the young man's home.

Although home didn't really describe it.

There was no warmth to the place. A poky kitchenette – basically just a gas cooker, a sink and a few wall cupboards – led directly onto a cramped lounge-diner housing a faded sofa and a folding table, taken up almost entirely with a TV. Off the lounge was the bedroom, the double bed against the wall on one side but still only leaving enough room for a hanging rail in lieu of a wardrobe, and a slim chest of drawers. Ida could smell the sourness of the bathroom before she even put her head in the door and wasn't surprised to see mould blooming on the wall.

Little wonder the lad had gone off on his travels. There wasn't much he would come across in terms of accommodation that would be worse than what he'd put up with during his time in Bruncliffe.

Feeling a pang of shame that anyone could rent out a property in such a state, she set about cleaning, glad to have something to take her mind off the awful news from Mire End Farm.

Because Ida felt terrible about what had happened to her cousin. Guilty even. Yes, they'd had their differences when the newly widowed Carol had arrived in Bruncliffe to stay with the Capsticks. Trouble was, they were both fanatical cleaners and there hadn't been enough at Croft Cottage to occupy two folk of such a persuasion. With tensions growing, Ida had been on the verge of taking drastic measures when Delilah had stepped in and secured Carol a position at Clive Knowles' farm as a live-in housekeeper.

The rest was history, Clive and Carol forming an unexpected attachment. Which really Ida should be taking credit for. But she couldn't help thinking, as she replaced the now-sparkling oven racks and started on the hob, that she was somehow to blame for the incident which had left her cousin at death's door. Because without Ida's interference, Carol would still be living in Thorpdale and a long way from the caravan that had blown up.

She stepped back, hands on hips to admire her work, and was struck by how clean the flat actually was. If you discounted the mould, which the lad couldn't be blamed for, Stuart had kept the place in good order. The oven hadn't been that bad and the cupboards weren't sticky or stained like in some houses. The carpet had been vacuumed regularly too, although that didn't disguise the fact it was at least a decade past its best.

It made Ida curious as to what Mr Procter, a man she wouldn't have taken for running up wanton expenses, had been thinking when he'd asked her to clean it. Still, she mused as she opened the cupboard below the sink, it wasn't her place to query his decisions—

The shiny bright red plastic broke her train of thought.

'That's my bucket!' she exclaimed, reaching in to pull out the item she'd last seen at Taylor's over three weeks ago. It was heavier than she'd expected, a duster draped across the top, further corroborating her suspicion. For not only had her bucket been stolen from the estate agent's, but a duster too, the rest of her cleaning supplies having been discarded on the floor of the cupboard, an action which had baffled Ida as much as the theft.

She pulled back the duster with an indignant humph and stared at the contents.

Files. Quite a few of them. And from Taylor's by the looks of things.

She pulled one out and flicked through it. Something to do with a rental property. Feeling none the wiser, she shoved it back in the bucket – *her* bucket – and found herself re-evaluating the lanky lettings agent, who'd seemed such a quiet lad. Yet here was evidence that he was a thief. He'd stolen her bucket and her duster and helped himself to a heap of Taylor's files at the same time, none of which made any sense. Especially not when he'd shunned the opportunity to steal a load of excellent quality cleaning supplies. Unless . . .

She pictured the heap of supplies she'd discovered on

the floor of the storage cupboard at Taylor's, jumbled there exactly like someone had upended the bucket they'd been stored in. Someone in a hurry.

And the duster?

It had been draped over the bucket, hiding the contents from view.

Readjusting the scenario in her head, Ida came to the conclusion that she'd had it all wrong. Stuart Lister hadn't stolen her bucket, per se. He'd stolen the files and then simply used her bucket and the duster to transport them unseen back to his flat.

Somehow that made it better and she found herself forgiving the lad, especially now she'd got her belongings back. But it still begged the question as to what the hell was in these folders that had made them worth stealing in the first place?

9

'I told you there wasn't much to see, O'Brien.' Sergeant Clayton was standing at the edge of the black mass which had once been home to Pete Ferris. 'That explosion did a good job of obliterating the lot.'

Samson merely nodded, continuing his careful walk amongst the ruins, wisps of smoke still rising from the twisted pile of melted metal and charred wood. Set against the backdrop of the vibrant green fells and the majesty of Pen-y-ghent, the remains of the caravan were a discordant note in what was turning into a beautiful sunny day.

'Stubborn as a mule,' muttered the sergeant with a heavy sigh, turning to Delilah, who was holding Tolpuddle on a short lead to prevent him walking on any hot ashes. 'He won't find owt the inspector didn't, and she found bugger all.'

'Did she give any idea as to what caused the fire in the first place?' asked Delilah. 'Was it arson?'

The sergeant narrowed his eyes, staring at her. 'Who would have any reason to want to burn that piece of crap down?' He turned to include Samson in his gaze as he came to join them. 'Unless you two know something I don't?'

'It's not public knowledge yet but Pete Ferris left a will,' said Samson.

Sergeant Clayton's jaw dropped. He glanced at the smouldering debris in disbelief. 'You're kidding me! Why would a man who was always broke pay out to have a will drawn up for that lot?'

'Search me. But he did. Matty's got us doing background checks to verify Pete's assets before the details are made public.'

'And the beneficiary?'

'Clive Knowles.'

'Well, now . . .' The sergeant removed his helmet and scratched his head, looking across the river in the direction of Mire End Farm. 'Not Pete's family, then?'

'Nope.'

'So let me guess, you're thinking some disgruntled relative might have done this?'

Samson shrugged. 'It's one possible theory.'

'Christ, O'Brien. Nothing is ever straightforward when you're involved,' the sergeant grunted. 'Two weeks down in London and you're seeing shadows in every corner.'

'You still think it was just kids mucking around, then?' Delilah asked.

'I'll tell you what I think,' replied the sergeant, rubbing his stomach, a loud rumble coming in response, 'I think that working with you pair is not helping my ulcer any!'

'Sorry,' murmured Delilah. 'We don't mean to badger you. But this case is a bit close to home, what with Carol being involved.'

'Case? Has Clive Knowles hired you?'

Delilah nodded and Sergeant Clayton let out another sigh.

'Can't say as I blame him. If it was my lass who'd been caught up in this, I'd want answers, too. It's a rum do all right.'

'So you *don't* think it was kids, then?' Samson was staring at the sergeant.

'Happen as I'm leaning towards it being something else,' he conceded, turning to Delilah. 'Something you and young Danny stumbled on yesterday up at the quarry.'

'The break-in? You think whoever did that is connected to this?'

'Makes sense. The inspector said the fire could well have been accidental as there was no sign of accelerant being used. So my theory is that someone was squatting here and things got out of hand. A candle left unattended. A camping stove knocked over. Suddenly there's a blaze which catches the gas cylinder and, boom!' Sergeant Clayton threw his arms in the air to further illustrate his explanation. 'Which is why I've got Danny back at the station trawling through computer files, seeing if we can't get a handle on whoever this person is who's been hanging around town. Because having seen that makeshift knife that was left in Quarry House, I don't think we're dealing with some frightened runaway kid.'

Delilah shivered uneasily at the memory of her solo stakeout. 'Poor Carol,' she said. 'She didn't know what she was walking in on.'

'Aye. Clive seemed to think she must have seen the fire and come over to investigate.'

'And then what? Someone attacked her?' Samson asked.

'Could be. The doctors haven't ruled out the possibility that her head injury was inflicted deliberately rather than incurred in the explosion.' Sergeant Clayton gave a pained smile. 'We all know Carol's not the type to shrink from confrontation, so maybe she saw someone fleeing and challenged them and got more than she'd bargained for. Which leads me to believe that whoever this is, they're dangerous. So I'm going to be asking folk to take extra precautions until we've apprehended this miscreant – make sure doors are locked at night and keep us abreast of anything out of the usual, that kind of thing. I'd appreciate it if you two could help spread the word.'

'Of course,' said Delilah.

'Right, well, I'd best get back to the station. You know how to get hold of me if you uncover anything I need to know about.' The last was aimed pointedly at Samson, who nodded before the sergeant walked back across the field towards the police car, parked up next to the vivid Mini.

Delilah waited until he was out of earshot before turning to Samson. 'You're not buying his theory, are you?'

Samson grinned. 'How well you know me.'

'Want to elaborate?'

He shrugged. 'Not sure I can. Just a gut instinct. There's been way too much drama surrounding Pete and his property for it all to be a coincidence.'

'You're sure that's not just the guilt talking?' Delilah said gently, thinking again of those missed phone calls.

'Possibly. But I find it strange that someone would break into a caravan and use candles or a camping stove when there was a perfectly functioning electricity supply, plus a gas cooker with a nearly full cylinder already there.'

'Fair point. So if we're presuming arson, the most obvious starting point would be Pete's will. A disgruntled relative, as Sergeant Clayton said.'

There was a slight pause before Samson nodded. 'Definitely worth looking into, especially as it ties in with what Matty's already asked us to do. Could be worth having another chat with Clive, too, just to see if he told anyone about his unexpected inheritance.'

'Poor Clive,' murmured Delilah, tears filling her eyes at the haunted look on the man's face when he'd left them to go to the hospital. 'If it turns out his loose talk was the cause of Carol being hurt, he'll never forgive himself.'

She felt an arm slip around her shoulders, Samson drawing her into his chest and placing a soft kiss on her forehead. But as she looked up at him, his focus was on the blackened remains of Pete Ferris's caravan. She sensed that whatever that gut instinct of his was telling him, this case was going to be more complicated than it seemed.

PC Danny Bradley was feeling more than a little frustrated. A caravan burned down in the middle of the night, the resulting explosion placing a woman in hospital, all possibly connected to something he'd uncovered, and what did his sergeant do? Stuck him on desk duty, combing through files and police alerts to see if there was anyone matching the profile of their mystery squatter.

The young constable would far rather have been at the crime scene, especially as Sarge had radioed to say Samson and Delilah had turned up. Although his boss hadn't voiced the arrival of the Dales Detective Agency duo in such non-descript terms. But instead of getting their input and being at the heart of the action, Danny was sitting in an office, staring at a computer screen. To make it worse, the downpour of the early morning had given way to brilliant blue skies, one of those days when it was almost criminal to be inside.

With a sigh, he continued scrolling through the latest bulletins from police forces across the region. So far, nothing had caught his eye and he was beginning to suspect he was searching for the proverbial needle in a very large haystack.

Someone on the run, possibly a felon, and probably dangerous.

The only possible match was a repeat offender who'd walked out of an open prison over in Lincoln a few days ago and was the subject of a large manhunt. Classed as a threat to the public with a history of violence, the man's description sounded right. But the dates didn't fit. If Sarge's theory was correct and the intruder at Quarry House was the same person who'd been squatting at Pete Ferris's caravan, then they'd been in the area for at least three weeks, possibly longer, whereas the escaped prisoner had only been at large for forty-eight hours.

Reaching the end of the police updates with no other likely contenders materialising, Danny pushed back his chair in exasperation. He was getting nowhere. In fact, the entire exercise felt like a waste of time. Through the outer office window came the gleam of sunshine. He needed no further temptation.

A brisk walk around the marketplace to clear his mind and then he'd get back to it.

Minutes later he was stepping out onto Church Street and taking a deep breath, the air so fresh after the recent rain, the wet stone of the Crag glinting in the sun. Already feeling more invigorated, he started striding up towards the cobbled square, where he found himself lured towards Peaks Patisserie. A coffee to accompany his walk. That would help. Just a coffee. No cake. Because the last thing the young constable wanted was to start emulating his sergeant when it came to the temptations of the sweeter kind.

'Morning, Danny! What can I get you?' Lucy Metcalfe was slicing up a tray of salted-caramel brownies behind the counter. And what a counter it was.

Bakewell tarts, Yorkshire parkin, lemon-and-ginger scones, a tea loaf (made even more delicious, in Danny's opinion, when eaten with a slice of Wensleydale), a sumptuous raspberry and white-chocolate cake, a chocolate fudge cake, an array of muffins and—

'Just a coffee to go,' he said, summoning his willpower.

'Nothing for Sergeant Clayton?' she asked in surprise, continuing to cut up the brownies, the knife hitting solidly against the chopping board with each strike. 'I happen to know he's a fan of the fudge cake.'

Danny grinned. 'I think you're doing him a disservice by suggesting he's only capable of having one favourite.'

She laughed, putting the knife down and wiping her hands on her apron before turning towards the coffee machine. And Danny felt his resolve crumble, like a poorly constructed drystone wall in a winter storm.

'Oh go on then,' he said. 'Make it two slices of the chocolate fudge cake.'

'Good decision!' She finished making his coffee, placing it on top of the counter before reaching for a knife. Not the large one she'd been using earlier but a longer, slimmer one, its edge serrated. 'Different cake, different cutting requirement,' she explained, spotting his focus on the blade as she expertly cut into the cake and transferred the slices to a box. 'You can tell a lot about a chef from the knife they use.'

Danny's head snapped up, his attention no longer on the delicious treat as his synapses fired, making unexpected connections. Knives. Blades. Identity . . .

'Why didn't I think of that before?' he murmured.

'What's that?' Lucy was handing over the box and holding out the card reader for him to pay.

'Folk being identified by their knives,' said Danny excitedly, tapping his credit card and grabbing his purchases before rushing out of the door, eager to get back to the task he'd been so anxious to leave.

Lucy Metcalfe watched him hurry past the window, down the cobbles and off out of sight, shaking her head in bemusement at how working in law enforcement in Bruncliffe seemed to have an odd effect on people, turning them from staid, dependable citizens into impetuous, unpredictable investigators. Although, she mused with a laugh, revising her hypothesis while cutting up the rest of the brownies, in the case of her sister-in-law Delilah, she'd already had those traits in abundance.

Across the other side of the marketplace on Back Street, Samson was opening the front door of the office building, one eye on Tolpuddle, who was pushing ahead of him into the hallway, the other on the orange Mini as it disappeared down the road. Having had a call from Baggy, Delilah was on her way to the garage to get the verdict on the Micra. And Samson was hoping the news was better than she was expecting.

For one thing, the little red car was a lot less conspicuous, something Samson had learned to prize in a life lived undercover. For another, it was a lot less powerful. While the steep roads in the area might make such an attribute in a vehicle unappealing to most, to a passenger in a car being driven by Delilah Metcalfe, it was something to be treasured. Definitely worth sacrificing the Mini's extra leg room for, in Samson's opinion. Because with Delilah at the wheel, he spent most of their journeys in discomfort anyway, one hand gripping his seat and his feet braced against the floor.

The brief drive back from Pete's caravan had been no exception, Delilah whipping around corners now the rain had cleared, the stone walls flashing past in a blur as the Mini reached speeds the Micra wasn't capable of.

'What do you reckon, boy?' Samson murmured, bending to pat Tolpuddle's flank. 'You hoping we get the Micra back too?'

There was a burst of laughter from the top of the stairs, Samson looking up to see Nina and the tall figure of Nathan Metcalfe watching his conversation with the dog in amusement.

'Nathan!' Samson exclaimed, delighted to see his godson. 'What are you doing here?'

Nathan was coming down the stairs, Nina behind him, his amusement changing rapidly into awkwardness in the way typical of adolescents.

'Erm, just came in to see how Nina was doing.' A flush of colour highlighting his cheeks, his head held slightly to one side, the lad was the mirror image of his father at the same age.

It was enough to transport Samson back to his teens, hanging out with Ryan Metcalfe at Ellershaw Farm, Ryan excited about the prospect of joining the army and heading off to exotic climes. Climes that would see him get killed in action, leaving behind a widow and child. Watching Nathan's approach, Samson knew how proud Ryan would have been of the young man his boy was becoming.

'And?' he asked as the lad reached the hall and bent down to make a fuss of Tolpuddle.

Nathan frowned up at him. 'And what?'

'How's Nina doing?' Samson grinned.

'I've been busy,' said Nina, stepping in front of Nathan with a grin to match Samson's, not in the least daunted by his teasing. 'I was supposed to be inputting new clients into the dating agency system but given what's been going on, I thought it might be more useful if I concentrated on verifying Pete Ferris's assets instead. You know, seeing as there was the fire and all.'

Samson nodded, impressed by her initiative. 'How did you get on?'

'According to the land registry, Pete is – or was – the rightful owner of the land. And as for the caravan, I got Ida to give me the number for her cousin, who cleared that up for me.'

'What's Ida's cousin got to do with this?'

'She's married to Pete's uncle.' Nina gave him the look that Bruncliffe locals reserved for folk unschooled in the region's genealogy.

'Of course she is,' he muttered.

'Anyway, according to Ida's cousin's husband, Pete was left the land and the caravan by his father some years back, a reward for sticking around when his old man got out of prison. Apparently the rest of the kids couldn't wait to leave town.'

'Not much of a reward,' commented Nathan. 'The place was a dump.'

'Were you in there?' asked Samson in surprise, knowing Pete wasn't one for inviting people into his home.

Nathan shook his head. 'Just saw through the door.

Remember last month when we went over to chat to him about the sheep rustling?'

Samson did remember. The way Pete's normally aggressive lurchers had lain down for Nathan, the lad having forged an affinity with them after they helped rescue him off the fells back in March. He remembered how Pete had been with the teen, too. When Samson and Delilah's questions had drawn a blank from the taciturn poacher, it had been Nathan who'd persuaded him to speak, whispering something to him which got him talking. Not much, mind, but more than he had been.

'Did Ida's cousin give any indication of disgruntlement amongst Pete's family about the will?' Samson asked, turning back to Nina.

'She seemed to think it wasn't an issue. In fact, she's of the opinion that Pete's brothers and sisters don't want any connection with their childhood. Which suggests it wasn't a happy one.'

'You can say that again,' said Samson, recalling the emaciated, whey-faced kids at school. 'Think they spent most of it half-starved.'

The two teenagers stared at him with the incomprehension of youth, the experience of the Ferris family so far removed from their own.

'Right,' Samson continued, 'that's all a great help, Nina. Thanks a lot.'

Nina flashed her grin then tipped her head towards the door. 'We're just heading out to scrounge some food off Dad. Want to join us?'

Samson was aware of his empty stomach, and the temptation of Kamal Hussain's exquisite curries was strong.

But out of the corner of his eye, he was also aware of the sudden frown that had darkened his godson's brow. Three was definitely a crowd in this instance.

'Thanks, but I've got work to do. Catch you later.'

The front door opened and slammed shut behind them and Samson was left alone with Tolpuddle.

'Beans on toast?' he offered the dog, who looked as disillusioned with the alternative to Nina's offer as Samson felt.

Together they went upstairs into the kitchen, the Weimaraner making it clear by a few strategic nudges that he wasn't prepared to wait for food any longer. So Samson filled the dog bowl before, stomach growling in complaint, he turned to start preparing his own meal. Reaching down a tin of baked beans from the cupboard, he emptied it into a pan and turned on the stove. And immediately he was thinking about the fire at Pete Ferris's caravan.

It was nagging him. That Sergeant Clayton was happy to go along with this reckless-squatter theory. Samson wasn't one for ruling out the unusual when it came to crime, but when there were facts which contradicted the logic an investigation was based on, then it was time to start considering other options. The ample gas supply and working electrics were big enough contradictions to make Samson uneasy about accepting the sergeant's line of enquiry.

As for the speculation that a disgruntled Ferris family member might have burned it down, it didn't really make sense. Apart from Nina's excellent work in establishing that Pete's bizarre bequest hadn't triggered any fury, even if it had, why would a relative destroy the caravan without contesting the will first? They could have destroyed what might become their own property.

His musings were interrupted by the opening and closing of the front door, followed by the sound of solid footsteps coming up the stairs.

'Afternoon, Ida,' he said, turning towards her as she appeared on the landing and strode into the kitchen. Only to place the red bucket she was carrying on the table with a thump. Then she picked up the red marker pen and wrote the words *Theft of Ida's bucket* in the corner of the white-board before promptly writing 'SOLVED' in smug block capitals next to it.

'You found your bucket!' he stated, incredulous.

'That scoundrel Stuart Lister had it,' she muttered. 'My good duster too.' She gestured at the bucket where a yellow duster did indeed lie draped across it. 'I was cleaning in his flat for Taylor's and found them stowed under the sink.'

'I didn't take Stuart for a thief,' said Samson with a smile. 'He must have just borrowed it for something.'

'Aye!' snapped Ida, glowering at his levity. 'Tha's right. He borrowed it to commit an even bigger crime.' At which she whipped off the duster and revealed a stack of files beneath it. 'From Taylor's,' she added as Samson stretched out to take one.

Details of a rental property. He flicked through another one. The same.

'Why on earth—?'

Ida was shaking her head. 'Buggered if I can make head nor tails of it. But I figured as I'd bring them here first seeing as tha's looking into the lad's whereabouts. Besides, that Mr Procter wasn't concerned about the disappearance of my cleaning kit when I reported it, happen as he won't be bothered about this lot being missing either.' The last was accompanied by a contemptuous sniff.

Samson was still trying to work out this Capstick logic, which he suspected made sense to a woman capable of holding a grudge as powerful as any blood feud, when the door opened and closed again, the footsteps up the stairs a lot lighter this time.

Delilah. Samson felt his heart skip and then start thumping, as bad as any adolescent on a first date. Fortunately he was saved the scrutiny of Ida's usual omniscience by her focus on the red bucket and its contents.

'What I can't understand,' she was saying, frowning at the files, 'is why the lad stole them when he knew he was going away. That just doesn't make sense.'

'Hi.' Delilah was in the doorway, a plastic bag in one hand and a notebook in the other.

'How did you get on? Is the Micra alive and well?' asked Samson, soaking in her appearance, feeling a daft smile making its way across his lips of its own accord.

'Unfortunately not. It's off to the scrap heap so I had to clear it out.' She held up the bag with a mournful look. Then her attention fell on the bucket stuffed full of files. 'What's this?'

'My bucket! The one as was stolen out of Taylor's,' said Ida, chest puffing up in pride at her detective skills as she pointed at the contents. 'I've discovered it was used to smuggle out that lot. Tha'll never guess where I found it.'

Delilah stared at the bucket for a second, eyes wide. Then she grinned. 'I don't know where exactly, but I'm betting our backpacking lettings agent was the culprit.'

'How did tha know that?' There was more than a hint of disgruntlement in Ida's tone at her challenge having been unexpectedly answered.

'This.' Delilah raised the notebook she was holding, stirring a memory Samson couldn't quite place. He'd seen it somewhere before, not that long ago. But couldn't think where. 'I know when he stole it, too,' she continued, looking pleased with herself. 'Which means I also know who we need to talk to next when it comes to the mystery that is becoming Stuart Lister.'

Before Ida or Samson could react to this bold declaration, Tolpuddle lifted his head from his bowl, sniffed, and let out a loud bark.

'Tha beans! They're burning!' cried Ida, hustling Samson out of the way to grab the pan and pull it off the stove as an acrid smell rose into the air. She cast the pan in the sink and ran the tap on it. 'Ruined,' she declared, giving him a baleful glare, her prognosis covering both the cookware and its contents while Samson watched in despair as his intended meal was washed down the drain.

Deprived of imminent sustenance, his stomach let out a grumble of distress.

'Come on,' said Delilah, turning towards the door. 'Let's go. I'll explain on the way and we can get something to eat when we get there.'

With Tolpuddle in his wake, Samson followed her down the stairs, way too hungry and way too intrigued to protest.

10

'I found it when I was clearing out the Micra,' Delilah explained, handing Samson the small notebook as they walked up Back Street under a soft-blue sky, a few puddles on the pavement the only indication of the morning's downpour. 'It was in the side pocket on the driver's side.'

Samson took it from her and with it came the memory of Arty Robinson, one of his father's friends, handing it to him through the car window outside Fellside Court. It had been earlier in the month, at a time when Samson had been caught up in trying to ascertain the true nature of Bernard Taylor's shocking death. Occupied with the case at hand, he'd shoved the notebook in the side pocket and forgotten all about it.

'Arty and the gang's stakeout notes!' he exclaimed as he flipped through the pages.

Yet another thing Samson had forgotten about. The spurious stakeout he'd set up for the group of pensioners who'd begged to be allowed to help the Dales Detective Agency in what they thought was an investigation into the estate agent's. Not admitting that he'd actually been tasked by Bernard Taylor's wife, Nancy, to determine if her husband was having an affair and about to leave her, Samson had sent Arty and his friends – Samson's own father included – to Peaks Patisserie to monitor the double-fronted building across the square, thinking the exercise was a harmless one, sufficient to keep them occupied. Looking at the precise notes before him, he realised he'd done them an injustice.

The pages were covered in elegant handwriting, detailing the comings and goings at Taylor's offices on the very day Bernard had died. Every single person who'd entered or exited the building that Saturday morning had been listed, along with meticulous comments as to their overall demeanour, the information neatly laid out in three columns headed *Time*, *Name* and *Appearance*.

It was a set of field notes as good as any submitted by the professionals Samson had worked with and he felt sudden shame that these amateur detectives had put such effort into a situation he'd contrived merely for their amusement. Only, perhaps their hard work had been worth it after all . . .

He stopped walking, Delilah and Tolpuddle coming to a halt beside him outside Turpin's solicitors on the corner of the marketplace as Samson focused on the final page of writing.

'This is about Stuart,' he said.

Delilah nodded. 'Yep. That's what caught my eye when I flicked through it.' She pointed at the last column. 'Pretty interesting take on how he was behaving from our sleuthing friends, too. "Subdued", "slouching" and "not keen to get to work" according to their observations.'

'I'm not sure that's all that revealing. I mean, how many lads in their twenties would look enthusiastic about heading to the office on a Saturday morning?'

'Possibly, but we're talking about Stuart Lister here. He's never struck me as the sort for late nights or going clubbing so I doubt he was hungover. Besides, there's more.'

Samson looked to where she was pointing and let out a whistle. 'They saw him again the next day, with Ida's bucket!' He glanced up at her. 'Walking away from the marketplace towards Church Street.'

'In other words, away from Taylor's and towards his flat, the day before he suddenly quit work.'

'So you think this was when he stole the files?' mused Samson, his curiosity more than piqued now.

'Makes sense. He'd have had the place to himself on a Sunday. Seems like our spies sensed he was up to something too – "hurried gait", "furtive manner", "not his usual self",' Delilah quoted from the detailed notes before grinning. 'Thank goodness for women's intuition.'

'How do you know it was—?' Samson stopped, because his colleague was tapping the notebook and the set of initials beneath the last entry about Stuart.

CR. EH.

Clarissa Ralph and Edith Hird, the sisters who shared a flat at Fellside Court and made up the female contingent of Arty Robinson's group.

'Seeing as they're some of the last people to see Stuart before he left town, I thought it would be worth having a chat with them, so I texted ahead and they're waiting for us in the cafe. They've already eaten but Edith said if we hurry, we should make last orders.' Delilah grinned. 'Reckon we'll be able to get something better than burned beans on toast.'

'Let's hope so,' murmured Samson, deep in thought as

they resumed walking, across the square, down Church Street and then up the steep incline of Fell Lane towards the retirement complex.

This case, which had seemed so straightforward, was now becoming a bit of a puzzle, thanks to the developments surrounding Ida's stolen bucket. And while Samson still didn't think Mrs Lister's worst fears about her son would be realised, there were definitely some questions that needed answering. Like what on earth was so special about those files that Stuart had gone to the effort of stealing them the day before he was set to take off? And why had he then just left them behind in his flat? It didn't add up.

The questions gave Samson enough to ponder that his hunger pangs were temporarily forgotten. The moment they stepped inside the striking glass entranceway of the retirement complex, however, he caught the scent of something delicious wafting from the cafe in the far corner, and his stomach started grumbling again.

Arty Robinson took one look at the pair of them as they entered the cafe in Fellside Court and broke out into a huge grin.

'You finally plucked up the courage, then, Samson?' he quipped, slapping the O'Brien lad on the back while Eric Bradley let out a laugh that caught his breath and set him coughing, his oxygen cannister bouncing in its trolley beside him. 'Ye gods, but you didn't hang around. Heard you only got back from London yesterday.'

Samson squirmed while Delilah looked mortified, the entire cafe able to hear the former bookie's pronouncements, a multitude of grey heads turning as he delivered them in a booming voice while ushering the visitors to the table his friends were lingering at post-lunch.

'Leave them alone, Arty,' admonished Edith Hird, but the smile the former headmistress gave the young couple was dusted with mischief.

'He's only jealous,' said Clarissa Ralph, giving Tolpuddle a warm welcome while dabbing at her eyes, which always dewed up in the presence of romance. 'Isn't that right, Arty?'

'Jealous?' queried Arty. 'Impressed, more like, that a rogue like him has managed to woo a fine lass like our Delilah! Must be all those pointers we gave him, eh Joseph?'

Arty had turned to Joseph O'Brien, who'd remained sitting at the table, quietly taking in the usual banter, a fondness in his gaze as he watched Samson and Delilah take the places that Edith and Arty were busy setting for them. He didn't need to look at their faces to see that Arty was spot on. There was a sense about them, an aura of completeness with a current of electricity humming beneath it. Like two parts suddenly made whole and brimming with life.

'I'm not sure buying roses from the Spar counts as solid advice,' said Samson dryly, finally finding his tongue. At which Delilah whipped round to face him.

'You sought advice about how to . . . how you could . . . ?' She stuttered into shocked silence, leaving it to Arty to fill in the gaps.

'Woo you? Yes, he did,' he said, his grin now triumphant. 'But for the record, Eric suggested the roses. I suggested a new pair of running shoes.'

Delilah's mouth opened. Closed. And then she nodded, her cheeks bright pink. 'Good call.'

'I'll make a note of that for next time,' said Samson.

'Next time?' Clarissa stared fiercely over the table at him, her normally placid demeanour ruffled by the suggestion of future betrayal.

'Sorry . . . I didn't mean . . . I wasn't implying . . . Delilah's the only one for me!'

A collective sigh went around the pensioners at the unintentional declaration of fidelity prised from Samson, and it was his turn to blush. He picked up the menu and buried his face in it. Which is when Joseph decided it was time to save his son from the merciless teasing.

'I'm sure you didn't call in to be abused, you two. What can we do for you?'

'Food first,' muttered Samson, lowering the menu. 'What's good?'

'The special,' said five voices in unison, Arty patting his rotund stomach in emphasis.

'It's homemade shepherd's pie,' elaborated Joseph. 'As good as your mother used to make.'

Needing no further recommendation, Samson nodded and was about to go and order when Delilah got to her feet and placed the black notebook on the table. 'I'll get the orders in, you can start bringing them up to speed.'

'Why, that's our stakeout book,' said Clarissa as Delilah walked away. 'Do you need us to do another one?'

'I hear you're looking into the fire at Pete Ferris's caravan,' said Arty. 'Nasty business. Is it something to do with that?'

'Hope to God it's not Barbara Hargreaves' missing laundry,'

wheezed Eric. 'I don't fancy watching a line of her smalls for days on end. Even if there are free meat pies included.'

The group burst out laughing, Samson shaking his head in disbelief.

'For a business that is supposed to be confidential, it never fails to amaze me how much everyone else seems to know about what we're up to,' he lamented.

'That's Bruncliffe, son,' said Joseph. 'The good and the bad of it.'

Samson caught his eye and Joseph knew he was thinking the same thing; that only a few weeks ago it had been the interfering nature of the townsfolk which had prevented the two of them, alongside Delilah and DCI Frank Thistlethwaite, from being killed. Joseph touched the cast on his left arm and the broken wrist he'd sustained up at Rainsrigg Quarry, the rough plaster serving as a testament to how much he owed the people of this town.

'Actually, it's none of the above,' continued Samson, lowering his voice, the pensioners becoming serious and leaning in across the table in anticipation. 'It's about the stakeout you did at Taylor's.' He opened the notebook and pointed at the third column. 'You saw Stuart Lister going into the estate agent's on the Saturday Bernard was killed and, according to your notes, he seemed "subdued". Then the next day, you crossed paths with him again. Can you tell me anything more about how he appeared on either of those occasions?'

The group shared a surprised look, as Delilah returned to the table with two generous helpings of shepherd's pie.

'You want to know about Stuart? The lettings agent?' clarified Arty, his tone incredulous.

'Yes. We're particularly interested in what you noticed about him on the Sunday,' said Delilah, placing a plate in front of Samson, who immediately picked up a fork and began eating like a starved man. 'Were you all together when you saw him that day?'

Edith Hird shook her head. 'It was just Clarissa and me. We were heading to Whitaker's to get the Sunday papers and he was walking towards us down Church Street.'

'We wouldn't have taken any notice normally,' chimed in her sister. 'Nothing more than a friendly "hello". We're not like Mrs Pettiford, constantly sticking a nose in business where it doesn't belong. But we'd seen him the day before and he was connected to the target of our stakeout so . . .' She shrugged.

'Plus he was carrying a red bucket. That made us curious.'

'What's wrong with a lad carrying a bucket?' queried Arty. 'Happen he had some cleaning to do, what with him going gallivanting.'

Edith tipped her head to one side. 'Perhaps. But there was something about him. He looked so hot and bothered.'

'In that huge jumper too,' added Clarissa. 'A lovely cable knit but on a fine morning when even I didn't have a coat on. It was just odd. There was definitely something shifty about him.'

'Which is why we made the notes.'

Delilah glanced at Samson, who'd cleaned his plate and was leaning back, a look of satisfaction on his face.

'Right,' he said, clearing his throat and tapping the notebook again. 'So you stand by your original observation that he was behaving oddly. "Furtive" was the word you used.'

Both sisters nodded, casting wary looks at the others, all of them more than curious now.

'What's this all about, son?' asked Joseph, voicing the question he knew his friends were thinking.

'Nothing really. Stuart cropped up in something we're looking into so we thought we'd do a bit of background research.'

Samson's perfunctory response didn't fool his audience.

'Into someone who's buggered off abroad?' asked Eric.

'Suddenly. Without telling anyone,' added Arty.

The glances around the table had become sharper, whetted by the scent of something mysterious. A case that needed solving.

'Is he in trouble?' Edith was frowning, her thin face made even more severe. 'Because he didn't strike me like the sort to get himself caught up in anything untoward.'

'Has he gone missing?' enquired Clarissa, eyes wide, hand over her mouth. 'I saw a documentary about those backpacker murders in Australia—'

'Seriously, Clarissa, you need to stop watching that true crime channel on YouTube!' Edith scolded. 'It's making you jittery—'

'That were his mother!' Arty's exclamation was accompanied by the slap of his hand on the table, silencing the sisters as he turned to his friends in excitement. 'The woman making the ruckus in the detective agency yesterday when Samson got home! Didn't Troy say she was a Lister?'

'Angela Lister,' agreed Edith, nodding.

'Stuart's mother,' said Clarissa, 'who was apparently looking distressed.'

'So he *has* gone missing,' concluded Eric.

'What . . . how . . . ?' Samson was watching the exchange in confusion.

'We went to the Fleece for the early bird special last night,' explained Joseph. 'And Troy was telling everyone about the commotion surrounding your homecoming. He happened to mention the lady who was shouting and carrying on. This Angela Lister. Seems his wife is related to her somehow.'

Delilah was nodding as well now. 'Of course. Kay's from over that way.'

'Of *course*,' muttered Samson, shaking his head at the easy acceptance of this tenuous relationship, which was so Bruncliffe in style.

'The name didn't ring any bells last night,' continued Arty, 'seeing as we were all more interested in hearing about how Delilah welcomed you home.' He grinned at Samson. 'But now we've put two and two together—'

'And got the wrong end of the stick. Stuart hasn't gone missing.'

'Well, what is it then?'

Samson looked at Delilah, who shrugged and then nodded. 'I don't see the harm in telling them,' she said.

'You have a very short memory as to the trouble this lot are capable of getting into,' he muttered.

'Unfair!' protested Eric. 'It wasn't us who got locked in a freezer.'

'Or jumped out of a fire in our boxer shorts,' added Arty.

'Or got shot at up at the quarry—' Clarissa broke off and looked at Joseph. 'Oh, actually . . .'

'Okay, okay!' Samson held up a hand, the other one

reaching into his jacket pocket. 'Mrs Lister came to see me because she doesn't believe Stuart went travelling. Even though she's just received this.' He placed the postcard on the table and they all leaned in to have a look.

'Thailand? I wouldn't have said he was the type to go that far.'

'How come it's not handwritten?'

'What a romantic view!'

'Whoever took this has an artistic eye!'

'It's not even got a foreign stamp!'

Passing the card between them, the friends kept up a stream of conversation until Edith turned to Samson.

'I presume you've already checked out this Postcard4Me to see if this is authentic?'

Samson nodded. 'Delilah looked them up. It all seems legitimate. Stuart must have logged on, uploaded one of his photos, and ordered the postcard. They print it off and send it on your behalf.'

Arty was staring at him in bewilderment. 'You mean you don't have to go and buy a postcard and find a stamp and take it to a postbox? This company does it all for you?'

'It's called progress, Arty,' said Eric.

'But that's the whole point of going abroad! Getting out of your comfort zone by having to interact in a language you don't speak. This . . .' he gestured at the card with a look of contempt. 'This is so impersonal.'

'Have to say I agree,' said Edith. 'But I don't think that's the crux of what Samson is trying to tell us. I'm guessing there's something about this card that has triggered the investigation?'

'The lack of kisses,' said Samson. 'Mrs Lister claims that

Stuart would have added kisses on a card to her. Hence the lack of them has strengthened her conviction that her son hasn't gone away at all and is, in fact, in trouble.'

There was complete silence around the table and then a clamour of voices. All apart from Clarissa and Joseph. She was looking at the photograph, the beach, the palm trees, the small bar in the background. And Joseph was watching her.

'What is it, Clarissa?' he asked quietly.

She turned to him, shaking her head. 'This view. There's something wrong with it.'

They had Samson's attention now, the rest of the group falling silent too as Clarissa placed the postcard back on the table and pointed at the panorama of the beach. 'Did you say this was Stuart's own photo?'

Delilah nodded. 'I checked the stock images at the website and it's not one of theirs, so yes, it has to be his.'

'But that can't be right.'

'Why not?' asked Samson.

'Because,' said Clarissa, tapping the card with conviction, 'I know for a fact this photo wasn't taken by Stuart Lister.'

11

The glow of the epiphany which had struck Danny Bradley while watching a tray of brownies being cut up had diminished to no more than a mere flicker of possibility an hour after he'd left Peaks Patisserie.

In truth, even that flicker was fading fast. He was getting nowhere.

The constable leaned back in his chair and stretched, letting his gaze drop from the computer screen and onto the plastic evidence bag on his desk. The ugly homemade knife he'd found up at Quarry House looked even more incongruous lying on top of a pile of papers and next to Danny's Bruncliffe United mug.

He picked it up and stared at what had once been a spoon. He'd been so certain this would be the breakthrough he needed in identifying the sinister squatter who'd been hanging around town. When he'd got back from his curtailed walk, he'd got straight to work, not even taking the time to indulge in the cake he'd brought back with him, confident that his search wouldn't take long. That this unique weapon would be the key he needed to find his man. Or woman.

But he'd drawn another blank. A long trawl through

police reports, trying to find a crime committed with something matching it, had yielded nothing.

He tossed the bag back onto his desk, where it bounced off a stack of files and fell to the floor. As he retrieved it, his gaze fell once more on the sharpened end of the spoon. And that stain.

Was it blood? He peered at it, turning it to catch the light better. But it was impossible to tell. What it needed was proper analysis in the lab, which he doubted would happen any time soon given current budget restraints, unless he could prove it was definitely connected to an ongoing case. Yet he hadn't been able to find any crimes linked to it—

Maybe that's where he was going wrong? Looking for crimes.

With a jolt of energy, he inspected the rusty smudge again. If he was right and it was blood, then the knife had been used to attack someone. Perhaps even kill them. And it would have left a very unique wound . . .

Hospital reports. Danny's fingers started flying over the keyboard once more. Ten minutes later he got his reward.

An incident report from Leeds General Infirmary entered on the police database, which fitted the timescale he was looking for. A man had been found unconscious on the pavement outside A&E on a Monday night three weeks ago, covered in blood from a chest wound consistent with being stabbed. The team on duty had stemmed the bleeding, stitched the wound and reported the matter to the proper authorities. But when a constable had turned up to the busy ward later that evening to interview the man, she'd found the bed empty and the hospital staff unable to say where their patient had gone.

What they had said was that the man was of Eastern European origin and that his wound had looked odd. While consistent with a blade, the opening suggested it wasn't an orthodox knife but rather something short and pointed.

'Like a sharpened spoon?' murmured Danny.

Sensing he was on to something, he found the relevant police report, and an even bigger surprise. The case had been sent straight to the desk of a senior police officer in the city.

Danny stared at the name for a few seconds, stunned by the coincidence. For the detective in question was none other than DCI Frank Thistlethwaite, cousin of Matty and an officer who'd recently had more than a passing interest in events in Bruncliffe.

Wondering what could have prompted someone of DCI Thistlethwaite's rank to pay such attention to an isolated stabbing incident, Danny picked up his mobile.

After seven months of investigations in which the inhabitants of Fellside Court had made regular appearances, Samson knew better than to outright dismiss the theories of his father's friends. No matter how preposterous they seemed. So when Clarissa made her startling announcement regarding the provenance of the image adorning the postcard from Thailand, his first instinct wasn't to query her.

Her sister, however, held no such qualms.

'How on earth can you tell it's not Stuart's photo?' Edith was asking with undisguised scepticism.

'Because he only set off three weeks ago,' Clarissa continued, indicating the picture of palm trees and serene beach. 'Ergo, this photo was definitely not taken by Stuart Lister.'

Edith gave an exasperated snort. 'That still doesn't explain anything.'

'Well, it's the truth!' shot back Clarissa.

'I think what Edith is trying to say is we just need a bit more clarification,' said Arty gently, while placing a hand on the former headmistress's arm. 'Isn't that right, lass?'

'A bit of logic wouldn't go amiss either,' muttered Edith.

'So are you saying that you can tell when this photo was taken?' asked Delilah, successfully drawing Clarissa's attention away from her sister and back onto the postcard.

'Not precisely. But I'm pretty sure this was taken over a decade ago, well before Stuart Lister set foot in Thailand.' Clarissa looked around the table at several blank faces, Samson's among them. 'The Boxing Day tsunami,' she said. 'I watched a programme about it last year and it showed how large parts of the beaches on Phuket were completely changed afterwards. Patong was one of them.' She shrugged. 'There's something about this photo that doesn't feel right. The trees, for a start. They're all very mature looking. Possibly too mature. And this,' she said, pointing at the aptly named Paradise Bar in the background before giving her sister a pointed look, 'is no longer there.'

Samson felt the stirrings of interest, the first sense that Mrs Lister might be on to something. Delilah meanwhile had her mobile in her hand and, after a few taps of the screen, she placed it on the table next to the postcard so everyone could see it.

'This is the same spot that Stuart's photo was taken from, courtesy of Street View,' she said, sending a murmur of surprise around the group.

The difference between the two images was striking.

While both portrayed an idyllic scene of sand and sea and palm trees, the landscaping wasn't the same, some trees missing from the version on the phone and others clearly planted more recently. But it was in the background that the biggest change could be seen, the small bar which made Stuart's photo so distinctive now an elegant hotel.

'The Paradise Bar,' murmured Edith. 'It's not there. Clarissa's right.'

'How often do they update the images on this?' asked Samson, picking up Delilah's phone to look at what seemed to be the more current panorama of Patong Beach.

She shrugged. 'Probably once a year. Maybe a bit longer for places like this. But either way, I think it's conclusive evidence that Stuart can't have taken that photo. And seeing as it's not available on the Postcard4Me website, then it has to have been uploaded from somewhere else.'

'Doesn't mean it wasn't Stuart that uploaded it though,' countered Samson.

'You mean rather than just take a photo while he was there, he searched the internet for an image of Patong Beach and somehow hit on one from before the tsunami by accident?'

Samson could tell from her tone that Delilah wasn't buying it. 'Perhaps he wasn't at Patong Beach?'

'That doesn't make sense, either,' said Edith. 'Why would the lad go to the bother of sending a postcard to his mother of somewhere he wasn't?'

'Because it looks nicer than where he is?'

'Or perhaps because he doesn't want folk knowing where he really is?' Arty's contribution brought silence to the group, broken only by the clatter of crockery and cutlery being cleared from tables in the background as the cafe emptied out.

'What do you think?' Delilah asked, turning to Samson. 'Does that sound like a possibility from what you know?'

'Could be. Mrs Lister mentioned Stuart's father hadn't featured in his life at all, but when I queried whether Stuart could have gone looking for him and invented a story as cover so he wouldn't hurt her feelings, she dismissed the idea out of hand.'

'Well, she would, wouldn't she,' said Edith softly. 'It would seem like a betrayal, I'm sure.'

'Sounds like that's it,' Arty said, dusting his hands in satisfaction and preparing to stand. 'Which means it's time for coffee and cake in the lounge.'

Tolpuddle, who'd been quietly sitting beneath the table the entire time, poked his head out, ears cocked at the magic word.

'Hold your horses, you two!' Delilah looked up from her phone. 'I've just done an image search for the picture on the postcard and drawn a blank. There's not a single photo the same as that online.'

'So?' Samson shrugged.

'So, where did Stuart get it from if it's not his? You can't upload something from the internet if it's not there in the first place.'

Arty let out a groan and sank back into his chair. 'Is anyone else's head hurting?'

Edith laughed. 'Some detective you are, Arty Robinson. Come on,' she said, standing up. 'Let's do as you suggest. Perhaps caffeine and a sugar rush are just what we need to crack this case.'

As Samson followed the others out of the cafe and down the corridor to the lounge, he found himself thinking that it was going to take more than hot beverages and sweet treats to establish the whereabouts of Stuart Lister. Because given the bucket of files Ida had brought back to the office, perhaps it wasn't just his location Stuart didn't want people knowing about.

Either way, it was beginning to look possible that Mrs Lister could be right. Her son hadn't gone travelling after all.

It was mid-afternoon before Sergeant Clayton finally made it back to the station and he was feeling weary. A conversation with Samson O'Brien and Delilah Metcalfe often triggered that reaction, mainly because they had an innate knack for making the simplest of cases complicated. The burning of Pete Ferris's caravan seemed to be shaping up the same way.

The sergeant's fatigue as he left the burned out carcass of what had once been the poacher's home hadn't been eased any by an impromptu game of chase with a ewe and her lambs on the Horton Road, as he ran up and down the verge after them, trying to herd them back into a field. The loud toot from the Taylor's Mini as Delilah and Samson drove past laughing had done nothing to aid his temper.

Noticing the collapsed section of drystone wall that was giving the animals access onto the road, Sergeant Clayton had stopped off in Horton to have a word with the farmer responsible. Which had led to the farmer airing his forthright views – this was the Dales after all, where sugar-coating was saved for doughnuts – about the lack of success the police were having in the ongoing investigation into the theft of quad bikes across the area in the last few weeks. The sergeant had taken the reprimand on the chin, ashamed of the fact that crime such as this, which was so important to his community, carried so little weight on the national level when it came to appointing resources.

So, little surprise then that when he pulled into the yard at the back of the station his heart had plummeted to see Mrs Pettiford flagging him down. Barely giving him the chance to get out of the car, the bank clerk began accosting him, demanding to know what he was doing to make the townsfolk feel safe hanging out their washing.

Not having a clue what the woman was talking about but knowing from bitter experience not to let his ignorance show if he wanted to get away from her this side of retirement, he simply fobbed her off with some generic phrases about taking law and order seriously and then distracted her completely by telling her about the possible presence of a criminal on the run in the area.

He'd had the satisfaction of watching her fall silent, soaking in every word of his warning, before leaving him abruptly, eager to get away so she could start spreading her latest bit of gossip. Thus, while he was hot, sweating and more than a little peckish as he entered the back office in the station, he was also feeling smug. Because he was confident that with Mrs Pettiford as the messenger, the whole of Bruncliffe would soon be alert to the necessary security measures they should be taking until this situation with the potentially dangerous squatter could be cleared up.

'Well, that's one job sorted—' He broke off, spotting

that young Danny was on the phone, and headed for the kettle instead. And was overjoyed to see a Peaks Patisserie box sitting by his mug.

Sergeant Clayton flipped up the lid of the box to see two slices of chocolate fudge cake, and knew right then that he'd been right to fight off recent attempts from police officers in other forces to seduce his constable away from Bruncliffe. The lad was worth his weight in gold.

'Right, great, we'll see you then,' Danny was saying, concluding his call.

The sergeant waited for him to hang up before pointing at the cake. 'What's this then? Your performance review isn't for another month.'

'Huh?' Danny looked over, puzzled, then saw the cake, which the sergeant had taken the liberty of putting on plates and was bringing over. 'Oh, that. I brought it back with me an hour or so ago but forgot all about it.'

Sergeant Clayton stifled a groan. Because he recognised the excited expression currently gracing the lad's face. And he also knew that no one forgot they had uneaten cake from Lucy Metcalfe's place unless there was something serious going on. 'Whatever it is you've been working on, just tell me it's not bad news,' he muttered as he took his seat.

'The exact opposite. I think we might have a break-through in the search for our squatter thanks to that knife I found. And you'll never guess who's possibly got an interest in it?'

'What, you mean as well as O'Brien?' asked the sergeant with a resigned shake of his head.

'DCI Frank Thistlethwaite!' Danny beamed. 'He's

coming over tomorrow to have a look at the knife and wants us to take him up to Quarry House and to Pete's caravan. He thinks there might be a connection to an unsolved murder on his patch in Leeds. You know, the one he arrested Samson for?'

This time the sergeant couldn't contain his anguish, the groan slipping from his lips as he let the fork he'd been holding fall onto the plate next to the untouched cake. 'One day,' he moaned, 'we might be able to go back to having cases in these parts that are bog-standard crimes.'

'Where would be the fun in that?' asked his constable as he got up and switched the kettle on.

Sergeant Clayton shook his head. Then he slid the fork into the cake and bit into a slice of heaven. It was almost enough to dispel the sense of foreboding clouding over him at the day's developments. Almost.

Leaving Fellside Court was never straightforward. There always seemed to be one more cup of tea that needed drinking, or another helping of cake being offered. Or the conclusion of a gripping episode of *Flog It* which the pensioners declared simply couldn't be missed.

Samson, Delilah and Tolpuddle finally made it as far as the entranceway when enough of the day had sufficiently passed as to merit it being called early evening. The sun was dropping lazily towards the horizon, still a long way from setting as the month of May reached its conclusion, and the sky had turned a pale blue, streaks of delicate cloud draped gauze-like on top of the fells. Wanting to prolong the walk home, instead of going out of the front door, Samson stepped out into the beautiful courtyard at the back. Sheltered on three sides by the building, it had a view up onto the hillside, the green so fresh, dotted with the white patches of ewes and lambs. With the birds singing, the cherry trees in the last stages of bloom and the air smelling of summer, Samson's heart swelled with joy. So much so, he slipped his hand around Delilah's.

'Crikey,' she said with a grin, glancing down at their intertwined fingers, 'that's a bit serious. You'll be kissing me in public next.'

Samson laughed. Then tipped his head towards the expanse of glass that looked out onto the courtyard from the lounge. 'I figured we'd give our audience something to smile about.'

Sure enough, several faces were behind the window, watching them leave, Arty clearly making some comment on Samson's display of affection as the rest of the group were laughing.

'They can't help it if they're incorrigible romantics,' said Delilah, as they walked around the side of the complex and out onto Fell Lane. 'Do you know they've managed to get me a full house for the first Silver Solos event next week? When they suggested the idea of a seniors' date night, I thought it would be just Clarissa who was keen. Turns out there's quite a market for love in later life.'

'Are they all going?'

'Yep.'

'Even my dad?' Samson's eyebrows shot up in surprise.

'You didn't think he would?' Delilah looked at him. 'It's been a while since your mother died . . .' she said gently.

'No, it's not that. I don't expect him to still be pining over Mum. It's just . . .' Samson faltered to a halt, stumbling on a topic he'd never talked about with someone before. He was about to change the subject, conditioned to decades of locking down his emotions when it came to his father. But then Delilah squeezed his hand. Just a simple pressure, applied to his grasp. He felt the words tumble out of him.

'He was always drunk. Or intent on getting drunk. And while he wasn't the violent type, he wasn't exactly husband material. So I suppose I've never imagined him in that way. As being attractive to someone else.' He shrugged. 'I guess I still haven't got used to his sobriety and the fact that the person he's become, the way he's changed his life around, might make someone else want to be with him.'

'I don't think your father has changed,' Delilah said softly. 'I know it's easy for me to say, given I wasn't the one whose childhood was spent with him, but I would suggest he's always been a good person with a warm heart. The alcohol just masked it all those years. But he's fought his way through all that. Is still fighting. And frankly I think it's surprising he hasn't got together with someone before now. Besides,' she added with a grin, 'you should be glad he's such a catch at his age. Gives you hope for the future.'

Samson let out a laugh, startling Tolpuddle, who let out a bark, and as they walked down past the police station, from where Samson had retrieved his drunken father many a time, he found himself marvelling that he could be taking amusement from an aspect of his life that had so long cast a black cloud over his soul. He stopped, pulled Delilah into his arms and kissed her. Outside the library. The sunshine, the birdsong, the soft air, Samson felt it all within him, caught up in the embrace and a burst of pure love.

'Do you know what I think, Delilah Metcalfe,' he murmured against her lips, 'I think I lo—'

'I know what *I* think!' retorted Delilah, cutting across him before he could complete his heartfelt declaration. She was leaning back in his arms and looking over his shoulder, her cheeks pink, a wicked look in her eyes. 'I think you're intent on giving Mrs Pettiford a heart attack!'

Samson glanced behind him and there was the bank clerk, standing in the doorway of the library, mouth open as she stared at them.

'Evening, Mrs Pettiford!' Samson called out, grinning over at her.

'Evening,' she said stiffly, the Bruncliffe politeness reflex overcoming her disapproval.

'It's a great evening for romance, isn't it?'

Mrs Pettiford's mouth closed. Her lips pursed. And she clutched her library books to her chest, like a talisman.

'Samson O'Brien!' whispered Delilah on a hiccup of a laugh, her face still crimson. 'No wonder she thinks you're the devil.'

She turned away from the library and the reproachful gaze of Mrs Pettiford, and started walking again, Tolpuddle alongside her. Samson fell into step with them and was debating whether to continue with the avowal of devotion he'd had curtailed, when Delilah spoke, her brisk tone making him think this conversational diversion was no accident.

'So, what's next in the Lister case then?' she asked, eyes fixed ahead, a lingering trace of rose on her cheeks.

'Well, it seems clear the postcard raises some questions. Not least as to why Stuart used such an old photo.'

'Or if indeed it was him who uploaded it.'

Samson nodded. 'Which suggests a couple of scenarios. Either he's disguising where he really is or someone else sent it.'

'Which is a lot more sinister.'

'Agreed. And then we have the bucket full of files found in his flat by Ida.'

Delilah finally looked at him. 'Do you think he might have been involved in something? That he left town because of his work?'

'Could be. In which case, I suggest we talk to Julie at Taylor's tomorrow. She seemed to have a good relationship with him. If anyone can shed light on Stuart's behaviour before he left town, it will be her.'

'I'll take that,' said Delilah quickly. 'I need to see Neil about the IT upgrade so I can arrange to meet him there and speak to Julie at the same time.'

'You're seeing Neil again?' Samson cursed himself the moment the question left his mouth, knowing how it must sound, and aware that some green-eyed part of him had fully intended it to sound that way. 'I mean . . . weren't you due to see him today?'

'I put him off so I could go out to Mire End Farm with you.' She pulled a face. 'I think I must have offended him, though, as he's not answered my calls or any of my texts.'

'He's probably just busy,' said Samson, inwardly grinning. 'But yes, that would be great if you can speak to Julie. In the meantime, I'll head over to the Happy House and speak to Mrs Lee. Ida seems to think she's the kind of neighbour who would have noticed if anything was up with Stuart.'

Delilah nodded. They continued across the square in silence until they reached Back Street, when she turned to look at him. 'It really is just work, you know. Me and Neil.'

'I know.' He reached for her hand and wrapped his fingers around hers. And tried not to think about how Neil had looked at her when he'd called into the office the day before. Because while Delilah might be telling herself things were on a purely professional footing between her and her ex-husband, Samson was pretty sure that Neil had other ideas. Hence his decision to move back to Bruncliffe.

Chiding himself for allowing Neil Taylor's shifty behaviour to spoil what was shaping up to be a lovely evening, Samson concentrated on the feel of Delilah's hand in his as they approached the office building. But when they reached the front door a couple of minutes later and heard raised voices coming from inside, he got a taste of what the future could be like. For one of the voices was the very topic of their conversation. The other was Ida's. And if Samson wasn't mistaken, she was humming. Loudly.

12

'I just want to leave Delilah a message!'

'Happen as there's no one here to take it.'

'Surely you could do it?'

'That's not part of my job description.' Ida Capstick was standing at the bottom of the stairs in the hallway of the office building, arms folded as she stared at the Taylor lad, whose face had gone an interesting shade of puce at her rigid refusal to accommodate his request.

She'd been about to leave for home when the doorbell went and she heard someone enter. Heading down the stairs, she'd been dismayed to see Bruncliffe's boy-band lookalike in the hall, that irritating smile of his already in place as she approached. She'd brusquely pointed out the office was closed but he'd persisted in trying to leave a message. She'd likewise persisted in refusing to take it, her contrariness driven by her intense dislike of the young man and his betrayal of Delilah, until his smile had morphed into a grimace of annoyance. With something else under it. Something akin to panic.

'You're just the bloody cleaner for God's sake! So tell Delilah—'

Ida slapped her hands over her ears and started humming, loudly and tunelessly.

'Listen, you old—!'

The front door opened before Ida could learn exactly what type of 'old' she was, Neil Taylor breaking off when he saw Samson, Delilah and Tolpuddle on the doorstep. Ida fell silent, refolding her arms, and doing her best to keep the grin in her heart from showing on her face.

'What's going on?' asked Delilah, while Samson was looking from one to the other, eyebrows raised. Tolpuddle, meanwhile, trotted over the tiles to Ida's side, an act of devotion which would see him rewarded with a Hargreaves' pie the following day.

'He's just leaving,' said Ida, glaring at the Taylor lad.

Neil smiled, a muscle in his cheek twitching at the effort. 'Indeed I was. It seems I missed office hours. But now you're here, Delilah, perhaps we could have a quick chat?' He inclined his head towards her office on the first floor.

Delilah looked at Ida, who was still blocking the stairs and had no intention of moving. And then at Samson, who was standing in his own office doorway, equally showing no signs of offering privacy. 'Erm, sure . . . but here's good enough. Save our legs,' she said with a nervous laugh. 'Is it about the meeting this morning? I tried to call you but—'

'Fine! Let's do this in public, then!' The tic in the Taylor lad's cheek had got worse, Ida finding herself mesmerised by the pulse of skin in what was normally a flawless facade. 'I'm terminating the contract for the IT upgrade.'

Delilah blinked, Samson's eyebrows shot up once more and even Ida found herself shocked. It wasn't so much the message – which was odd enough, given that Delilah had spent months getting Taylor's system sorted and the project was nearly at completion. It was more the delivery. Gone was the courteous, flirty manner of a man intent on making a conquest of his ex-wife, which Ida had observed on every occasion he'd called in of late, a manner which Delilah had seemed oblivious to. Instead the words were blunt, the tone unvarnished, and Neil Taylor had transformed into his late father, the inherited ruthless streak showing up through all those layers of gallantry he was so keen to hide behind. A streak Ida suspected Delilah had borne witness to more than once during the latter part of her short marriage to the man, and yet had never spoken publicly about. The respect Ida already felt for the lass intensified as she watched her trying to deal with this sudden shift in relations.

'Are you serious?' Delilah finally asked.

'Totally. I'll make sure you're recompensed for the work thus far but I don't want you to take it any further.'

'But it's so close to being finished. Why would you want to—?'

'This isn't open for discussion, Delilah!' Neil snapped, causing Tolpuddle to emit a low growl and take a step forwards. For a split second, Ida debated putting a hand under the Weimaraner's collar but decided it might be more interesting not to. The growl had done the trick, though. When Neil next spoke his tone was more restrained. 'Just wind up the project and get everything back to how it was. Now, if you'll excuse me . . .' He started towards the door.

'Hold on a sec!' Delilah stepped after him, a dangerous flush on her neck which Ida recognised. The lass was at the very edge of her control. She took a deep breath before speaking again. 'Look, it's not that straightforward. It's going to take time to reinstate everything—'

'You've got to the end of the week. Anything over that,

and Taylor's won't be paying.' With a curt nod of his head, Neil Taylor left, the door closing behind him.

Ida and Samson caught each other's gaze in shared surprise, waiting for the outburst, only Tolpuddle brave enough to pad across to the figure still facing the door with her fists clenched, shoulders raised, back radiating tension. The Weimaraner wasn't fazed. He leaned against Delilah's leg, and her hand dropped to his head, fingers uncurling, arms relaxing as she stroked him. When she turned round, her smile was ironic.

'How the hell did I ever marry that man?' she asked, with a strained laugh.

Samson shot Ida another glance, both wrong-footed by her response.

'You're not cross about the contract?' he ventured.

'Mad as hell,' said Delilah. 'All that work for nothing. What a waste of time. But what you saw just there . . . Neil at his finest . . . that did me good. Reminded me that he can be a right b—'

'Blighter,' Ida interjected.

Delilah grinned. 'Yes, a right *blighter* when he wants.'

'But what caused all that?' Samson was shaking his head.

'Happen as it's my fault,' said Ida. 'He called in to leave a message and I wouldn't let him. Guess that wound him up.'

'He could have texted. Or phoned. Delilah's been trying to get in touch with him all day. Seems odd that he calls in on the off chance she's here and then goes ballistic and terminates the contract when she arrives.'

Delilah shrugged. 'Who knows. But what I will say is that whenever Neil acts like that, it's not because he's angry. It's because he's afraid of being caught out. He was exactly the same when I confronted him about his affairs.' She grimaced at the memory. 'A nervous Taylor is a ruthless one.'

'No excuse for rude behaviour,' huffed Ida.

'Is humming included in that?' Samson asked, with feigned innocence.

Ida glowered at him, getting a grin in return.

'It still begs the question, though,' continued Samson, turning to Delilah, 'as to what could possibly have happened in the last twenty-four hours to make Neil so uptight about you working on the IT system. Yesterday he was talking about taking you to the Coach and Horses to discuss it. Today he doesn't want you anywhere near it.'

'I'm as in the dark as you are.' Delilah sighed. 'But whatever prompted this, I guess I know what I'm going to be doing for the next few days.' She started towards the stairs, intent on beginning work.

'Not so fast, young lady.' Ida put out a hand, stopping her on the bottom step. 'Tha's no need to start dancing to the tune of that popinjay tonight. Tha should be taking this lad out for a meal, more like.' She jerked a thumb at Samson, who was grinning. 'A nice meal, mind. Happen the Coach and Horses is a grand idea. And don't go saying tha can't afford it as I've seen tha accounts.'

Delilah burst into laughter, throwing her arms up in surrender. 'Okay. Come on, Samson. Seems you have a date.' She led the way to the door, Tolpuddle behind her. Samson made to follow but then turned back.

'Thanks, Ida,' he said, planting a kiss on her cheek. 'You're a star. Solving the mystery of your stolen bucket and now giving Delilah romance advice. I don't know what we'd do without you!'

Ida almost smiled. She watched them leave, the same suffusion of joy she'd felt that morning on arriving at the office coursing through her. They were a grand couple, she thought as she went back up to the kitchen to collect her bag. They deserved each other.

Allowing herself a final satisfied glance at the whiteboard with her solved case up there for all to see, she gathered her things and left the building. As she cycled home in the soft evening light, however, her contentment turned to worry. The news from Leeds about her cousin, Carol, wasn't good. While the operation had gone well, she was still in a critical condition and not out of the woods by any means.

This worry was further compounded by Ida's domestic concerns. George had sent a rare text from his mobile that afternoon, the act itself an indication that something was wrong. Normally the antiquated device lay discarded in the dresser drawer, despite her repeated requests that he keep it to hand while out in the barn just in case of an accident. Fortunately, it hadn't been such a calamity that had driven her brother to use the phone. Instead it was an urgent need for food, George asking her to pick up some more bread as they were out. And another packet of ham. That was two loaves consumed in three days along with enough ham to feed a family for a week.

Worms. It had to be.

On the plus side, however, she mused as she rode up past Fellside Court on her way to Thorpdale, whatever was ailing her brother and making him eat so much, at least he'd stopped muttering on about those blasted ghosts.

*

Date with Evil

In the hallway of his parents' home, Neil Taylor caught sight of himself in the mirror above the antique walnut console and had to concede that he wasn't looking his best, his pale features giving the appearance of a man meeting death. Which, since he'd heard Rick Procter's news about the business the day before, pretty much summed up how he felt.

Financial irregularities. A fancy way of saying his father had been corrupt. It made Neil sick to the stomach. Not so much the corruption, but the idiocy of being caught. And leaving behind a trail that could contaminate the Taylor family.

It already had. The deal Rick had negotiated for the business was way below market value, but Neil didn't have a leg to stand on. In fact, he was counting himself lucky they had a buyer lined up because the enterprise his father had spent his entire life building was now a liability for whoever was stupid enough to take it on.

It certainly wasn't something Neil wanted to deal with, any notions he'd had of taking over having withered overnight. Nor was it something he considered his mother capable of handling, despite her misguided notions of transforming herself into an entrepreneur. As if she'd be up for running something like the estate agent's on her own when she'd been a housewife all her life.

All of which made Rick Procter a blessing in disguise.

So it had been a fit of panic which had torn Neil from a fitful sleep in the early hours when he'd remembered the work Delilah was doing for Taylor's. Lying in his childhood bedroom, he'd suddenly seen the implications.

If Rick had discovered something malignant in Taylor's system in the few weeks he'd been helping run the ship, then there was every chance that Delilah, with her meticulous attention to detail, could come across the same hiccup. And every chance that hiccup would be brought to the attention of Samson O'Brien. A man Neil had no reason to trust. A man with connections to the police.

Neil and his mother would be ruined, possibly even sent to prison.

Likewise, danger lay in Rick Procter getting wind of the fact that someone else had access to Taylor's confidential concerns. He'd run a mile from the sale and Neil would be left with a worthless business.

Which is why it was imperative to make sure Delilah was nowhere near the IT system. If that meant throwing the baby out with the bathwater, Neil was prepared to do it, because his sense of self-preservation was far stronger than any affection he might feel for his ex-wife. Or anyone, for that matter.

So he'd deliberately avoided her attempts to make contact all day, instead calling in at the office at an hour when he thought she might not be there. The plan had been to leave an impersonal message, because despite the brevity of their marriage, Delilah knew him. She would know if he was lying. She would demand answers to his sudden termination of the contract.

That crone of a cleaning lady had scuppered everything.

Still, thought Neil, gazing at his reflection before brushing his hair back off his forehead and dampening down his eyebrows with a wet finger, it was done. Delilah was off the job. And Taylor's was about to be sold.

'Is that you, love?' His mother's voice floated out from the kitchen, along with the smell of roasting beef.

Setting his shoulders back and fixing on his smile, he

walked down the hall, prepared to finalise the deal. All he had to do was get his mother on side and the paperwork could be drawn up and processed before the week was out, without her being any the wiser as to the real reasons why they'd had to sell.

Neil was confident. This was his mother. She was putty in his hands.

'Evening,' he said, walking into the kitchen. Nancy Taylor was at the sink, dressed immaculately as always, but with a sadness about her that had arrived with her husband's death and lingered still. 'Something smells delicious.'

'Beef Wellington,' she said, her face lighting up at the sight of him. 'Your favourite.'

He put his arm around her and kissed her cheek. 'That's perfect. Because we've got something to celebrate.'

'Like what?' she asked, frowning, the dark smudges under her eyes and the thinness of her features mapping her grief.

'I've found a buyer for the business.'

Her frown deepened. 'But . . . I thought you'd agreed I could . . . I mean, I know I don't have the experience but with your help . . .'

Neil let his smile grow to its dazzling best. 'It was too good an offer not to. Trust me, Mother. We can't turn this down.'

And he set about persuading her to give away the culmination of years of hard work, hers and his father's, not caring that he was giving away her dreams along with it.

While Neil Taylor was busy washing his hands of his father's corruption, the folk of Bruncliffe were busy barricading themselves in for the evening. For Mrs Pettiford had done as well as Sergeant Clayton had hoped, even exceeded those expectations in some ways. Having of course used her position in the bank, distributing the news over the counter with a side helping of banknotes, she'd also stopped by Peaks Patisserie at an hour when she knew it would be full and made her announcement in the loudest of voices. Then she'd gone over to Shear Good Looks, her ex-daughter-in-law's salon, waiting until the hair dryers were all off before broadcasting what she'd been told. After that, it was simply a matter of making sure she 'bumped into' some key components of the Bruncliffe grapevine and pretty soon her job was done.

Thus, by nightfall, the entire town was aware there was an unspecified evil at large – for most of them knew better than to take the town gossip's embellishments at face value and that the chance of it actually being a serial killer on the lookout for his next victim was highly unlikely – and that precautions needed to be taken.

Those precautions took various forms. For most it was simply a matter of locking the back door before going to bed, something of a rarity for many. For others, sufficiently disconcerted by Mrs Pettiford's missive, extra measures were taken: quad bikes stowed in barns rather than in the yard; cars locked and alarmed; a golf club unearthed from the attic and placed by the bed; or, in the case of Will Metcalfe up at Ellershaw Farm, the key to the shotgun cabinet placed on his bedside table. Because Will had heard that his sister and Samson O'Brien were investigating this supposed squatter who had the town on high alert, and knew from experience that where those two were involved, danger tended to follow.

Date with Evil

Out at Mire End Farm, no such safeguards were being put in place. In fact, the farmhouse was in complete darkness, apart from a small lamp in the kitchen, left on to keep the aged sheepdog company. His master was oblivious to the supposed threat to his community. He was too concerned with the threat to the woman he loved.

Under the bright lights of the hospital in Leeds, Clive Knowles was sitting at the bedside of his beloved, watching the slow rise and fall of her chest while the machine next to her beeped and clicked, and measured her fight to stay alive. The incongruity of it shook him. His Carol, so robust, so fearless, a woman not given to shrinking from life, was now reduced to a frail thread of existence, teetering on the brink of death.

'I'll find who did this,' he muttered, his rough hand holding the unresponsive square shape of hers. 'I promise you, Carol. I'll find them and they'll pay.'

13

Wednesday was glorious, as befitted the first day of June. From the minute the sun burst over the Crag, it cast its warmth down onto Bruncliffe in sufficient quantities for the arrival of summer to be proclaimed. With the blue sky arching over the fells and the sound of birds filling the air, as the townsfolk emerged onto the streets to go about their daily business, the perilous thoughts of the evening before were banished. Laughed about, even. For on a day such as this, nothing untoward could happen.

Sitting in the compact living space in Mr and Mrs Lee's flat above the Happy House takeaway, Samson O'Brien had to agree, although his opinion wasn't purely based on the meteorological splendour he could see through the window. His verdict on the day came from the fact that his morning had started with two breakfasts. A quick slice of toast at the office and now this.

'More?' Mrs Lee was standing in front of him, baby on her hip and a big smile on her face, holding out another plate of what she'd said were called *youtiao*, a type of doughnut stick Samson had fast acquired a taste for.

'Please. They're delicious!' he exclaimed, glad that for

once he hadn't drawn the short straw when it came to interviewing someone as part of an investigation.

Despite Ida's best intentions when she'd shooed Samson and Delilah out of the office building the evening before, their 'date' at the Coach and Horses had of course turned to business and the Stuart Lister case, and over the course of a very enjoyable meal, they'd organised their schedules for the following day. Samson had suggested he interview Mrs Lee first thing before the Happy House became busy, while Delilah had overcome his protests and insisted on sticking to her original plan of talking to Julie at Taylor's, adamant that she would still be able to get the work on the IT system done before Neil's deadline. They'd also agreed that an initial look through the files Ida had brought back from Stuart's would be a good idea, preferably when they got back from their meal.

When they'd returned to the office building, however, the files had lain untouched, neither of them in the mood for admin. A shot of heat flushed Samson's cheeks at the thought of what they had been in the mood for . . .

'Are you okay?' Mrs Lee was looking at him with concern. 'You look hot. Want me to open the window?'

'Erm . . . yes, great,' muttered Samson, forcing his mind back onto his work.

Mrs Lee crossed to the opposite wall and leaned over the sofa to lift the sash, before returning to take a seat across from him at the small table tucked into the corner next to the kitchenette. On the other side of the kitchen area, a flimsy looking concertina door led into what Samson presumed was the bathroom, while between the table and the sofa another door no doubt led to the bedroom. Judging by the faint sound of a radio audible from below where Mr Lee was already preparing food for the day's business, the sound-proofing wasn't at a premium. Which suggested Mrs Lee might know a fair bit about the activities of her former neighbour.

'So, you want to talk about Stuart?' she asked, bouncing the baby on her knee, a rice cake clutched in his chubby hands, his gappy grin revealing three teeth.

Samson nodded. 'What sort of neighbour was he?'

'No trouble, if that's what you mean? He didn't have parties or anything.' She shrugged. 'He was polite. Friendly. Tolerant.' She nodded at her baby and smiled. 'This one is teething. Which means he cries a lot. Stuart never complained about it.'

'Do you think he could hear it?'

She laughed. 'Of course! These walls are like paper!'

'So could you hear him?'

'Yes. When he walked around. But it wasn't much.' She cast a hand at her own tiny living space with a wry look. 'There isn't far to walk.'

'Did you notice anything unusual in the week or so before he left town?'

She shook her head. 'No. Although I was surprised he never said he was going.'

'He didn't say a word to you?'

'No. If I hadn't seen him leave, I wouldn't have known he was gone.'

Samson looked up from his notes. 'You saw him leave? When?'

Mrs Lee scrunched up her face, consulting a mental calendar. 'Let me see . . . it was in the early hours, I know that. As for the day . . . a Tuesday? . . . Yes! It was a Tuesday because I remember the restaurant had been crazy busy the night before, given it was a Monday, so my husband was more tired than usual. We were in bed and the wind woke me. Rattling the window. I was lying there, worried it would wake him too, and that's when I heard Stuart.'

'He was in his flat?'

'Yes. Moving around. It was two o'clock in the morning, so I was surprised.' She grinned. 'I thought he had company, you know.' She winked at Samson, who grinned back. 'Then the baby started crying so I got up and carried him through here. That's when I heard Stuart leave.'

'Was it definitely Stuart?' he asked.

'I'm sure of it.' She dipped her head, dimples in her cheeks as she smiled sheepishly before tipping her head towards the front door. 'I looked. Not to be nosey. Just because . . .'

Samson twisted to see the door. The angle it was at would give anyone standing there a view along the landing and down the stairs.

'He was carrying a rucksack,' she added. 'I came back in and then went to the bedroom window.' Now the smile slipped back into a grin. 'Perhaps *that* was nosey. But I saw him walk up Church Street to the marketplace.'

'At two in the morning?'

'Yes. I thought it was strange. No trains or buses at that time, but maybe he was meeting someone.'

Samson looked towards the closed door, behind which was the window in question, and Mrs Lee pre-empted his request. 'Do you want to see?' she asked, already standing with the baby in her arms, gesturing for him to follow.

Together they entered a cramped bedroom, a double bed pushed against the wall, a cot crammed in at the end of it. Beneath the window, a dark stain suggested a constant battle with damp. The damp was winning.

'It's the same in the hallway downstairs,' said Mrs Lee, noticing Samson's focus. 'We asked the landlord to deal with it but he just ignored us. And now we don't know what will happen.'

'What do you mean?'

'Since Mr Taylor died. We're waiting to see who the new landlord is. If they decide to sell . . .' Her face contorted in worry.

'Bernard Taylor was your landlord?' Samson asked, surprised and appalled in equal measure. The place was in dire need of investment.

Mrs Lee nodded. 'Officially there's an agency in Skipton in charge. But they sent us an email by mistake last month, just after Mr Taylor died. It was about the future of the property and the company that owns it – Royal something-or-other . . .' She waved a dismissive hand. 'I forget the name. But Mr Taylor was listed as the contact. We're hoping whoever takes over will be better.'

Thinking that if Neil Taylor was to take on this aspect of his father's business, Mrs Lee's hopes might well go unanswered, Samson crossed the bedroom to the window and looked up the road towards the town centre. From here, Mrs Lee would have had an unrestricted view of someone walking up to the marketplace, the street lights on either side enough to offer illumination. But it didn't answer the question as to what had made Stuart start his adventure in the dead of night.

'Why are you so interested in Stuart?' Mrs Lee asked. 'Is he in trouble?'

'No, not that I know of.' Samson turned to face her. 'His mother has asked me to check up on him. She doesn't think he went travelling.'

'His mother is worried about him?' Mrs Lee glanced down at her now sleeping baby, a frown rippling across her forehead as though she could already imagine the day when her son would move beyond the security of her own arms, and how troubling that could be.

'That's why I'm going over his movements before he left town. To be able to reassure Mrs Lister. So now I can tell her that you saw him leave with your own two eyes.'

'Oh.' Mrs Lee was still frowning, but looking towards the front door now, as though remembering that night. 'Only, I didn't.'

'Didn't what?'

'See him. His face. I only saw his back as he went down the stairs and then up the street.'

'But you were sure it was him? He was the right height, right build?'

'Yes . . . although with the rucksack it's hard to say and then . . .' She broke off, a look of puzzlement on her face. 'There was something strange. When he walked up the road, a gust of wind blew his hood down.'

'And?'

'His hair. It was under the streetlight and it looked different. Blond maybe.' She shrugged, not sounding confident. 'It could have just been the lighting.'

Samson looked out of the window again, imagining the scene. Stuart Lister walking away, rucksack on his back, head uncovered. The artificial light stark against the darkness, making things seem bleached, turning mousey to blond. More than possible. It still left the overriding question though: Where was the lettings agent going at that hour in the morning?

'It was a huge shock. He just left without telling anyone.'

As the morning sun transformed the marketplace into something akin to a Mediterranean piazza – albeit with North Yorkshire temperatures – Julie was sitting behind her desk in Taylor's, a coffee from Peaks Patisserie in her hands and a pecan-and-maple tart on a plate in front of her. Brought along by Delilah to encourage conversation, the bribe hadn't been needed. The minute she'd mentioned she wanted to ask some questions about Stuart Lister, the receptionist had been more than happy to open up. Desperate, even, to talk about him.

'Don't get me wrong,' she continued with a sad smile, 'I'm over the moon for him. Getting away from here, doing something so different. It's just . . .'

'Odd?' suggested Delilah. She placed a restraining hand on Tolpuddle, who was stretching forward, showing keen interest in the neglected pastry.

'Out of character, yes. Totally. Stuart never once mentioned having a desire to go abroad. I mean, I know we didn't work together long, but trust me, working here . . .' Julie broke off and glanced towards the office at the back, the door open, the room empty. 'I don't want to speak ill of the dead but Mr Taylor wasn't the easiest of bosses. So Stuart and I, we kind of bonded. If that makes sense?'

Delilah nodded. Bernard had been her father-in-law. She knew precisely what Julie meant.

'So apart from the shock of Stuart going, was there anything else that struck you as unusual or noteworthy? In the weeks or days leading up to his departure?'

The receptionist took a sip of coffee, forehead crumpling as she thought back. 'No. And that's odd in itself. Surely if he was planning this, especially if he was planning it in secret, you'd think there would have been something in his behaviour that would have given the game away. But there wasn't.'

'No unexplained absences? No phone calls he stepped outside to take?'

'Nothing. Unless,' she added with a laugh, 'you count him having a morning off for some root canal work at the beginning of last month?'

'Do you happen to know the date?'

'Seriously?' Julie's eyes widened. 'You want to know about him in that detail?'

Delilah shrugged. 'We're just trying to establish his movements, so I'm looking into anything we can get. The more evidence we can put in front of his mother that there is nothing suspicious about her son's sudden departure, the more chance we have of easing her concern.'

'Okay, well in that case . . .' Julie turned to her computer and pulled up a file. 'It was the first Friday in May. The day before . . .' She glanced over her shoulder to the empty office once more.

'The day before Bernard was killed,' stated Delilah, keeping her voice matter of fact, even while her brain was doing somersaults. So much of their investigation into Stuart

Lister seemed to keep coming back to the death of the mayor. 'I don't suppose you know which dentist it was?'

'The one down by Herriot's surgery.'

'Turner's.' Delilah added to her notes. A simple call would corroborate the root canal treatment. 'Anything else?'

'There is one thing, but it's going to sound silly . . .' Julie paused, then opened a drawer in her desk and pulled out a piece of paper. 'I was off work with a migraine on the Monday after Mr Taylor died and when I came in on the Tuesday morning, Mr Procter showed me this. It was the only notice Stuart gave that he was quitting his job.'

The note was handwritten and brief in the extreme. Owing to the pressures arising from Bernard Taylor's death, it stated, Stuart Lister was leaving his position with immediate effect to go travelling.

Delilah glanced up at Julie, unsure as to what was triggering the receptionist's uncertainty. 'What about it?'

'Well, it looks like Stuart wrote it. I mean, that's his handwriting for sure. But it's just . . . it says "Bernard Taylor". We never called Mr Taylor that. Not even behind his back. And I certainly don't think Stuart would have been so familiar in his leaving note.'

Delilah stared at the note and the receptionist blushed. 'I told you it was silly,' she muttered.

'Not at all. Can I take a copy of this?' Delilah had her phone out, taking a photo as Julie nodded.

'Will you let me know if you discover anything?' There was a wistful tone to the receptionist's voice. 'If you find out where he is? I'd love to be able to contact him.'

'I promise. Right,' said Delilah, standing up, Tolpuddle

getting to his feet beside her, 'I'll leave you to get on with your work. Thanks for your time.'

'You're welcome. How's the Mini behaving, by the way?'

'Brilliantly. Although I think Samson would prefer it had a bit less oomph! He's not the most relaxed of passengers.'

Julie laughed. 'Shame it doesn't have a dashcam as well as a GPS tracker – could be an entertaining watch. I could see what has him so terrified.'

'The Mini has a tracking system?' Delilah asked, intrigued.

'Yes. Mr Taylor insisted.' Julie rolled her eyes. 'To make sure his employees weren't using the company car for their personal errands. Not that Stuart would have taken advantage. Don't worry – I switched it off before I gave you the keys.'

'Was Stuart the only person to drive it?'

'Pretty much. Mr Taylor preferred his own car. He thought the Mini was too garish.'

'So does that mean you can tell me when Stuart last drove it and where he went?'

'No problem.' Julie's fingers were already skimming across the keyboard, her eyes on the computer screen. 'I know for a fact the last time the car was used was on the Monday before Stuart left, but as to where he went . . . oh, that's odd. The file's been deleted.'

Delilah leaned over her, the receptionist pointing at the final line of data, several days before the date she'd mentioned. 'You're sure it was used on the Monday?'

'Certain. Because the keys were put back in the wrong place.' She pointed to a box on the wall. 'They're supposed to be left in the key safe along with the house keys but they were thrown in my desk drawer. Took me an age to find them when Neil said you were going to be needing them.'

'So who deleted the file?' asked Delilah.

Julie shrugged. 'We all have access to it. Made the tracker a bit useless for policing how the car was used, but we never pointed that out to Mr Taylor. Like I said, Stuart wouldn't have taken advantage anyway. But if you think about the date . . .'

'Bernard was already dead, so that just leaves Stuart.'

They both fell quiet, and in that silence, the front door opened. Tolpuddle let out a low growl.

'Delilah! What a sight for sore eyes.' Rick Procter entered the building, handsome face lit up with a smile, a warm laugh greeting them as he approached. Then he spotted the Weimaraner, continuing to growl softly despite Delilah's hand on his collar. 'And the ever faithful Tolpuddle. Still not a fan, I see.'

Delilah gave an apologetic shrug, her dog's deep-seated aversion to the property developer something he had in common with Samson O'Brien.

'So, Julie,' Rick continued, switching his attention to the receptionist, 'I hope these two haven't been giving you the third degree!'

His smile was still in place. Even so, Julie turned to her computer and cleared the screen, looking guilty at being idle. 'Sorry, Mr Procter, we were just chatting about Stuart.'

'Stuart Lister?' Rick turned back to Delilah, frowning. 'Is he in trouble?'

'Not so far as I know,' she said, with a smile of her own, even if it took more of an effort these days, her opinion of

Rick not as favourable as it had been before she started working with Samson. 'Just making a few enquiries. His mother seems to think he might not have gone overseas.'

'Oh. Right.' Rick's frown deepened.

'You don't seem surprised,' said Delilah, watching him.

He glanced at Julie, and then shrugged. 'I didn't know the lad that well but the little I saw of him, he didn't strike me as your typical backpacker.'

'That's what everyone seems to be saying.'

'Let's hope we're all wrong, then, and that he's happily sunning himself on a beach somewhere.'

'Agreed,' murmured Julie.

'Now, if you'll excuse me, ladies,' said Rick, glancing at his watch and turning towards the office at the rear of the room, 'work is calling.'

'Before you go,' said Delilah, 'when's a good time for me to come in and finish off the IT system?'

'The IT system?' This time Rick did look surprised.

'I've been overhauling it. Or I was, until Neil terminated the contract yesterday,' she added with a wry shrug.

Rick shook his head. 'He never mentioned it. But it shouldn't be a problem. What do you need?'

'Access to the main terminal to reinstate everything. It shouldn't take more than a few hours. I just need to co-ordinate the updated files with what you've been working on in between times. But don't worry,' she said, recognising his flash of concern, something she was accustomed to dealing with in her IT business, 'any changes which have been made to the system since I started working on it will be flagged and we'll be able to go through them together to make sure nothing gets lost.'

'Right.' Rick gave a tight smile. 'You had me worried there. Thought all our hard work over the last few weeks was about to go up in smoke.'

'Not a chance!' laughed Delilah.

'So, erm . . . would Saturday morning work? I'll be mostly doing viewings so the office will be all yours. Perhaps I could treat you to lunch afterwards? Purely business,' he added, his smile growing warmer.

Delilah found herself smiling back, his charm hard to resist despite her reservations about him. 'That would be perfect. I'll see you then.'

With a final word of thanks to Julie, Delilah headed for the exit, a firm grasp still on Tolpuddle's collar. She was just pulling the door open when Rick caught her up, careful to keep Delilah between him and the dog.

'Just one last thing,' he murmured, low enough that the receptionist couldn't hear, but loud enough to be heard over the rumble from Tolpuddle's chest. 'Why did Neil cancel the upgrade, do you know?'

'Search me.'

'He didn't say?'

'Not a word. Just marched into the office yesterday and ordered me to put everything back as it was.'

Rick gave her a long look as though weighing her up. Then he glanced over his shoulder at Julie before leaning in close, his voice almost down to a whisper, while Tolpuddle's growl went up another notch. 'Look, this is going to be common knowledge soon so I might as well tell you. I'm buying Taylor's. So if there's anything going on I should know about . . .' He spread his hands wide in supplication, appealing to her.

'You're buying this place?' Delilah's words came out in a hiss of surprise, but even as she said them, the wisdom of Rick's business decision was clear. The buying and selling of property would fit his portfolio perfectly. She nodded. 'Good move. Although I didn't think Nancy would sell.'

Rick gave a grin. 'Everyone has their price. But,' he added, expression becoming serious, 'I'd hate to find out I'd paid over the odds for something that has hidden flaws. You're sure Neil never said anything about why he changed his mind about the IT contract?'

'Quite sure. Why? Has something made you think there might be more to it?'

He stared at Delilah for a moment and then gave a brief nod. 'Let's just say there's been a few things. I didn't want to say in front of Julie because she has the lad on a pedestal, but there's something about Stuart Lister's sudden departure that doesn't sit right with me.' He spread his arms wide. 'It's not my place to say any more. But keep me posted if you uncover anything during your investigation into his whereabouts, will you?'

'I'll do my best,' said Delilah, noncommittally, not sure what Samson would make of her informing Rick of their progress and at the same time, dying to know what had made Rick Procter sound so dubious about the former lettings agent.

Relief came over the property developer's face. 'Good. Thanks. And as for the IT upgrade, I'm sure I don't have to tell you that Neil Taylor isn't the most professional person I've ever dealt with. Not that I'm saying I don't trust him, but . . . sometimes I'm not sure what his game is.'

There was a loaded silence in which Delilah found herself nodding. 'I understand.'

'I knew you would. And if you could keep all this quiet for now?'

'My lips are sealed.'

Rick's smile returned full beam. 'Great. I owe you. At this rate I'll have to upgrade our lunch appointment on Saturday to something a bit more upmarket than the Fleece.' He reached out to squeeze her shoulder but the warning bark from Tolpuddle made him pull back and instead, lean across to open the door.

Head filled with everything she'd just learned about Taylor's and its employees, Delilah stepped out into the sunshine of the marketplace, keeping a firm hold on Tolpuddle as they set off up the cobbles for Back Street, aware that he was straining back towards the estate agent's. His growl didn't subside until they reached Turpin's on the corner, by which time Delilah was already on her mobile to Turner's, the dentist's Stuart Lister was supposed to have visited. And by the time they reached Plastic Fantastic, Barry Dawson waving at them as he rearranged a selection of mops outside his shop, she was hanging up, musing over yet more news. Which is when the bright orange car sitting outside the office caught her eye, the little black box on the dashboard visible through the windscreen.

When Samson returned half an hour later, it was to find two members of the Dales Detective Agency team sitting in the Mini: the canine one looking hungry; the human one holding a file and tinkering with the GPS system, looking like she was fit to burst with excitement.

*

Rick Procter had watched them go, the blasted dog pulling at the hold she had on him, head twisted over his shoulder, malevolent gaze fixed on Rick, while Delilah sauntered off up the marketplace like she didn't have a care in the world. Like her life wasn't hanging in the balance.

Which it was.

The Taylor peacock had seen to that. Thanks to him, Delilah Metcalfe's future was looking very precarious. As was Rick's own.

He turned from the doorway and fought to keep his smile in place as he approached Julie at her desk.

'When did you last have a day off?' he asked.

She looked up in surprise. 'Erm, not for a while, what with Mr Taylor . . .'

'I thought as much.' Rick nodded sympathetically. 'Look, I know things have been a bit fraught lately, and me along with it.' He gave an apologetic laugh. 'So what do you think about taking the rest of the week off? An extra few days by way of thanks, paid of course.'

'But . . . what about . . .' She cast her hand at her desk, covered in files. 'And Mrs Taylor? Don't we need to tell her?'

'Let me deal with all that. You just start thinking about what you're going to do with your long weekend. Perhaps take your mother somewhere nice?' Rick's smile was all concern now, Julie lapping it up.

'Oh, Mr Procter. That would be lovely. Thank you! I'll just finish up—'

'No finishing up!' he said, leaning across her to close down her computer. 'Your holiday starts now.'

She laughed at the spontaneity of it. Gathered her things,

thanked him again, grateful tears in her eyes as she hurried from the building. Rick calmly locked up after her before crossing the reception area, entering the rear office and closing the door. At which point he grabbed the peace lily that sat atop the filing cabinet and flung it across the room, shattering the plant pot and spilling soil everywhere.

He stared at the destruction, shaking, feeling his entire life's work collapsing into a similar heap of debris.

Stupid bloody Neil Taylor! He was just as much of a liability as his father. All this time Delilah Metcalfe had had access to Taylor's computer files and that idiot had never thought to tell Rick.

The news had changed everything. All the evidence Rick had spent the last few weeks disposing of. The tracks he thought he'd covered, which Bernard Taylor had so carelessly left behind. Delilah was about to unearth it all with one keystroke when she reinstated the system.

Could unearth it at any minute, seeing as she was in possession of the original digital files.

Rick placed a hand on the filing cabinet, feeling the world tip and tilt beneath him. Was this it? Had he finally run out of options? Or could he wriggle out of this like he had everything else—?

The sharp edges of something beneath his palm pulled at his attention. He raised his hand to see a key, lying in the dirt-marked circle where the plant had been.

Feeling like a boxer on the ropes, he picked it up, inserted it in the cabinet's lock, and turned it.

A spare key. Kept under the plant pot by blundering Taylor senior. A key his employees probably knew about.

Cold with fear, Rick bent down and pulled open the

bottom drawer, the empty suspension files taunting him as they had the last time he'd looked in there. It was a space which had once held some extremely incriminating paperwork. The Kingston Holdings files. Details of sham rental properties used by Taylor and Rick to launder the proceeds of their criminal partners' drugs business.

He slammed the filing cabinet shut, thinking back to the Sunday after Taylor's death, when he'd come to the office to retrieve the documents which could land him in prison. The way the plant had been on the floor when he'd entered the room. The way the files had been missing.

At the time, he'd presumed the fallen plant had been an accident and the Kingston Holdings files had finally been removed to a safer place by his incompetent partner before his untimely passing. But this key, the cold metal now lying in Rick's palm, suggested a different story.

Had someone beaten him to it? Were the files in the hands of someone who could wreak havoc with them?

The meek-seeming Julie? Or that battleaxe of a cleaner, Ida Capstick? If she was involved, then O'Brien and Delilah wouldn't be far behind. Or was it that drip of a lettings agent? Had he been one step ahead all along? Snooping where he shouldn't have been . . .

Frustration and fear boiling up in equal measure, Rick could no longer deny the net was closing. So close now, he was starting to feel the cords tightening around him.

This was it, then. Plan B. The nuclear option.

He stared at Taylor's desk, an elegant design of metal and glass, a computer monitor on the surface, the PC unit tucked away neatly in a drawer designed to house it. In itself, the deed he was contemplating would be so simple with the access he'd been granted. So easy to execute. But the consequences if it went wrong . . .

It couldn't go wrong. He wouldn't allow it to. So think!

He made himself reflect back over his conversation with Delilah, trying to reassess it in the light of these latest revelations. Did she know? Had she been here on a scouting mission, already privy to information which could ruin him?

He thought not. She'd seemed genuinely surprised at the news of the sale so at least Neil had managed to keep that quiet. She'd also seemed to be telling the truth when she said she didn't have a clue why the IT contract had been terminated. And as Rick had known Delilah all her life and knew she could be read as easily as an open book, he trusted his gut on this.

Fair to say she was in the dark, then. Which meant O'Brien probably was too. But there was every chance that could change between now and Rick's deadline tomorrow, given Delilah was working on the IT system. He would have to keep a close eye on her to make sure she showed no signs of coming between him and his escape. If she did, this time Miss Metcalfe would not be spared.

14

Samson heard the Mini starting, quickly followed by an impatient honk of a horn. From behind the wheel, Delilah was beckoning him to hurry up.

Having stayed with Mrs Lee for a bit longer than had been strictly necessary, chatting about life in general and consuming a few more of the delicious *youtiao*, he'd then sauntered across town to Peaks Patisserie to pick up something for lunch. With the warm sun overhead, it was the kind of day for eating outside, even if it was only on a couple of chairs in the yard behind the office with the Royal Enfield and Tolpuddle for company.

Delilah seemed to have other ideas.

'Get in!' she commanded, leaning across to open the passenger door as he approached the car.

'Thought you might fancy—'

'Make sure your seatbelt's on,' Delilah interrupted him as he held up the bag containing their intended lunch, excitement radiating from her. 'And have another look at this en route.'

She thrust the file she'd been holding on his lap, the one he'd found on the floor of the Mini the day before, and he just had time to stow the bag of food in the rear footwell before she was pulling off.

'Want to tell me what this is all about?' he asked, as they left the cobbles behind and turned down Church Street, Tolpuddle letting out a bark at something outside.

Delilah grinned. 'A root canal that never happened, and a hunch,' she said. 'According to Julie at Taylor's, the only odd thing in Stuart's behaviour was that it wasn't odd. She made the valid point that he wasn't behaving secretive at all in the lead-up to his sudden departure and the one thing out of the ordinary was that he took a morning off for a root canal. So I phoned the dentist.' She cast an arch look at him. 'Stuart never had an appointment there the morning in question. And has never had a root canal.'

'How the hell did you get them to tell you that? I thought patient confidentiality—' He broke off, her grin even more Cheshire-cat like. 'Let me guess,' he muttered, having learned that the social connections between individuals in Bruncliffe were a lot closer than the theoretical six degrees of separation. In Delilah Metcalfe's case, it was often as few as two. 'A cousin who works there?'

'Brother's sister-in-law, actually. Will's wife Alison? Her sister is Stuart's dentist. She was able to confirm he lied to Taylor's about his absence.'

'Why would he do that?' mused Samson. 'Couldn't he have just taken a morning off to do whatever it was he was up to?'

'I suppose he might have been doing some preparation for leaving and didn't want to raise any red flags? Or maybe he just didn't want to use up paid holiday. But it does seem to suggest something underhand. And as for the hunch,' Delilah continued, tapping the GPS system on the dashboard. 'Guess where Stuart's last journey was on the day before he took off?'

Samson looked at the file and then at the screen of the navigation system, a map already on the display. 'Henside Road?'

'Correct.'

'Why is that of interest to us?'

'Because whatever Stuart was doing at Henside Road, it was important enough for him to access the tracking system on Taylor's computer system when he got back and delete the record of his journey.'

Delilah's smile was positively smug. But Samson didn't blame her. This was all good detective work and added to the increasing enigma that was Stuart Lister.

'That definitely comes under the heading of interesting,' he said. 'As does the fact Taylor's have a tracking system on this car. Are we being tracked now, do you know?'

'No. Julie's turned it off, but it would have been active when Stuart last drove it.'

'But if he deleted the information, how come you know where he went?'

Delilah's smile became almost unbearable and she tapped the GPS again. '"Deleted" is such a naive concept when it comes to IT. I accessed the original data stored in here.'

'And that's taking us to Henside Road,' said Samson, impressed with his partner as he flipped open the file.

But when they got past the Hardacres' farm on the Horton Road and Delilah put her foot down, the car snaking around the twists and turns between stone walls, he had to accept that reading was going to have to wait. He was too busy holding on to his seat.

*

As the Mini cleared the last of the cobbles, Ida Capstick was just arriving in the marketplace, hot and bothered on her bicycle. She watched the car go by, Delilah and Samson in the front, unaware of her presence. Not so Tolpuddle. His gaze caught hers and she saw him bark. As if he knew she had a pie for him in her basket.

Already late, she'd figured a few more minutes at the butcher's wouldn't make a difference. As for why she was late? Her brother and his blasted appetite, followed by a personal errand.

Having brought home the extra supplies George had asked her to buy the day before, Ida had been handed another list this morning as she was about to leave. Biscuits, bread rolls, some cooked chicken and some chocolate bars. She'd taken it without a word, reluctant to challenge him when she knew it could easily derail him for the day. But such was her concern about his health, she'd been unable to stay silent. He'd been at the back door, hand on the knob, heading for the barn as she spoke.

'Is there summat up with thee?' she'd demanded, raising her eyes from the list of provisions. 'Tha's eating enough for a pregnant woman!'

George shook his head, shifting from one foot to the other. 'I'm fine. Just need more food.'

She watched him, aware something wasn't quite right, but not sure what it was. 'No stomach ache?' she asked, grasping at straws when it came to the symptoms of a parasitic infection.

'I'm fine,' he'd repeated. He looked at the old digital watch on his wrist and she knew she was unsettling him, taking him away from the schedule that so rigidly defined his life. A minute late getting out to the barn, and he would start to fret and panic.

'Good,' she'd said, nodding, smiling. Reassuring him. 'As long as everything's all right.'

He'd nodded back. He was about to go when she forestalled him one more time.

'Did tha hear anything last night? A flute or the likes?' As she'd said the words, she'd realised how daft she sounded, the idea of a flautist out in the depths of Thorpdale in the middle of the night. But for the past two mornings the vague memory of soft music floating through her open window and permeating her dreams had been with her on waking.

George had stared at her, troubled no doubt by the illogical query. 'Heard owls,' he said.

She nodded, regretting having asked. 'Most likely that,' she muttered.

He'd turned to go. Paused. Then his face had lit up. 'Carburettor's fixed!' he volunteered, happily.

'Excellent!' said Ida, meaning it. She knew it was a big deal. Over the last week, she'd seen him out in the barn walking frustrated circles, one accusatory eye on the mess of parts on the bench from the Fordson Model N as it defied his attempts to get it working.

George had given one final nod and then was gone, out the door and across the yard, pace faster than usual as he tried to make up for the seconds their conversation had delayed him.

She'd watched him go, her worries for his well-being no less vivid than they had been. It wasn't normal for a man to be eating so much, not without something ailing him.

Deciding there was nothing she could do for now, she made a promise to herself that if his exceptional appetite showed no signs of abating by the end of the week, she would call the doctors and make an appointment. Although how she would get George to attend it was another thing.

With a sigh, she'd packed her things and headed out, her bicycle already in the yard where George set it out for her every morning. But as she'd cycled out of the dale, the westerly wind no more than a gentle whisper on her face on this finest of mornings, the fells a carpet of green, Swaledale lambs gambolling in the distance, Ida had been unable to take the usual contentment from her commute. She was too worried about her brother. What was it about him this morning that had been odd?

It was only as she'd reached the outskirts of Bruncliffe and met Tom Hardacre driving past in his new John Deere, the yellow wheels flashing bright in the sunshine, that she'd realised. George hadn't uttered a single tractor statistic when she'd been grilling him. Not one.

Whatever was ailing him, he clearly wasn't stressed about it. In fact, just the opposite. His joy at finally getting the vintage carburettor working had been plain to see. Perhaps that's what was driving his hunger? Happiness?

Ida had allowed herself a soft laugh at the idea and, in a slightly lighter frame of mind, headed into town to sort her personal errand. Which is where she was returning from when the Mini went past.

She was glad Samson and Delilah hadn't seen her. She felt self-conscious enough as it was, her flustered state owing nothing to the glorious weather or her exertion on the bicycle. She cycled across the busy marketplace, head down, focused on getting across it as quickly as possible. A sharp right at the top, and she was onto Back Street, and thankfully a bit less in the public eye. But not quite enough.

Troy Murgatroyd was standing in the doorway of the Fleece, head back, eyes closed, soaking in the rays of the sun, a smile on his face.

The clank of her bicycle going past had those eyes flicking open, acknowledgement taking a couple of beats.

'Ida!' he exclaimed. 'I almost didn't recognise you!'

She hurried on, waiting for the sarcasm. But the good weather had worked its trick on the mercurial temper of the landlord, no insults hurled after her as she turned up the ginnel and round to the back of the office building.

At least Samson and Delilah were out, she reassured herself, as she let herself into the yard, parked her bike and opened the rear porch.

The sound of youthful laughter floated down the stairs. Nina was at work, young Nathan up there with her. Ida found her courage failing and she turned to leave, her cowardly retreat stalled only by the fact she was standing in the exact spot where she had been subjected to a violent attack mere weeks ago. The thought of how she'd soldiered on through that particular ordeal, not allowing injuries to stop her, was enough to bring forth her usual resolution. For what was this present predicament compared to that?

Chin up, she walked up the stairs in defiant steps. Despite the churning in her stomach.

'Morning,' she grunted as she reached the landing and turned towards the kitchen.

They were both sitting at the table, looking at something

on Nina's mobile, heads bowed over the screen. Then Nina glanced up. She stared. Her mouth opened. And Ida froze.

'Wow!' exclaimed the teenager, nodding, standing up and approaching. 'Ida! I love your trousers! Where did you get them?'

Ida Capstick tried not to let her relief show. 'Wilson's outdoor shop on the High Street,' she muttered, suffering Nathan's attention now too.

'Combats,' he said with approval. 'Good choice. You can never have too many pockets.'

Ida glanced down at her covered legs, the numerous pockets having been the deciding factor in her purchase that morning, and nodded. A brief tip of the head, no more. Then she stared at the kettle on the counter.

'Tha's not got a brew on yet, lass? It's gone past time,' she observed with her usual asperity as she set about rectifying the matter.

But Nina just smiled back at her. Unfazed. As though she knew that, inside, Ida Capstick's smile was as dazzling as the sunshine pouring down on Back Street.

With such a fine day gracing the Dales, some would have said it was criminal to be sitting inside. If solicitor Matty Thistlethwaite concurred, he wasn't letting it show as he sat behind a glass table in his first-floor office at Turpin's, watching his latest client. Fingers steepled in front of his lips, he was digesting the news she'd just imparted. And as always, he was taking his time to formulate a response, careful in his words and his deeds despite his relative youth.

'I think it sounds a little low,' was what he finally said.

'Current market value would suggest something a bit more substantial.'

Nancy Taylor nodded. 'Thanks for your honesty. I didn't mean to put you in an awkward position given this is such a small town, but I really value your advice.'

Matty spread his hands wide and smiled. 'Not that awkward. I don't have any business with Rick Procter so it's not a conflict of interest. And as for the opinion of folk, so long as I know I'm acting ethically, that's all that matters.' He reached for his coffee, a tactic he used to give his clients space to think, something he'd found reduced the tension in matters dealing with money, where tempers could often be raised.

Not that Mrs Taylor was likely to be such a case. Dressed in a stylish black trouser suit, understated jewellery completing the outfit, she was a classy lady, in manner as well as appearance. The complete opposite to her deceased husband, who'd been coarse, boorish, and, given what Matty had learned over the last couple of months, possibly more than a little shady in his business dealings.

It was her husband's business which had prompted Nancy to set up this meeting.

'So, do you think you'll sell?' Matty asked.

'I'm tempted not to. Bernard spent so long building up Taylor's, it seems disrespectful to let it go without a fight. But Neil isn't interested in helping me run it. In fact, he's pressuring me to agree to the sale.' Nancy sighed. 'I don't know what's best to do.'

Matty poured them both more coffee from the cafetière, using the time to marshal his own thoughts. Because he knew what was coming. Nancy was about to ask him for his opinion.

Rick Procter buying Taylor's. In one respect Matty's point of view on the matter was crystal clear: he'd rather Procter didn't get his hands on another flourishing Bruncliffe enterprise, further cementing the man's power over the town. But it was easy for Matty to hold that view when he wasn't the one looking to assume control of a business he knew nothing about, while dealing with the grief of losing a spouse.

Across the table, Nancy was toying with her cup, forehead pulled tight into a frown. But despite the sorrow etched on her features, there was a steeliness about her, a resolution Matty had never noticed before when she'd been the shadow behind her husband, the silent accompaniment smiling in the background as he carried out his official duties.

'Do you think I'm capable of taking it on?' She was looking at him now, giving him that same frank regard with which she'd waited for his verdict on the price she'd been offered for Taylor's.

'Yes.'

Nancy looked surprised and then gave a short laugh. 'To the point as always. Although it seems you're in the minority when it comes to evaluating my commercial capabilities. My son doesn't share your faith in me.'

Far too prudent to air his personal thoughts on Neil Taylor and the man's qualifications as an expert on business acumen, Matty simply nodded.

'It's only natural he's cautious, though I have to say I'm surprised he's settled for such a low price. But you're a good judge of people, Nancy. I'd say that's of paramount importance when operating a business that sells homes. The paperwork side of things can always be learned.'

'Right. Well, I'll bear that in mind. Although I don't have long to think it over – Rick wants a decision by the end of the week.'

'What's the hurry?'

Nancy shrugged. 'I think he's feeling stretched, helping me out and trying to run Procter Properties at the same time. It's understandable.'

'Either way,' cautioned Matty, 'I think you should get an independent evaluation before you proceed any further. Deadline or no deadline.'

'Thanks.' Nancy gave him a grateful smile. Then she reached into her handbag and took out an envelope which she placed on the table. 'While I'm here, I've taken the liberty of removing Bernard's will from the firm of solicitors he usually dealt with. I'd like you to take charge of it, if you would.'

This time Matty's professional demeanour deserted him and his eyebrows lifted, his coffee cup paused partway to his lips. 'Why . . . I mean, of course, but . . . why me?'

'You've just said I'm a good judge of people.' Nancy smiled then shook her head. 'To be honest, I didn't have a lot of faith in the crowd Bernard chose. They seemed to be taking forever to provide documentation, dragging their heels over every little thing. It was very frustrating. Plus they're based all the way over in Leeds.' She rolled her eyes. 'Why Bernard couldn't have used you I don't know. He was happy enough to use Turpin's before you took over, even though old man Turpin never seemed very thorough in my book. But no, all our legal affairs had to be moved to some flash premises an hour and a half away.'

'I'll have you know this is flash by Bruncliffe standards,' said Matty, gesturing at their surroundings with a grin.

Nancy replied with an apologetic laugh. 'I definitely didn't meant that as an insult, Matty. In fact, I can't think of anyone I'd trust more. Which is why I notified the Leeds firm of my intentions yesterday.' She pushed the envelope towards him and rose to leave. 'I know I can rely on your discretion. And you can rely on *all* my business from now on out, including Taylor's if I decide to keep it on.'

His client was at the door before Matty remembered his manners and hurried over to escort her down the stairs and from the building, so caught up was he in the enormity of what had just occurred. Nancy Taylor had bestowed her business on him, overturning the decision her husband had made when Matty Thistlethwaite first took over Turpin's on his return to his hometown. Within a week of buying the practice, the young solicitor had lost all of Taylor's accounts. And Rick Procter's too. It had been a hard blow and the following months had been a struggle. But gradually Matty had developed new contacts and word had got round that while the Thistlethwaite lad might look like he was straight out of school, he had a wise head on him, and a closed set of lips. Which in a town like Bruncliffe was valued more than anything.

Taking a seat back at his desk, Matty's attention was elsewhere, mulling over the conversation he'd just had and the possible business it could bring, so it was somewhat on autopilot that he reached for the envelope Nancy had left behind. He flicked it open, pulled out the pages and, within a few minutes, found his focus sharpening. Two words in particular had caught his gaze.

Kingston Holdings.

Instantly he recalled the face of a nervous young man sitting across from him a matter of weeks ago, asking about a possible shell company. Stuart Lister, the lettings agent at Taylor's. And here was the same company name, turning up in the last will and testament of the lad's boss, Bernard Taylor.

Feeling the first stirrings of disquiet, something told the solicitor that his lips were going to have to remain even more firmly sealed than usual.

15

'It's a wild goose chase,' muttered Delilah, arms folded as she stared at the large farmhouse with an air of grievance. 'I've brought us all the way out here for nothing.'

Standing next to her, Samson was finding it hard to disagree. All her excitement about a possible lead in the Stuart Lister case didn't seem justified now they were at the property purported to have been the lettings agent's last official visit.

Having endured Delilah's driving out through the stunning but sinuous Silverdale, the sheep on the fellsides reduced to white blurs against the green on a route which culminated in the death-defying sudden drop and precipitous climb of Henside Road, Samson felt he was owed more than this. An unoccupied rental property in the middle of nowhere.

'It's up for let again.' He pointed at the lilting estate agent's board by the front door, no doubt a victim of the wind which was whipping over the surrounding fells unimpeded. 'According to this,' he continued, consulting the rental contract in the file in his hand, 'the last tenants only took on the property back in November. Barely six months and they're gone already.' He glanced around at the uninhabited landscape stretching into the distance. Despite the blue sky and the bright sunshine, there was a chill to the air which hadn't been felt in the town. 'Can't say I blame them. It would have to take a certain person to want to live this far away from it all.'

'You mean unlike living in the metropolis of Thorpdale?' Delilah asked with a grin.

'Fair point,' said Samson, laughing, acknowledging the comparison to the remoteness of his childhood home. 'But at least Twistleton Farm is protected by the fells around it. Here it just seems so . . .'

'Bleak?'

Samson nodded. 'And exposed.'

A lapwing rose in the distance, wheeling up above the barren hillside, its call fluctuating as it ducked and dived through the sky.

'Beautiful though,' said Delilah.

'Well, it must have something going for it. Taylor's are asking people to fork out a lot to live here.' Samson held out the property specs from the file for Delilah to see and she let out a low whistle.

'Eighteen hundred a month?' She looked back up at the house in wonder, the ivy-covered porch and the unkempt lawn not reflecting the price tag, while the eerily blank windows gave the entire building a forlorn appearance.

Samson continued reading. 'Six bedrooms, three reception rooms, a bespoke kitchen—' He broke off, puzzled. 'Whatever that means.'

'It means an Aga and some hand-built cupboards that cost a fortune,' said Delilah with a dry laugh. 'Folk thinking they're getting the real country experience because they've got a cooker our grandmothers couldn't wait to get shot of. Come on.' She gestured towards the path that led around the building, Tolpuddle already heading off on it, nose down sniffing the ground. 'Let's have a look out the back and see if we're missing something.'

Footsteps crunching over gravel, they made their way to the rear and arrived in a yard. To the right, a long outbuilding stretched away, roof lower on one side than the other, giving it a lopsided look, while the back of the house projected the same sense of emptiness. Abandonment even.

'Is it just me, or is this place creepy?' murmured Delilah, gazing up at the lifeless windows.

Standing there in the sunshine, with her head tilted backwards, the wind playing with her hair, she caught Samson's breath, the sheer perfection of her. He found himself drawn towards her.

'I tried to tell you something yesterday,' he said, putting an arm around her shoulders and lowering his face to hers, 'before Mrs Pettiford interrupted us. Thing is, Delilah Metcalfe, I think I lo—'

Tolpuddle's sudden bark made them both jump, breaking away from each other as it echoed around the yard, shattering the silence and sending a couple of pheasants squawking into the skies.

'What is it, boy?' Thoughts of romance abandoned, Samson turned towards the Weimaraner, who was at the nearest of the three doors that were spaced along the outbuilding. The dog was looking stressed, scrabbling at the wood, sniffing like crazy.

He barked again, stretching up on his back legs to push the door with his front paws. With a loud screech, it grated along the uneven floor, opening enough to allow him inside.

'Tolpuddle! Come here!' shouted Delilah, as she followed Samson over to the building. 'We'll be done for trespassing if we're not careful.'

They reached the door, Samson pushing it open even further, and stepped inside.

It was a workshop of some sort, a workbench in the corner, rusting tools on a set of wonky shelves above it. At one end, a high window of eight panes of glass was set into the stone wall, letting in light despite being smeared and dirty. Beneath it, Tolpuddle was turning circles, nose to the ground, and growling.

'Whatever's the matter with him?' asked Samson.

Delilah shook her head. Reaching her dog, she placed a hand on him, feeling the tremors of agitation rippling through his body as he continued to investigate the oil-stained concrete. 'Easy, Tolpuddle,' she murmured, stroking him. 'Easy, now.'

'Can you see what set him off?'

'Must just be an old scent. Probably a badger or a fox got in here.'

'Or a human.' Samson was studying the dust beneath the window, where a half-set of footprints had caught Tolpuddle's attention, his nose twitching frantically over them. The dog let out another bark, softer now, friendlier, turning to look up at Samson, tail wagging. 'This place isn't so scary after all, eh? You big softie.'

'Whoever they were,' said Delilah, pointing at the smears on the windowsill where someone had disturbed the dust as they grabbed hold to pull themselves up onto tiptoe, 'they were trying to see out.'

Samson glanced back down at the ground, placed his feet on top of the prints and then stretched up. Delilah was right. Not only did he now have a view out of the grime-covered glass, but someone had helpfully wiped a small patch clean on one of the panes at exactly the right height for him. He was looking out onto the yard and the back door of the farmhouse.

'Someone was curious,' he murmured, lowering himself back down. 'Although what there is to be curious about out here, God knows.'

'Well, before someone gets curious about a bright orange Mini being parked out front, I think it's time we left.' Delilah was leading a much calmer Tolpuddle towards the exit.

Samson followed, but as he tugged the door closed behind him, he paused. 'Is this what set Tolpuddle off?' he asked, running his hand over a series of scratches in the wood, a good way up the door.

'What are they?'

'Claw marks. From a dog, I'd say.'

Delilah immediately looked at her Weimaraner, afraid he'd caused the damage when he'd been clambering at it, but Samson was shaking his head.

'Not from Tolpuddle. They're too deep. This was a dog much bigger and more powerful than our lad. I'd say a Rottweiler maybe, or something even bigger.'

'Crikey. We were lucky the tenants had already moved out then,' said Delilah with a laugh.

But Samson was still staring at door of the outbuilding, his attention sharpened, seeing things he'd missed before.

Things he'd never have missed if the delights of Delilah Metcalfe hadn't been filling his mind.

'Whoever they were, they were security conscious,' he said. 'Look. Someone had a heavy-duty padlock on here at some point.'

Delilah leaned over to see several screw holes in the door and on the frame, the mark of metal left on the wood. 'Seems a bit excessive for an old workshop,' she murmured.

'Agreed,' said Samson. Intrigued, he checked the next two doors, finding similar markings. 'A guard dog, three lots of padlocks and,' he added, staring at a square yellow box high up on the wall, 'an alarm on a barn.'

'Hi-tech surveillance too.' Delilah pointed at a small camera above the back door of the farmhouse. 'Bang up to date, as well. I'd say that was installed no more than three or four months ago. Certainly this year.'

Samson was flicking through the rental file, pulling out the inventory. He ran his finger down the list and nodded. 'No mention of any alarm or CCTV on Taylor's property details. So I'd say you're right. The tenants had all of this fitted.'

'It's hardly surprising, though, is it?' Delilah cast a hand out at the steep fells rising around them. 'Anyone moving out here from the city would be spooked enough to up the security a bit. And none of this tells us anything more about Stuart Lister and whether or not he's truly gone travelling.'

'Apart from one thing,' said Samson. 'If this place is so innocuous, why did Stuart feel the need to delete any evidence that he'd been here?'

*

While Samson and Delilah were pondering the significance of the rental property on Henside Road, the sun warming their backs, Clive Knowles was a long way from his beloved fells and farmhouse. Slumped in a seat in the hospital canteen, he was fast asleep, his head propped against the wall, a half-eaten meal congealing on a plate alongside an untouched mug of tea on the table before him. Shooed out of the ward by well-meaning nurses, he'd been encouraged to go and get something to sustain himself after an overnight vigil at Carol's side. A proposal he'd only agreed to on the condition that someone would come and get him if her situation changed.

Two forkfuls in and the fatigue had hit him. Several more and his body started shutting down despite his fear that something would happen to the love of his life if he failed to remain awake. But anyone observing the farmer in his deep slumber could tell that even in his dreams he was being tormented with anxiety. Limbs twitching, the occasional soft grunt escaping from his lips, he resembled a man far from peace.

Which was true. For his delirious brain was busy conjuring up images of his fiancée trying to protect a flock of pink sheep from a pack of wolves. While she swiped at the snarling beasts with an old walking stick, Clive was doing his best to reach her, running across fields which seemed to suck at his feet, making his progress laborious and dangerously slow. Too slow. For the wolves were upon her now, Carol still valiantly fighting them even as they dragged her down. He shouted. Saw the lead wolf turn, and then it was upon him, pulling at his sleeve, sinking its teeth into his arm—

'Mr Knowles!' Another shake of his arm, fingers gripping enough to cut through sleep. 'Mr Knowles!'

Clive surfaced blearily. He experienced a second of complete bliss at escaping imminent death before reality crashed back upon him, the concerned face of the nurse standing next to the table making him realise that his own demise was nothing compared to the possible loss of Carol.

'Is she okay?' he gasped.

'You need to come with me.'

He was on his feet and following her in a tortured heartbeat. Down interminable corridors, all the way to the intensive care unit, not daring to ask any further questions. Not wanting the answer he dreaded delivered in such a sterile environment. Through the door, onto the ward, and there was Carol, machines still beeping, features still ashen. But her lips were moving.

'She's been trying to say something,' explained the nurse. 'Which is a good sign in itself. And while she's still not out of the woods by a long chalk, she seems determined to communicate. We thought you might be able to make out what she's saying.'

Clive sank into the chair by the bedside, took Carol's limp hand in his.

'It's me, love,' he said, as she continued to murmur, her bandaged head tossing restlessly now on the pillow, her fingers fluttering in his grasp. 'Take it easy. I'm not going anywhere. You just concentrate on getting better.'

More incoherent mumblings. He leaned closer to catch the words but heard only snippets of sound from a rambling mind.

'Don't fret yourself, lass,' he murmured, stroking her forehead.

Whatever was occupying Carol's thoughts continued to plague her, however, as her lips began to move even faster, Clive able to decipher the word 'meatballs' closely followed by 'cannabis'. He was struggling to make sense of any of it when her grasp tightened on his, stout fingers closing around his hand with the strength he associated with this phenomenal woman. This time when she spoke, she was perfectly lucid.

'Phone Pete,' she said.

Then her grip slackened, her body stilled and she fell silent.

'Carol!' Clive was on his feet, panicked, fear coursing through him.

'It's okay, it's okay!' The nurse, gently calming him even as she checked on her patient with practised efficiency. 'She's coming round but it could take a while. In the meantime, whoever Pete is, he must mean a lot to her. Is he a relative? Do you want me to try and get hold of him?'

Clive shook his head, mute with shock. Because the only Pete the farmer or his fiancée knew was firmly beyond the reach of modern technology. So why was the dead poacher occupying Carol's subconscious thoughts?

The Dales Detective team made the most of the weather on the way back to the office. As they turned out of Henside Road into Silverdale, Delilah pulled the Mini over and the three of them got out to have an impromptu picnic in a field with the provisions Samson had brought from Peaks. In the distance, Pen-y-ghent rose out of the fells, an unblemished blue sky over it, while oystercatchers called out in the sunshine. With the warmth encouraging them to linger, none of them were in any hurry to get back to work, Samson and Delilah lying in the grass while Tolpuddle investigated a nearby beck. In fact, if it hadn't been for Delilah's mobile going off, Samson would have prolonged their sojourn in this idyll all afternoon. As it was, his passionate intentions were rudely curtailed by a command from Ida. Frank Thistlethwaite was at the office and wanted to see them. Immediately.

'This had better be good, Frank,' Samson muttered as he entered the office building, holding out his hand to the detective.

Frank grinned. Then he reached out to remove a bit of grass from Samson's hair, one of the bushy eyebrows that marked him out as a Thistlethwaite raised in humour. 'Been lying down on the job?' he asked.

Delilah blushed, Samson grinned back at him.

'Is there somewhere we can talk in private?' continued the DCI, turning serious.

Samson went to lead the way into his office but as he pushed open the door he was met by a glare from Ida, ensconced behind his desk and busy talking to a client. From upstairs came the sound of Nina working away on Delilah's computer.

'We need bigger premises,' he muttered.

'It'll have to be the Fleece,' suggested Delilah, already heading back outside to the pub across the road.

They found a table at the rear of the main bar, offering all the privacy they might need, the cold interior of the pub far from busy on a midweek afternoon when the sun was shining. Perversely, Troy Murgatroyd's mood didn't reflect the drop in business. Instead he was politeness itself as he served the coffees without any scathing comments, the glorious weather having had its usual positive effect on his volatile humour.

'So, what's up?' asked Samson as the landlord returned to the bar, leaving them in peace.

'This.' Frank held out his mobile, a picture of an ugly homemade knife on the screen.

Delilah recognised it immediately. 'That's what Danny found up at Quarry House. Have you discovered who it belongs to?'

'Not as such. But we might know who it was used on.'

'We?' queried Samson.

'Bruncliffe's very own Constable Danny Bradley. He had the bright idea of searching hospital records to try and locate the owner and came across a report of an unidentified male being admitted to Leeds General three weeks ago, with wounds consistent with a blade like this. It just so happens, I've an interest in the same case.'

Delilah stared at the photo and then at Frank. 'You think there's a connection between this stabbing and our mysterious squatter?'

'Nothing concrete as yet but my gut is telling me Danny's spot on. It's also telling me that he was right to draw a link to what was going on at the allotments.' He gave a rueful grin. 'And there was me dismissing Uncle Seth's concerns over stolen eggs and cabbages as trivial.'

'So does that mean we're looking for someone who's come here from Leeds?'

The detective shook his head. 'Not necessarily. Just

because the victim was taken there doesn't mean that's where the stabbing occurred. It could be they chose Leeds General because it's a bigger hospital. Easier to slip away from, which our man did, unfortunately. Which means it's more than possible the crime was committed in this area.'

'This is Bruncliffe!' protested Delilah. 'Surely someone would have heard or seen something if that were the case?'

'Unless it's something that spilled over from the city. Something involving organised crime?' mused Samson. 'Is that what you think this is?'

Frank gave a nod of appreciation. 'Not much gets past you, O'Brien. Although it's too early to say for sure. But this isn't your regular blade of choice and the fact the victim didn't stick around for the police to take a statement makes me think there's more to this than a drunken argument that escalated into violence. Which is why I've submitted the knife to forensics for analysis. Fast-tracked. Because if we're right, then whoever was loitering up at the quarry and possibly also at Pete's caravan is a dangerous individual, with at least attempted murder, and perhaps murder, to his name.'

'Murder? There's another case linked to this?'

'I believe so. I've an unsolved killing on my books I think could be associated somehow with the knife attack.' Frank paused, contemplated his coffee, and looked back at Samson with a wry smile. 'It's the murder I tried to pin on you.'

'Luckily, I'm not one for holding a grudge,' replied Samson dryly, even though the events of three months previous were still raw. Being arrested in Peaks Patisserie with much of Bruncliffe looking on was an experience he didn't want to repeat.

But now he found himself thinking back to the crime-scene photographs splayed out on the desk in the interview room at police headquarters in Leeds, where he'd been taken at the time. The glossy images had shown a man, staring blankly into eternity, a jacket pulled tight around his throat. Samson's jacket, lost in an escape from a Rottweiler while trespassing on a property he'd been investigating in the Roundhay area of the city. Little wonder DCI Thistlethwaite had thought he'd found his culprit when he traced the murder weapon back to Bruncliffe.

'I thought that man was strangled then chucked in the canal?' Samson remarked. 'Not exactly the same MO.'

'I'm not looking at the method. I'm looking at the victims. Both my unidentified corpse and the person who was stabbed are Eastern European.' Frank's comment drew sceptical looks from his companions but he shrugged them off. 'I know I'm clutching at straws, but while I have a murder victim whose fingerprints and DNA aren't ringing any bells with Europol, I'm willing to work a hunch when it comes to the knife. Which is why I called in. Besides wanting to warn you as to the type of person you might be dealing with here, I wanted to know if you've got any further on the burned-out caravan.'

Samson shook his head. 'Apart from establishing that Pete's last will and testament probably didn't provoke an arson attack from a family member, we haven't got any further.'

'Distracted by other things?' The grin that accompanied the question transformed Frank from solemn detective into handsome rogue.

'Another case, actually,' muttered Delilah, cheeks flaming.

'Hopefully nothing that could get you shot?' Frank's tone was noticeably softer.

'Not a chance!' said Samson with a laugh. 'An overly concerned mother insisting we investigate her son's where-abouts. There's a few oddities to it, but nothing dangerous.'

'Good to hear. As for whoever is behind this piece of work,' said Frank, pointing to the photo of the knife, 'like I said, they need treating with utmost caution. So if you do come across anything related to Pete's caravan or what-ever was going on in Uncle Seth's allotment—'

'We'll call you straight away,' confirmed Delilah.

Frank smiled. 'Pleased to hear it. Now, onto something a lot less menacing. This Speedy Date night you've roped me into—'

'Less menacing!' Samson's bark of laughter startled Tolpuddle, his sleepy face appearing over the edge of the table, while Delilah glared at her partner.

'Is there something I should know?' asked Frank, looking from one to the other.

'Ignore him,' said Delilah. 'You'll have a great time.'

But despite her protestations, the twinkle in Samson O'Brien's eyes left the seasoned detective wondering just what he'd signed up for.

16

'Why am I only hearing about this now?'

Rick Procter's terse demand was met with sullen looks from the two men standing in the barn doorway of Twistleton Farm, the early evening light casting up onto the fells, turning them golden. It was a stunning location, the farm buildings surrounded by hills on three sides, with only sheep for neighbours. The isolation of what had once been the O'Brien home had been the attraction for Procter Properties. That and the fact it was owned by a drunkard and therefore a cheap buy. As far as the locals were concerned, it was currently under development to become a high-end residence. In reality, it was up and running as a cannabis farm and turning out a steady supply. Despite this latest hitch.

'Well?' he snapped, anger and fear rising in him in equal measure.

One of the men stared at the ground, the other shrugged his huge shoulders. It wasn't insolent. But it was bordering on it. And it reflected the growing shift in Rick's relationship with these hired hands, given to him to oversee operations by the crime syndicate he was in partnership with.

'So you're saying the men we've been looking for are connected?' he persisted, trying to rein in his temper. Aware he couldn't afford to burn bridges just yet. 'And probably together?'

'Brothers,' muttered the smaller of the two, his foreign accent rasping over the word. He flicked his head towards the barn, shadowy figures moving around in the gloom behind him. 'One of the workers told us.'

Rick glanced in the same direction and then looked away, his conscience more than able to cope with what he was endorsing but not liking to dwell on it. A workforce that came supplied, no questions asked. That didn't get to leave the premises at the end of the shift. That didn't get paid. And which spoke next to no English.

But this string of disasters was forcing him to dwell on the matter. First a worker escapes from the premises on Gunnerstang Brow just after it's been set up, while Rick is still dealing with the fallout from the sudden death of Bernard Taylor. Then, with police crawling all over the quarry and the surrounding area, further hampering efforts to trace and catch the escapee before he can alert the authorities to what's going on, another man breaks out from here in Thorpdale. With several miles and a lot of bleak, empty countryside between the two, Rick had been happy to accept the claims from the men in charge that these were isolated incidents, staffing issues caused by momentary lapses in supervision.

Such lapses should have been punished, of course. Like they had been after the trespass at the property near Roundhay Park in Leeds, only the presence of a Rottweiler keeping the intruder from discovering the true purpose of the house undergoing renovation. The trespasser, in what Rick now accepted was a freak of coincidence, had been O'Brien; the guard responsible had paid for his carelessness with his life. As the dead man's former colleagues, the guards – because that's what these men currently standing in the evening sunshine at Twistleton Farm really were – were well acquainted with that fact.

Yet they seemed unperturbed.

Perhaps because they were also well acquainted with the growing concern from above over the troubles besieging Rick's operations. The incident in Leeds had resulted in the hasty closure of the profitable venture and the relocation to Henside Road, the orders coming direct from the Karamanski brothers in Bulgaria. Those orders may as well have had 'final warning' written all over them.

Which is why Rick's relationship with these guards had shifted. Like wolves in a pack, they could sense he was wounded, and they were circling him, waiting for the right moment to strike. When he'd arrived at the remote property earlier, to see if there was any news on the search for the latest runaway, they'd been almost brazen when admitting the full extent of their bungling.

Not only were both breakouts connected, they'd informed him, but the initial one up at Gunnerstang Brow had seen one of the guards stabbed in the process. What was worse, the man's colleagues had taken him to hospital and dumped him there.

'This guard that was injured,' Rick asked now, brain whirring, trying to assess how much damage had been caused, 'which hospital did they take him to?'

'Leeds,' grunted the larger man.

At least they'd had the sense to go further afield, somewhere anonymous. But still, a knife wound in a hospital, even a city-centre one, wouldn't go unremarked. 'Were the police involved?'

The guard shook his head.

'So what happened to him?'

This time the man's shrug was accompanied by a sardonic leer. 'He got treated and left. No problem.'

But it was a problem. A huge problem. Because now what had been two isolated incidents had turned out to be a concerted effort on the part of one individual. Breaking out of Gunnerstang through violent means and then coming all the way here to free his brother. Rick was no longer looking for lost and vulnerable illegal immigrants. This had the markings of something more calculated. Which would make finding the men – and silencing them – even trickier.

On the plus side, however, one of them had stabbed someone, so they were hardly likely to go throwing themselves on the mercy of the local authorities.

'And the dog? You said he was hurt in the escape. What did you do with it?'

The man put his fingers to his temple and mimed a gunshot, while his colleague's focus reverted to the floor.

Finally some sense. The last thing they needed was a wounded Rottweiler on the premises.

'Right,' said Rick, with more authority than he felt. 'Replace the dog if you need to. But sharpen up. If there are any more mistakes around here, there'll be trouble.'

The guards nodded slowly, then turned back into the barn, the shorter of the two kicking out at one of the workers who'd slumped exhausted over a bag of fertilizer.

Rick averted his gaze. Lifted it across the yard and out down the dale, taking deep breaths.

The clock was ticking. He could hear it, each second like a thump in his head. By ten o'clock tomorrow morning it would all be done, but until then he either needed the two escaped workers caught and silenced, or he needed them to stay hidden. Because he would only get one shot at what he was planning. If it didn't come off . . .

He forced the thought aside. Concentrated on the problem in hand. Two brothers, then – did that change anything? Did it change where they would go?

Rick focused on the horizon, on the stone rectangle of Croft Cottage at the start of Thorpdale, the only habitation for miles. It had seemed the obvious place for an escapee from Twistleton to head for. So much so, Rick had called in the other day at a time when he'd known Ida wouldn't be there, hoping to get a look around the place without any protest from her witless brother so it could be eliminated as a possible hideout. But 'Brains' Capstick had had other ideas, turning aggressive, spouting his tractor nonsense.

Rick had been planning on another visit. Perhaps with Ida at home so he could play the role of concerned employer in light of the panic being spread around town. Encourage her to allow him a quick look in the barn, for her own protection, and in doing so, determine once and for all that the man he was looking for was long gone.

Only now he was looking for two men. With a history of violence. Were they really likely to be still cowering at Croft Cottage undiscovered? It didn't seem feasible. Most likely they were out of the area already, heading back to wherever they'd come from. Or rather, been taken from.

Besides, even if by some chance they were still there, surely they would put up a fight if one of the Capsticks stumbled on them? These weren't the kind of men to react kindly to being backed into a corner. And any confrontation would be uneven, Ida and her brother against a couple of desperate illegals. Even Brains and his giant wrench would struggle to overpower two blokes with at least a knife between them.

So perhaps it was best to leave Croft Cottage and its occupants well alone. No point stirring things up. Not when there was so much else at play. Besides, a bit of spilled Capstick blood would only be a bonus.

In a better frame of mind, Rick turned to leave. And then halted, pulling out his wallet.

'Here,' he shouted, beckoning the guards back over to him.

They came with the wary looks of feral dogs.

'Thanks for telling me everything,' said Rick, holding out a couple of fifties. 'I appreciate it.'

Eyebrows raised, the smaller of the pair took the money for both of them. 'Thanks,' he muttered in return.

They watched Rick leave, two silhouettes against the fellside, still visible in his rear-view mirror as he drove down the dale. Yes, the clock was ticking. Which is why he was keeping them sweet. Because any hint of what he was planning and they'd use it as leverage to save their own skins. There was no such thing as loyalty in this game. As they were going to find out very soon.

*

As Rick Procter's Range Rover sped down the dale, it had to brake for a lone cyclist riding up it. Ida Capstick lifted a single finger off the handlebars in acknowledgement of her new neighbour's cheery wave as he drove by. But even the presence of that man in such proximity to her home couldn't sour her mood.

She'd had a more than satisfactory day and as she wheeled into the yard of Croft Cottage, the sun on her back, she felt nothing but contentment. They were finally getting somewhere with the huge amount of work at the detective agency, and while she hadn't actually solved any cases in the last twenty-four hours, she'd fielded calls and managed to get a start on the filing system the business so badly needed.

Which is why she'd allowed herself the rare treat of knocking off early. A quick stop at the Spar to pick up some potatoes to go with the mound of Hargreaves' sausages she'd bought that morning, and she'd been on her way. Home well before her usual hour and in plenty of time to make sausage and mash for George. She was hoping that by treating him to one of his favourite meals, she could somehow abate the raging hunger that seemed to be consuming him.

Propping her bike against the wall of the house, she allowed herself one final moment of pleasure as she looked down at her new trousers. Because, if she was truthful, which on the whole she was, it was these combats that were the source of her gratification. Not only were they comfortable and practical, but the pockets! Marvelling at how she'd got so far through life without appreciating the wonder of having multiple compartments in the same garment, she was turning towards the back door when she heard music.

Tilting her head, she caught the notes, faint but sure.

The flute. The one she'd thought she'd been imagining. Creating a magical sound which floated out over the evening, conjuring up love and happiness and the joy of life—

Embarrassed by her own wistfulness, Ida frowned in the direction it was coming from. The barn. Which didn't make sense because George didn't listen to music. He found the offerings on the radio distracting with their sudden changes in tempo and rhythm and had never shown any inclination to discover a genre that might appeal to him. Yet here was Ida listening to the most beautiful of refrains, and it was coming from his workspace.

Drawn towards it like a child of Hamelin, she crossed the yard and reached for the closed door. Pulled it open. And froze on the threshold as the music came to a sharp halt.

There was a moment of silence, broken only by the cluck of one of the hens behind her, George staring out from the gloomy interior in shock.

'Well, I'll be damned!' Ida finally muttered, taking in what was before her.

For sharing her brother's precious sanctuary were two men. One of them – in his late twenties, she'd guess – was sitting in the old kitchen chair, a grey cast of pain to his thin face above the hoodie he was wearing, a flute held partway to his mouth. The other, the older of the two but still no more than mid-thirties, was standing over by the bench, fierce intelligence in his dark gaze, a screwdriver grasped in his right hand, and a marked tension to his wiry frame, which was swamped by a Bruncliffe rugby top.

While the presence of the men was surprising in itself, it was the hoodie and the rugby top which caught Ida Capstick's attention. Turns out she *had* solved a case that day, as she'd just found Barbara Hargreaves' missing washing. But as she was discovering with this detective lark, while she'd solved one case, she'd opened another. Because as to the identity of the two men, she didn't have a clue.

Except, Ida suddenly realised with growing dread, perhaps she did. And if she was right, she and her brother were in deep trouble.

The feeling of quiet optimism was still with Rick Procter as he reached the outskirts of Bruncliffe. Yes, the news the guards had broken had contained some worrying elements. The injured man being treated at A&E for a start. That was a possible lead the authorities might chase. But time was, for once, in Rick's favour and he was confident he would be done and dusted with the town before anyone came calling for him in connection with some unidentified man's hospital record over in Leeds.

And on the plus side, after his visit to Twistleton Farm he was now convinced that the escapees had left the area and were not going to pose any further risk to his business. The biggest risk they'd pose would be to any unsuspecting person who encountered them.

Rick allowed himself a wry smile, feeling strangely calm as he drove through the town, acknowledging the greetings of folk with a raised finger off the steering wheel, back in his persona of local boy made good. Perhaps his unexpected serenity arose from the thought that he would soon be able to forget about all those balls he'd been so busy keeping in the air for so long.

Leaving the Range Rover around the corner on High Street, he let himself into Taylor's and crossed to the office. He'd been making good headway with the loose ends, removing evidence that could incriminate him, leaving nothing to chance so that the next day would go smoothly. There remained only two more items to deal with. Delilah Metcalfe, who, thankfully for her, had showed no signs so far of having uncovered anything out of place in Taylor's IT system. And the other thing . . .

He glanced out into the main room, to the desk that had been unoccupied for some time.

Perhaps he'd let nature take its course in that instance? Save him getting his hands dirty?

Using the power button on the keyboard, he turned on the computer and sat down. This was going to be the biggest deal of his life. He needed to make sure he knew exactly what he was doing.

The men stared at her. Ida stared back. George did his nervous shuffle between them, like a boxing referee separating opponents before a bout. All the while, that hum of menace vibrating around the barn.

'Evening,' said Ida, manners in place even as she was trying to assess the situation. Because she sensed there was real danger here, which her brother wouldn't have been able to fathom.

The squatter in Quarry House. The clothes, taken from

Barbara Hargreaves' back yard. The warning which had ripped through Bruncliffe like an out-of-control heather burn on a tinder-dry fellside – a violent criminal on the run.

What if Sergeant Clayton had got it wrong? What it there were *two* violent criminals . . . ?

In that moment, standing there in the barn in the solitude of Thorpdale, Ida Capstick felt afraid. She thought about her mobile in her bag out in the yard. Then remembered. Her amazing combats. She began inching her hand down to the thigh pocket on her right leg, reaching for her phone—

'No!' The older of the two men, the one wearing the rugby top, stepped forward, the screwdriver clearly a weapon now, the crackle of violence in the air.

Ida took a step back, phone out, fingers bringing it to life even as she kept her gaze on the men. On George too, who was looking confused, agitated. Beginning to murmur rapidly to himself.

'No!' the man said again, coming towards her, an intense energy about him, his slight build not fooling her.

She didn't have time to look at the screen. She hit the first entry in her contacts. Lifted the phone, heard the dialling, backing up the entire time. Trying to calculate if she could outrun this man. Aware that would mean leaving George behind—

'No!' the man shouted one last time, lunging for her with the screwdriver—

'Zenith IN5F Carburettor STOP!' her brother screamed, pulling at his hair, feet shuffling, maximum agitation. 'STOP!'

The man froze, dropped the screwdriver, turned to George. 'Gasoline four-point-four litre, three-speed gearbox,' he murmured, hand out as he approached him, pacifying him with the lull of his voice the way Ida's father used to pacify a spooked ewe.

'*Ida? Ida? Are you there?*' Delilah in Ida's ear, wondering why she wasn't speaking.

George calming down, the man next to him, leading him to the bench, to the carburettor. The man's fingers dark with engine oil and grease.

'*Ida? What's going on?*'

The carburettor. Fixed. The way George was placated, the quiet murmuring between the two of them . . .

'*Ida? Is everything okay?*'

Ida opened her mouth. Aware of the three men turning to watch her. She forced a smile for their sakes. 'Everything's fine, lass. Sorry. Must have hit call by accident.'

She hung up, and in doing so, placed her trust in the dark-haired man with the bright eyes. Because anyone who could win the confidence of her brother by reciting tractor statistics had to be worth trusting. Even if they were criminals on the run.

17

'What did Ida want?' Samson turned from the hob, lifted the pan of chilli onto a trivet, and began to serve it into two bowls.

He was standing in Delilah's kitchen in the small cottage up on Crag Lane, the window above the sink giving a spectacular view out over Bruncliffe below. Having decided to spend the night there rather than in the more makeshift quarters at the office, they were planning on finally working through the files Ida had discovered in Stuart Lister's flat. Once Samson had cooked tea.

'She didn't mean to call,' said Delilah, soaking up the sight of him in an apron from her vantage point at the table, tucked into the corner by the archway to the lounge. 'Probably fumbled it getting it out of one of her many pockets!'

Samson laughed. 'Never thought I'd see the day when Ida Capstick turned up for work in combats. Weird thing is, they really suit her.'

They'd arrived back at the office from their meeting with Frank Thistlethwaite to find Ida discussing the merits of her new trousers with Nina. Once they'd got over the shock of her attire, they'd held a brief catch-up with their colleagues, bringing them up to speed with the latest developments in the possible squatter scenario and the investigation into Stuart Lister. Nina, in turn, had pointed out a new case which had been added to the board. Herriot had called in while they were with Frank, the vet wanting them to look into the ownership of a Rottweiler he was treating.

'This Rottweiler of Herriot's,' said Samson, returning back to the topic they'd been discussing when Ida's call had interrupted them. 'Someone just dumped it at his surgery?'

'That's what he told me on Monday. I can't decide if that's inhumane or not? I mean, whoever it was, at least they're getting the poor thing treatment.'

'Still a form of abandonment though. Some folk aren't fit to own dogs,' muttered Samson. 'Are they, Tolpuddle?'

On the other side of the archway, the Weimaraner lifted his head from where he was lying on the rug, an eyebrow raised as though expecting something more substantial than mere chatter when his name was mentioned.

'So, do we take it on?' asked Delilah. 'Given we're a bit overstretched at the moment and I really need to make inroads on Taylor's blasted IT system if I'm to hit Neil's deadline?'

Samson shrugged as he placed the bowls on the table and took a seat opposite Delilah. 'Why not let Nina have a shot at it? She can call Herriot, get as much detail as she can from him. Let's see what she comes up with.'

'Great idea. I'll let her know first thing. She'll be over the moon to have her own case.'

'Hopefully one that can't possibly get her into trouble,'

grinned Samson. 'I don't fancy having to tell her father she's been injured while on our payroll.'

Delilah grinned back at him. 'I reckon that'd be worse than having Will on your back!'

The mention of her overprotective brother drew a wry smile of acknowledgement from Samson. 'Talking of Will,' he said, 'does he know about . . . you know . . . us . . . ?' He waved his fork between the two of them.

'About you making a dishonest woman out of me?' Delilah raised a provocative eyebrow. 'Seeing as most of Bruncliffe knows by now, I can't see how he'd have failed to have heard. Although,' she added, 'he's been roped onto the council for the Swaledale Sheep Breeders' Association and has been all over the place this week judging shows, so I suppose there's a chance he's still in the dark. Why? Are you expecting him to turn up at the office demanding a duel to restore my honour?'

'Wouldn't put it past him.'

'Don't worry, Tolpuddle will protect you,' laughed Delilah, glancing over her shoulder at the grey form, now splayed out on the sofa, paws in the air, belly exposed, and fast asleep.

'That softie?' Samson smiled at the snoozing dog. 'I'd be better off with Herriot's ownerless Rottweiler!'

His words triggered a shudder from Delilah, remembering a certain act of trespass involving a guard dog of the same breed. 'Don't even joke about it! I still have nightmares about that time in Leeds. I was sure you were a goner.'

'You mean the time you ran off and left me to fend for myself against a slobbering savage?' Samson's pained look was worthy of Tolpuddle.

'I didn't run off! I was just faster getting to safety than you, that's all. Anyway,' she continued with a cheeky grin, 'you should be counting your lucky stars we didn't have to have a repeat performance today out at that rental property. If your theory is correct about there having been a Rottie or the like over there, I wouldn't rate your chances in a foot race right now with two weeks of soft London living under your belt. You'd have been caught for sure!'

Samson started laughing, then broke off, his head tilted, struck by her comment. 'Huh. That's interesting. The Henside Road house . . . a mislaid guard dog . . .'

Delilah could tell he was busy making connections. 'You don't honestly think there could be a link to Herriot's abandoned dog and the scratches on that barn door?'

He shrugged. 'It's certainly a coincidence. When did Herriot say the dog was left with him?'

'Sometime last week.'

'It'd be good to know when the tenants left Henside Road. See if the dates match.'

'I'll make a note to ask Julie in the morning,' said Delilah, pulling out her mobile.

'What about injuries? Did Herriot say what they were?'

'A cut leg, from what I can recall. He said it was infected . . .' She paused, laid down her phone and frowned, remembering the conversation from two days before that already seemed like years ago. 'Actually, there was something unusual. He mentioned the dog had been dosed up on ketamine.'

'*Ketamine?*' Lowering a forkful of chilli, Samson stared at her. 'That bloody drug. Getting as common around here as Rottweilers!'

Delilah shrugged. 'To be honest, I didn't really take it in at the time as I was so busy. But now I think about it, it's doubly odd, especially as vets are about the only folk I can think of who have legal access to ketamine. Which begs the question—'

'Why would a vet need to take their own animal to another vet?' Samson was nodding. 'So we're talking illegal access to ketamine and ownership of a guard dog . . .'

'Someone selling drugs?'

'Or making them . . . ? In a remote rental property . . . ?'

'At Henside Road?' Delilah gave a surprised laugh. 'That's a hell of a leap!'

'Is it?' Chilli forgotten now, Samson was leaning across the table. 'All the security systems. The heavy-duty padlocks which had been on the outbuilding. Something fishy was going on out there.'

His logic was irrefutable. But still Delilah found it hard to believe. 'So what are you saying? That the last lot of tenants were running a drugs farm? And that Taylor's knew nothing about it? What about the six-monthly inspections? How would they have got around those?'

'Maybe they didn't.' Samson shrugged. 'Because maybe they didn't have to.'

Delilah's mouth dropped open. 'You're not seriously suggesting they had inside help? Who?'

'Stuart Lister.'

The name fell into silence. And then Delilah was laughing. 'Don't be daft! He's not the type.'

'Not the type? He quit his job suddenly, left town without even telling his mother where he was going and has since sent back a postcard, the provenance of which we've established is extremely odd. If not dodgy. Add to that, exhibit A in the corner over there . . .' Samson pointed at the red bucket by the sofa. Ida's bucket, filled with the files Stuart had stolen from Taylor's. 'All in all, I'd say young Stuart Lister is certainly shaping up to be the type who's done something illegal.'

Still Delilah was shaking her head, thinking of the lanky lettings agent who wouldn't say boo to a goose. 'It just doesn't fit. He's too . . . nice!'

Samson nodded. 'Yes. He's nice. But he was also at Henside Road just before he left. And for some reason, he deleted the GPS file of his visit. I think the sooner we start looking at the contents of that bucket, the better.'

Standing in the corridor outside the intensive care unit, the city skyscape beyond the windows being turned glorious beneath the colours of a setting sun, Clive Knowles was trying to work out what to do.

Was it a fool's errand to go haring off home on the basis of a few whispered words from his fiancée? Looking for what, exactly? Meatballs, cannabis and a mobile phone?

He wasn't even sure about the latter. He scratched his head, ran a hand over his unshaven face, bristles rough under his fingers, and felt the fatigue gnawing at him, preventing him from making a lucid decision.

In his calmer moments, he viewed Carol's outburst earlier in the day as nothing other than the ramblings of an incoherent mind. Best ignored, his time and energy better spent here, by her side, encouraging her to emerge from the deep sleep that held her tight.

But since her bizarre utterances, not a single murmur

more had passed Carol Kirby's lips, and the flicker of hope Clive had experienced at her unexpected speech had dwindled back into desperate concern. To the point where he was beginning to clutch at straws.

What if she *had* been trying to tell him something? He'd mulled over this possibility as he watched her inert form, the click and beep of the instruments surrounding her lulling him into a meditative state. Which is when he'd remembered her coming home from across the fields one day a few weeks ago, a bucket in one hand and a rubbish bag in the other.

She'd been cleaning Pete's caravan in the wake of the news that it had been bequeathed to Clive in the unfortunate poacher's will. She'd started to offload the bucket on the kitchen table, eager to show him the items she'd brought back, but Clive had had no time to be regaled by whatever it was she'd deemed worthy of keeping. Because that had been the day Delilah had mobilised them all – the hitman had been due in town and Clive had been in a state of high tension.

Sensing his fraught mood, Carol had quickly stowed the items away and given him her full attention, helping him get ready for the following day. But what Clive did remember was that the first – and only – thing she'd pulled out of her bucket in front of him was a tin of meatballs.

Was that what she'd been referring to in her muddled state? The meatballs from Pete's caravan? And if so, was it possible that she'd also brought back a supply of cannabis, the poacher having been more than partial to smoking it? If that were the case, Clive found himself reasoning, how did the request to phone Pete fit in?

It took him a little while to work it out. To realise that he'd taken her whispered words to be an instruction, while instead, Carol may have been listing yet another item she'd found in the caravan.

Pete's mobile phone.

But even after all this conjecturing, the fact remained that Carol's mumblings may well have just been her injured brain simply reciting the objects she associated with the site of the accident which had caused her coma. Certainly not enough to justify abandoning her to go and check what she'd brought back in her bucket that day. Not when the round trip to Mire End Farm and back took the best part of four hours, and there was every chance that it would lead to naught. Four hours in which the worst could happen and he could lose her.

The thought of her passing without him there . . .

No matter how he reasoned it, however, as he'd sat by her bedside over the last few hours, he'd found himself plagued by the thought that whatever had been important enough to pierce that coma was perhaps worth investigating. Might even lead him to catching the bastard who'd caused the explosion at Pete's caravan.

Outside the sun had slipped even further down, splashing crimson and purple across the clouds. Night was coming. The hours of dark, the hours most associated with danger and death.

He'd go, Clive decided. But not until dawn. When the sun rose again, he'd set off. The roads would be quieter. He could maybe do the journey in a fraction of the normal time. And hopefully Carol would never even know he'd left her side.

Content he'd made the right decision, he returned to the ward and resumed his vigil beside the silent form lying in the bed.

As night began to settle on Thorpdale, Ida was in the place she loved best. Her kitchen. Sausages spitting in the frying pan on the range, potatoes mashed and ready for serving while the gravy bubbled next to them, she was keeping busy, not allowing herself to dwell on what she was doing. Or the possible consequences of it.

'They're good people,' she muttered to herself, turning to place the teapot on the table, mugs and cutlery already laid out.

She allowed her glance to lift from the tablecloth to take in the two men sitting in the seats usually occupied by the Capstick siblings.

The older of the two brothers – for now she'd had a chance to study them in better light she could see the likeness in the aquiline nose, the dark deep-set eyes, the same high cheekbones – nodded at her, smiling, gratitude in his gaze. The younger one, the one who was slouched in the chair, protecting his side, sweat on his forehead, he only had eyes for the food, staring at the meal in progress with the look of someone who hadn't been fed properly in a while.

George had done his best, Ida making sense now of the extra supplies he'd been demanding. Ham, bread, fruit. He'd been sneaking it all into the barn for his new-found friends. How long had it been going on? When she'd asked him he'd not been able to give a precise day, his internal calendar not structured the same as the one from Bruncliffe

Auction Mart that hung on the wall beside the dresser. So she'd done her own calculations, based on the way food had been disappearing from her fridge and her concerns over George's possible tapeworm. He must have found them on Monday. It was now Wednesday evening. But the look – and odour – of the lads suggested they'd been on the run a lot longer than that. At least two and a half weeks, because that's when the clothes had been stolen from the Hargreaves' back garden.

So Ida had made a snap decision out in the barn. The men, whoever they were and wherever they'd come from, were in dire need of help. The younger one especially. He was clearly injured – ribs, Ida suspected, from the way he was holding himself. So she'd told George to bring them inside, opening up her hearth and home the way Bruncliffe folk did in a crisis.

But it hadn't been easy. The two strangers had been wary, eyeing her nervously as they'd finally followed her across the yard, only to linger by the back door, hesitant to commit to entering the kitchen as though afraid it was a trap. It wasn't like they could communicate either, no grasp of English on their part beyond the tractor statistics and Ida not even beginning to guess what language they were speaking. Something Eastern European, possibly?

Deciding the language of food would be one they had in common, Ida had started cooking, putting the potatoes on to boil, heating the teapot, sorting out crockery. Still they'd watched her from the doorway, murmuring between them, while George set the table, grinning the entire time. Finally, when she'd placed the sausages in the hot frying pan and they'd started sizzling, the aroma of Hargreaves'

Yorkshire links filling the room, the two men had inched forward, unable to resist any longer. George had pulled out chairs, seating them like a maître d' at the best of restaurants, and they'd sat waiting in silence since.

'Pour the tea, George,' Ida said, turning back to the range and beginning to dish up.

George did as he was told, still grinning, his excitement at similar levels to when he'd taken possession of the Little Grey tractor late last year. Then Ida was placing plates in front of their two guests, mounds of mash, three sausages each for starters with more in the pan, and a large jug of gravy – Ida being of the belief that you could never have too much gravy.

The younger man watched his plate arrive, cutlery already in his hands, and bent down eagerly to start eating. But a brusque comment from the other man made him pause. Then they both looked at Ida.

'Thank you,' the older man said, the younger one nodding in agreement.

'No need for thanks,' muttered Ida, taking a seat by the range, strangely touched. 'Eat up while it's hot.'

And so they started eating. The clink of cutlery. The occasional sigh of contentment. The tick of the grandfather clock. It could have been a scene from any country kitchen after a long day on the farm. But for the fact Ida Capstick had no idea who these men were, nor if they represented any threat. One thing was clear, however: the younger lad was in need of medical attention, wincing with pain as he ate.

A hospital was out of the question. She'd had trouble getting them into her house. They'd spook entirely if she tried to get them to A&E at Airedale. So Ida settled on the next best thing. While the two young men were making the most of her hospitality, she snuck her mobile out of her pocket and sent a text to the only person she could think of to help. Hoping that she wasn't going to embroil another Bruncliffe resident in a situation which she might have misjudged completely.

Grigore was nervous. This strange woman and her strange brother. Could they be trusted?

So far, the brother had proved reliable, a docility to him which had allayed even Pavel's initial fears. Since he'd discovered them a few days ago, he'd been bringing them food and drink, and they'd passed the time comfortable in each other's company, Grigore helping him with the faulty carburettor, glad to be doing something that resembled the life he'd left behind.

But while they might feel confident that the brother wouldn't do anything to alert anyone to their presence, the sister was a different entity entirely.

Fierce was the first word which had sprang to mind when she'd appeared in the doorway, that granite expression on a face which consisted of so many angles. Shocked but yet resilient, reaching for her mobile despite the threat Grigore posed.

He was ashamed to think of how he'd reacted, willing to attack a woman, one almost old enough to be his mother. But she'd stood her ground, only relenting from making the call when she saw her brother calming down, saw how familiar Grigore was with him.

She was loyal, to her brother at least. Whether she would

extend the same loyalty to them remained to be seen. Yet here they were, accepting her hospitality. Accepting the meal she'd prepared. Too hungry and tired not to. But that didn't mean he had to lower his guard. And so he watched her out of the corner of his eye. Watched Pavel too, shovelling his food down like a condemned man.

'Easy, brother,' he murmured. 'Don't make yourself sick.'

Pavel grunted, another forkful of potato heading for his mouth.

Over by the stove, the woman had taken out her mobile, her fingers flicking across it, sending a text. When she glanced up, she caught his gaze with her own stern regard, a defiance in her, as though she knew she'd just done something perhaps she oughtn't have.

She'd contacted the police. He was sure of it. This had all been a trap.

The food Grigore had been relishing suddenly tasted like sawdust, soured by the panic building in his chest. But what could they do? Pavel was in no state to start running, even if Grigore could persuade him to leave the comfort of the table, the kitchen that felt so like home. Even the woman who had cooked for them, reminding him of his own mother with her no-nonsense approach to everything.

He cringed again at the thought of himself brandishing a screwdriver at her.

Him! Threatening a woman! This is what he'd been reduced to. What the Devil had reduced him to.

It was the Devil who'd made him so suspicious too, tainting everything so that even a genuine act of kindness became blighted with mistrust. If that's what this was, a genuine act of kindness.

Date with Evil

Grigore finished the last morsel of sausage and set his cutlery on his plate, reached for the mug of tea and managed to make himself drink some of it, the brew strong enough to curdle his stomach. Then he nodded towards the woman.

'*Thank you*,' he managed again, the two words about the sum of his English.

She was on her feet instantly, reaching for the frying pan, holding it out, clearly offering him more. He shook his head, patted his stomach, smiled. Tried not to let his concern show. Because if she had betrayed them, best she didn't know he was aware of it.

Satisfied he was full, she placed the pan back down and reached instead for the teapot. There was no communication this time as she filled up his mug, presuming he would want more. He nodded again, but made no move to drink it as she resumed her seat and took out her knitting. He wasn't sure his guts needed the punishment.

Pavel was still eating, face flushed, both through fever and through unaccustomed sustenance. When had he last eaten like this? That last night at home in mid-September, Mama insisting on feeding him up before he headed off to the city to make his fortune. Little had they known that there was no fortune to be made, only misery and deceit. And crime.

A small groan escaped his brother's lips, a hand going down to his side. He needed a doctor. But how that could be arranged, Grigore had no idea. Nor did he know what their next steps would be. Right now, with the clock ticking in the background and the comforting click of the woman's knitting needles, he could feel sleep creeping at the corners of his consciousness.

He moved in his chair, rousing himself. And as he did so, he got a waft of his stale clothes, his unwashed state, and was embarrassed. What he would give for a bath and a good night's rest. Luxuries he'd taken for granted only four months ago.

'Wonderful,' muttered Pavel, finally finishing and sitting back in his chair with a wince. 'As good as Mama's cooking.'

Again the woman was on her feet, offering more. Pavel raised a hand, shook his head, smiled. And then her brother was next to the table, two bottles in his hand.

'*Yorkshire beer*,' he said, placing them on the table, glasses alongside them. Doing that jig he did when he was happy, the same jig he'd done when they'd got the carburettor working the day before.

Pavel was already pouring the amber liquid into his glass, eyes alight at the unexpected treat.

'Drink up!' he said with a tired smile.

But Grigore was wary. Alcohol wasn't the best option right now. He needed his wits about him.

'Come on, brother. Everything's fine. We're safe,' insisted Pavel, raising his glass to their hosts.

And Grigore found himself taking the bottle, watching the beer flow into his glass in an act which seemed so normal in this weird situation. He nodded, lifted it in salutation, and raised it to his lips. Took a long drink.

Which is when he heard the car door slam, the patter of footsteps and the back door flying open. He'd been right. They'd been betrayed.

Dropping his beer, Grigore grabbed a knife from the table and sprang to his feet.

18

'Sorry, Ida, I came as quick as I could—'

The apology came at the same time as the back door flew open and there was Ana Stoyanovic, staggering back in shock as the older of the brothers leaped up from the table, brandishing a knife towards her.

'It's okay!' Ida exclaimed, her words aimed at both parties as she rushed to place herself between her guests and the new arrival. 'She's a friend. A nurse.' She was pointing now, at the younger man, the way he was holding himself. 'Nurse,' she repeated, hoping the word was recognised across the language barrier.

The older brother's panicked gaze was flicking between them, unsure of where the threat lay. But then it came to rest on Ana's face. That beautiful face, the perfect cheekbones, the green eyes, all framed with golden hair.

Ana Stoyanovic was the closest to an angel on earth Ida Capstick had ever met and had the nature to go with it. But in this instance, it wasn't Ana's angelic qualities that Ida was after. It was her nursing qualifications and the fact that she was from Serbia, which, in Ida's limited knowledge of linguistics, might provide some key into the language these brothers were speaking and hence, their origin.

'She's a friend,' she repeated.

There was no need. The man was letting the knife fall back to the table, staring at Ana, drinking in the sight of her. If she represented danger, he'd clearly decided to let fate take its course. The irony wasn't lost on Ida that her own stern features had failed to elicit such an effect.

'Hello,' said Ana, entering the kitchen, pulling the door closed behind her, a flush of pink on her alabaster cheeks at the intense attention.

The man said something to her and she shook her head. He said something else and this time she nodded. Said something hesitant in return.

'Tha can understand them?' asked Ida.

'A little,' said Ana, her attention turning to the strained features of the younger brother. 'I'm guessing this is the one who's injured?' She approached him, all business now in that way nurses have, and he mutely accepted as she lifted his hoodie and gently examined his side, the lad trying not to flinch at her touch.

When she stepped back, her face was grave.

'He has several broken ribs at least and I wouldn't rule out a partially collapsed lung. Ideally, he should go to hospital for a CT scan—'

Ida was already shaking her head. 'Tha's wasting tha breath. They won't go. I'm sure of it.'

Ana looked at the two men, taking in their dishevelled appearance, and then turned back to Ida. 'Want to tell me what's going on here?'

'Actually,' said Ida, feeling relief at sharing this burden, 'I was rather hoping tha was going to be able to help me get to the bottom of that.'

*

While Ida was trying to get to grips with her mystery guests, Samson and Delilah were trying to make some kind of sense out of the files she'd brought back from Stuart Lister's flat in her bucket.

With the kitchen table proving too small, they'd relocated to the lounge and spread the folders out across the rug, Tolpuddle still sprawled on the sofa from where he was watching them with sleepy bemusement. Sitting cross-legged on the floor, they were flicking through the documents, making the odd comment and frowning a lot.

'Are you feeling this?' Samson eventually asked, as he finished reading another file and dropped it on the rug before leaning back against the couch and stretching out his legs. 'That there's something odd going on here?'

Delilah nodded. 'Definitely. But what exactly?'

Over thirty files, all for rentals on Taylor's books. All for properties being rented to the same company.

Kingston Holdings.

The jolt of recognition had captured Samson's attention from the very first file, the name leaping off the page at him. Because Kingston Holdings was, according to the conversation he'd had with Mr Marsden at Yorkshire Lockers several weeks ago, the company owned by the mystery benefactor who'd paid for the lockers at Bruncliffe College. The same lockers Samson was looking into as part of his endeavour to find out who'd framed Nathan. With ketamine.

Again, that connection.

Interest more than piqued, he'd opened another file. Found the same company listed as the tenant. Likewise with the next. And the next . . . While the rest of what he was seeing didn't make sense, that name was ringing bells.

'Have you come across this Kingston Holdings before?' he asked, keeping his tone casual.

Delilah shook her head. 'You?'

'Nope.' The lie slid off his tongue easily, her closeness to Nathan and her legendary temper still making him wary of revealing the possible link. 'Seems odd for one entity to be renting so much property in a backwater like Bruncliffe.'

'Agreed,' said Delilah. 'But it's not illegal. Certainly not something Stuart would have felt he had to hide.'

'So what are we missing then?' asked Samson, frustration rising. 'Because the lad went to the bother of stealing all this lot, so there's got to be something here. Some anomaly that can help us crack this.'

'What we need is a spreadsheet.' Delilah was already standing up, going over to her bag for her laptop. 'It'll enable us to better collate all this data.'

Samson watched her with a grin, loving her passion, the way she got so fired up about life, the way she—

'What?' she said, aware of his focus on her as she resumed her seat on the floor, computer on her lap.

'Has anyone ever told you that you're sexy when you go all geeky?'

She gave him a mock glare. He pulled her towards him. 'How about we take a break?' he murmured, kissing her, his intentions clear.

'What about the files,' Delilah protested feebly.

'They'll wait.' Samson had her face between his hands now, his kisses more insistent. 'We've got far more pressing matters to tend to.'

'Like?' she raised an eyebrow, a grin forming on her lips.

He felt the world contract, aware only of her in his arms. 'Like the fact,' he said quietly, 'that I've been trying to tell you I lo—'

'Oh my God!' Delilah snapped out of his embrace, eliciting a surprised bark from Tolpuddle, the flush on her cheeks having nothing to do with Samson's overtures. 'The anomaly!'

She was up on her knees now, laptop abandoned as she burrowed through the pile of folders, flicking them open, scanning them, discarding them. Until she found the one she was looking for.

'Here! This! I thought I recognised the address.' She tapped the front page of the file she was holding. 'This isn't a rental!'

In the face of her excitement, Samson reluctantly brought his attention back to less amorous matters. 'What do you mean?' he asked, taking the folder from her and reading the details. A large former farmhouse with way more bedrooms and bathrooms than the average family required, it was an imposing property.

'I mean, I happen to know this particular house isn't being rented. It was sold a year ago to an architect who's just moved up from London with his family.'

'You're sure?'

'Definite. I did his website for him three months ago and went over there for a meeting.'

'He couldn't have rented it out through Taylor's since? He wouldn't be the first to settle in the Dales only to realise the reality of rural living isn't for him.'

Delilah leaned over his shoulder and pointed to the date

on the contract. According to the paperwork, the rental period had commenced the previous June. And was ongoing.

'I think he'd have noticed if the tenants were still living with him, don't you?' she said with a smug smile.

Samson let out a low whistle. The anomaly. She was right. For some reason Taylor's had an ongoing rental property on their files which wasn't really a rental property.

'Do you remember where it was, exactly?' he asked.

She gave a dry laugh. 'It's in the middle of bloody nowhere! Down one of the side roads on the way up to Bowland Knotts. Even with a GPS I had trouble finding it. Why? You think location is important?'

'Maybe.'

'Well in that case, let's get organised!' Delilah opened her laptop and began drawing up a spreadsheet, leaving Samson to accept that, for now, they were back at work.

'Transylvania?' Ida couldn't keep the surprise out of her voice at the revelation. 'In Romania? That's where they're from?'

Ana Stoyanovic nodded, while George was appraising his new friends with open awe.

'Home of UTB tractors,' he murmured, reaching for the only fact from his vast store of statistics which could match this exotic location. 'And Dracula.'

Across the table from him, the man they now knew as Grigore gave a smile of recognition, raising the glass of beer he'd been given to replace the one he'd dropped.

But beyond naming the oldest brother as Grigore and the youngest as Pavel, and discovering where they hailed from, Ana's attempts to find out more about the men had hit a brick wall.

'So tha's not sure how they got here?' Ida asked. 'Or why they've been sleeping rough?'

Ana shook her head. 'Trouble is, I don't speak Romanian and they don't speak Serbian. So we're having to communicate in Hungarian.'

Ida simply nodded, unable to comprehend a life where languages could be so easily interchanged. She had trouble enough making herself understood when talking with her cousins down in Sheffield, and that's when they were all speaking English!

'That said,' continued Ana, 'my Hungarian really isn't up to it. I only have a smattering. And they . . .' She looked at the brothers and shrugged. 'I've tried using Google translate with them but they're not cooperating. I think maybe they just aren't in the mood to talk.'

'They're scared and they don't trust us,' said Ida. 'And I can't say as I blame them. Whatever the poor souls have been through, it's not been pleasant.'

One look at the two men was enough to confirm that. There was a permanent edginess to them which even a good feed of sausage and mash and a strong brew hadn't been able to completely eradicate. While Pavel was looking more relaxed, nursing his second beer of the evening, his older brother remained ill at ease, taking no more than occasional sips of his drink as though reluctant to let his wits be dulled.

'I'm wondering if what they've been through is even worse than we can imagine,' murmured Ana. 'It strikes me that they may have been trafficked.'

'Trafficked?' Ida heard the disbelief in her own voice –

the mere notion that folk were capable of trading people like cattle such an alien concept to her. 'Round here?'

'It's more common than you think. Car washes, nail bars, building sites.' Ana shrugged. 'I don't see why Bruncliffe would be immune.'

Ida stared afresh at her guests. They both looked shattered. And George was starting to get restless, beginning to rock slightly in his chair, the odd tractor statistic slipping out. He'd had more than enough human interaction for one day.

'Right, then,' she said, going with her instinct. 'Let's get them washed and to bed. We can sort everything else out in the morning.'

'You're letting them stay here? Without knowing anything about them?' Ana's questions held more than a hint of doubt. 'Is that wise?'

Ida grunted. 'Not sure as to how wise it is, lass. But it's the right thing to do. Like tha said, it's highly likely them boys have been to hell and back. Least we can do is give them a bed for the night.'

'But what if one of them is the man Sergeant Clayton is looking for? Mrs Pettiford was in the cafe this morning saying he's wanted for murder!'

'Has Lucy not taught thee yet to ignore anything that old gossipmonger says?' muttered Ida, knowing that Ana's part-time work in Peaks Patisserie exposed her to more than was healthy of the local tittle-tattle, and her relatively recent arrival in town meant she hadn't yet learned to sort the wheat from the chaff. Mrs Pettiford was definitely chaff.

'Constable Bradley found a knife, Ida,' Ana said gently. 'One that had been used. That's not gossip.'

'Aye, so I heard. Doesn't mean these lads are connected.'

The look Ana gave her suggested she could tell Ida wasn't even convincing herself. Which she wasn't, because there was the small matter of the clothing the men were wearing and where it had come from . . . But she wasn't about to confess that to Ana. It would mean even more pressure to bring in the authorities.

Ana wasn't quite ready to acquiesce to Ida's plan, however. 'So I'm guessing you don't want to call the police,' she said. 'But at least tell Samson and Delilah.'

'No. Not tonight. Happen as we've all had enough for one day. I'll sleep on it and decide what's best tomorrow.'

There was a long pause, Ana turning her cool gaze onto the two men, assessing them openly. Pavel smiled back, a hint of cheekiness in his look despite his pain. Grigore just stared at her. Unfathomable.

'Well, if you're sure this is what you want to do,' Ana finally said, turning back to Ida, 'in that case, let's get Pavel started on some medication. Ibuprofen and paracetamol alternated every two hours for now and we can see about getting him to hospital in the morning. In the meantime, I'll help you get the beds ready.'

Grateful for Ana's pragmatism and offer of assistance, Ida got to her feet, noticing the way Grigore recoiled the moment she moved, grasp tightening on the bottle he was holding, preparing to use it as a weapon. The man was a tinder box of tension and she was about to let him stay the night under her roof.

Putting on a brave front to cover her own concerns, she led Ana out of the kitchen and up the stairs. The best way to take her mind off what could turn out to be the daftest decision she'd ever made was to do a bit of housework. There were sheets to be found, bedding to be taken out of storage and baths to be run. After all, Ida assured herself as she showed Ana where the spare linen was kept, there was nothing like a hot bath and a good night's sleep for soothing the nerves.

She spoke Hungarian. This Serbian angel who'd appeared out of nowhere. A smattering of it, anyhow, not quite as much as Grigore and Pavel who'd grown up in a region where so much of the population was of Hungarian descent, their own grandparents included. Her grandfather was Hungarian, too, she'd said.

He hadn't got round to asking anything else, mesmerised by her beauty, the perfection of that face. As she'd lifted Pavel's stolen clothing to examine him, Grigore had felt a rare moment of intense jealousy, wishing he was the one with the broken ribs.

It hadn't been easy to resist answering her stilted questions, when all he wanted to do was interact with her, spend the rest of his life talking to her. But the questions were too dangerous. Who were they? Why were they here? What had happened to them? A muttered warning to his brother and they'd both sat there like mutes, making out that it was language which was keeping them from answering, even when she'd resorted to a translation app on her mobile. In reality, it was a lack of trust.

And a sense of shame, too, on Grigore's part. What would this woman think of them when she found out what they'd done? That Pavel had fallen for a human trafficking scam and that in trying to bring him home, Grigore had murdered someone and left another to die a lonely death.

What kind of man would she think he was? The worst of men.

So he'd kept his mouth closed as she struggled with her broken Hungarian and her digital dictionary, allowing her nothing more than their first names and their place of birth. Even that felt like a lot after so long living in the shadows. But he'd got her name in return.

Ana.

He'd stowed it away along with all the other precious things he'd tried hard to protect from the brutality he'd been exposed to over the last few terrible months.

Now at last the questions had stopped, but Grigore sensed the danger was far from over. It seemed like Ana and the older woman, Ida, were deciding what to do. And they weren't in agreement. He listened to their words, trying to grasp which way the wind was blowing from the tone, trying to be prepared for a dramatic exit when all he wanted was to go to bed, the good food and home comforts making him sleepy.

Then the women were getting to their feet, the sudden movement making him flinch, grasp his beer bottle . . .

Ida was watching him, a flicker of concern on her face. Then she gave one of those nods she was fond of, a sharp tilt of the head that brooked no nonsense. This was it. She'd made a decision. And suddenly Grigore found he didn't care any more. Whether it was the effect of the small amount of beer he'd consumed or whether it was simply that he was happy to resign his fate into the hands of the goddess called Ana, he didn't have the energy to determine. Instead, he watched as the two women left the room.

Footsteps up and down the stairs, the sounds of furniture

being moved, the gush of water following. A bath being run?

Minutes later Ida returned and beckoned for Pavel to follow her. Pavel looked at Grigore. Grigore shrugged. And Pavel headed out of the kitchen.

It was too late for worrying. It was too late for running.

'Grigore!' Ida's brother had shifted into the chair opposite him at the table, placing a new bottle of beer in front of him, and was now jigging in his seat with excitement and pointing at himself. 'George!'

'George, Grigore,' said Grigore smiling, pointing at the pair of them in turn.

'Grigore, George, George, Grigore, UTB tractors, Dracula!'

This new litany brought forth a laugh from Grigore. Then the door to the hallway opened and in came the angel, a smile on her face at the sound of laughter.

'He is liking you,' said Ana with open approval as her gaze rested on Grigore and made his heart flip.

At last, he thought as he watched her join them at the table, a beer in her hand, something good had come out of the entire tragedy. In the course of a single evening, his life had gone from the depths of hell to something resembling paradise.

But as he clinked his bottle against hers and took a long drink, a wave of guilt crashed over him, turning the beer sour in his mouth.

How could he be sitting here enjoying the company of this angel when he'd left a man to die? What about the promise Grigore had made to him?

Should he speak up now and fulfil the oath he'd made?

Even as he was thinking it, the voice in his head was telling him it was too soon. Too early to place such trust in these people. And besides, it mattered little whether Ida and her brother were the good people he suspected they were – they would be no match for the Devil and his henchmen. A few more days, give Pavel time to recover so they could be ready to run – or fight – if necessary, and then Grigore would talk. He would tell them everything. But until then, the man they'd left behind would have to take his chances. If he was still alive.

19

The Capsticks' guests were accommodated downstairs in the room at the front of the house, a space which had always been saved for 'best', seeing usage only when esteemed folk visited, such as the vicar, balancing a cup of tea on his knees while sitting on the settee making small talk with folk who didn't really do God. More recently, it had been the last resting place for both Capstick parents, a bed being brought down so Ida and her mother could nurse her father through the cancer that eventually took him, before it was Mrs Capstick's turn to lie in the bed and watch the fells in the distance as her life slowly dipped below the horizon.

George and Ida had seen no need to take the double bed out. It was more hassle than it was worth just to liberate a space neither of them used, content as they were to spend their time in the kitchen or, in George's case, in the barn. So after their baths, their two guests were shown to the freshly made bed, sheets smelling of Dales sunshine, blankets and bedspread smelling of lavender, a couple of pairs of George's pyjamas folded over a chair.

Neither of the brothers cared that their berth for the night was overlooked by a plethora of Capsticks past and present, staring down on them with angular jaws and pinched faces from above the fireplace. With stomachs full for the first time in months, bodies washed of grime and a moderate amount of alcohol melting their limbs, Grigore and Pavel gratefully turned in for the night. They were asleep in no time at all, long before Ana Stoyanovic drove off into the night and Ida and George crept up the stairs, avoiding the ones that creaked out of respect for their lodgers.

Half an hour later, the cottage was quiet, only Ida left awake, staring out at the stars and wondering what torments the two lads had been through to bring them starved and wounded to her door. Wondering also what Ana had meant when she'd been taking her leave and had enigmatically said she might know someone who would be able to help with the language barrier and persuade the reticent brothers to talk.

It would be some time before sleep would claim the final occupant of Croft Cottage. And when it did, it wasn't the most restful, a combination of excitement and fear fuelling Ida Capstick's troubled dreams.

At an hour when dawn was a lot closer than dusk, the lights were still burning in the cottage on Crag Lane. With a weary sigh, Samson leaned back against the couch, stretched his legs out along the floor and ran a hand over his face.

'So,' he said, 'what have we got?'

'A headache,' muttered Delilah, sitting cross-legged next to him, computer on her lap.

They'd finally finished combing through the files Stuart

Lister had taken from Taylor's, reading them multiple times, cross-referencing them, pulling out any inconsistencies, and entering everything onto the spreadsheet Delilah had produced on her laptop. She'd also drawn up a rough map, locating the position of every property, Samson currently looking over her shoulder at thirty red dots scattered across the Bruncliffe area, each one representing a rental. All of them in remote locations.

Delilah was right. It was a headache of mammoth proportions.

'Let's start with the rent,' he said.

'Astronomical!' Delilah pulled the spreadsheet back up on the screen and pointed at the third column. 'Starting at a minimum of four grand a month and going up to a whopping seven thousand.'

'And we thought eighteen hundred a month for Henside Road was a lot,' murmured Samson. 'At this rate Taylor's is pulling in the best part of a million every six months for this lot.'

'That's the other thing,' continued Delilah. 'The contracts were all started at different times, yet all of the rent is paid on the same day. Six-monthly, in advance, payable on the first Thursday in June and the first Thursday in December. Don't know why, but that seems a bit odd to me.'

'Agreed. Plus it's a heck of a lot of money to have to shell out upfront.'

'Next, the tenants. Or tenant, I should say.'

Samson was nodding, looking at the relevant column, thirty entries under it, all identical: Kingston Holdings. The same company was renting every single property.

'And if that wasn't bizarre enough, we get to the owners.'

Delilah twisted the laptop so he could get a better view. 'I happen to recognise pretty much all of these names.'

'You know them personally?' Samson felt a glimmer of hope that they could simply contact one of the men listed – for they were all men – and ask them what was going on.

'Yes. Or did, to be precise. They're all dead.'

He did the classic double take. Looking from the screen to Delilah's face and back again. Trying to take it in. 'I don't understand.'

'Death?' said Delilah with a wry smile. 'Or what's going on here? I can help you with the former, but the latter . . .' She threw up her arms in surrender. 'I haven't got a clue about that.'

'Let me get this straight. You're telling me that the names you recognise on here all belong to men who are now deceased?'

She nodded. 'Frank Lambert? That's Nancy Taylor's father. He died at least ten years ago. And Tom Dugdale? Annie Hardacre's uncle. He used to farm next door to us. I was only a nipper when he passed away.' She shrugged. 'I can't give exact dates for the rest but I know the names. And I know they're no longer in a state to be renting out property. Property they never owned in the first place.'

Samson was still staring at the screen, trying to get his head around it. 'Any chance it's a coincidence?' he asked. 'People with the same names but alive?'

Delilah's look was sceptical. 'One or two maybe. But this many?' She shook her head. 'Besides, if these were genuine owners, some of them would live in the area and I'd know them. I'd know that there was a Fred Lambert or a Tom Dugdale alive and well. But the only folk I know with these names are all dead and long buried.'

'What the hell . . . ?'

'Don't know about you,' said Delilah, getting to her feet, 'but I need a brew.'

Samson got up too, following her through to the kitchen to sit at the table while she put the kettle on.

'How do we start to make sense of it?' she asked over her shoulder, as she reached down a couple of mugs and a packet of Hobnobs from a cupboard. At the rustle of the wrapping, a sleepy-looking Weimaraner padded hopefully into the kitchen.

'Perhaps we go back to where we began,' suggested Samson. 'With Stuart Lister. I think you have to agree now that the fact he stole these files doesn't look good.'

Delilah gave a reluctant nod. 'None of his behaviour is looking ideal right now.'

'Or the timing of it. He stole the files the day after Bernard died, made a visit to Henside Road the following day, which he tried to erase all trace of, and then left town at two o'clock in the morning.'

'You think this is all connected to Bernard's death, then?' asked Delilah, joining him at the table with two mugs, the packet of biscuits and a Dog-gestive for Tolpuddle.

'It's looking that way. Whatever scam Stuart was involved in, he seems to have got spooked when Bernard died.'

'Perhaps he thought it would be uncovered in the aftermath? Whatever this "it" is.'

'Maybe we hit the nail on the head at the outset? Drugs of some sort? We've already established that the set-up at Henside Road was more than a bit fishy.'

Delilah was shaking her head. 'Henside Road was a genuine rental. So even if our wild speculation about what was going on out there is somehow on the mark, it can't explain the thirty properties we've just been looking at. You can't make drugs in a place other folk are living in.'

'Fair point,' muttered Samson. He sighed, the late hour and the complex puzzle sapping his energy and muddling his thoughts.

They fell into a weary silence, the only sound the tick of the kitchen clock and the contented crunch of Tolpuddle enjoying his midnight snack. Samson was about to suggest they call it a night when he noticed Delilah was regarding her mug of tea with a look of contemplation, as though she was debating whether or not to say something.

'What is it?' he asked.

A slight flush rose up her cheeks. 'I was just thinking that we're not the only ones who suspect Stuart might have been up to something.' Her focus was still fixed on her mug, an air of confession creeping into her tone. 'I wasn't going to bother mentioning this because I know how highly you rate him,' she continued, with more than a hint of irony, 'but Rick Procter was in Taylor's this morning when I was talking to Julie.'

'Oh. And? Tolpuddle bit him?' Samson asked hopefully, leaning over to pat the Weimaraner and getting an appreciative nuzzle in return.

Delilah grinned, her gaze finally meeting his. 'He settled for a prolonged growl. But the reason I'm bringing it up is because Rick seems to be concerned about Stuart's sudden disappearance.' She raised a hand to forestall the riposte that was already forming on Samson's lips. 'I know you won't set much store by that, given the source, and I have to admit, Rick's gone down considerably in my estimation too in the last few months, but he was genuinely worried.'

'In what way?'

'He said there'd been a few things . . . He didn't go into specifics but it was clear he thought Stuart had been up to something dodgy.'

'Ha!' Samson's laugh was filled with derision. 'Give me a break! That's just Rick playing the model citizen, making it look like he's taking good care of Nancy's business while she's grieving.'

'Think it probably has more to do with the fact that Nancy's business will soon be his . . .' Delilah let her words hang in the air, an eyebrow raised in Samson's direction.

He stared at her in disbelief. 'Rick's buying Taylor's?'

'I heard it straight from the man himself. Kind of puts a different spin on his concern, doesn't it?'

'How come he told you?' asked Samson, still dubious.

'He hadn't planned to, but when he heard Neil had cancelled the IT system update out of the blue, he wanted to know why. Telling me about the sale gave him a legitimate reason to ask.' She shrugged. 'His exact words were that he didn't know what Neil's game was. What with that and the suspicions he's obviously harbouring about Stuart's behaviour, like I said, Rick was genuinely concerned. So much so, he's asked me to keep him posted on our investigation.'

'And have you?'

Delilah gave him a frank look. 'No. I don't intend to either.'

Samson nodded, unsettled in so many ways by what she'd told him. The thought of Rick confiding in her. The thought of the property developer getting his claws into yet another of Bruncliffe's enterprises. Despite his intense loathing of the man, however, Samson had to admit there was something intriguing in the conversation Delilah had relayed. Not least the fact that Rick shared Samson's own wariness when it came to Neil Taylor's motives for being back in town. Knowing better than to drag that topic back up, he focused on the case.

'So Stuart is ringing alarm bells all over,' he mused. 'But by doing what?'

'Something that's generating a lot of cash,' said Delilah, 'if those rental fees Taylor's is charging are genuine.'

'Cash,' murmured Samson, 'a lot of cash.'

He was thinking about past cases, his work with the National Crime Agency. The way cash was the currency of so many of the criminal networks they'd busted. And suddenly he was seeing the holdall Nancy Taylor had brought to the office just before her husband died. A holdall stuffed full of banknotes, one hundred and twenty-five thousand pounds' worth, to be exact, which Nancy had asked the Dales Detective Agency to ascertain the origin of. Slapping his palm against his forehead, Samson wondered if they had just done exactly that.

'I can't believe I didn't make the connection before!' he exclaimed. 'Where you get one, you always get the other.'

Delilah looked at him, eyebrows raised. 'I'm not following.'

'What if we're right about Henside Road? What if there really was some kind of drugs farm out there which Stuart closed down before disappearing? If you're selling drugs on that scale, you're going to be generating a lot of—'

'Cash,' interjected Delilah, nodding, seeing where he was going. 'Which you then need to make legitimate . . .'

Samson was already on his feet, getting the laptop, bringing it to the table. 'How about this for a system to legitimise it?' he asked, pointing at the spreadsheet, at the bizarre single tenant and the deceased property owners. 'The proceeds from the sale of the drugs neatly incorporated into mainstream banking systems, no questions asked. Like I said, where you get one, you have to have the other. Drugs and money laundering.'

She glanced up at him. 'That's an awful lot of cash from one drugs farm.'

'Who said there was only one?' he muttered. 'Stuart Lister had access to a raft of isolated houses. He could have been running more than one manufacturing site with ease. Then the income gets nicely washed in these sham rentals.'

'Crikey! No wonder he stole the files!' murmured Delilah, shocked. 'A sophisticated criminal racket. And right under everyone's noses!' She paused, thinking everything through, and then looked at Samson, her face turning grey as she came to the same conclusion he'd just reached. 'Bernard Taylor. He must have been involved for this to have worked.'

'I'm afraid I'm inclined to agree. That holdall Nancy found was probably part of it. His monthly cut or something along those lines.'

Delilah was stunned into silence. Staring at the spreadsheet, seeing the logic of what Samson was suggesting yet not wanting it to be true. He watched her struggling to assimilate this new version of reality with someone she'd known all her life. A man who'd been her father-in-law.

'I always knew he was a bit shady,' she murmured, 'but this . . . And Stuart! I just can't believe it.'

'Seems Mrs Lister had it right all along,' muttered Samson bleakly. 'Her son didn't go globetrotting. He ran off before he was caught.'

More silence, Delilah digesting it all. When she spoke it was with her usual compassion. 'The poor woman. And poor Nancy. This is going to shatter them.'

Samson just nodded. For he was thinking it wasn't only the two women who were going to have their lives destroyed when the news broke. The tight-knit community of Bruncliffe would be torn apart, too.

A sliver of light, beginning to slant through the airbrick high up the wall, sufficient only to signify another dawn. Another day.

How many had he spent in this pitch-black pit? He'd lost count. Hunger had seen to that. And fear. In the corner something scuttled across the shadows. He no longer reacted. He was too weak. Too tired. Too thirsty.

Another day, he muttered into the dark. Another chance that salvation would come. Because it had been promised, admittedly no more than a hoarse whisper through the airbrick pledging help, but he was someone who put great faith in promises. Even though he knew the clock was ticking.

For he'd seen the face of the Devil. The man who'd put him in this hell. There was no way he'd be allowed to live much longer.

From outside the thick walls came the high-pitched bleat of a lamb followed by a shrill cry. A lapwing. A flash of pride cut through his misery at the recognition of the haunting sound.

Another day. He could survive another day. For he was an optimist. Blindly so. And this was Bruncliffe.

He lay there, delirious, in pain, watching the meagre light crawl slowly across the damp walls, and knew it was only his faith in Bruncliffe that was keeping him alive.

20

The dawn was magnificent. Against a sky of fragile blue, the long, low cloud that spanned the hump-backed length of Pen-y-ghent had been turned a vivid pink.

The exact same shade of pink as the Texel sheep in the field before Clive Knowles. Leaning on a gate at Mire End Farm, his old sheepdog sitting next to him, he was watching his flock and thinking of Carol. The way she'd laughed when she'd seen his theft-prevention measures, the dye coming out slightly stronger than he'd intended.

How he wished she could see them now. The lambs running around on their special morning energy. The larks singing their hearts out up above. Even the discordant clack of a pheasant seemed a sound heaven-sent after so many hours cooped up in the intensive care ward. Life beyond the confines of Carol's bedside was fit to burst, a juxtaposition Clive was finding hard to cope with.

It seemed wrong that everything was going on as normal when she was fighting to stay alive.

He glanced at the bucket full of miscellaneous items by his feet. Would one of them do the trick and reveal the identity of the scoundrel who'd brought this tragedy upon his fiancée? Clive didn't really have much faith that it would, but there was little else he could do.

Just as he'd vowed, he'd left the hospital in the last vestiges of the dark, making the most of the quiet roads to arrive back at Mire End Farm as the day was breaking. Entering the empty farmhouse had been a shock. Not quite empty, the dog rising arthritically from the cold hearth to greet him with a slow wag of his tail, no sign of distress at having been looked after by a neighbour in the forced absence of his master. But even if the fire had been roaring that June morning, the house would still have felt wintry. For what had become the beating heart of it was missing.

Overcome with emotion, Clive had forced himself to concentrate on the task at hand. Find the things Carol had brought back from Pete Ferris's caravan. He'd been stumped where to start, remembering only the meatballs with clarity. So he'd made his way towards the larder, spying Carol's cleaning bucket in the porch in passing and deciding that, seeing as it had been used to transport Pete's belongings here, it would be a useful guide as to whether he'd retrieved everything.

He'd spotted the meatballs straight away on the top shelf of the larder. Next to them, three tins of dog food of a brand he didn't recognise. Both lots went in the bucket. Then he was afforded a stroke of luck – or rather, he was afforded the benefit of living with someone as organised as Carol Kirby. With the farmhouse spick and span in a way it had never been during Clive's long years of single occupancy, there weren't many places to look. So when he'd pulled out the kitchen dresser drawer where the key to the caravan was kept, he was rewarded by a neat stack of items that literally smelled of Pete, the sweet odour of cannabis hanging over the lot. Among them, a mobile phone.

Clive had gathered it all up and headed out into the dawn.

A dawn Carol couldn't share with him, he thought, feeling melancholy descend as he took in the majesty of the scene. Although he knew what his ever pragmatic fiancée would say about it – being an adherent of proverbs, a morning sky this colour would have her muttering about shepherd's warnings.

It was one hell of a warning in that case.

Bending down to give the dog one last pat, he picked up the bucket and turned towards his battered 4x4, intending to head for town. But the pink cloud tugged at him. So he laid the bucket back down, took out his mobile, and figured out how to take a video.

It took three attempts – during which he succeeded in filming his boots, the dog and a bit of the gate – before he managed to capture the idyllic scene at Mire End Farm. Five minutes after that, with the sun yet to haul itself over the mass of Pen-y-ghent and a cluster of brooding clouds developing to the west, Clive was heading for Leeds. Via Bruncliffe.

After an extremely late night, Tolpuddle was by far the freshest of the Dales Detective Agency trio as they arrived at the office building on Thursday morning at seven prompt. Having finally collapsed into bed in the early hours, neither Samson nor Delilah had slept well, troubled by the magnitude of what they'd discovered. Consequently they were looking far from rested as they wearily climbed the stairs towards the kitchen. The sound of a vacuum being run around Delilah's office and the strong smell of polish told them Ida had also arrived before her normal time.

'Not a word about what we found, remember,' murmured Samson as they rounded the landing and headed for the kitchen.

Delilah gave a reluctant nod. She wasn't at ease keeping Ida out of the loop when it came to what was happening in their ongoing cases, not after she'd put so much effort into helping run the business in the past couple of weeks. But what they were dealing with was so sensitive and the consequences so grave, Delilah had seen the wisdom of Samson's suggestion that they keep it to themselves until they were able to corroborate what Stuart Lister's stolen files implied.

That a major drugs and money-laundering organisation had been operating in Bruncliffe with the compliance of the mayor and his lettings agent.

With a lifetime lived there, Delilah didn't need telling what this could do to the community. Distrust, suspicion, accusations; once sown, they could tear the fabric of the place apart and destroy all that was good about the Dales town. It wasn't something to be triggered without having as many facts in place as possible first. Which is why Samson was heading straight to see Matty Thistlethwaite, the solicitor having agreed to squeeze him in at eight, before Turpin's opened its doors.

'Morning!' The vacuum had been turned off and Ida Capstick was joining them in the kitchen, taking in their shattered appearances with a wry look. 'Been burning the candle at both ends, I see,' she muttered, making the wrong assumption.

Delilah was about to protest their innocence but Samson intervened.

'Guilty as charged,' he grinned, pulling Delilah into him for a kiss.

'Hmph!' Ida reached for the kettle.

Released from Samson's embrace, Delilah felt her cheeks burn. 'You've been here a while, already, Ida,' she noted, trying to cover her perverse embarrassment at being accused of something she'd actually been guilty of the morning before. 'What's got you in and cleaning so early?'

'Burning the candle at both ends, too?' Samson asked with a cheeky smile.

Ida shot him a look. 'Got things to be getting on with.' She busied herself making tea, an abruptness about her that was even sharper than normal, mugs clattering onto the counter.

Samson raised an eyebrow at Delilah, who shrugged. But she'd also noticed that Ida's tea ritual wasn't up to its usual standard. For a start, the pot hadn't been warmed and she was already pouring on the boiling water. Then she started stirring the tea with a teaspoon, clearly not intending to leave it for the requisite brewing time. There was definitely something the matter—

The realisation came with a blast of self-reproach. Ida had hinted she was having domestic problems on Monday, yet with everything that had occurred since – the return of Samson and the Stuart Lister case, not to mention the fire at Pete's caravan – Delilah hadn't once enquired how things were going at Croft Cottage.

'I've been meaning to ask you,' she said now, a touch of contrition in her words, 'how is George getting on? Is he still convinced you have ghosts?'

Samson was staring at Delilah, confused, while Ida whipped round, a frown drawing her face into even more angles than usual.

'Don't know what tha's wittering on about, lass. Nowt wrong with George.'

'Oh, sorry, it's just you said he'd been spooked by something—'

'Tea!' Ida thumped two mugs on the table and turned back to the sink, the conversation clearly at an end. Samson's phone pinged loudly into the uncomfortable silence.

'Crikey, everyone's up early today!' he announced with forced levity as he glanced from Delilah to Ida and then to his mobile. 'It's Ana, wanting to know if I have contact details for Manfri.'

'Manfri?' asked Delilah with surprise, the Gypsy and his siblings having left town back in April. 'I've got his mobile number but he won't be in the area. It's the Appleby Horse Fair this weekend so they'll be up there already.'

'Good point.' Samson was nodding, even as he was copying the number Delilah was displaying on her phone. 'I'll let her know.'

'Did she say what she wants with him?'

Samson grinned. 'Why? You jealous?'

Delilah laughed, thinking it was a fair question, given the charisma and brooding good looks of the man. That and the fact he'd saved their lives. 'Not at all. Just curious.'

'I'll ask her.'

At the sink, Ida had gone still, her back to the room, teapot in her hands as she paused in the process of emptying it out.

Another ping. A quick response. Samson smiling as he read out Ana's message.

'So, no need to worry. She's not after a date with him. Apparently she's come across some Romanian refugees over in Skipton who need help but don't speak English. She thinks Manfri might be able to translate—'

From the sink came a sudden crash, a curse and the sound of breaking ceramic, Ida leaping back, a cut on her hand from one of the many shards the teapot had been reduced to.

'Ida!' Delilah exclaimed, rushing forward. 'Are you okay?'

'Nowt but a nick,' muttered Ida, already holding her hand under a running tap, turning the water pink. 'No need to fuss, lass. Just a stupid lapse in concentration.'

Samson had opened the cupboard above the cooker and taken out what passed for a first-aid box – raising an eyebrow in Delilah's direction on seeing it contained several bars of chocolate alongside painkillers and antiseptic cream – and was pulling a plaster out of a packet.

'Sorry,' Ida said, eyes cast down as she dabbed the cut dry. 'I've broken tha teapot.'

'The teapot's not what matters,' Samson said softly, peeling the backing off the plaster and laying it across the cut before placing an arm around her thin shoulders. 'What matters is that you're okay.'

Ida looked up finally, her gaze resting on his and then turning to Delilah, and she seemed on the verge of saying something, but then she just gestured at the two mugs. 'Don't forget tha tea. And if tha's going out, take an umbrella. There's bad weather coming.'

Samson looked towards the window and its framed blue sky in incredulity, but before he could challenge the accuracy of this forecast, Ida spoke again.

'Oh, and that were on the back doorstep when I arrived.' She was pointing to a bucket beneath the table. 'From Clive Knowles according to the note. I'll leave thee to it. Happen as it's time I was gone.'

And with that she left the room.

'Is it just me or does she seem out of sorts?' murmured Delilah, as Ida's solid footsteps descended the stairs.

'Definitely,' agreed Samson, 'And what was all that about George and ghosts?'

'Something she mentioned the other day. George was claiming he was hearing noises around the house, and was getting very stressed about it. Poor Ida was worried about him. So I thought I'd see if that was what was bothering her.' Delilah shrugged. 'I might drive over to Croft Cottage this evening. Try and have a chat with her.'

'Good idea. In the meantime, let's see what Clive has brought us.' Samson was lifting the bucket out from under the table, Tolpuddle immediately thrusting his nose in it, sniffing, and then sneezing dramatically, a piece of paper blown onto the floor in the process. He sneezed again before staggering back against the cooker, a befuddled expression on his face.

'Crikey, what set him off?' asked Delilah, rubbing the Weimaraner's head.

'This.' Samson held out a margarine tub, the lid lifted at one corner, a sweet, grassy odour rising from within. 'Why on earth has Clive left a tub of dope on our doorstep?'

'Along with two tins of meatballs and a brochure for

286

caravans,' added Delilah, taking the items out and lining them up on the table. 'Not to mention some dog food, a mobile phone and—'

'Shotgun cartridges!' exclaimed Samson, who was holding a second margarine tub and staring at the contents in surprise, while Delilah picked up the piece of paper Tolpuddle had expelled from the bucket.

'Hopefully this will explain everything,' she said, turning the page over. Torn from a promotional notepad, 'I'Anson Quality Feeds' stamped across the top, it was covered in an almost undecipherable scrawl.

'Apparently Clive thinks these might be important for our investigation into the fire at Pete's caravan,' said Delilah, squinting at the writing. 'He says they're things Carol brought back with her when she went to clean it a few weeks ago.'

'So these are all Pete's. At least that explains the dope,' Samson mused, regarding the odd selection of items, shaking his head. 'What is it about the women of the Capstick clan and buckets full of miscellaneous things? I don't suppose Clive says why he thinks they might be relevant?'

'Something about Carol still being in a coma . . .' continued Delilah, as she twisted the note to get more light on it. 'Oh, Carol spoke! Only a few words, but she mentioned some of this lot.' Delilah lowered the page and looked at the range of Pete's belongings on the table, eyes wide with disbelief. 'Clive thinks that must mean there's a clue here. To the person responsible for the explosion.'

Samson snorted. 'Seriously? Some meatballs and a glossy magazine selling caravans? There is the phone, I suppose, if we can find a charger for it . . .' He ran a hand through his hair and glanced at his watch. 'Look, we don't have time for this now. I need to get to Turpin's and you need to get cracking on Taylor's IT system if you're going to hit Neil's deadline. Plus, there might be something on there that could back up our suspicions about Stuart.'

'I doubt it,' said Delilah. 'I don't think even Bernard was dense enough to ask me to work on the system if he knew there was evidence of his criminality on there. But I'll keep my eyes open.'

'Good. As for this lot, we'll try and make something of it later.' He cast a sceptical glance over Carol's haul. 'If in fact there is anything to be made of it.'

'Agreed, although I think I'll just put these two out of reach.' Delilah picked up the margarine tubs and placed them in one of the wall cupboards. 'Last thing we need is a dog getting high or chewing through a shotgun cartridge!'

'You wouldn't be that daft, would you, Tolpuddle?' Samson ruffled the dog's ears, getting a look of affection from the Weimaraner.

'How little you know him,' retorted Delilah.

Samson grinned, pulling her into his arms. 'I'm looking forward to the opportunity to get to know him better. And his owner. Let's get away when this case is over. Go the Lakes or over to Robin Hood's Bay?'

She nodded, and he kissed her, but even as she felt herself dissolve into him, part of her was wondering about the future, a scenario she hadn't allowed herself to dwell on over the past few days. How long would Samson O'Brien be content to stay in Bruncliffe playing at detective when his real career was beckoning down in London?

'Work,' she murmured, pulling gently away from his embrace. 'You don't want to be late for Matty.'

Samson gave a reluctant sigh. 'Right, I'll come straight back when I've finished at Turpin's and update you.' He kissed her once more and then moved towards the doorway. 'In the meantime,' he added, 'mum's the word.'

Delilah had no need to be reminded. She'd never felt less like sharing the details of a Dales Detective Agency case. Because no matter how this one turned out, she couldn't see it being anything less than toxic.

The new day had brought a crisis of conscience at Croft Cottage. As he eased the door closed behind him, his brother still fast asleep beneath the stern faces above the mantlepiece, Grigore was resolute about what he had to do.

While Pavel had slept well, the painkillers giving him enough relief to escape into slumber, Grigore had managed only a few hours before he was pulled into consciousness by guilt. There was no excuse for delaying. His concerns about trusting the people who'd given them a home for the night seeming unjustified when weighed in the balance against a man's life. He needed to raise the alarm before it was too late. If it wasn't already.

He entered the kitchen, ready to tell all, only to find it empty. The clock ticking into silence. On the table were two places set ready. On the worktop, eggs in a box, a loaf of bread, a frying pan, and a piece of paper featuring an arrow pointing at the fridge. He pulled open the fridge door and saw a hand-drawn picture of a frying pan left on top of a blue-and-white plastic bag. Inside the bag were bacon, sausages and . . . He blinked. Took out the cylindrical black item next to them, inspecting it with awe.

'Sângerete,' he whispered. Blood sausage. A staple in his native Transylvania. While this wasn't as fat and smelled less garlicky, it was clearly a local alternative.

Any final doubts he'd been harbouring about the wisdom of what he was about to do were banished. For how could these people not be good when something as wonderful as sângerete was part of their breakfast routine.

He closed the fridge. Food would have to wait. He had things to say first.

A noise outside took his attention to the window and the shambling form of George approaching across the yard. He was muttering to himself. When he entered the kitchen and saw Grigore, his face split into a smile.

'Fordson Model N working good morning!'

Grigore smiled back. 'Ida?' he asked.

George shook his head. So Grigore tried the next best thing.

'Mobile?' he asked hesitantly, holding his hand to his jaw, mimicking a phone.

'Mobile!' declared his host gleefully, as he placed a piece of technology on the table which wouldn't have been out of place in a museum. There was nothing smart about it, texting and calling the limit of its function. Which meant no translation app.

Suddenly Grigore realised the magnitude of his task. How was he going to sound the alarm when he couldn't even communicate effectively. Then his eyes fell on the notepad on the table, a pen next to it, the tools used to make the note he'd understood so clearly. Pulling out a chair, he gestured for George to sit down, taking the seat opposite. And with careful thought, Grigore began to draw.

'So tell me, what's so important that it couldn't wait until a more civilised hour?' Matty Thistlethwaite's complaint was delivered with a smile as he sat across from Samson, the pair of them in armchairs in the corner of the solicitor's office. He leaned forward and poured coffee from the cafetière that had been waiting on the low table when his guest arrived.

Samson shrugged, out of his depth and not sure where to start. Having extracted everything they could from the files the night before, the Dales Detective duo had decided the next course of action should be to get some expert help. But expert help they could trust and which wouldn't involve the authorities. They'd both agreed that going to the police at this stage could mean putting Nancy Taylor and Mrs Lister through unnecessary trauma if Samson and Delilah's suspicions were proven to be unfounded.

Hence Samson was sitting in Turpin's, trying to get answers to questions he didn't even know how to ask, and all without revealing too much. Which was difficult when dealing with a man as astute as the young solicitor.

'How easy is it to find out if a company is a shell or not?' he finally said.

Matty blinked. A flicker of something – recognition? – rattling his habitual composure. Then he was taking a sip of coffee, considering his reply. When he spoke, it was in measured tones.

'As I said to someone not long ago in reply to the same

question, there are two answers. Often such entities are easy to spot if you know what you're looking for. But if you wish to find out anything beyond merely identifying them as such, then that's a completely different ball game.' He lowered his mug back to the table and fixed Samson with a steady gaze. 'Perhaps you'd care to tell me more about the specific company you're looking into?'

There was a beat of silence, and then Samson threw caution to the wind.

'Kingston Holdings.'

This time the reaction was more noticeable, Matty inching forward in his armchair, no hint of surprise on his face but the movement in itself suggesting to Samson that he'd hit a nerve.

'You've heard of them?' he queried.

The solicitor gave a non-committal shake of his head. 'Before I say anything further, I need to know how you came across this company.'

Samson felt his heart rate kick up, the same way it always did when a case was being cracked open, Matty's response telling him that there was something in this. That the speculation he'd indulged in with Delilah into the early hours could possibly be right. But how much to divulge?

Matty smiled, as though reading Samson's thoughts. 'You can trust me. You know that. Whatever you tell me will never leave this office.'

'Even if what I tell you puts you in an awkward position? Possibly with the police?'

A slight shrug of the shoulders and the solicitor smiled again. 'I've come to expect nothing less than high drama where you're concerned, Samson.'

Samson laughed, conceding the point. And conceding that Matty Thistlethwaite was someone he'd trust with the greatest confidence. So he started talking.

'Thing is,' he began, 'Delilah and I have come across some files which are linked to a company called Kingston Holdings. And to Taylor's. They've given us reason to believe that something very dodgy was going on there before Bernard's death.'

'Define dodgy.' No smile from Matty now. Just intense concentration.

'Drugs and money laundering.'

The bald statement afforded Samson the rare sight of seeing Matty Thistlethwaite's thick eyebrows shoot up his forehead, before he reached for his coffee once more. 'Is that all,' he murmured dryly. 'Go on.'

'Well, as a result of our investigation we've come to the conclusion that the person behind all of it was none other than Taylor's lettings agent, Stuart Lister.'

This time Matty's reaction was to burst into laughter, Samson now the one in a state of surprise.

'What?' he asked. 'What did I say?'

'Stuart Lister,' said Matty, shaking his head. 'You couldn't be further from the truth.'

21

Delilah's morning turned out to be very fragmented. She'd only just sat down and pulled up Taylor's IT system on her PC when there was a clatter of two pairs of feet on the stairs. Through the open office door, she could see Nina and Nathan making their way to the first floor, both laughing.

She met them on the landing, their youthful energy almost tangible as they greeted her, Nathan crouching down to make a fuss over an equally exuberant Tolpuddle. Already tuned in to the ways of the office, Nina headed straight to the kitchen and the kettle. As she turned back from filling it, she noticed the table and the miscellany of items ranged across it.

'What's all this?' she asked.

'Some of Pete Ferris's belongings.' Delilah saw her nephew's head snap up, attention leaving the belly rub he'd been administering to the Weimaraner, the dog letting out a low whine in protest.

'I thought everything was destroyed in the fire,' said Nathan, straightening up and crossing to Nina's side.

'Carol Kirby was cleaning over there a few weeks ago, when Clive found out he was inheriting it. She brought this lot back with her, thinking it was all worth saving I suppose.' Delilah shrugged, watching the teenagers inspect the items.

'Interesting smell,' said Nina, nose twitching as she sniffed the caravan brochure, a grin on her face. 'Pete must have liked his tobacco with an edge.'

'I couldn't possibly comment,' said Delilah, grinning back.

'Was this all there was?' Nathan wasn't sharing the joke. Instead he was picking up each belonging in turn, a despondent look to his face.

'That, plus some shotgun cartridges and some of Nina's "edgy tobacco", both of which I've put out of reach of a certain hound.'

The lad shook his head mournfully. 'Not much of a legacy,' he muttered. 'Some bloody meatballs, dog food and a stash of dope.'

Delilah let the oath slip, knowing her nephew had set store by the poacher, even while many in the town shunned the man. No surprise when he'd saved Nathan's life. She put her arm around the lad's shoulders, a gesture that was now quite a reach for her as he continued to grow.

'These aren't the things Pete would have wanted to be remembered by,' she said gently. 'He left his most important possessions to you.'

'The lurchers,' muttered Nathan, giving a nod, tears threatening. He brushed a hand over his eyes, Nina turning to put the kettle on, giving him space. 'Yeah. They're a bit special all right.'

'As for this stuff,' Delilah cast a hand over the table,

'I've no idea what they signify, but perhaps you two can put some work into it today?'

'You mean, work on a case?' asked Nina.

'Two cases, actually. Clive brought these here because, despite her comatose state, Carol mentioned some of them. Which has led him to believe there might be a clue here as to who and what caused the fire. So get your thinking caps on and work out how, if at all, these things could have been linked to what happened at Pete's caravan.'

Nina was nodding, already regarding the objects with a more critical eye.

'And the second case?' asked Nathan.

'Right up your street with your love of dogs,' grinned Delilah. 'Herriot had a Rottweiler abandoned at his surgery and wants us to track down the owners. So I'd like you to call round to see him and get as much background as you can. But whatever you do, Nathan, don't fall in love with the damn thing! I'm not sure how Lucy would feel about you bringing another mutt home. Especially one that size.'

Nathan gave a twisted grin. 'No worries on that front. I'm not mad keen on Rottweilers. Had a bad experience with one once.'

Nina glanced at him quizzically but he just shrugged, offering no further explanation.

'Thankfully,' said Delilah, 'this one will be safely locked up in a pen, so you should be fine. If you discover anything of interest, mind,' she continued, feeling the need to include a warning, just in case the Rottweiler did turn out to be connected with whatever Stuart Lister had been involved in, 'make sure you report back to either myself or Samson straight away. No going solo and getting into trouble.'

'Like you do all the time, you mean?' quipped Nathan, his grin having become cheeky, while Nina was attempting to smother a smile.

Realising she'd be fighting a losing battle if she tried to deny the accusation, Delilah murmured something about needing to get back to work and made a tactical withdrawal. With the teenagers already mulling over the assortment of objects from Carol's bucket – ably assisted by Tolpuddle, who was nosing one of the dog-food tins as though he knew the contents – she returned to her office to concentrate once more on Taylor's IT system. That deadline of Neil's was ticking away, the pressure mounting to get the job finished. And now she had the added intrigue of seeing if Samson had been right. Perhaps there might be some concrete evidence in the electronic files which would help strengthen their case. Although she rather suspected it would be like looking for a needle in a haystack.

Ten minutes later, she stumbled across a pitchfork.

Targeting her initial search on the phrase Kingston Holdings, she'd retrieved the digital copies of the files Stuart had taken from the office, and discovered her former father-in-law had indeed hidden his misdeeds in plain sight. Not only that, but as Delilah opened up the first file, expecting an exact replica of the one she'd already read, she saw a detail which had been excluded from the paper version.

A bank account number for the owner of the rental. Or rather, the fabricated owner of the faux rental.

Leaving the file open, Delilah clicked on the next one. Another bank account number. She clicked on a third.

Again, a series of numbers . . . she paused. Stared at the screen and then flipped back to the original file, a buzz of excitement building—

'Have you got a charger for this?' Nina was in the doorway, holding up Pete's mobile.

'Oh, right, erm . . .' Gathering her wits, Delilah nodded. 'Have a look in the filing cabinet in Samson's office. Ida put a load of old chargers and the like in there last week. There might be one that fits.'

She watched Nina scamper down the stairs, before returning to the computer. Placing the three open windows in tile formation, she ran her gaze across all of them. All different properties. All different supposed owners. Yet the bank account details for all three were the same.

Heart beating fast, she opened up the remaining files. By the time Nina came back up the stairs, Delilah knew she'd discovered something fundamental.

'None of them are the right sort,' the teenager said, leaning on the doorframe. 'You okay if I take Pete's phone back to the restaurant? I'm sure we've got one that's a match.'

'Yeah, sure, whatever,' murmured Delilah, staring at the screen, transfixed.

'I might even scrounge some samosas out of Dad while I'm there,' grinned Nina, before turning back down the stairs, this time with Nathan behind her.

The door closed below. Delilah was barely aware of it. She was too focused on the details in front of her.

It was astounding. Every single one of the thirty properties being rented by Kingston Holdings had identical bank details. And she was looking at the account number.

This was where Kingston Holdings was sending its money. They could locate the actual bank with this.

Then her eyes caught on another detail. The rental due date. She didn't need to check her watch. She knew what day it was – the first Thursday in June. Which meant the next payment was due today. In a matter of hours, in fact, because the contract bizarrely stipulated a time. Ten o'clock.

Reaching into her desk drawer, Delilah pulled out an external hard drive. It was time to make a backup copy of the entire system, one that could be put in a safe place. Because with what she'd just uncovered, she had the feeling there were going to be plenty of other gems hidden in this particular haystack.

'He came to see me, not long before he went travelling,' Matty Thistlethwaite was explaining, all trace of laughter gone from his face. 'He sat in that very chair you're in now and asked me exactly the same question about exactly the same company. Which would lead me to conclude that Stuart Lister isn't the person you're after.'

Samson was reeling. 'Stuart asked you about Kingston Holdings? When?'

'Early May if my memory serves me correctly,' said the solicitor, consulting his mobile and nodding. 'Yes, of course, the first Friday in May. The day before Bernard Taylor was killed.'

'Christ!' Samson sank back in his chair, comparing the date against what he knew. 'The dental appointment . . .' he muttered. 'Stuart told the office he was going for root canal treatment and came here instead. He didn't want anyone knowing he was talking to you.'

'That figures. The lad was a trembling wreck.'

'So what were you able to tell him?'

'At the time, nothing. All we agreed was that I'd look into this Kingston Holdings and get back to him.' Matty spread his hands wide. 'The next day Bernard died and a couple of days after that, I heard Stuart had left town.'

'And now?' asked Samson, having noted the solicitor's turn of phrase. 'What can you tell me now about Kingston Holdings?'

There was a long sigh. Then Matty dropped his gaze. It was a while before he spoke.

'I'm sorry, Samson. I'm not sure I can say any more. Client confidentiality and all that.'

Samson nodded. The comment in itself telling him plenty. Matty knew all about Kingston Holdings. In fact, he was working for someone connected to it.

'I respect you too much to pressure you into talking, Matty. So let me turn the tables. How about I tell you what I know about Kingston Holdings.'

And so he told him. About the files found in Stuart's flat detailing the faux rentals, and the enormous sums of money going through Taylor's on a six-monthly basis. About the suspicion that genuine rental properties were being used to make drugs. He even mentioned the link between the company and the school lockers.

When he finished, Matty was stony-faced.

'If that's true . . .' the solicitor murmured.

'Then Bruncliffe is in trouble. And possibly Stuart Lister too. Because if he isn't actively involved in this, then he knew about it. His visit here, his visit to Henside Road, the files he stole from Taylor's. Which begs the question, where is he now? All we have to prove he left the country is a postcard we can't verify the origin of. And having heard what you have to say about the lad, I'm beginning to think his mother was right to come to us with her concerns.'

'Mrs Lister has hired you to find him?'

'Yes. She called in on Monday. I have to be honest, we didn't take it too seriously at first, but now . . . What you've just told me changes everything.'

'I had no idea. I genuinely thought he'd gone abroad.' Matty was looking perturbed. 'That whatever he'd stumbled on, he didn't want to deal with.'

Samson grimaced. 'I think he did try to deal with it. That could be the problem. Which is why I could do with knowing whatever you've discovered about Kingston Holdings.'

Matty glanced down at his hands, clearly torn.

'Listen,' Samson said softly, leaning forward. 'I know this isn't easy for you. I know how seriously you take your duty to your clients and they respect you for it. But you have to ask yourself the question, is it better to be known for your discretion, or for your propriety?'

'Damn it, you know how to work a man!' muttered Matty, with a wry smile. He gave a brisk nod and then stood up, crossing to his desk to pick up an envelope before returning to his chair. 'After Stuart's visit, I did a bit of digging into the company. All I was able to ascertain was that it's incorporated in the British Virgin Islands, which I would suggest means it's safe to say that Kingston Holdings is indeed a shell, as you suspected. But when I heard Stuart had gone away, I didn't trouble myself with it any further. So you can imagine my surprise when this was brought to me yesterday.' He pulled a sheaf of papers out of the enve-lope and passed them across the coffee table. 'It's Bernard Taylor's will. Turn to the last page.'

Samson did as he was told. He scanned down the text, his eyes drawn immediately to one of the final clauses. Breath caught, he read the details.

'Nancy?' He looked up shocked. 'She owns Kingston Holdings?'

'As of her husband's demise, yes. She inherited what's known as a beneficial ownership in the company from him.'

'So . . . are you saying . . . she's involved in all this?' Samson struggled to get the words out, the idea so prepos-terous.

'Given that she appointed me to execute the will, I'd say not. She'd hardly have brought an incriminating document like this so close to home if she was aware it contained elements of a questionable nature. In fact, I'd hazard a guess that Nancy hasn't even looked at the contents and has no idea about her newly acquired status.'

It was a logic Samson couldn't fault, given the woman they were talking about. He just couldn't picture Nancy as someone who'd get caught up in criminal activity. Especially when there was the small matter of her having authorised an investigation into the cash she'd found in Bernard's wardrobe. But ruling her out created another problem. Because if Stuart Lister's disappearance was indeed suspicious, given that Bernard Taylor had been lying in a morgue at the time, the deceased mayor could hardly have been involved.

'This beneficial ownership,' said Samson, 'does it mean Nancy is the sole owner of Kingston Holdings?'

Matty shook his head. 'Not at all. There could be a dozen more beneficial owners out there and you'd never know because they're hidden beneath layers of trustees. That's the whole point of the system – to hide the identities of the people who are really behind entities like this.'

Samson let out a low whistle, brow knotted. Across from him Matty was nodding.

'You're thinking there's someone else out there?' said the solicitor.

'There's got to be. Just who?'

'I think,' said Matty in his most sober tone, 'this might be something for the police.'

Samson found himself agreeing. Because after this conversation, it was clear that Stuart Lister could be in real trouble and needed to be found. If it wasn't already too late.

No matter which way he looked at the piece of paper, George Capstick couldn't understand it. And when he didn't understand things, the panic began to build, slowly closing up his lungs, making his heart thunder . . .

He'd come in from the barn to check on their guests as Ida had instructed, and had found Grigore inviting him to sit at the kitchen table, at which point his new friend had started drawing on Ida's notepad. George had been about to warn him that Ida didn't take too well to her shopping-list paper being used for anything beyond its designated purpose – especially not when the user had grease all over their hands – but there had been something resolute about the man's face. So George had sat and waited and then looked on in puzzlement as the pad was turned to show him four drawings, Grigore clearly trying to explain something.

Half an hour on, George still didn't understand. On his feet now, pointing at the scrawl on the right-hand side of the page, the last of the drawings. A black square with what looked like a person within it and some sort of looming mass outside.

'TE20 Continental four-speed gearbox what's that?' he demanded again, resorting to his favourite tractor's statistics as the stress rose inside him.

Words came in reply. Grigore speaking, but not making sense. Although George could feel the sharp edges of frustration gathered around the foreign sounds.

Grigore was getting upset because George wasn't doing things right.

A deep sigh from Grigore, his hand running over his face, and then his pen pointed at the first image once more. They were going to go over it all again. Even though there was no point. George looked out of the window towards the barn, knowing he was off schedule, the morning sliding into chaos that tore at his fragile equilibrium.

He forced himself to look at the pictures. He knew the first one, a dark blotch with four legs.

'2088cc three-point linkage dog!' he repeated, having verified his deduction last time by barking, at which Grigore had nodded. But after that, things became more difficult.

He stared at the second sketch. It looked like grass and water. Two figures on it.

Grigore tapped the page and spoke again, the sound a sliding jumble of vowels and consonants that George's mind refused to organise into something comprehensible. He shook his head. Focused instead on the third picture.

It resembled a cow with a person's body. Horns. Two legs. And a tail. But George couldn't think of anything—

'Devil!' he suddenly exclaimed.

'*Diavol!*' exclaimed Grigore, nodding vigorously.

But the excitement faded as quickly as the fireworks at Bruncliffe's Bonfire Night celebrations. A devil. George looked at his friend in puzzlement.

Grigore gave another sigh. Tapped the fourth and final picture. Saying something . . . This time there was a sliver of recognition from George. Like a piece of a jigsaw that doesn't quite fit but suggests the shape of the one you're looking for . . .

He cupped his hand over his ear. 'Unsynchronised gear say it again.'

'Steward.'

George blinked. Suddenly it was as clear as day. 'Steward?' he repeated back.

Grigore jumped up out of his chair, grinning. Nodding. Happy. Then he ran the pen across all four images, a torrent of language issuing from him, the grin melting into something like panic.

George Capstick, an expert in panic, stared at the page and felt the stress continue to build, making him rock, making him mumble. Because he had no idea what a dog, a devil and a steward had to do with anything. Or why they should be so important to Grigore.

He was going to have to get help. Even if that meant he would have to use his mobile.

*

The dark had become marginally less dark. His pain had become noticeably greater. As had his thirst. He had to accept now, as the thin band of light tracked across his cell, that they weren't coming back.

How long had it been since they last put food and water in? A day? Two?

At first it had been regular – meagre amounts but what felt like twice a day. Overhead there had been footsteps. Voices. Then everything had gone ominously quiet. The supplies had reduced in frequency and quantity. Often just a heel of bread and a small bottle. But now . . .

It could be his mind playing tricks, blinded by the agony pulsating from his left leg. Or had they really stopped coming?

He reached for the water, held the bottle against his lips and tipped it up carefully, taking only the smallest amount. He'd started rationing it when it had dawned on him that they might not be coming back. Lips wet, throat still parched, he shook the bottle, trying to gauge how much he had left. Knowing it was also a gauge of how long he had left.

Not much, was the brutal answer.

It was getting harder to be optimistic. Despite the firm promise he'd been made. Despite his faith in Bruncliffe.

22

'So you've got everything in hand?' Rick Procter was standing in his office, looking down into the courtyard of the Low Mill complex his company owned, keeping his tone cordial as he spoke into his mobile. 'Nancy's agreed to sell?'

'Everything's under control,' came the reply, ringing with false bonhomie. 'Although it will be Monday before the paperwork can be sorted. I presume that's no problem?'

From his vantage point on the third floor of the former mill, Rick had a view out across the slate rooftops of Bruncliffe, all the way to the towering gables of the Victorian town hall. He let his gaze drift to the far side of the imposing building, to the property where, at this moment, he could imagine Neil Taylor squirming as he tried to weasel his way out of an awkward situation.

Like hell had Nancy agreed to the sale. Rick could tell from the way her son was talking. And from the fact that not a murmur about the impending handover had been heard around town. Because news that Taylor's Estate Agents was about to be bought by Procter Properties would have been impossible to contain once the cogs began turning to make it happen. A secretary working on the paperwork.

The gossipy clerk from the local bank. A leak would have sprung somewhere. Even Neil himself would have been unable to resist boasting about the excellent deal he'd negotiated for his mother. If it had actually been going ahead.

In ordinary times, Rick would have been seething at the duplicity. But right now, this suited him. Let the Taylor peacock stew. Let him be so focused on pulling off this deal that his concentration, and that of his mother, was elsewhere. Just for the next few hours. Then it would all be irrelevant. Rick would be gone and Taylor's would collapse, Neil and Nancy left with nothing but debt and scandal and a name that would be tarnished forever.

Still, no harm heaping a bit more stress on the lad.

'Monday I can cope with,' said Rick. 'But I'm warning you, Neil, anything beyond that and you'll have to find someone else to deal with your father's mess. Understood?'

He hung up on the professions of compliance at the other end. Let his gaze drop to the courtyard below and the range of boutique establishments on the ground floor. Since the first day of trade, they'd been exceeding even Rick's expectations when it came to the desire people had to splash money on the likes of hand-made chocolates and designer clothing. Above them, the apartments and offices were all rented out, the development of executive homes and townhouses on the adjacent plot all complete and sold.

It was a successful project. The jewel in Procter Properties' crown. In a few minutes he would be walking away from it and never coming back.

He experienced a pang of regret. All that work, the legitimate side of his business where he had so excelled, about to be forsaken because he'd got in over his head.

No point dwelling on it. He turned from the window and focused his thoughts. At ten o'clock the transfer would be made. Thirty payments, dressed up as biannual rental fees, would be electronically relayed into Taylor's account. From there, the money – the true origin of which Rick had never been stupid enough to enquire about – would be dispersed to another account, after which it would be wound through several offshore banks, no doubt, before winding up in whichever establishment the Karamanski brothers kept their legitimate finances. Washed clean. No hint of the crime that had generated it.

Rick and Bernard had set the system up several years ago and it had run smoothly ever since. Handling the finances of the likes of Niko and Andrey, you made sure you got it right.

Only this time, that wouldn't be quite how it would unfold.

This time there would be a glitch in the system. A gremlin that would divert the funds into a different account. One registered far away from Bruncliffe. Or Bulgaria. One only Rick had access to.

Simple enough, especially since Rick's interim management of Taylor's gave him access to all areas. What wasn't so simple was making sure he was well clear of the town before the Bulgarians had a chance to react, because once they realised what had happened, they'd be on him like greyhounds on a hare. So timing was of the essence. Divert the money. And then get the hell out of the country, the false passport and emergency cash he had stashed in a safe place sufficient to make good his escape until he could get to his newly acquired wealth. Then he would be living the good life. In the sunshine.

It would work, he told himself. He'd head home one final time to get his belongings and then pick up the passport and cash. After that, he'd do the deed and be nothing more than a footnote in the history of his hometown. A quick glance at his watch and he allowed himself a smile. The clock was finally ticking in his favour.

Peace and quiet reigned over the three-storey office building on Back Street. The only occupants were closeted in the back room on the first floor, a grey shape curled up asleep in the dog bed in the corner, and a hunched figure sitting at the desk, focus on the computer screen in front of her.

With Nina having texted to say they'd gone to Herriot's to get the details on the abandoned Rottweiler, Delilah had been left alone to concentrate on Taylor's IT system. In terms of her official remit, she was almost done. But in terms of finding something to solidify the suspicions brewing against Stuart Lister and Bernard Taylor, things were going very slowly. Apart from the cloned bank account details in the Kingston Holdings files, she'd found nothing else of interest so far.

Problem was, there was so much to sift through, none of it stored in the most efficient of ways. Files within folders within further folders, some of the information duplicated needlessly. Normally the internal workings of her clients' systems weren't something she concerned herself with – her job, as she always informed them, being simply to design and install the wardrobe, while they chose how to arrange the clothes within it. From what little she'd seen of Taylor's, there were a lot of clothes strewn on the floor.

Leaning back in her chair to stretch her back, she was

contemplating taking a break when the flashing email icon in the corner of her screen caught her eye. An email from DC Green. Curious, Delilah opened it. She skimmed the initial text, Jess Green explaining that she'd been unsuccessful in getting the email to Samson and thought it important enough to forward to Delilah instead. Beneath that, the original message explained that a photograph was attached which had come to light as part of the investigation into Samson's old boss, DI Warren. A photograph Warren had put through official channels for digital enhancement. Only trouble was, Jess and her team had no idea what it related to. Could Samson help?

Brief and to the point. Except for the conclusion.

Looking forward to having you back
working in London soon!
Cheers, Jess

Delilah found herself focused on the words, taking in their implication. Samson wasn't intending to stay in Bruncliffe. It was already decided. Yet he hadn't said a thing.

Would it always be like this? The constant worry that he would up and go. That her world would never be enough to contain him.

She let her gaze fall back on the computer screen, eyes unfocused as she clicked on the attachment and waited for it to load. When she did snap back into the present, it was to see a section of a photograph, enlarged, pixels visible, a ghostly visage staring back at her.

The sharp cheekbones, the gaunt face. Even with the

blurring, she would have known him anywhere. She was looking at the skeletal features of Pete Ferris. Or the reflection of him. For through his image she could see a stone wall, the back of a house.

He'd been looking out of a window, taking a photo, and had caught himself in the glass. All thoughts of Samson's impending departure banished from her mind, Delilah leaned forward, her attention caught by the white line cutting across the middle of the image.

Wood. Part of the window pane. At least two small panes, possibly more. And in the bottom one, a smudged circle where someone had tried to clean the glass.

She knew straight away where it was. Where Pete had been.

Henside Road.

He'd been in the old workshop, taking a photo out of the window that looked onto the rear of the house. What had he been doing there? More importantly, what had he seen that triggered his desire to record it digitally?

She stared at the screen, letting her eyes cross every inch of it and saw nothing of note until she reached the bottom right-hand corner. A blur of black in the frame. Something captured just out of sight. It looked like part of an animal. A dog, maybe? A big one to have been in the shot.

A Rottweiler? Like Samson had suspected from the scratches on the workshop door.

Brain racing now, Delilah sat there for a few minutes, trying to make sense of it all. For some reason, DI Warren, who had nothing to do with Bruncliffe other than his connection as Samson's old boss, had requested part of a photo be digitally enhanced by his own police department, ostensibly as part of a case. The result of that enhancement revealed a reflected image of Pete Ferris at Henside Road.

Pete, whose caravan had just been burned down.

Henside Road, where a drugs farm may have been operating.

From the floor below came the sound of the front door opening and closing. She was on her feet in an instant, running towards the stairs.

'Samson! Come and see this—'

She broke off in disappointment. Instead of her partner making his way up the stairs, it was the sturdy figure of her oldest brother. He was scowling.

'What's this I hear?' he demanded before he'd even reached the landing. 'O'Brien's back in town and you two are virtually living together?'

'Morning, Will. Lovely to see you, too,' Delilah said with added sarcasm, preparing for yet another lecture on the perils of dallying with a man widely considered to be a reprobate.

'Well? Is it true?' he growled.

She nodded, feeling the heat rushing up her cheeks, her chin jutting out in familiar familial defiance.

'About bloody time!' laughed Will, his frown flipping into a grin as he pulled his shocked sister into a bear hug. 'I know I had my reservations about O'Brien but he's proven himself a good lad.'

Delilah was still trying to process the abrupt change in demeanour when he released her and headed for the kitchen, filling the kettle and putting it on before opening the fridge and helping himself to a small pork pie.

'Make yourself at home, why don't you!' Delilah quipped, as he dropped heavily onto one of the chairs.

'Been out with the sheep all morning and I'm starved. But I'd far rather that than traipsing round shows like I've been all week, trying to judge the top tup! Some folk can get a tad touchy if you don't choose theirs.' He gave a dramatic sigh and then grinned at her. And she felt her heart warm. After so long at loggerheads, over her marriage to Neil Taylor – Will's opinion of the man having been made clear from the outset and which she now had to admit had been right – over her refusal to give up her businesses when divorce crushed her spirit and her finances, and more recently, over her willingness to welcome Samson back to Bruncliffe, it was a joy to see him so unreserved in her company. Like the old days, when their brother Ryan was still around . . .

'So, where is Bruncliffe's answer to Lothario? I've got a favour to ask him. Is he hiding out somewhere in case I'm after his blood?'

Delilah laughed. 'Funny you should say that! I think he is a bit worried about how you might react. But no, he's over at Matty's on a case—'

Realising she'd already said too much, this new laid-back Will having caught her off guard, she abruptly shut up. While she trusted him implicitly with most things, she didn't trust him to keep quiet about this. Not when it would have such an impact on the town. But her brother was already on the scent, watching her with narrowed eyes.

'What case?' The growling tone she was more accustomed to had returned. 'Nothing that'll get you into trouble like that awful do up at the quarry?'

'No. Not at all. Just a bit of . . . background work.'

Will let her words drift into silence, still watching her as the kettle boiled to a stop. Then he shook his head, rising from his seat to make the tea. 'Don't know if I should be impressed or appalled that you can spend so long with someone who lied professionally for a living and yet still be so bad at it yourself. Never take up poker, little sis. You've more tells than a lame Swaledale in an auction ring!'

Delilah knew she couldn't argue with his assessment. So she changed the topic. 'What did you want with Samson, if it wasn't to run him through with a rapier for dishonouring me?'

'The next best thing.' Will gave a sly grin. 'I want him to be the judge for the sheep section at Bruncliffe Show.'

'You really do hate him,' laughed Delilah. 'Tom Hardacre did it last year and still has folk not speaking to him as a result.'

'Aye. All the more reason to choose someone who wouldn't care about that. Plus Samson was a good judge of stock when he was out in Thorpdale. He had the makings of a grand farmer. Still could be if he put his mind to it.'

'Only if he lives somewhere where there's sheep.'

'What the hell do you mean?' Will whipped round to face her, and Delilah was immediately kicking herself. What was it about her brother today that was making her a lot less circumspect than usual? 'Is he not staying around? Is this . . .' he waved the teaspoon he was holding vaguely in the air, 'this *thing* the pair of you have going on, is it not serious?'

Delilah knew she was beetroot, heat burning her neck. She managed to keep her voice calm. 'That part of it is none of your business, Will. As for the rest of it, all's I'm saying is don't go banking on Samson being in Bruncliffe forever like the rest of us. Not everyone is content with a life lived in one place.'

Will stared at her for a moment, then dropped the teaspoon in the sink with a clatter before nodding. 'Fair point. But just mind you don't get hurt again, that's all.'

He held out a mug to her like a peace offering before turning to resume his seat with his own. As he did so, his gaze fell upon the whiteboard, taking it in for the first time: the neat lines of Ida's writing, the haphazard additions around the edges as they'd had to add more cases to it, the postcard sticking out over the edge.

'Blimey! You've got a lot on.' He was soaking in every word, scrutinising it, Delilah sensed, to see whether there could be any hidden danger for his sister in there. His sister whom he still failed to acknowledge was no longer the toddler chasing round after her five brothers, but a grown woman capable of—

'What's this, then?' Will's exclamation broke in on Delilah's internal grievances. He moved across to the board and took down Stuart's postcard, and stared wistfully at the photo.

'Part of an ongoing investigation. A mother worried her son has gone missing. Remember the lettings agent at Taylor's?'

Her brother glanced up at her. 'The tall lad who was almost killed by a tractor last November? Wasn't he supposed to have gone backpacking or the like?'

Delilah just nodded, not wanting to reveal anything more in case she let something slip.

'So is this where he's gone? Patong Beach?' Will was turning the postcard over, reading the brief message, frowning. Then he turned it back and studied the photo closely, brow furrowed. 'How the heck did he get hold of this?' he finally asked.

'I presume he used a camera,' said Delilah with a grin.

But Will wasn't laughing. He was shaking his head. 'You're not following me, sis. I mean how did he get this exact photo?'

A chill ran up Delilah's spine. There was something in the way her brother was looking at the postcard. How much to tell him? She decided to take a gamble.

'Actually, there is a bit of a mystery around it,' she confessed. 'We thought Stuart took it himself sometime during the last couple of weeks and uploaded it to the company that sent the postcard. But Clarissa Ralph at Fellside Court reckons that can't be true because the photo—'

'Was taken much longer ago than that.'

'You saw the same documentary then? About the tsunami?' asked Delilah.

Will shook his head, tapping the postcard. 'Didn't need to see no documentary, lass. Happen I was there when this were taken.'

Delilah's jaw couldn't have dropped any further. 'What . . . ? How . . . ?'

'That trip to Thailand after we finished school. Remember? A gang of us went from the rugby club. Spent most of the trip drunk or hungover or recovering from sunburn. Epic!' He grinned. 'That's when this were taken.'

She'd forgotten. Her oldest brother's first trip away from

home. She'd still been in primary school and there'd been so many comings and goings since. But now she cast her mind back, she could remember her mother had been beside herself with worry that something would happen to him, the first of her children to fly the nest – even if it was only for a week!

'So, like I said,' Will continued, frown back in place, 'how the hell did Stuart get a hold of this photo?'

Delilah shook her head, nonplussed. 'You're telling me you know who took it?'

'Aye. I can remember it like it were yesterday. Bloody idiot had been near driving the rest of us mad with his preening and his strutting. Why the hell we agreed to let him come, I don't know – he was barely old enough. But we did, and then he kept prattling on about capturing the dawn when all we wanted to do was capture a bit of fun and frolics.' He winked at Delilah. 'So finally, on the last morning, he went out and took it. And made a bloody good job of it too, I have to admit. But then, he was always a bit artistic. Didn't know one end of a yow from t'other but I guess you don't need that to be a graphic designer.'

The chill on Delilah's arms became a cold hand around her heart. 'So who took it, Will?' she said, forcing out the question she was dreading the answer to.

Will looked at her in surprise. 'Why, that nincompoop you insisted on marrying, that's who. This here is Neil Taylor's photo. No doubt about it.'

23

She got rid of Will as quickly as she could, wanting nothing more than silence. Time to allow the roar in her head to subside. Leaning back against the sink in the kitchen, Delilah closed her eyes and forced herself to focus.

Neil Taylor had taken the photo that appeared on the front of the postcard Mrs Lister had received from her son. Which begged the question, how had Stuart gained access to that photo?

Delilah could see three possible scenarios. Somehow Stuart had got his hands on the image without Neil knowing, which didn't seem convincing. So that meant Neil had given it to him, which in turn could suggest Neil was involved. A silent partner, who'd known all along what his father was mixed up in? Or . . .

It was the third possibility which made Delilah go cold. What If Neil hadn't given anyone the photo of Patong Beach? What if he was the person who'd sent that postcard? The photo. The lack of kisses Mrs Lister had complained of. Even the peculiar use of the name Bernard on the resignation note Stuart left behind at Taylor's. They all suggested this could be the case. That Neil Taylor was continuing to operate the criminal organisation his father had set up.

The implications were stark. If Neil was acting solo, then everything they'd thought about Stuart Lister needed revising. His stealing of the files. His visit to Henside Road. Could he have simply been investigating something suspicious he'd stumbled across during his work?

In which case, the fake postcard took on a sinister twist and Stuart was in deep trouble. If not already—

Delilah's eyes snapped open, her mind unable to accommodate the concept that her ex-husband might be a murderer. As well as a major player in a drugs network. It was enough to make her feel sick. No wonder Neil had demanded she cease work on the IT system and reinstate it immediately. Had he realised the mistakes his father had made? The evidence that was lying within those digitally recorded files?

So, Neil Taylor or Stuart Lister? Which one was the criminal mastermind?

It was going to be difficult to establish. But it needed to be done, because if it was Neil who was behind everything, then efforts really needed to be concentrated on finding the lettings agent. And quickly.

She turned her focus to the whiteboard and as she let her eyes drift over the cases, she began to see connections.

For starters, her overhaul of the IT system could be linked to the files Stuart took, which had been found in Ida's stolen bucket.

She moved across to the board and took up the red pen. Uncapped it and drew arrows between the three cases. Then she wrote the words *DC Green photo/Henside Road* and added an arrow from there to the investigation into Pete's assets, which in turn she connected to the fire at his caravan.

She considered the board afresh for a moment, thinking about the Henside Road tie-in, before drawing more lines, from DC Green's photo to the stolen files and then on to Herriot's mysterious Rottweiler. A Rottweiler which Pete had also come across. Another line added.

The whiteboard was looking busy now, a network of interconnected cases laid out in plain sight. Delilah stared at it, letting the possibilities play in her mind. Seeing more that could be included. For if Pete had a connection to Henside Road, then he also had a connection to Stuart's stolen files. Files which Samson believed could hold the answer to the cash found in Bernard Taylor's wardrobe . . .

Her gaze fell to the table below the board. The collection of motley items laid out on it. She picked up the caravan brochure, flicking through it. Noticing the circles drawn around some of them. High-end statics with wood-burning stoves and floor-to-ceiling windows. The prices were way beyond Pete's reach. Unless he was planning on a new income stream? From a source that could be dangerous?

In that instance, Delilah was back in front of the poacher's caravan, seeing the lurchers left for dead outside, hearing Samson shouting to call for help. Help that was already too late. Pete Ferris's death had never sat easy with Samson, something she'd put down to guilt. But now?

She let the brochure fall back to the table, took the pen and wrote *Pete's suicide?* on the right-hand side of the board. Then she drew a final series of arrows before adding several circles around *DC Green photo/Henside Road*.

If she was right about that photo then the Dales Detective Agency was investigating a number of cases which all overlapped. And if that were true, Stuart Lister was at the heart of it, either on the side of the angels or as a devil incarnate. But how to tell?

Henside Road. Of course! His final visit there had been erased on the GPS system at Taylor's. If she could get access to a computer in the estate agent's, she could see who had logged on the morning the file was deleted. If it was Stuart himself, then she had her answer. If it wasn't, then she was going to have to face the fact that she'd been married to a criminal. And Stuart Lister was in need of rescuing.

Heart thumping, she glanced at her watch. Five minutes before opening time, but Julie might be in early. She scrolled through the contacts on her mobile and made the call. No answer. So she tried another number as she crossed to her office to rouse a sleepy Tolpuddle. The phone answered on the second ring.

'Hi. It's Delilah. I've come across something I need to verify immediately. Is it okay if I pop over?'

Help was coming, thought Ida Capstick with relief as she stood in the queue in the Spar, her basket laden down with bread, milk, cheese, several tins, plus fruit and vegetables. Enough food to feed a family. Which is exactly what she'd suddenly acquired. She was even going to nip into Hargreaves' for more provisions before heading back to the cottage.

After a night of very little sleep – part of her too afraid to close her eyes, worried she and George might be murdered in their beds, and the other part too wound-up after all the excitement – she'd risen just as the sky started to show the pink streaks of impeding dawn. Accepting rest was now beyond her, she'd made the decision to head into town and get her work done early. Work made considerably lighter by not having to clean Taylor's, Mr Procter having messaged to say it was closed for two days. She'd be home before much of the morning had passed. And before the clouds building out to the west brought the glorious sunshine of recent days to a stormy end.

But the impending change in the weather wasn't the main push for her to get back to Croft Cottage. She also had underlying concerns about leaving her brother on his own with the two Romanians, despite him having apparently already spent several days in their company unbeknownst to her. The entire time she'd been fulfilling her cleaning duties that morning, the photo Delilah had shown her of the crude homemade knife found up at Quarry House kept tormenting her.

What if she'd got it completely wrong? What if the men weren't victims of some brutal trafficking organisation as Ana had mooted? The more Ida thought about it, the more the notion seemed far-fetched. Bruncliffe wasn't that sort of place. But if that was the case, was she in fact harbouring dangerous fugitives?

It was a worry which had made it even more difficult not sharing news of her new lodgers with Samson and Delilah when they'd arrived at the office. Ida had been hoping she wouldn't bump into them, given her early start, and so when they'd turned up, her guilt at not confiding in them had manifested itself in grumpiness. Which in itself had made her even more churlish.

Still, she consoled herself as she placed her basket down on the counter and began lifting out the items while the person ahead of her paid, help was on its way. Manfri, of all people. Ana Stoyanovic had played a blinder with that one. Not once had Ida thought of the brooding Gypsy as someone who could help them with the language barrier they were facing. If Ana managed to press upon him the urgency of the situation, he might be persuaded to leave the horse fair up in Appleby and travel down to Bruncliffe. She wondered what was the soonest they could expect him. Surely he could be here by noon?

Hopefully, then, she wouldn't have to keep her secret from Samson and Delilah much longer. But until she knew more about the brothers, she wasn't prepared to say anything that might bring the authorities running. In the meantime, she'd take her chances that she'd misjudged them completely. After all, she prided herself on being a pretty good judge of character —

'Goodness, Ida! You've got enough there to feed the five thousand!' Mrs Pettiford had appeared behind her, a cocker spaniel by her side, and was having a good look at Ida's purchases. 'Even the loaves and the fishes,' she said, smiling at her own cleverness as she pointed at the tins of sardines. 'Are you and George entertaining?'

Ida placed the last item on the counter, took her time getting her purse out of her side trouser pocket, and then turned to the town's gossip. 'Happen as we are,' she muttered. 'A couple of illegal immigrants. Eastern Europeans.'

She saw the ripple of surprise, followed by the swift calculation, Mrs Pettiford assessing the verity of the statement and discounting it.

'Oh, Ida,' trilled the woman with a laugh as false as the blue skies outside. 'You are funny. Illegal immigrants!'

Ida paid for her shopping, and left the Spar, content in the knowledge that sometimes the truth could prove the most effective way of keeping something hidden. She'd barely stepped away from the shop doorway when her mobile rang, the name on the screen enough to turn that contentment to concern.

George. For the best part of a year his mobile had lain unused and now he'd had recourse to it two times in as many days.

'Is everything okay?' she asked, dispensing with small talk.

'Four-speed gearbox Grigore's drawing!' came the frantic reply. 'Dog devil steward!'

'George,' Ida said, with a serenity she didn't feel, 'I'm on my way home. Just stay calm. I'll be there soon.'

The reply was emphatic. 'No! Four-cylinder gasoline we need Ana!'

'You want me to call Ana?' Ida asked, noting the use of 'we'.

'Dog devil steward, Grigore's drawing, we need Ana,' came the confirmation.

The call ended. Ida left there on the marketplace, staring at the phone and trying to think of the last time George had asked for help that wasn't hers. Thinking also that whatever was going on at Croft Cottage, her brother wasn't feeling threatened. He was feeling frustrated. Whatever Grigore was trying to communicate clearly wasn't getting through. And George had sensed it was important enough to ask for assistance. But for once, not from Ida.

Feeling a weight lifting off her that she'd been carrying unaware for her entire life, Ida turned towards Peaks

Patisserie. Ana was on a day off from the nursing home where she worked and was helping Lucy out. Ida was sure Lucy would be able to spare her for an hour.

It was only then she noticed the figure cutting across the cobbles, head down, a grey shape shadowing her. Delilah, Tolpuddle on a lead having to trot to keep up with her.

The lass was in a hurry. Looking tense.

A sudden gust of wind took the sandwich board outside Whitaker's newsagents, sending it crashing over with a bang. And Delilah whipped round, eyes wide. Her reaction making the dog nervous too.

Something was up.

Ida watched them turn the corner at the bottom of the square, heading for Church Street. Going to see Danny at the police station maybe? Whatever burden the lass was bearing, it was a heavy one. One Ida instantly wished she could share. Because that's what friends did, she'd discovered in the last seven months. Yet, there she was, not sharing her own troubles.

By the time she reached the cafe and began walking up the steps, Ana waving to her through the glass, Ida had decided what she was going to do. She was going to go back to the office and tell Samson all about Grigore and his brother. But first, she was going to buy a new teapot.

As she entered Peaks Patisserie, fat drops of rain began to fall. The storm she'd been anticipating had arrived.

So much for Ida's earlier warning about taking precautions. As Samson stepped out onto the marketplace from Turpin's the rain was thumping down, borne across the square on a howling wind which would have made short work of any umbrella. Bruncliffe's detective, however, seemed oblivious to this summer tempest as he made his way towards the office.

He was kicking himself for not seeing it sooner. Stuart Lister wore a cut-price suit, lived in a grungy flat dripping with damp and showed no signs of a lifestyle that could remotely be called lavish. Hardly an indicator of a man making a lucrative living from illicit means. Which left the burning question. If Stuart wasn't involved in whatever murky business was being conducted out of Taylor's, then who was?

Because someone was. With Bernard out of the picture, Stuart should have felt confident to come forward with his suspicions. Instead, he'd stolen the files and taken himself out to Henside Road. After which, God knows what had happened to him.

Which meant someone else had to be pulling the strings.

Samson's first thoughts when musing over the issue with Matty had been Rick Procter. He was ideally positioned and there was the link between Kingston Holdings and the school lockers Procter Properties had fitted. But perhaps Bernard had bought the lockers and Rick merely installed them. Plus, why would the property developer have told Delilah he suspected there was something iffy going on at Taylor's if he was part of it? No matter his personal opinion of the man, Samson's training made him analyse the evidence objectively. And he had to be honest, there was very little evidence to go on. In fact, with the revelations from Matty having turned everything about the case upside down, they were back at square one. But one thing was sure, Matty had been right when he'd said it was time to call in the police—

'Oh! Quick! Catch it!' Barry Dawson's desperate cries tore Samson from his ruminations as a blue mop bucket, plucked from the colourful display outside Plastic Fantastic by the strengthening wind, went clattering past him, off the pavement and down the street.

Samson ran after it, managing to trap it against the kerb outside the pub. He picked it up and returned to the shop where Barry had just finished bringing the rest of the stock inside.

'Thanks, Samson. Think it would have got to Skipton if you hadn't caught it,' said Barry, reclaiming his merchandise as they both took refuge in the doorway. 'By the way, I've not had a chance to say it yet but congratulations. You know, on you and Delilah . . . being a couple.' The shopkeeper blushed.

'Oh . . . thanks,' said Samson, caught off guard.

Barry shrugged. 'You're so much better for her than that Neil Taylor. Mother always used to say about him that the apple doesn't fall far from the tree—'

Another fierce gust of wind tore down the street, causing him to break off as it sent a couple of slates careening off the roof of the pub to smash onto the pavement below.

'There's worse coming,' Barry said ominously, staring up at the glowering sky. 'Not a day for being out and about – this one is going to cause damage. Thanks again.' Bucket clutched to his chest, he hustled into his shop, closing the door firmly behind him.

Samson stepped back out onto the pavement and into the rain, deep in thought. Thinking about Neil Taylor. About the graphic designer's odd behaviour, his cancellation of the IT upgrade and the abrupt change in his attitude to Delilah when he'd last called into the office. And as for those other business opportunities he'd professed to be chasing . . .

Perhaps Barry's mother was right and the apple hadn't fallen far from the tree after all.

Was it possible? Had Neil stepped in to fill his father's shoes? Samson hadn't considered him as a potential accomplice, partly because he'd been blinded as to the reason for Delilah's ex-husband's return to Bruncliffe. Too quick to credit past relationships for his presence. But what if it hadn't been Delilah that had brought Bernard's son back?

With a sense of trepidation, Samson entered the office building, thinking that the storm wasn't the only thing about to wreak havoc. When he ran his latest theory past his partner, things could get volatile.

'Delilah?' he called out, shaking the worst of the wet off him onto the mat before heading for the stairs. He was on the second step when he saw the postcard pinned to his door.

He turned. Went back down to retrieve it. Stuart's postcard. With an added post-it note stuck to the front.

> *Neil Taylor took this photo! I*
> *think Stuart is innocent!*
> *D xx*

Samson stood in the silent hallway, realising the case hadn't just been upended. It had been torn wide open. And that the crimes which could be laid against the door of Delilah's ex-husband were looking to be more than just serial philandering.

*

'Sorry for bothering you at home.'

With the rain beginning to hammer down, Delilah was standing under the cover of a grandiose porch of one of the executive houses which had been built as part of the Low Mill redevelopment. Situated at the end of the cul-de-sac, it was bordered by stone walls around the front, offering it a fair degree of privacy from its neighbours. Holding the front door open with a warm smile upon his face was Rick Procter.

'It's me who should be apologising, for making you come over here in the wet. But like I said on the phone, I've given Julie the rest of the week off and I'm heading to a site visit in Skipton, otherwise there'd have been someone at the office to let you in.' He gestured at the empty space by her side, his smile turning apologetic. 'And thanks for being so understanding about Tolpuddle.'

'No problem. Not everyone is a dog person. Besides,' she laughed, 'I've left him in good hands. He's probably being spoiled rotten as we speak.'

Rick's smile grew wider, his gaze flicking over her shoulder as a frantic yapping set up in the background. Before Delilah could turn to see what had caught his attention, he was focused back on her, stepping forward and draping an arm around her shoulders, pulling her into a sideways hug with the affection that had characterised their relationship for years. Before Samson came back.

'Come on in out of the wet,' he was saying, 'and I'll get you the keys for Taylor's.'

Mrs Pettiford was on a day off. With her sister having flown to Venice for a long weekend – something the bank clerk was trying not to dwell on given that the closest she'd ever got to that romantic destination was a work trip to Birmingham, the so-called Venice of the North – she'd volunteered to look after Lady, her sister's cocker spaniel. Least she could do seeing as the dog had almost died last time she was tasked with its care.

Rather than driving them apart, however, that near-death experience had forged a bond between dog and woman that certainly hadn't been there before. And now Mrs Pettiford actually enjoyed walking the yappy spaniel. Particularly as it gave her an excuse to snoop around areas of town she wouldn't normally be so bold as to venture into.

But that enjoyment was negated when the weather turned inclement.

Blue skies had given way to black, the summer breeze had turned into a gale, and the rain was pouring down. Luckily she'd thought to bring an umbrella with her. An umbrella which had emboldened her even further, given that it shielded her prying eyes from view. Although right at this moment, it was making her rather conspicuous.

She was struggling to keep hold of it. With a lead and a shopping bag in one hand, the other was fully occupied with trying to stop the damn thing from turning inside out, all while Lady raced around her legs, the conditions having sent her into even more of a yapping frenzy than usual.

'Stop barking!' Mrs Pettiford demanded, looking down at the spaniel.

And just like that, the umbrella was gone, snapped out of her hand in a momentary lapse of concentration and sent tumbling down the cul-de-sac that she'd turned into. It flipped over itself multiple times, lifted into the air and then came to a halt right at the bottom of the road, wedged into a corner between two perpendicular stone walls.

Mortified, Mrs Pettiford hurried after it. Mortified because while she'd been happy to walk down here under the cover of her umbrella, she was now exposed and her nosiness clear for all to see. For what earthly reason could a woman of her limited means have for being in this particular cul-de-sac where the rich and famous of Bruncliffe dwelled?

She scurried past the opulent driveways, the expensive cars, the huge houses, barely allowing herself a glance at the lifestyles she so coveted, until she reached the umbrella. Which, just as she stretched out her hand to take it, snapped back up into the air like a living entity.

It sent her and Lady jumping back in fright, the dog yapping, before Mrs Pettiford was able to grab the handle and turn to leave. Face crimson.

As she turned – Lady on her left, making her turn to her right – she was looking straight into the driveway of the last property. A gleaming Range Rover parked on the gravel. A porch like something out of *Gone with the Wind*. And Rick Procter with his arm around Delilah Metcalfe, whispering into her ear and leading her into the house.

Shock was the first reaction. It was a mere matter of days since the bank clerk had seen the Metcalfe girl behaving in a very wanton fashion right outside the library. With Samson O'Brien. Yet here was the same woman, dallying with Bruncliffe's most eligible bachelor.

The girl had no self-respect.

As she walked back up the cul-de-sac, umbrella tightly grasped, Mrs Pettiford did try to give the lass the benefit of the doubt. But it was the absence of the Weimaraner that did it. That dog, which was Delilah Metcalfe's constant shadow – Mrs Pettiford could think of only one reason why it might have been left behind.

When she turned out onto the main road, she checked her watch. She had time to go home and change into dry clothes before hitting Peaks Patisserie. Besides, there was no point in venturing there before ten if she wanted this snippet of news to have maximum impact.

'You're sure you don't mind letting me have access to Taylor's while you're not there?' asked Delilah, following Rick along polished parquet flooring to the far end of the impressive entrance hall. They went through a pair of double doors and into a kitchen which was every bit as opulent. Granite surfaces gleaming, appliances all high-spec, a professional looking coffee machine hissing away gently. And two mugs of coffee on the breakfast bar.

'I mean, should we let Nancy know?' Delilah continued.

Rick shook his head, casting a wink back over his shoulder. 'The place is as good as mine. She won't care. Besides,' he continued, pausing and turning to face her, a hand resting on the breakfast bar, a small frown now accompanying his smile, 'you said it was urgent.'

She nodded. Offering nothing more.

He gave her a wry look. 'No point in me asking what it is you've discovered?'

She grimaced. 'Sorry, Rick, but until I've got on the system and checked things out, I really can't say.'

'Just answer me this then – is it something I need to be concerned about? Given that I'm on the verge of buying the place?'

It was a fair point. The man was in the process of taking on a business which was possibly mired in crime. The least she could do is give him a bit of warning.

'When is the sale set to complete?' she asked.

'Monday.'

She nodded slowly. 'Perhaps consider dragging your heels a bit. Give yourself a bit of breathing space, just until Samson and I get to the bottom of whatever this is we've stumbled across.'

The flash of annoyance which darkened Rick's face was understandable.

'Right,' he said tersely. Then he shrugged. Gave a smile. 'I'll take your advice, Ms Metcalfe, and be grateful for it. In the meantime, have you got time for a drink?' He was gesturing towards the mugs, the tantalizing smell of coffee drifting up from them. 'I took the liberty of making it in advance because I knew you were in a hurry.'

She was about to refuse, eager to get to the estate agent's and check the GPS files. But Bruncliffe manners kicked in. Besides, she thought as she took a seat on one of the stools at the breakfast bar, she owed him. Because if her suspicions were right, there was going to be nothing left of Taylor's by the time the sale date came round.

'It's Hawaiian,' Rick was saying, as he passed a mug into her hands, 'pure Kona. What do you think?'

An aficionado of the instant variety, Delilah hadn't got a clue what he was talking about but took a drink, the flavours of spice and fruits coating her tastebuds. It was sublime. 'Wow,' she said, blinking, 'it's gorgeous.'

'Should be. Cost a bloody fortune!'

'Not like you can't afford it. Bruncliffe's self-made man

and all that.' The comment came out slightly more barbed than she'd intended but to her relief, Rick laughed. Whatever reservations she now had about the man and his ambitions, he was easy company. 'So, any other expansion plans in the pipeline?' she asked, finding herself genuinely interested.

'A few. None I can talk about just yet.'

'Round here?'

He shook his head. 'Nah. I'm looking further afield.'

She shook her head, impressed. It was hard not to be when she could remember him as a teenager, declaring that he was going to be so successful, he'd able to retire by fifty. While she didn't share his single-minded approach to life, and found herself less inclined to spend time with him of late, she could still appreciate all he'd achieved.

'All jokes aside, Rick,' she said softly, 'you've really made something of yourself. You should be proud.'

Rick placed his mug on the counter, a strange look on his face. 'I'll go get those keys,' he muttered.

He walked past her, back out into the entrance hall, and Delilah swivelled round in her seat to take in the ultra-modern kitchen. There wasn't a thing out of place. It was like a show home. A little bit on the sterile side for her tastes, no personal touches. She swivelled back and sloshed the last of her coffee onto the counter.

Cursing her clumsiness, she looked around for a roll of paper towel. But the surfaces clearly weren't intended for such prosaic items. She got off the stool, almost tripping over her own feet in the process, and crossed to the nearest drawer. Pulled it open. And saw a couple of splashes of colour inside. Something fluffy.

Shock hit her first. The recognition of those feathery concoctions, the yellow stem, the purple thread, the lethal barbs designed to ensnare . . .

A Waterhen bloa and a snipe-and-purple. Two fishing flies. Exquisitely crafted by her brother Ryan and last seen in an old tobacco tin in Nathan's possession, just before that same tobacco tin was found filled with ketamine in his school locker.

Anger followed hot on the heels of shock. Rick. He had the flies in his house, just sitting in a drawer like trophies. Explaining their presence was going to take some doing.

'Here you go.' Rick was back in the kitchen, holding out a set of keys. As she swung round to face him, the flies in the palm of her hand, he simply nodded. 'Ah, I see you found them. How careless of me to leave them lying around.'

'Whatsh . . . Ryanshfliesh . . . ?' Delilah shook her head, her tongue feeling thick, slurring the words she was trying to form, the slate floor starting to dip and sway.

'You might want to sit down,' Rick was saying, crossing the room towards her. 'That coffee has a bit of a kick to it.'

He went to take hold of her arm. She tried to shake him off but her arm was heavy, her legs folding, deflating beneath her like they'd been punctured.

'Whatveyoudone?' she mumbled.

'Something I always hoped I wouldn't have to,' came the reply, as Delilah Metcalfe slipped into darkness.

24

'Delilah?' Samson's voice echoed up the stairs, the very stillness of the building telling him she wasn't there. Even so, he went up to the first floor and stuck his head in her office.

Empty. No one behind the desk. The dog bed unoccupied. He didn't need to go into the kitchen, seeing from the landing that the narrow space was devoid of life.

Not a soul in the place. That hadn't happened in a while.

He glanced down at the postcard in his hand. Where had she gone? Out to get fresh air? Because he knew the impact this revelation must have had on her. The idea that Neil Taylor was somehow involved in the crimes they were unearthing would have hurt her as much as the divorce. That she could judge a person so badly.

Samson had to admit to being sideswiped by the revelation too. While he had no time for Neil Taylor, he hadn't taken him for the sort to be in cahoots with criminal gangs. Not because he thought the lad was honest or anything. More that he just didn't feel Neil had the gumption. Or the nerve. Because it took nerves to pull off something like this. To run a clandestine operation right under the noses of people who'd known you all their lives.

No wonder Delilah had felt the need to get out of the office.

He was heading down the stairs when his phone beeped. A text. From Delilah.

Gone for a run. Love you.

He stared at the words, the meaning totally clear – she'd done as he'd thought and gone to clear her head. But it was the subtext that had him frozen. That fifth word. The magnitude of it.

For the past couple of days he'd been trying to tell her he loved her and she'd shunned his declarations. He'd got the sense it was perhaps too soon. Yet here she was throwing the concept casually into a text, of all things.

It seemed strange. Or was he just feeling slighted at her decision to make her first commitment of this sort to him through digital means?

Deciding this line of thought could wait until Delilah got back – at which point he would tell her how he felt despite her objections! – he continued down the stairs, focus back on the postcard and the case in hand. It was time to call in the police. He scrolled through his contacts and was about to make the call when the front door flew open and DCI Frank Thistlethwaite entered the hallway. PC Danny Bradley was right behind him.

'Talk of the devil,' said Samson, grinning. 'I was just about to call the station.'

Frank didn't grin back. 'Devil might just be the right word. We need to talk.'

*

She hadn't been fully under, her body jerking against him when he picked her up as though she was doing her utmost to fight, her lips still murmuring away. Had he got the amount wrong? Or just not waited long enough for the drug to take effect?

Not having time to hang around and find out, he'd carried her to the Range Rover, the 4x4 backed up to the house, boot open and waiting. After he'd seen that busybody from the bank staring in at them from the gateway earlier, he wasn't taking any chances. What the hell had she been doing out in this weather and down a bloody cul-de-sac of all places?

He forced himself not to think about it. About how his carefully laid plan had gone a little awry. About what he was being compelled to do because of it. What choice did he have? Whatever is was Delilah had found on Taylor's IT system, Rick had known she wouldn't let go until she got to the bottom of it, her tenacity having been something he'd always admired in her. Look at the way she'd found the damn fishing flies he'd stupidly kept hold of. Trophies he'd forgotten were there and which had nearly scuppered everything.

No chance of that happening again. They'd be disposed of along with every other piece of incriminating evidence. Which brought him back to Delilah Metcalfe and her bloody tenacity, the reason he was currently driving through Bruncliffe in torrential rain with her unconscious in the boot of his car. It all felt rather surreal. But so was the idea of stealing a million pounds from an organised crime gang.

Another thing he didn't need to be dwelling on right now.

Just take it step by step. First up, get the false passport and emergency cash. Then he'd dispose of his unexpected company, before completing the final act. The audacious theft that would end his life in this town.

With the rain falling in sheets across the windshield, he turned the Range Rover onto the marketplace and towards Church Street. He was heading for his safe place. Where he stowed items he wouldn't want recovered should Her Majesty's Revenue and Customs ever decide to make a dawn raid. Last thing you needed in that situation was someone opening a safe to reveal fraudulent documents and bundles of unexplainable banknotes.

Bouncing off the last of the cobbles, the Range Rover curved around the corner, splashing through the large puddles pooled across the road, and then turned up Fell Lane. It was like a river, water streaming down the middle of the tarmac, runoff from the fells that gave the street its name.

Diabolical weather. But good in a way. At least this would mean there would be no one out and about to hinder him. Because who would be mad enough to go out in this?

Rick indicated right and turned down the driveway towards his destination.

'You have to be joking?' Arty Robinson was standing in the entrance hall of Fellside Court, the normally magnificent view offered by the towering glass window that stretched the full height of the building reduced to a watery blur. 'You want to go out? In this?'

Joseph had to admit his friend had a point. After all, the cherry trees in the courtyard were being whipped by the wind, the last of their blossom stripped and sodden on the ground, while one of the silver birch in the copse next to the car park was bending in a way that threatened imminent disaster. And as for the rain, it was like something out of an apocalypse movie. But when a man had to go, a man had to go. As did a dog, apparently.

'Blame him,' said Joseph, pointing down at Tolpuddle, who was pulling at the lead and whining softly in the canine equivalent of crossed legs. 'He needs a walk. It won't take long. And sure, it's only a bit of water.'

As he said it, a squall hit the glass in front of them, dousing it afresh and setting up a low moan as the wind wormed its way through the door.

'It's a sight more than a bit, lad!' grumped Arty. 'What do you need me for, anyway?'

'For the company?' Sensing he wasn't winning the argument, Joseph decided to throw in a bit of bribery. 'Would it help if we hit the cafe straight afterwards? We could get a sneaky morning coffee. A slice of cake maybe?'

'Slices. Plural,' haggled Arty.

'Done,' said Joseph.

As they stepped out into the storm, wet through in seconds despite their waterproof jackets, Arty had a sense that he'd settled the deal too low.

Tolpuddle didn't like the rain. And wasn't a fan of the wind either, the sudden sounds making him jumpy. On top of that, he was feeling a bit anxious. Because she had been anxious. When she'd left him here he'd sensed it radiating from her, creating ripples that disturbed his environment.

So when the two men finally led him outside, across the

courtyard and into the copse where the trees were clattering and groaning, he was quick about his business. Not wanting to spend any longer in the fierce elements than he needed to. He was trotting back across the grass beside them when the vehicle came around the corner and parked, right in the middle of the courtyard. The car door opened and closed and a man got out.

The wind was blowing from the west. Tolpuddle was downwind. So he caught the scent the minute the car door opened. Two scents. One he hated. And the other, faint but unmistakeable—

He was off. Tearing out of the soft grasp on his lead. Ignoring the exclamations. Sprinting across the grass, onto the slabs, past the cherry trees. Not caring about the rain. Not caring about the noises. He was barking too loudly to hear them.

He saw the man turn, almost at the big wall of glass. But Tolpuddle didn't care about him. Not today. All Tolpuddle cared about was the smell coming from the car.

She was inside. He knew it.

So he went up on his back paws, barking, scratching at the car window, trying to get in to her.

Behind him were voices, shouting.

'Call that bloody dog off!'

'Tolpuddle! Calm down! Tolpuddle!'

'Get him off my car!'

Then a hand on his collar. He pulled against it, determined to stay where he was, trying to guard her. But there were several hands now, tugging him back, away from the car. His claws slipping and scratching down the metal. While he barked and barked and barked.

'Come on, lad! Easy does it!'

Pats on his side. More soothing words. The man was getting back in the car. Staring at him. Tolpuddle went even crazier. Snarling now, doing his best to break free as more people gathered around him.

'Hold him, you two! Don't let him go!'

'What's got into the big fella?'

'It's that bloody Procter. He hates him.'

Then the vehicle started backing up, pulling away, Tolpuddle barking until he thought his heart would burst as he watched it disappear out of sight, taking her with it.

'Bloody dog!'

Rick's heart was pounding, sweat on his forehead, a pulse throbbing in his temple as he thumped the steering wheel in fury. He'd pulled up outside the library round the corner from the retirement complex, not trusting himself to drive in this state.

Delilah's stupid mutt. He'd known she was in the car. And with all that commotion going on, drawing the pensioners to windows and even out into the courtyard, Rick hadn't dared leave the vehicle unattended. Which meant he hadn't been able to get into the manager's office, or its hidden safe with its crucial contents. His careful plans had been ripped apart by Delilah Metcalfe and her bloody dog.

'Damn it!' He thumped the steering wheel again, this time his hand hitting the horn and setting off an impatient blare. Across the road, Sergeant Clayton was just leaving the police station, the sound drawing his attention.

It was enough to calm Rick. The last thing he needed was the local copper sticking his nose in.

Forcing a grin, he acknowledged the sergeant's concerned look, signalled all was okay and pulled away from the kerb. He drove slowly through the town, thinking hard. He was going to have to accept that the fake passport was out of reach – a repeat attempt to retrieve it would incur the attention of the old fogeys, who would be sure to give him the third degree about what had just occurred. And the cash? He had a reserve stash, not quite the two hundred thousand he'd been planning on, but enough to tide him over.

A glance at the dashboard clock. Twenty-five minutes before the transfer would be made. Time enough to dispose of his unwanted passenger. But not time enough to access his alternative funds. He'd have to rejig his schedule. Divert the transfer and then get the cash. Use his real passport to flee to the continent and take it from there. With the amount he'd soon have in an offshore bank account, he was confident he'd be able to get his hands on some forged ID.

There was only one snag. He'd be hanging around the area longer than was wise after he'd stolen the Bulgarian's money. What he needed were some distractions. Something to cover his tracks and give him time to clear town. A genuine scorched-earth policy.

'We got a match!' announced Frank Thistlethwaite, dropping a plastic evidence bag on Samson's desk before taking a seat, a look on his face that Samson recognised from his own life on the force. The thrill of being on the chase. Of seeing your quarry ahead.

Sitting next to him was Danny Bradley. Although the young constable was fidgeting so much it could hardly be

Date with Evil

called sitting, excitement bubbling through his words when he spoke.

'It was the blood on the blade!' Danny pointed at the crude knife inside the bag, the dark stain on the tip visible. 'The DNA from that was a match for a fugitive on Europol's Most Wanted list!'

'A Bulgarian,' added Frank soberly. 'With links to human trafficking.'

'Christ!' muttered Samson.

Frank nodded. 'And if that wasn't grim enough, once we knew the nationality of the bloke who'd been treated in Leeds General, I took a punt and contacted someone from the equivalent of the NCA over in Sofia and they were able to put a name to my Eastern European murder victim from a photo.'

'The one found in the Leeds and Liverpool Canal?' Samson asked in surprise.

'With your jacket around his neck,' corroborated Frank. 'He was suspected of having been involved in the same gang, plying the same heinous trade.'

Samson stared at the knife, trying to configure the connections. 'So someone who was in Quarry House left behind a weapon used to stab a bloke who was treated in Leeds and who happens to be a wanted fugitive. And that stabbing victim was in turn linked to a man found dead in Leeds, draped in my jacket. Both of them Bulgarian. Both caught up in the same criminal organisation.'

'And both with established links to a Europe-wide trafficking ring. An interesting tangle of relationships, don't you think?' Frank leaned forward. 'All of it leading back here to Bruncliffe.'

'So you think whoever was hiding out in Quarry House could be involved with that somehow?' Samson asked, his mind making furious calculations at the detective's revelations.

Frank nodded. 'We're leaning that way. We managed to get a partial print from the shaft of the knife but it didn't register on any database. And given this new slant on who was on the receiving end of that homemade blade, we're thinking that the person who made this knife wasn't a criminal on the run after all, but rather an illegal immigrant, having escaped from God knows what.' He spread his hands wide. 'We were hoping you might have come across something, anything, in your investigations into both the thefts at Uncle Seth's allotment and the fire at Pete Ferris's caravan which might help us find whoever this person is—' He broke off, staring at Samson. 'What is it, O'Brien? You've got that look on your face like you're on the scent of something!'

It was Samson's turn to lean forward across the desk. 'Human trafficking. I'm just thinking that it normally goes hand in hand with organised crime. Like drug farms.'

'And? Don't tell me you've stumbled across one of them over here?' said Frank, with a dry laugh. A laugh which faded as Samson nodded, sending those trademark Thistlethwaite bushy eyebrows shooting up.

'A drugs farm in Bruncliffe?' Danny was so fired up he was almost out of his chair.

'Yes, although we suspect it's not just one but an entire network. And a sophisticated money-laundering scheme to back it up, all run out of Taylor's estate agents. That's why I was about to call you.'

While Danny was staring at Samson with an open mouth, Frank was already processing the information.

'Bernard Taylor was involved in this?' he asked.

'Bernard, and it would appear his son Neil has taken up the reins.' Samson pushed the postcard across the desk and explained the background to the case. By the time he'd finished, Danny's mouth had been open so long, he was in danger of it staying that way permanently.

'Jesus!' the young constable finally muttered.

Frank's reaction was more perceptive, frowning as he spoke. 'And this Stuart Lister you claim uncovered all of this? He's now missing?'

'That's what we believe. His visit to Henside Road was followed by a swift and uncharacteristic decision to go travelling. I'm now inclined to believe he's in trouble.'

'Could he be the person who was squatting at Quarry House?'

'It doesn't add up,' said Danny, shaking his head. 'The reported injury at Leeds General was the evening before Stuart left town. And besides, if he wanted to arm himself, why would he go to the effort of making a knife when he would have had access to a proper one from his own kitchen?'

'Fair point.' Frank's frown deepened. 'In which case, we've got a drugs ring working out of the area with an Eastern European gang supplying trafficked labour, and Neil Taylor is at the heart of it. And from the sounds of it, your missing Stuart Lister is indeed in serious trouble. If not already dead—'

A loud crash came from the doorway and the three men spun round to see Ida Capstick standing there, face ashen, a shopping bag on the floor and bits of shattered pottery around her feet. From the fact that one of the fragments

347

was a spout, Samson deducted that Ida had broken her second teapot of the day.

Tolpuddle couldn't stop trembling. Back inside Fellside Court, the dog was whining softly and shivering, despite Clarissa Ralph having brought down her best towels and given him a good rubbing to dry off. They'd tried to get him upstairs into Joseph's flat, but the Weimaraner started growling every time they attempted to move him towards the stairs, pulling back against his lead, his head fixed so he could stare out into the courtyard.

'What on earth's wrong with the poor thing?' asked Edith Hird.

Arty shrugged. 'A reaction to such a massive adrenalin burst maybe?'

'An allergic reaction to Rick Procter more like,' muttered Eric, patting the dog, the affection having no effect on the animal's obvious stress.

Joseph shook his head. 'It was odd. I've seen him in Rick's presence before but never like that. I don't think I'd have had the strength to hold him back even if I didn't have one arm out of action. And besides, he didn't actually go for Rick. He went for the Range Rover.'

'Well, whatever it was,' said Arty, 'we should maybe get him home. Delilah will know how to calm him down. Did she say where she was going when she dropped him off?'

'Taylor's,' said Joseph.

'Right, we'd best head over there.' Arty looked out of the glass at the incessant rain, down at the out-of-sorts Tolpuddle, and sighed. 'Let's go and get soaked again.'

*

Out at Croft Cottage, communication was still an issue, despite the presence of Ana Stoyanovic. Having left the cafe straight away – Lucy Metcalfe making no objections to her temporary waitress taking time off, knowing that Ida wasn't one to ask such things lightly – Ana had driven through terrible conditions to reach the remote dale. Rain lashing the windscreen, she'd had a tight grip on the steering wheel of her elderly Renault Megane as she negotiated the narrow, wall-lined lanes, the floodwater at worrying levels and rising, while the windshield wipers struggled to keep her view clear. And as she'd turned into Thorpdale, she'd been treated to the spectacular sight of a large ash tree in the field next to the road being felled by the wind. Crashing sideways, it landed across the telegraph wires and snapped them in two, leaving the broken ends whipping around in the gale.

Glad to turn into the safety of the Capsticks' yard, Ana had parked up and hurried across to the kitchen, where she'd found George Capstick in a very agitated state, rocking on his heels and muttering away to himself, while Grigore was sitting at the kitchen table, pointing at a notepad. The Romanian's face had lit up when she walked in, an openness to his manner which hadn't been there the evening before. As though he trusted her now.

That delight had quickly transformed into frustration as the limits of Ana's Hungarian became apparent. Limits which couldn't be augmented by the digital means Grigore had eschewed twelve hours earlier, the Capsticks' internet connection having been taken out along with the phone line, and data provision non-existent in the isolated location.

Staring at Grigore's drawings, Ana had never felt more

regret at having learned so little of her grandfather's native language.

'I don't understand,' she said again, in the one phrase she knew fluently.

Grigore threw the pen on the pad and looked anxiously at the clock. Whatever he was trying to communicate, there was a sense of urgency about it. Then he nodded at her. Tried to smile. But the worry was eating at him.

'Dog, devil, steward,' muttered George over her shoulder, he too staring at the drawings as though their meaning would suddenly become clear.

Ana checked her phone. She'd called Manfri as soon as Samson had passed on the Gypsy's number, the neighing of horses and the sound of busy activity audible in the background. Despite not knowing her from Adam, the minute she'd mentioned Ida and Bruncliffe and the predicament the Romanians were in, he'd agreed to help, promising to be on the road just after nine.

It was now a quarter to ten. He couldn't be more than forty-five minutes away.

'Help,' she said to Grigore in her broken Hungarian. 'Help comes.' She pointed at her watch, sweeping her finger round from the minute hand to the number six, trying to make him understand.

He just nodded. Sadly. As though that might be too long to wait.

Footsteps overhead, dragging him out of the semi-conscious stupor he'd slipped into. Then the door had opened, blinding him with the light from the corridor. He'd thought it was water. Food. But instead there was a soft whump of sound, something heavy landing on the dirt floor. Then the door was closed again.

He waited for his eyes to readjust, for the vivid aura behind his eyelids to fade. Then he peered across the dark. A mass of black, more dense than the rest of the black. Unfathomable from this distance. So he shuffled forward, biting his lip against the stabbing pain as he inched over the damp soil, fighting to keep himself from passing out.

Closer now, he reached out a hand. Touched the lump. And felt the soft yield of flesh. Someone else. Thrown in here with him. Were they dead? Not long if so, his searching hand meeting bare skin, feeling the warmth.

A murmur. A woman's voice, the sound no more than a whisper.

Whoever she was, she was alive. But barely conscious.

And then she spoke again, a collection of slurred consonants and vowels but distinguishable nevertheless.

'Tolpuddle . . .'

He jerked back, realising who his new cellmate was. And a surge of optimism coursed through him. He'd been right to have faith. Help had arrived. All he needed to do now was wake it up.

25

'I should have told thee earlier.' Ida Capstick hung her head as she finished speaking, the heat of shame on her cheeks. Samson having given up his seat, she was sitting behind his desk, the two policemen opposite.

'And *I* should have realised something was up,' said Samson, putting an arm around her shoulders. 'You weren't yourself first thing.'

It was an understatement, he realised. Any day in which Ida managed to smash two teapots was definitely a day where she was out of sorts. But then, taking in a couple of unknown men George had found hiding in the barn was more than enough to have triggered that. Having listened to her startling account of what had unfolded at Croft Cottage the night before, Samson also realised that Ida was more than capable of keeping confidences when she needed to, not a hint of the drama having passed her lips that morning.

Ida grunted. 'No excuse,' she muttered. 'Ana said as how it could be trafficking those lads were caught up in. But I didn't really credit it. I just didn't think it were possible. Who would do such a thing?'

'That's what we're working on finding out,' said Frank Thistlethwaite. 'So do you know anything about these Romanians other than their names, their nationality and that they've been on the run?'

'They weren't right keen on talking last night. Happen as I don't blame them. But I do know they stole Mrs Hargreaves' washing.'

Samson noticed a note of triumph creep into Ida's voice. But Frank wasn't showing any interest in the case of the missing laundry.

'What about this drawing you said one of them was doing in an attempt to communicate?' he continued. 'Are we getting anywhere with that?'

Ida shook her head. 'George was muttering on about a dog, devil, steward or some such like, and Ana just texted me to say she can't make sense of owt on it either. I've asked her to send us a photo but with the internet down, don't get tha hopes up of it arriving anytime soon.'

'Understood. But given that this Stuart Lister might be in trouble, we can't afford to hang around.' Frank turned to Danny Bradley. 'Danny, I want you to ask Sergeant Clayton to round up Neil Taylor. Nothing heavy-handed. Just tell the lad we need to talk to him. Until we have concrete evidence we don't want to go playing our cards just yet.'

'I'm on it,' said Danny, getting straight onto his radio.

'Meanwhile,' continued the detective, pulling out his mobile, 'I'm going to see if I can rustle up someone who speaks Romanian to go and chat with our two mystery men now they seem willing to talk—'

'No!' Ida's blunt exclamation was enough to make Frank pause, phone in hand. 'Don't go sending police out to Thorpdale. It'll spook them. And George. Besides, Manfri will be there before long. Tha'll get some answers then.'

'Is that the same Manfri who helped with the sheep-rustling case?' Frank was looking at Samson, who nodded. The detective ran a hand through his hair, his handsome features contorted into concern.

'I think Ida's right,' said Samson. 'We won't be able to get any more out of those men than Ana has and as for a professional interpreter, this is the Dales. You're probably looking at Leeds or Bradford so at least an hour's wait, even if they can come immediately. Manfri is our best bet. And if the Romanians have been through what we think they have, they might respond better to someone who isn't official—'

'Anyone for samosas?' Nina and Nathan were in the doorway, hair dripping, puddles of water forming at their feet. Nina was grinning despite being soaked, and holding up a fragrant smelling bag. She froze, seeing the sombre faces, sensing the tension. 'Sorry. Didn't mean to interrupt.'

'No need to apologise,' said Samson. 'We're just in the middle of something.'

'Anything we can help with?' asked Nathan, eyes wide, desperate to be involved.

Frank shook his head. 'Not this time, son. Best leave this one to us.'

The lad bristled and he looked on the verge of a sharp retort when Nina's hand met his arm, giving it a squeeze.

'Tea?' she said brightly. 'All round?'

'That would be perfect.' Samson gave the pair of them a smile. 'And thanks.'

The teenagers turned away, Nina's intervention not enough to prevent Nathan muttering loudly about being treated like kids. But Frank was right to be reluctant to let them loose on this case. Until more was known about exactly what was going on in Bruncliffe, they were safer out of it.

'Right,' said Frank, briskly back to business, 'let's leave the Romanians to Manfri for now, but I want to be kept abreast of anything he gets out of them. So Ida, keep in touch with Ana and tell her to notify us if anything comes out of their conversation or the drawings. Meanwhile, O'Brien, before we go pressing any panic buttons, I'd like to have a look at the evidence you've come across for this crime syndicate. You know I can't go calling in more resources without having seen something concrete to substantiate your claims.'

'I totally understand,' said Samson. 'But you'll have to wait for Delilah to get back. I don't have access to her computer.'

'And where is the delightful Ms Metcalfe?' For a moment Frank's face relaxed into a smile.

'Gone for a run.' As he said it, Samson looked at his watch. It had been a while. Considering she knew they'd just uncovered something explosive. Normally her inquisitive nature wouldn't allow her to miss a second of an investigation. 'She should be back any minute.'

Ida made a noise of dissent, shaking her head at him. 'Tha's got tha facts wrong, lad. Delilah's not out running. For a start, I saw her in the marketplace with Tolpuddle, and she wasn't dressed for heading up on the fells. And for another, those blasted trainers of hers are still lying in the middle of the rear porch. Happen I know that for sure as I tripped over them coming in.'

Samson stared at her. Then his eyes dropped to the postcard. Lying on the desk. Post-it note visible, written in Delilah's clear style. He looked at the bottom line. Thought about the text she'd sent . . .

That was it. That was what had unsettled him about the text. Her use of the word love and . . . he looked back down at his mobile, checking what she'd written. While from the hall came another voice.

'What's with all the serious faces?' Will Metcalfe was standing there.

'Doesn't anyone ever knock in this bloody place?' muttered Frank.

'Only offcumden,' retorted Ida.

Samson was oblivious. Staring at the text. The lack of kisses. He glanced at the post-it note. Kisses. He flipped the postcard over, seeing Stuart's message to his mother, the lack of kisses which had made her suspect its origin . . .

'When did you last see Delilah?' he demanded, wheeling round to face Will.

'Earlier this morning. Why? What's wrong.'

'Did she say anything? Anything at all about the case we're working on?'

Will shook his head. 'Not really. Although we did chat a bit about that.' He pointed at the postcard.

'What about it?' Frank's tone was every bit as sharp as Samson's.

'I told her I recognised it. That Neil had taken it.' He

shrugged. 'She said it was part of a case but wouldn't say any more. Pretty much kicked me out after that. Why?' He turned around, scanning the room, finally registering his sister's absence. 'Where is she?'

Frank looked to Samson. Samson looked at the text message. And felt his entire world start to crumble.

'Who does he think he is?' Nathan was muttering as they entered the kitchen, his annoyance at DCI Thistlethwaite's officious behaviour intensified by a sense of embarrassment he didn't understand. Or rather, understood but didn't want to face.

'A high-ranking detective in the police force?' quipped Nina with a grin. 'Come on,' she said, filling the kettle as he slouched against the doorframe. 'Whatever is going on down there is clearly serious. You can't blame them for wanting rid of us. Besides, there are ways of getting involved without them realising.' Her grin developed a mischievous twist. 'I've found the fine art of being invisible indispensable over years at the restaurant. Offer to do menial tasks like making tea or clearing tables, and suddenly they don't notice you and you get to overhear all sorts!'

Nathan let out a reluctant laugh. This is what she did to him. Made him laugh. Made the sun shine when dark thoughts threatened. He pushed himself off the doorway to start helping her but as he did so, his gaze went to the whiteboard. And he froze.

It was covered in red arrows. Arrows linking all the cases. The missing lettings agent, the stolen files, Bernard Taylor's cash, even Heriot's Rottweiler which they'd just been to see.

He let out a low whistle, Nina turning to see what had prompted it.

'Crikey!' she exclaimed, staring at the amended whiteboard. 'This must be what's got them looking so solemn downstairs.'

Nathan was nodding. 'It's all connected.' Then his gaze fell on the two new entries and he went cold.

'What is it?' Nina was watching him.

'Pete's suicide. Whoever did this has put it on the board.'

'And?'

'They've linked it to Henside Road.' He pointed at the only item which had been circled vigorously, aware his hand was shaking. 'How can he have died because of Henside Road? Was it because of me? Did that have something to do with him taking his own life?'

Nina's look had turned incredulous. 'Don't be daft! How on earth could you be responsible for that?'

'Because that's where Pete found me, when I ran away from home in March. At a property out on Henside Road. He made me promise not to tell anyone, ever.' Nathan gulped, fought the panic rising in him, and gestured at the network of arrows. 'So I'm *not* daft. I'm somehow involved in all of this.'

Nina looked from him to the board and back again. 'Okay – before we go downstairs and announce this, let's do a little digging of our own first.' She tapped the words that had been highlighted by the circle. '"DC Green photo/ Henside Road,"' she read out. 'That's Delilah's handwriting and she clearly thought this was important. So where would we find a photo from DC Green?'

'Probably in an email? Which we could access on Aunt

Delilah's PC,' said Nathan, 'except I don't know her password.'

'Luckily,' said Nina, her grin back in place, 'I do.'

'There's no one in there. And I'm not willing to stand out here getting soaked any longer, hanging around on the off chance Delilah might turn up,' grumbled Arty, nose pressed against the wet glass of Taylor's as he peered into the dark interior while the rain lashed against the window.

'So where is she?' asked Joseph, likewise staring into the empty estate agent's, even the small office in the back abandoned, the door open to reveal just a vacant space.

Between the two men was Tolpuddle, the Weimaraner's shivering more pronounced out in the storm, the lead quivering in Joseph's good hand.

Arty shrugged. 'No idea. But you can't say we haven't tried to find her. Two unanswered calls, a text message and now this. So I vote we call it quits and get this lad back to the office. What's the betting she's there, waiting for the rain to ease off before coming to collect him. Like any sensible person,' he added grumpily.

Joseph looked down at Tolpuddle, the low whine the dog was still persisting with audible above the wind. Arty was right. The office was their best bet. At the very least, Samson might be there.

He nodded and the pair of pensioners made to turn away when they were hailed from across the square.

'Is Neil in the office, do you know?' Sergeant Clayton was striding towards them.

Joseph shook his head. 'You're out of luck, I'm afraid. The place is all locked up.'

The sergeant knocked loudly on the glass and rattled the door anyway, before emitting a large sigh. 'Have you seen him around?'

'Not today,' offered Arty. 'But Delilah was supposed to have a meeting here earlier. She might know where he is. We're heading over to the office now. Want us to ask her?'

'As a matter of fact, I'm heading over there myself so I'll walk with you, if you don't mind.'

'I don't suppose there's any point in us asking what—'

'Not this time, Arty.'

The grave tone of the sergeant didn't invite any further digging. Instead, Arty shot Joseph a look as they made their way across the wet cobbles. Something was up. Something serious. Enough to make even Arty forget to grumble about the atrocious weather.

Nerves shredded and stress levels at maximum, from the ginnel on the opposite side of the square Rick Procter watched the men leave. Finally. He gave it another thirty seconds, the maximum he could spare, before jogging across the cobbles and letting himself into the estate agent's, firmly locking the door behind him.

Heart thumping, clothes dripping, he hurried towards the back office.

That had been close.

When he'd got to the entrance of the ginnel, having left his Range Rover tucked out of sight behind the chemist's, he'd nearly died at the sight of Boozy O'Brien and his mate standing at the door of Taylor's, trying to get in. If it had been just the two pensioners, Rick would have brazened it out, got rid of them and got on with his business. But the damn dog was there. And Rick couldn't afford another scene like the one in Fellside Court earlier.

So he'd waited in the mouth of the ginnel. All the time checking his watch, the minutes ticking away, his stomach in knots. And then Sergeant Clayton turned up. Rick hadn't been able to catch what he'd shouted, the wind whipping the words away. But he was clearly looking for someone. Him?

Doubtful. Not this soon. Even if Delilah's absence had been noted, why would anyone point the finger at him? Unless that Mrs Pettiford had been spreading her gossip?

Don't think about it. Not now. Focus.

Closing the office door, he carefully laid the small rucksack he was carrying on the floor, sat at the desk, and woke up the computer. Fidgeted impatiently while it roused itself, and then logged on to the business bank account. One minute to ten. This was it. This was when he changed his future, forever. His past too. For Bruncliffe's history would be rewritten with a single click of a mouse.

A calm descended over him. He stared at the screen. At the clock in the bottom right-hand corner. And as the hour finally arrived, he watched the numbers changing in the bank account.

In reality, it took more than a single click. But it was still speedy.

Rick Procter rose from his old partner's desk a very wealthy man. One who now had a massive target on his back. There was no time for dallying. A last pit stop to pick up his alternative source of cash, tie up the last few loose ends and then he'd be gone.

Taking a small device from the rucksack, he laid it under

the desk and turned it on, allowing himself a smile. He wasn't the only one for whom the clock was ticking. In ten minutes, Taylor's would go up like a roman candle.

'She's missing?' Will Metcalfe demanded. 'How can she be bloody missing in Bruncliffe?'

'How long has she been gone?' asked Frank, ignoring Will's insistent questions.

Samson checked the text. 'Forty minutes. A bit more maybe?'

'At least that. I saw the lass crossing the marketplace at just gone nine,' said Ida.

'That's an hour, then! She's been gone an hour and you didn't notice?' Will's questions were becoming more irate. 'What the hell is going on?'

'She's got Tolpuddle with her,' said Ida into the growing tension.

Samson nodded, that knowledge offering some respite. Because he knew the Weimaraner's loyalty had no bounds.

'For Christ's sake, tell me what's going on! This is my little sister we're talking about.' Will slammed his hand on the desk, bringing silence to the room.

Frank turned to him. 'It's possibly nothing, but we've reason to think there's a criminal organisation operating out of the town—'

Will didn't wait to hear any more. He whirled round. His voice dropping to a whisper. 'You'll be the bloody death of her, O'Brien.'

Samson wasn't capable of a reply, his throat dry, his skin clammy.

'It might be a false alarm, Will,' Danny Bradley was saying.

But then the front door opened and in walked Sergeant Clayton, with Joseph and Arty behind him. Between them was a very anxious-looking Tolpuddle.

'No sign of our man at home or at work,' Sergeant Clayton said, addressing Frank, while taking in the significant gathering in Samson's office.

His words were met with no response. Everyone in the room staring at the dog.

'Tolpuddle,' Samson managed, the Weimaraner scurrying over to him to be enveloped in a hug, trembling and whining softly. 'How come you've got him, Dad?'

'Delilah left him with me.'

'You've seen her? When?'

'About an hour ago?' Joseph looked at Arty for corroboration, the pair of them feeling the stress, knowing this was about something serious.

'Was she going for a run?' Even as he asked the question, Samson knew the answer was standing there shivering in his arms. Tolpuddle. Delilah wouldn't have left him behind.

'No son, she was heading over to Taylor's—'

'Shit!' Frank Thistlethwaite grimaced at Samson. 'Could she be with him?'

Ida let out a low moan.

'Who? Who is she with?' Will's fists were curling dangerously.

'Neil Taylor,' said Samson. 'We think Delilah might be with Neil. And we think she might be in danger.'

26

He'd taken a gamble. Used up the last of his precious water rations in a drastic bid to wake her up. He'd debated the wisdom of his actions as he'd guided the water over her face, doing his best in the dark to make sure it hit the target. But the thought of who she was outweighed his concerns. The thought of what she was capable of.

His rash deeds didn't seem to be having much effect, however, apart from provoking a bit more moaning.

So he shook her. Gently at first, eliciting a few more groans. So he gave her another shake. This time it was a bit harder and she rolled out of his frail grasp and flopped over onto her back.

There was a grunt of exhaled air and then quiet.

Despair clutched at him. It wasn't working. She wasn't going to save them. He'd wasted his water for nothing.

He clasped his arms around himself, felt tears on his face.

While beside him, in the back pocket of a pair of jeans, two sharp barbs had been crushed by the change in position of the supine figure. Originally intended for much smaller prey, they were nevertheless strong enough to pierce the fabric and strike soft flesh. Which, in turn, was strong enough to pierce the fog clouding her brain.

*

Delilah felt herself returning. Pulled back from a dizzying fall into unconsciousness through an awareness of something stabbing her, sharply. An insistent pain that demanded her attention.

She went to move an arm to see what it was, but her arm wouldn't cooperate, heavy and lumpen. So she opened her eyes, blinked. Closed them. Opened them again.

It was pitch-black.

She heard a mumble, realised it was herself, her tongue thick, her lips rubbery.

Fear kicked in then, enough of her brain awake to sense the danger here. The incongruity of the situation. For she was lying flat on her back on a damp floor, in the dark, and couldn't remember a thing about how she'd got here.

'Tolpuddle,' she murmured, some hazy memory forcing its way in. Then she was trying to sit up, her limbs uncoordinated, aware of a foul smell, the scent of death and decay—

'Take it easy.'

The hoarse whisper came from the blackness, shocking Delilah into movement. In a tumble of legs and arms, she was scrabbling away from it, her scream no more than a whimper. Then her watch caught on her trousers and the light came on and in the ghostly glow of the dial, she saw an apparition.

A haggard face, more skull than flesh, staring at her through sunken eyes.

'It's me,' he croaked. 'Delilah, it's me.'

She stared in horror, recognition dawning before her watch went out, plunging them back into darkness. Whatever this hell was, it had provided her with the answer she'd set out looking for. Stuart Lister was innocent. Because why else would he be down there with her?

They found the photo with ease, the image appearing on the screen the minute they woke Delilah's computer up.

'It's a close-up of a window of some sort? Someone's reflection in it?' Nina was saying, regarding it with confusion.

Nathan, however, knew exactly what it was and was doing his best not to be sick. He was back in that small workshop, shivering, starving, in pain. And desperate to be home.

'It's Pete Ferris,' he muttered.

'And what's that?' asked Nina. Her finger was resting on a black mass to the left of the shot, on the other side of the glass.

'A Rottweiler,' murmured Nathan. She turned sharply, staring at him. 'It tried to attack me.' He shrugged, trying for a nonchalance he was far from feeling. 'That's why I'm not so keen on them.'

'So is this where Pete found you?'

'Yes. It's an old workshop in an outbuilding round the back of a farmhouse on Henside Road. I was hiding there and somehow Pete and his lurchers came across me and brought me home.'

She looked back at the screen. 'And this photo? Do you remember it being taken?'

Nathan shook his head. 'It was all a bit surreal. One minute I was looking out the window, because I heard voices outside. Then the dog tried to attack me, so I was banging on the glass to get help, and just as I thought I was a goner, the Rottweiler turned tail and went running back to the two men by the house. Which is when Pete snuck up behind me and shoved me to the ground.'

'This all sounds really odd.' Nina was really staring at him now. 'Why would he do that?'

'He said it was because we might get done for trespassing. He'd been poaching.' Nathan shrugged. 'I was too tired, cold and scared to care.'

Nina looked at the photo again. 'While I still think you're daft to believe you had anything to do with Pete's suicide,' she said, putting her hand on his shoulder and squeezing it, her voice edged with excitement, 'I do think you're right about being involved in whatever is going on. We should let Samson know about this.'

Nathan wasn't about to argue. He was too transfixed by the warmth her touch was generating.

Downstairs in the office building, things were in chaos.

Will Metcalfe was going spare, Ida looked like she was about to collapse, while Frank Thistlethwaite was trying to impose some sort of order.

Samson was watching it all with a sense of detachment, crouched down, hugging Tolpuddle tight to his chest, the dog unrelenting in his soft whining, mirroring Samson's own agitation. Will had been right. Delilah had ended up in danger yet again and it was all his fault.

'She's still not answering her phone,' his father was saying. 'I'll keep trying.'

'We need to find her,' said Will, pacing the hallway.

'We need to find Neil Taylor,' countered Sergeant Clayton. 'I'm going to get an alert out across the region.'

'Great,' said DCI Thistlethwaite. 'But if this is about drugs and money laundering like we suspect, then we're dealing with very dangerous people. We need to be careful how we approach it.'

'Sod careful!' growled Arty Robinson, wielding his mobile. 'I've just sent out a general alert on the WhatsApp group that saved Samson's backside last month. I've told anyone who's seen Delilah to shout.'

Several phones pinged in unison as his message duly arrived.

All the while Samson was trying to reassure himself. Delilah was sensible. Even if she had gone to see Neil, she wouldn't be stupid enough to confront him. Not given the magnitude of this case. But . . .

But Delilah wasn't cut out for poker. That beautiful face of hers was incapable of hiding her feelings. So even while she might have set out with the intention of merely testing the water where her ex-husband was concerned, Neil would have seen her disdain, her anger. And that would have placed her in peril. For if Stuart Lister had been got rid of so easily, Delilah would be no different.

Samson's guts churned at the memory of the last time he'd seen Neil Taylor. In this very hallway, the man's flirting of the day before suddenly rendered into hostility as he demanded Delilah stop working on Taylor's IT system. Hostility which had been confusing at the time, but now made so much sense. He'd known Delilah was a danger. That the IT system held evidence of his crimes. And in the balance against that, whatever affection he held for his ex-wife counted as nothing.

'Samson?' A voice cutting through his anguish. Nathan on the stairs, Nina next to him, both of them beckoning him and looking agitated. 'There's something up here you really need to see.'

Ana Stoyanovic was taking a break from her disastrous attempts at interpreting. The tension in the kitchen of Croft Cottage had got too much, with Grigore growing more frustrated at his inability to get his point across and Ana under mounting pressure to elicit something from him, given Ida's alarming updates about what was going on.

Drug farms and human trafficking, with Neil Taylor at the heart of it all. And now the latest news . . . Delilah was missing and possibly in danger. Lovely Delilah Metcalfe, one of Ana's favourite people.

It was hard enough to take in without Ida suggesting that Grigore's drawings might be crucial. Life-saving, even. If only Ana could understand them.

No surprise, then, that the atmosphere in the kitchen had become strained, especially when exacerbated by George rocking anxiously while muttering the same three words over and over. Nor had it helped that when Pavel had finally appeared, looking a lot better after a bit of rest but clearly still in pain, he'd been angry with his brother, a heated discussion arising between them.

Ana got the sense the younger brother didn't want to tell them whatever it was Grigore was trying to express. Judging by Ida's texts, it was seeming very likely that the brothers had indeed been trafficked as Ana had suspected.

In which case, it was little wonder they were reluctant to talk. After an experience like that, trusting anyone would be difficult. But Pavel needn't have worried, she thought wryly, because no one understood what Grigore's drawings were supposed to communicate anyway.

Fifteen minutes and the cavalry would be arriving in the form of Manfri. Not a moment too soon. Until then, Ana needed some fresh air. Which meant – given it was pouring down despite being officially summer, the climate of her new home never failing to amaze her with its crazy weather – she was standing in the front porch with the door open. Situated on the far side of the house from the kitchen, it smelled of polish and window cleaner and looked like it got very little use. But the views were amazing, hills stretching up on either side the full length of the dale and, far off in the distance, a blur on the horizon that she knew must be Twistleton Farm. The old O'Brien place.

She let her gaze lift to the cloud-covered fells, white torrents visible where swollen springs were roaring down the hillside.

There'd be serious flooding, for sure. She might even have trouble getting back to town, her Megane not exactly an all-terrain vehicle. As she had the thought, a Range Rover went past at a speed not suited to the road surface or the conditions, the vehicle bumping and rocking over potholes and sending up plumes of spray. She recognised both the vehicle and its driver.

Rick Procter. She ducked back instinctively, her ex-boss at Fellside Court never someone she liked encountering.

'Devil!' exclaimed a voice in her ear, making her jump. George Capstick had entered the porch behind her and was pointing at the Range Rover as it headed further into the dale. 'Twenty horsepower Ida says he's the devil!'

'Rick Procter?' Ana asked, thinking it an apt description. George nodded. 'Dog devil steward.'

Ana stared at him. 'Devil,' she murmured, thinking of Grigore's drawings. The one that looked like a cow on two legs. She began searching through the photos on her mobile, all the while thinking that this was ludicrous. Because what possible connection could Rick Procter have to two Romanians who'd turned up at the Capsticks' out of the blue?

As she clicked on the image she'd been looking for, one of Rick standing next to her at the Bruncliffe Christmas lights turn on, she let her eyes drift once more towards the horizon and the collection of buildings which had once belonged to Joseph O'Brien. Then she was rushing towards the kitchen.

There had to be a way out.

Still groggy, her legs wobbling when she tried to move, Delilah had managed to manoeuvre herself into a seated position, back propped against a damp wall. Next to her, Stuart Lister was slumped in pain, the lettings agent having uttered little more than his initial rasped greeting as he lapsed in and out of consciousness.

How long had he been here? Days? Possibly weeks?

She couldn't focus her thoughts enough to calculate when he went missing, a mist of confusion still clouding her brain. Not enough confusion to protect her from the certainty that she had no one to blame but herself for landing in this predicament.

Rick Procter had played her like a fish, luring her in and then incapacitating her. It must have been the coffee, that bloody blend he was prattling on about, all the while knowing he'd laced it with God knows what.

She wasn't sure who she was more angry with, Rick or herself. For not only had she gone along to his house like the trusting fool she was, but she'd failed to let anyone know where she was going. No note left for Samson, an unintended omission when it came to Joseph, telling him only her intended final destination of Taylor's.

All of which meant that when her absence was noted, no one would know where to start looking for her.

Panic surged, the musty smell clogging her throat, her chest tightening at the certainty that Rick Procter had no intention of letting them live. Feeling the terror overwhelming her, she forced herself to concentrate on the practical.

Getting out.

Pressing a button on her smartwatch, she shone the feeble light around the small room where they were being held. It was a cellar of some sort. Thick stone walls, the floor left as dirt, patches of water beginning to seep up through it, no doubt caused by the torrential rain outside. The only openings were an airbrick right up against the high ceiling and the door.

The door was locked. The airbrick too small to get through, even if they could reach it. And given Stuart's condition, on the off chance they did manage to escape, she didn't think he was up for running.

She let her watch go dark. Listened to Stuart's troubled breathing. He was asleep. Or unconscious. Careful not to disturb him, she took a gentle hold of his wrist, the pulse faint beneath her fingertips. She didn't need a medical degree to know he was close to dying.

They had to get out of here. And soon. There was no other choice.

Through the quagmire that had become her thought process came a pinprick of realisation. The door. She'd presumed it was locked. She hadn't tried it.

She looked across the blackness to where she knew it was, bracing herself for an effort her body wasn't ready for. And realised there was the smallest amount of light, a tiny ray, no more than a glimmer, coming from that corner of the room.

Not trusting her legs to work, she rolled onto all fours and started across the floor to investigate. There had to be a way out. Because otherwise they were both going to die.

The reaction was visceral. Ana Stoyanovic laid her phone on the kitchen table in front of Grigore without saying a word and the Romanian jerked up out of his chair, knocking over his mug of tea, staring at the screen in horror.

'Devil?' asked Ana.

'*Diavol!*' Grigore nodded, eyes wide, glancing at his brother. They exchanged some frantic words, Pavel leaping to his feet too, looking like they were about to flee.

She'd scared them. Made them think that perhaps they weren't safe here. No wonder when she was showing then a photo of a man who clearly terrified them, yet there she was, smiling next to him. They thought she was connected to him. To whatever they'd escaped from.

'It's okay,' she said, gesturing for them to sit back down. 'It's okay. You're safe.'

Behind her George was murmuring anxiously, pulling the doors open in the bottom of the dresser and rummaging inside, while the spilled tea dripped slowly onto the floor. More hasty words between the brothers, Pavel agitated, while Ana wondered how she could reassure them, let them know that they were in no danger. That she hated Rick possibly as much as they did.

Then George brushed past her, something in his hand. A wrench. A large one. In one smooth movement, he brought it down on the image of Rick Procter staring up out of Ana's phone, smashing the glass into a craze of jagged lines and eliciting shocked noises from the three onlookers.

'Dead Devil!' he grunted. Then grinned.

Grigore was the first to start laughing.

Pete Ferris. Staring out of Delilah's computer at him, from what Samson was pretty sure was the outbuilding at Henside Road.

Nina and Nathan had taken Samson into the kitchen first, shown him the whiteboard and Delilah's handiwork. That had been enough to send his mind reeling. But then they'd brought him into Delilah's office and shown him the photo DC Green had sent up.

How the hell had Pete Ferris wound his way into the Met investigation into Samson's old boss?

'It's Henside Road,' murmured Nathan, mistaking silence for confusion.

Samson glanced at his godson. 'How do *you* know that?'

'That's where Pete found me. When I ran away. He must

have taken that photo when I was with him.' The lad shrugged, as though he'd just made some inane comment about the weather. Not possibly cracked a case wide open.

By pure fluke, while fleeing town after being falsely accused of dealing drugs at school, Nathan had ended up at Henside Road, possibly when it had been operating as a drugs farm. So too, by the sound of things, had Pete Ferris.

'Why don't you take me through exactly what happened that day,' said Samson, struggling to keep his voice calm.

Nathan began talking, telling him about the Rottweiler, the voices, the men outside. And then Pete's strange behaviour.

'These two men,' said Samson, 'can you describe them?'

'It was dawn, I couldn't really see them. But I know they weren't speaking English.'

'Did you see anything else? Anything that seemed out of place? Drugs or anything?'

Nathan shared a surprised look with Nina, shaking his head, while Samson headed for the door, wanting another look at the whiteboard in the kitchen.

'What's this all about? I mean, don't you think it's time we were told?' Nina was asking, the two teenagers following him across the landing.

It was a fair point. Especially now it seemed as though Nathan might be a witness should the case ever be prosecuted. Should Delilah and Stuart ever be found—

'We're investigating a possible drugs racket in the area,' said Samson, cutting across his own morbid thoughts. 'We were looking into Neil Taylor's involvement in it and, in the process, Delilah has . . . gone missing.'

Nina gasped while Nathan took on the fierce look all the Metcalfes seemed to adopt in a crisis.

'And somehow this is connected to me and Pete being at Henside Road?' he asked.

'I'd say so.' In the kitchen now, Samson turned his attention to the whiteboard and the mess of arrows, knowing the answer was in there somewhere.

She'd seen it. Delilah had got the photo from DC Green and made the connections, spotting the possible link between all this and Pete. He glanced down at the table, saw the caravan brochure splayed open, the circle around the luxurious static.

Pete Ferris had been dreaming big. Or planning on a windfall.

Back to the board, Bernard Taylor's holdall of cash. Blackmail of some sort? He'd thought that once before and dismissed it. Perhaps he'd been rash?

'This might be worth a look,' Nina was saying, reaching for Pete's phone, which was on the table, charging. 'I mean, Pete's holding a mobile in that photo, so maybe whatever he was taking a picture of is on here?'

Samson nodded, not really hearing. Too busy making links and connections, trying to figure it out, hoping it might yield a clue as to where Delilah was. Wondering what the hell it was that was nagging at the back of his mind. Something Danny and Frank had told him – something to do with the stabbing victim and the dead man in Leeds . . .

When Nathan spoke, he almost missed it.

'If Henside Road is connected to Aunt Delilah's disappearance,' asked the teen, 'why aren't you talking to Rick Procter?'

'Rick? What's he got to do with this?' Samson stared at his godson.

'He was there. Outside. Talking to the men. I was about to bang on the window to get help, even though I didn't think he'd be pleased to see me, you know, after that incident at school. But Pete threw me to the ground before I could.' He shrugged. 'He had a couple of dead pheasants with him. I think he thought Rick would prosecute him for poaching.'

'You're certain it was Rick?'

Before Nathan could reply, Nina was holding out Pete's phone. 'No doubt about it,' she said, pointing at the image on the screen.

Taken through a grimy window, it was clear enough. Rick Procter. Blond hair gleaming. Standing by the back door of the property on Henside Road. Next to him were two burly men and Bernard Taylor. And on the far left of the shot, a hint of a shadow, no more than a blur on glass. A blur which would be digitally enhanced to produce the photo on Delilah's computer.

Pete Ferris, signing his own death warrant.

Nina swiped the screen and another photo popped up. The interior of a barn, huge piles of sacks stacked up against a wall. She zoomed in. 'Fertiliser?'

'Used in making cannabis,' said Nathan.

They both stared at Samson. Who was struggling to stay upright. Because suddenly everything was clear – should have been so clear all along if he hadn't allowed himself to be blinded by prejudice – and with it came the awful realisation that Delilah, his wonderful Delilah, was in so much more trouble than he'd thought. There was no chance of her relying on lingering marital affection in her present predicament. And what was worse, they'd wasted precious time in their search for her.

'We've been looking for the wrong bloody person!' he shouted.

He turned round, haring for the stairs, just as the front door opened and all hell broke out down below.

27

Frank Thistlethwaite had plenty of experience under his belt when it came to being a serving policeman. But nothing had prepared him for how Bruncliffe reacted in a crisis. When the front door of the office building opened and Neil Taylor walked in was no exception.

Will Metcalfe was on him in a flash, a strong hand around the man's throat, thrusting him up against the wall. 'Where is she? What have you done with her you bast—'

'Easy, Will! Let him speak!' Sergeant Clayton was trying to intervene, pulling at Will's arms, Neil being choked further in the process, while Arty Robinson was squaring up, threatening to beat the lad senseless.

Over it all came a commanding shout from the stairs.

'Let him go, Will!' Samson O'Brien, standing there, a fierceness to him that brooked no argument.

Will released his grasp, Neil slumping to the floor, coughing.

'We need to make him talk,' protested Arty, standing menacingly over him.

Then Ida looked up from her phone, voice leaden. 'I've had a text from George. Grigore has identified the person he calls the devil. He says it's—'

'Rick Procter,' said Samson, coming down the final few stairs, the teenagers behind him. 'We've been looking for the wrong man.'

'Rick?' Sergeant Clayton shook his head. 'I thought you said Neil was the ringleader.'

From his seated position, Neil was watching them, eyes wide. 'What the hell are you all talking about? I just called in to speak to Delilah. What's going on?'

Frank held up the postcard. 'This,' he said. 'Did you take this photo?'

Neil nodded, genuine surprise on his face. 'Years ago. On a trip to Thailand. Why? What's that got to do with anything?'

Frank looked at Samson, who was shaking his head.

'Bulgarians,' he said grimly. 'Bruncliffe Manor. We should have spotted the link.'

And instantly Frank was back at the stately home outside town where he'd helped investigate the death of Bernard Taylor, killed during a shoot at which the mayor and his partner, Rick Procter, had been hosting some very unsavoury types. From Bulgaria.

A sense of dread filled the detective, knowing that having overlooked something so obvious might yet have fatal consequences. 'But I don't understand,' he muttered. 'How can it be Procter? The postcard . . . ?'

Samson turned to Will Metcalfe. 'Was Rick on that trip?' he asked quietly.

'Yes,' said Neil, before Will could speak. 'Because I took that photo with Rick's bloody camera! He was the only one with a digital and I wanted to try it out.'

There was a hole of stunned silence. Into which several mobiles pinged.

'Christ!' Arty was staring at his phone. 'Lucy's just updated the WhatsApp group. Apparently Mrs Pettiford was in the cafe earlier, spreading gossip about Delilah being a hussy.'

'And?' demanded Sergeant Clayton impatiently.

'She was basing her opinion on the fact she saw Delilah going into Rick Procter's place. At a quarter past nine . . .'

Samson snapped into life, Frank seeing the formidable force he must be out in the field.

'Ida, get another message on the WhatsApp group. Let's find the creep. Danny, revise the official bulletin for the region. We're looking for Rick Procter. Probably in his Range Rover—'

Joseph O'Brien let out a low groan. 'Oh, lord. He was at Fellside Court. He must have had Delilah with him in the car!'

'The dog!' Arty clutched a hand to his heart, face turning grey as Nina helped him to a seat. 'Tolpuddle was trying to tell us she was there. That's why he went for the bloody Range Rover.'

'And we pulled him back,' murmured Joseph in horror.

'What time was this?' Samson demanded.

'Just after nine thirty?'

Sergeant Clayton slapped his forehead. 'Procter was parked up outside the library about then. I remember thinking he looked a bit agitated. He must have just been leaving Fellside Court.'

Samson checked his watch. 'Less than an hour ago. He can't have gone far.' He turned to the sergeant. 'We need a list of every property Rick Procter or his business owns. And,' he swivelled round to Neil, 'a list of every rental on

Taylor's books. He could have taken her to any of them. And Ida, we could really do with some progress with the Romanian lads. Tell Ana to do her best to interpret those drawings. They could well be the key to finding Delilah and Stuart.'

'I've got nothing more than dog, devil, steward from them so far,' muttered Ida, 'which makes bugger all sense —'

'Steward or Stuart?' asked Nathan.

Ida stared at him. 'Stuart! George thought Grigore was saying "steward" but what if he was saying "Stuart"?'

'That would mean Grigore knows where Stuart is,' said Danny excitedly. 'Which could mean he knows where Rick is taking Delilah.'

'We need to get over there, now!' Samson said, as a cacophony of phones trilled again.

'Rick's been spotted!' Ida was holding up her mobile. 'He went past Croft Cottage a few minutes ago, heading for Twistleton Farm.'

Samson was already moving for the door. 'Frank? You got a car?'

'Right outside.' Frank hurried after him, Will and Sergeant Clayton following, the sergeant issuing instructions as he ran.

'Stay with Taylor, Danny. Get that list from him and if he gives you any grief, arrest the bugger.'

The constable's resigned groan was drowned out by the closing of the front door.

Delilah had a conundrum to solve. The door to their prison was fastened tight. Yet there was no keyhole. She'd crawled over and used the light from her watch to inspect it, finding that there was indeed illumination leaking through from whatever was outside, but it was through a hole way too small to take a key.

Perplexed, she rattled the door again. It remained firmly closed. A door with no visible way of locking it, yet it was indeed locked. A bolt on the exterior? There seemed to be a bit too much give in the door when she pushed against it for that. Unless . . .

She bent down and peered through the hole. There was a black horizontal stripe cutting across it. A latch bar. Like she had on all of the internal doors in her cottage. With the handle removed on this side, so there was no lever sticking through to be able to lift the bar. That's what the hole was. Where the missing lever had been.

If she could get something to poke through there and lift the bar, they would be free!

She turned, twisting her watch to illuminate the darkness, seeing nothing but dirt and stone. And Stuart, mumbling deliriously.

He was going downhill fast. They were running out of time.

A wave of despair threatening to engulf her, she collapsed into a seated position. A stab in her backside. Sharp. The same sensation she'd had when she came round. Able to move better now, she reached into the rear pocket of her jeans and felt feathers. And steel.

Ryan's fishing flies! How had they got there? Rick, getting rid of the evidence in one fell swoop? Forcing herself not to dwell on what that meant, she carefully removed them and inspected the two delicate creations. Thread and feathers and two hooks. If she could bind them together, they would be the right length to poke through the door and lift the latch.

From overhead came the sound of heavy footsteps. From outside came the sound of a lapwing calling. And from the corner came the stuttered breathing of Stuart Lister. Driven on by a sense of urgency, Delilah got to work.

Rick Procter was almost done. Bending down to the cupboard under the sink, he retrieved the cash, hidden in an old tin amidst the pile of junk in there. Sometimes hiding things in the open was the best bet, especially in the hovel of a house that belonged to Twistleton Farm. Not that it would be around much longer.

Crossing to the table, he placed an incendiary device on the floor, set the timer and let himself out.

Sheltering from the rain in the barn doorway, the two guards were watching him with that innate suspicion a lifetime working in crime gave people. He waved. Calmness personified. They had no idea that he'd already doused the far side of the barn with petrol and the trigger for that fire was on a much shorter fuse. Which meant it was time he was gone.

The diversions he'd set in place would cover his tracks long enough to ensure that by the time O'Brien figured it all out – which he would; that was the nature of the man – Rick would have left this miserable excuse for a summer long behind and be sunning himself in the Caribbean. And Delilah?

Overhead a lapwing sang its strange song and Rick let his eyes follow it across the ominous sky. Anything rather than think about Delilah Metcalfe.

He crossed the wet yard, nodded at the men, and got in his Range Rover. He'd done it. He'd pulled off the biggest deal of his life.

'"Stay with Taylor"!' Danny Bradley muttered into the pouring rain.

As he escorted said Taylor to the top of Back Street, water dripping down the back of his collar, his shoes saturated, Bruncliffe's constable was more than disgruntled.

Yet again his sergeant had sidelined him when things got interesting. It was enough to make Danny think twice about the offers he'd had to move to a different force, Frank Thistlethwaite having made it clear there was a place for him in Leeds should he want it.

Mood as sour as the weather, he followed Neil Taylor onto the marketplace and down towards the estate agent's. When they reached the two huge windows situated either side of the entrance, it took a second for them to process the flickers of scarlet decorating the name etched into the glass.

'Fire!' Danny was the first to react, spotting the flames in the office at the back. It already had quite a hold, streaks of red licking across the floor and up the walls. Snatching the keys from Neil's frozen hands, he opened the front door.

'You're not going in there?' exclaimed Neil. 'Don't be mad!'

'Call the fire brigade!' was all Danny shouted over his shoulder as he entered the building.

Smoke, thick and suffocating, spilled around him as he hurried across the reception area. But when he reached the small office, the fire was fierce. Heat scorching, the crackle and spit of wood burning. The entire room was in flames. A couple of frames on the wall were already crumpled and warped, a photo of Bernard and his wife in a plastic mount on the desk was melting, as was the computer screen. No one but an idiot would have gone in there.

Luckily, thought Danny as he pulled off his wet jacket and wrapped it around his head, the Bradleys were known for carrying a rogue idiotic gene. Because there was vital evidence in that room, and if Rick Procter was guilty, the prosecution were going to need every bit of proof they could lay their hands on to make sure he got his just deserts.

Face covered apart from his eyes, Danny stepped into the flames, heading straight for the desk. The floor underneath it was burning fiercely. If what he was after had been there, he was too late. But the desk, made from glass and metal, was showing few signs of damage yet, which gave him hope. So, shirt pulled over his hand, he opened the bottom drawer, the handle burning into his skin.

Not there.

The other side. Another burn, the drawer squealing open. There inside, in a purpose-built space, was the PC unit. Protected in its metal shelter. He ripped the cables out of the back, lifted it out and turned to go, and saw a splash of green on the floor by the door.

A plant. Without a pot, roots exposed, white flowers wilting. Somehow it had survived the fire so far. Danny didn't think twice. He scooped it up and hurried out into the marketplace where a substantial crowd had gathered, the wail of approaching sirens carrying over the howling wind.

*

'There's a fire at Taylor's.' One hand on the dashboard to steady himself as Frank tore along the rain-soaked roads towards Thorpdale, Samson was looking at his mobile. Ida had just updated the WhatsApp group, adding Samson and Danny Bradley in at the same time.

Frank spared a brief glance at his passenger before pinning his attention back on the tricky job of keeping the police 4x4 on the tarmac, the windshield wipers swiping furiously, visibility seriously impaired. The Leeds-based detective had proved himself every bit as good a driver as Delilah. From behind came the wail of another siren, Sergeant Clayton and Will on their heels.

'He's getting rid of evidence,' muttered Samson, the fear in his gut blossoming. Because Delilah was evidence.

'We'll get to her in time. And the lad, too.'

There was conviction behind Frank's words. As the car swerved around a deep puddle, tyres almost on the verge, Samson tightened his grip on the dashboard and prayed that Frank Thistlethwaite was as skilful at predicting the future as he was behind the wheel.

'We can't just sit here!' Arty Robinson was pacing Samson's office, the colour of his face suggesting his pulse was higher than it should be. 'Taylor's is literally burning. Delilah and Stuart are in danger. We need to get out there!'

'Take it easy,' murmured Joseph, concerned for his friend. Feeling stressed himself, he couldn't imagine what it was like with a dodgy heart. 'There's nothing we can do and worrying will only give you a coronary.'

'Doing nothing is more likely to kill me!' Arty shot back.

'Tha needs to stay calm,' said Ida, the tension on her

own face belying her advice. 'Happen as they might need us yet.'

'For what? More tea?' muttered Nathan.

Even Tolpuddle was on hot bricks. Still whining. Turning circles by the front door.

'I think we all need to have more faith,' said Nina into the tense silence. 'This is Delilah Metcalfe after all. She's more than capable of looking after herself.'

Ida nodded. 'Aye lass, tha's right. We need to have faith in our Delilah.'

The faith that her friends were showing in her wasn't being shared by Delilah at that moment. With her watch dangling from her teeth, the light it cast swaying over her hands, she was trying to bind the two fishing ties together. But it was tricky work and her fingers felt fat and clumsy in the aftermath of whatever Rick had given her, not nimble enough for the task she was attempting.

'Damn it!' she muttered as the hook of one of the flies slipped across the body of the other and pierced yet another finger.

'You can do it.' A hoarse whisper from beyond the circle of light around her. Stuart was conscious. 'I know you can.'

She grimaced. Wishing she shared his conviction.

She adjusted her grasp on the flies. Another go. What choice did she have. It was their only hope. Concentrating hard, teeth clamped on the watch strap, she carefully poked the barb of the second fly into the threads binding the first. This time it caught. She pushed a little further, wanting it tight, but afraid of snapping the threads. It slid in.

She'd done it! The two flies now formed a length of

metal, about three centimetres long. All she had to do now was poke her improvised lever through the hole and lift the latch.

As she turned towards the door, two things happened. Her watch light faded into nothing, plunging them into darkness. And she caught the faint smell of smoke.

28

The rain was still falling heavily, blown against the windows of Croft Cottage in ferocious gusts. In those conditions, against a glowering sky, the thick plume of smoke rising to the north wouldn't have been immediately visible. But the wind had shifted. Twisting round so that it carried down the dale, bringing the smell to the sharp nose of George Capstick.

'Fire!' he declared, rushing into the kitchen from the yard, where he'd insisted on keeping watch to see if the Devil went past again. 'Fire! Twistleton Farm!'

As George disappeared out into the hallway, Grigore stared at Ana, who grabbed the pen and drew flames on the notepad, pointing in the direction of the farm. It triggered another drastic reaction.

Shouting something to Pavel, Grigore started for the door.

'Where are you going?' Ana demanded, throwing herself in front of him, her hand on his chest. 'We've been told to stay here.' She pointed back to the chair he'd vacated.

Because the updates from Ida – via texts to George's phone now that Ana's had been smashed in the interests of communication – had been shocking. It wasn't Neil Taylor the police were looking for. It was Rick Procter.

The suspected mastermind behind the drug farms and the trafficked labour working them, he'd been seen with Delilah before she went missing and was now at Twistleton Farm. Ida had passed on a warning from DCI Thistlethwaite that Ana, George and the two brothers needed to stay out of it. That they should wait for the police to arrive because Rick was too dangerous for them to tackle alone.

But Grigore wasn't having any of it. He shoved a finger at the last of his drawings, the one that looked like a person locked up. Then he gestured towards the farm, agitated, his brother too.

'Help!' he declared in Hungarian, tapping the notepad. 'Help!'

Ana didn't know what to do, part of her terrified at the thought of confronting whatever was going on up there. Another part knowing they should help if they could.

The decision was taken out of her hands. Coming back into the kitchen, George Capstick stepped around Ana and opened the back door. He had a shotgun in one hand and the large wrench, a first-aid kit, and his outdated mobile in the other.

'Liquid-cooled vertical L-head time to go,' he said, giving the first-aid kit and the mobile to Ana, before calmly passing the shotgun to Grigore and the wrench to Pavel.

Ana followed them out into the pouring rain, texting Ida as she went. A minute later, she was standing next to the two brothers on a platform rigged up behind an ancient grey tractor as George drove them out of the yard and into the storm. Turning to the north on the flooded track, they could see smoke, black and dense, billowing into the sky.

*

'Fire at Twistleton,' Ida announced grimly, fingers flying over her mobile as she relayed Ana's message to the WhatsApp group.

Nina took a deep breath, while Nathan let out a low curse, Tolpuddle whining in unison.

'I'll get on to the fire brigade,' said Joseph.

'We should go over there,' insisted Arty again. 'They need us.'

'Maybe Arty's right,' said Nina. 'If Delilah's in there . . .'

'Tha's not going anywhere,' said Ida. But even she looked uncertain as she turned to stare out at the unrelenting rain.

For the occupants of the two cars which had just turned into Thorpdale, Ida's message was made redundant by the pall of black smoke drifting towards them.

Samson's heart contracted in pain at the sight of it.

Fire at Twistleton. Was Delilah in there? If she was . . .

Frank didn't say anything. Just put his foot down, demanding even more of the 4x4 as it bucked and rocked across the rough track. Up ahead, in the distance, a grey tractor was already heading for the farm. And coming towards it, at speed, was a Range Rover.

It was the barn which was in flames, the fire audible now, roaring and popping, the smoke swelling up and out, turning the dark sky even darker. But the passengers on the Little Grey weren't looking at the inferno as they approached the farm. They were watching the Range Rover coming down the narrow track towards them.

George wasn't slowing down. Shoulders hunched

forward, he had the determined set of a man prepared to see something through. Even if that something was a game of chicken with a powerful 4x4.

Ana felt a warm arm tuck around her. Grigore. Next to her. Looping his left arm around her waist, grasping the platform on the far side of her and bracing her body against his. Preparing to crash. At speed.

The tractor wasn't swerving. The imbecile was going to kill them both.

Rick Procter gripped the steering wheel of his 4x4, staring through the rain at the ancient machine coming straight for him. Brains Capstick driving, some people standing on the platform behind him. The fire had brought out the bloody hero in them. And messed up Rick's plans.

Then he saw the flashing blue lights in the distance, the dark blur of two cars approaching.

It wasn't the fire. They were here for him.

Rick Procter had never been someone to go down without a fight. Trusting his top-of-the-range vehicle, he yanked on the steering wheel.

The Range Rover swerved across in front of them, the boot missing the front of the tractor by millimetres as the 4x4 bounced off the track and through a gateway, into the fields.

George was already braking, throwing his passengers forward. Shouting at them. 'Off! Off!' Gesturing at the fire consuming the barn.

They all jumped down and began running towards the burning building, people staggering out of it, screaming, crying.

Behind them, George had reversed the Little Grey and was heading for the gap in the stone wall where Rick Procter had disappeared.

'Pull over! Pull over!' Samson shouted, seeing the tractor coming back towards them, blocking their route, the roof of Rick's Range Rover visible above the stone wall to the right as it tore across the field.

Frank slammed on the brakes, Samson having the door open before the car was truly stopped, heading for the fire. His sprint was slowed by a strong grasp on his arm. Will Metcalfe had leaped out of the car behind and was alongside him.

'Leave Delilah and Stuart to me!' he was yelling, pointing at the fleeing Range Rover. 'Go get that bastard!'

'No!' Samson made to shrug him off, his focus on the flames visible on the barn's gable wall, the people milling around outside, the cries of distress. 'Delilah's in there—'

'And I'll get her out. But arresting Procter, that's your *job*, Samson. You're a copper.'

Samson hesitated, torn. But Will just nodded and pushed him towards the tractor which was already in the field. 'Go!'

Forcing himself to turn his back on the scarlet flames tearing at the roof of the barn, Samson started running after the Little Grey. Heart pounding, lungs heaving, he managed another burst of speed and then he was jumping up, catching hold of the platform and hauling himself onto it.

'It's me, George!' he shouted over the roaring engine.

George just nodded. Attention firmly fixed on the Range Rover, which was pulling away.

*

Third time lucky. Kneeling in front of the door and working by touch to preserve what was left of her watch battery, Delilah slid the fishing flies back into the hole. This time she felt the end hook catch around the bar on the other side. Carefully, slowly, she lifted her homemade latch.

A clunk. Then the door was falling open away from her, flooding the room with light.

And smoke. Thick smoke.

Hand clamped over her mouth, she got to her feet and stepped out into what was a narrow corridor, slate floor, a bare bulb overhead. To the right, a set of stone steps, another door at the top of them. It was from there that the smoke was coming.

She climbed the steps, a hand on the wall, eyes stinging, legs still wobbling. The door handle was warm to her touch. She turned it. No luck. The door was locked. Properly. A mortice lock removing any chance of her repeating her trick with the fishing flies.

She placed her ear to the wood, feeling heat beneath her cheek. And hearing the roar. The fire was close. Coming closer. Then an almighty bang. Something major giving way, shaking the building.

Hurrying back down the stairs, she continued past the small room and found herself in a much larger space. More slate flags. Marks on the wall where shelves had once been. A storage place of some sort. It was empty now, save for an abandoned sandwich board lying on its back in the corner. What really caught her attention though, was the window.

Set high up in the wall, the top touching the ceiling, it was a narrow oblong. Large enough for a person to fit through. All they had to do was get up there.

Smoke swirling around her ankles, she hurried back to get Stuart. He was already near the door, crawling towards the light, pain engraved into his gaunt features.

'The place is on fire!' she exclaimed. 'We need to get out as soon as possible.'

'My left leg,' he croaked. 'I can't walk. Leave me and go and get help.'

She glanced over her shoulder to the steps leading up out of the corridor. To the gap under the top door where the grey tendrils seeping under it had turned black.

They didn't have long.

She turned back to Stuart, placed both her hands under his shoulders and muttered, 'This is going to hurt.'

Slowly, her arms screaming at her, the bullet wound in her left shoulder feeling like it was being ripped apart, she began to drag him across the cellar floor, towards their only chance of survival. From overhead another deafening noise, the impact of something huge. As the walls shuddered and dust fell from the ceiling, Delilah knew their time was fast running out.

DCI Frank Thistlethwaite made a snap decision. With O'Brien – a serving Met police officer – on the tractor chasing Rick Procter, getting the occupants of the barn to safety was now the priority. And so he ran towards the burning building, Sergeant Clayton in his wake. When they entered the yard, the heat from the flames fierce despite the pouring rain, a dark-haired man wearing a Bruncliffe rugby top had already unrolled a hose attached to the house and was dousing the doorway to the barn.

A doorway through which people were running. Terrified

men. Looking gaunt, clothes in rags. Ana Stoyanovic was there, gathering them to safety under the shelter of an old woodshed while Will Metcalfe was frantically moving between them, calling Stuart's and his sister's name. Meanwhile another man, pale and clearly in pain, was standing with a shotgun in one hand and a wrench in the other, guarding two thickset blokes who were seated back to back on the rain-soaked concrete of the yard.

'Is everybody accounted for?' Frank demanded, scanning the huddle of people clustered around Ana.

'I can't see Delilah or Stuart!' Will shouted, panicked, beginning to move across the yard towards the flaming doorway.

'No!' The man in the rugby top had dropped the hose and grabbed Will's shoulder, pulling him back, saying something in a language Frank couldn't recognise. But the gist was clear.

'He's right, Will! It's too dangerous!'

As Frank said it, there was a screech of wood and metal and the central beam of the structure collapsed, bringing the roof down in a thunderous roar.

'Delilah!' yelled Will, breaking free from the man's hold and lunging forward, only saved from throwing himself into the conflagration by the much more substantial form of Gavin Clayton.

'You can't go in there, Will!' the sergeant was saying, wrestling the famer away from the fire. 'There's no point. It would be suicide!'

Frank looked at the ruined barn and knew Sergeant Clayton was right. No one was coming out of that alive.

29

The storm had turned the land sodden, not only from the rain pouring out of the sky, but from the water streaming down the sides of the fells that surrounded them. Even the Little Grey was struggling, in constant danger of becoming bogged down, its thick tyres tearing up clumps of turf as it chugged across the field. Up ahead, the Range Rover was fishtailing and bucking dangerously over the uneven terrain as Rick pushed it to its limits.

He was pulling away from them.

If they didn't catch him soon, it would be too late. Samson knew this land like his own body, he'd worked it from childhood, trying to keep the struggling farm afloat while his father was trying to drink his grief away. And he knew that if you veered to the right before the next gate, you could cut back across the fields and onto the road, coming out just before Croft Cottage.

If Rick made it that far, he would be gone.

'Come on,' he murmured, willing more out of the old tractor, which was already way past its limit.

But then Rick made a mistake. He went straight through the open gate, ignoring the route to the right, which was nothing more than a sheep trod to the unsuspecting eye.

George cast a glance over his shoulder, eyebrows pulled into a frown.

'Badlands!' he shouted.

It was George's ironic name for the terrain that had been the bane of every farmer who'd ever tried to eke a living out of Twistleton. An expanse of land that nothing would grow on. Not because it was too arid, like the genuine Badlands. But because it was too wet.

As they followed the path of the Range Rover through the open gate, for the first time in over fifteen years, Samson found himself looking at Twistleton Bog.

They were still following him. Trundling along on that scrapheap of a tractor, gradually falling further and further behind.

Rick focused back on his driving as the Range Rover bounced and slid across the wet terrain. Far off, on the other side of this vast field, he could see another gate. According to his GPS, once he reached that, he should be able to cut across to the right and come out on a dirt track which would lead him back to the main road at the start of Thorpdale.

And to the Caribbean.

He grinned. It had been a close call. But he'd done it. O'Brien would have no chance of catching him now, especially not with this flat stretch of land ahead. The Range Rover would make mincemeat of it.

He pressed down on the accelerator. Felt his wheels bite, thrusting the 4x4 faster, further. Not paying attention to the reeds outside. Not paying attention to the cotton-grass.

If he'd been a genuine Dalesman, he'd have known he'd

just driven straight into a bog. As it was, he only realised when the wheels lost traction, slamming the vehicle into a massive deceleration and throwing him violently against the doorframe. He lost consciousness just as the Range Rover started to sink.

George halted the tractor a safe distance from the bog and they jumped off. Already the 4x4 was listing over onto the driver's side, sliding down into the reeds.

There was no sign of Rick.

Beginning to cross the mire, keeping the reeds under his feet, Samson shouted back at George. 'Get the tow rope!'

But George didn't move. 'Dead Devil,' he said, staring at the sinking Range Rover with a blank expression.

Samson paused, turned. Saw the resolution on George's face, that Capstick stubbornness. 'We have to save him! We need him alive.'

An ominous groan as the Range Rover tipped even further. If Rick was in there, he was already underwater.

'George! Please!' Samson was thinking frantically, trying to conjure up the right pressure to force his old neighbour to act. When he spoke, it was in desperation. 'Who's going to help me get this place back on its feet if you're in prison for manslaughter?'

George stared at him. That piercing look which Samson remembered from his youth, when it was just the two of them, up all hours lambing, getting the harvest in. Days he'd never really appreciated until they were part of his past.

'Three-point-linkage you're coming home?' asked George.

Samson nodded.

'Promise?'

'I promise,' said Samson.

With a cross between a giggle and a yelp, George jogged back to the tractor.

Frank Thistlethwaite watched the grey tractor coming back towards them. And wondered how he was ever going to be able to break the news.

The barn was still burning, the roof fully collapsed, but the house had been saved. Gavin Clayton had found an incendiary device beneath the kitchen table just before it was due to ignite. And from what they could tell, language being something of an issue, everyone who'd been in the barn had been accounted for. Except for . . .

The rain was finally easing off as the tractor pulled up. Samson jumping down, running over towards them. Frank steeled himself.

'Where are they? Did you get them out?' Samson was looking around, taking in the group of people with Ana, the two men on the ground still being guarded. Then his eyes came to rest on Will Metcalfe.

The farmer's face was streaked with soot and tears.

'Delilah?' Samson asked.

'I'm so sorry, Samson. I couldn't—' Will broke down into helpless sobbing.

Disbelief on his features, Samson turned back to Frank. 'Tell me you got her out.'

Frank shook his head. 'The roof fell in. There was nothing we could do.'

*

Samson's legs went from under him. He felt an arm under his, a man in a Bruncliffe rugby top, helping him to a pile of logs, sitting him down. Ana saying something before hurrying over to George and the unconscious Rick Procter on the back of the tractor. A huddle of folk in the old woodshed, looking terrified. The two blokes on the floor, being guarded by a man with a shotgun and a wrench. And coming up the track at a jog, Manfri, the Gypsy having arrived too late.

Too late to help them find Delilah and Stuart.

He stared at the ruined barn. Memories tumbling. His mother, laughing as he played in the hay. His father showing him how to chop wood. Happy memories of his childhood were precious in their scarcity. And now, this had wiped them out.

For this would forever be the place where he had lost her. Whatever love had remained for him at Twistleton Farm had been turned to ash by the fire.

Rick Procter's fire.

Self-recrimination tore at Samson's heart. He shouldn't have listened to Will. He should have come straight to the barn. For Delilah. His love for her the only thing that mattered in his life. He could have saved her. Instead he'd saved Rick Procter. Prevented him from being drowned in the bog. A man whose evil had torn so many lives apart.

Samson got to his feet. A cold anger consuming him. The world beyond that, nothing more than background noise. He walked past Manfri having an animated discussion with the man in the rugby top. Past Will, still sitting there, tears flowing. Past Sergeant Clayton, talking into his radio. Towards the tractor.

Ana was there, Frank next to her, the property developer beginning to come round, propped on the edge of the Little Grey's platform, blood streaming down his temple.

Samson was aware of Frank turning, saying something, putting an arm out to stop him. It was useless, the rage overwhelming now. He brushed the detective aside and reached for Rick, hands grabbing his sodden jacket, jerking him towards him, right arm already pulling back.

'Stop!' George. Pushing between the two men. Insistent. 'Stop, Samson. Save Delilah!'

He was pointing, at the man in the Bruncliffe rugby top, at Manfri, who was saying something to Ana. Something urgent.

'Grigore knows where Delilah and Stuart could be,' the Gypsy was insisting.

Like a man surfacing from the depths of the ocean, Samson came back to himself. Hearing sounds. Smelling the fire. He let go of Rick, walked over to Manfri.

'They weren't here?' he asked. 'They weren't in the barn?'

The man in the rugby top was shaking his head, pointing into the distance, over the fells. And Samson felt a shaft of optimism break through the darkness in his heart.

'So where are they?' he demanded.

A rapid exchange between Manfri and Grigore and then the Gypsy was speaking again.

'He says there was a man locked up in the place he escaped from. Unfortunately he doesn't know where the building was exactly, but it's somewhere near a quarry—'

'That's what the final drawing was,' Ana exclaimed. 'A man in a quarry!'

Manfri nodded. 'Grigore never saw him but was able to

make contact through an airbrick. Their communication was basic but he's certain it's this man you're looking for, the one called Stuart.'

'And if Stuart's there, Delilah might be, too!' said Frank

'But there's loads of quarries in these dales,' said Sergeant Clayton. 'How the hell do we know which one to go to?'

Samson whipped round to Rick, who'd slumped back on the platform. 'Where are they?' he shouted.

'He's in no state to talk,' protested Ana. 'He needs to go to hospital.'

But Rick was trying to answer. Mumbling incoherently. 'Delilah . . . too late . . .'

At that moment, Samson's phone started to vibrate.

'I can't do it . . .' Stuart Lister's weight collapsed back onto her and the pair of them tumbled to the cellar floor.

It was the fourth time they'd attempted it. The fourth time they'd failed. The window was too high and Stuart was too weak.

Having dragged the rickety old sandwich board across under the window, Delilah had opened it up and then lain it down on its side, providing an A-shaped platform to stand on. It wasn't the most solid of bases, but it had taken her weight. Standing on tiptoe with one foot on either side of the A, she'd just about been able to get her fingers to the window latch, pushing it open.

She'd thought they were safe then. That the dense smoke coiling into the room was no longer a concern. That the heat building up didn't need to worry them.

But Stuart wasn't able to pull himself up and out through the opening. His left leg was hanging at an odd angle and he had very little strength left, on the edge of blacking out.

Delilah felt the awful reality of the situation. The smoke getting thicker now, both of them coughing, eyes streaming, she had a decision to make. Save herself. Or die with Stuart. Because no one knew where they were. There was no help coming.

'One more try,' she said. She hauled herself back to her feet, legs wobbling, her head thumping, injured shoulder throbbing.

Stuart was shaking his head. Pain dragging at his features. 'I can't . . .'

Delilah wasn't taking no for an answer. Taking hold of his hand, she pulled him upright once more, and helped him up onto the sandwich board. But this time, she stepped onto the A-frame behind him. It wobbled and groaned, adjusting to the increased load.

'When I say go,' she said, 'give it everything you've got. It's our last chance.'

Stuart placed his hands flat on the wall in front of him and gave a resigned nod, lip caught between his teeth, agony on his face as his left leg hung useless.

'Go!' she shouted.

He pushed off his right leg, hands aiming for the window ledge, and as he did, she grabbed his thighs and shoved up with all her strength. Kept shoving, as he began to pull. Up a bit further, more effort, his right foot on her shoulder now, his body wriggling. Then he was through the window. A grunt of pain as he fell outside.

He'd done it!

Her turn now. Straddling the A-frame, she stretched up

onto her tiptoes, reaching for the window ledge, and with a loud crack, the sandwich board split in half, throwing her backwards. Arms flailing, she fell to the floor, her full weight landing on her left arm, smashing it against the slates. The pain was instant, searing from where her watch encircled her wrist, shooting up into her elbow.

She twisted onto her back, dazed. From somewhere came the sound of frantic beeping. Her smartwatch. Another one destroyed. Not that she would need to replace it this time. Because as she lay there fighting nausea and watching the smoke gather around her, she knew there was no way she was going to be able to escape the fire with a broken arm.

'It's a text from Delilah's smartwatch!' Samson shouted, staring at his phone. At the message that could change everything. 'An automatic alert. Telling me she's been in an accident.'

'Does it show where she is?' demanded Will.

'There's a hyperlink—'

'There's no data signal here,' said Ana.

'We need coordinates,' insisted Frank.

'It's got coordinates,' said Samson, 'but they're useless without—'

'A map!' Sergeant Clayton slapped an Ordnance Survey map down on the bonnet of his 4x4 and began unfolding it. 'Aways handy to have one in the glovebox. Now where's this lass at?'

It was a combination of coordinates and landscape that gave the answer. As Samson traced his finger across the gridlines, he recognised a feature that echoed Grigore's statement.

'Here!' he exclaimed, pointing at the spot. 'Quarry House, Gunnerstang Brow!'

Even as he said it, his burgeoning hope turned to dread. They were the other side of Bruncliffe from Rainsrigg Quarry. A good fifteen minutes in the current conditions with the flooding on the roads.

'The WhatsApp group,' Ana was saying, wielding a mobile that looked like it was out of the Ark. 'I'll text Ida and have her send out an alert for anyone in the area to head up straight away.'

'Let's go,' said Frank, jogging towards his car. 'Will, Samson, with me. Sergeant Clayton, I'll leave you to coordinate the emergency services here.'

They were in the car and tearing along the track, almost at the main road when they heard the sirens. Two ambulances and a couple of fire engines came into view, turning down the track towards them. As they passed the bright red trucks, Samson felt the earlier dread turn to outright panic. Fire. So far Rick had covered his tracks with fire. What if he'd done the same at Quarry House?

Constable Danny Bradley was slouched on the window seat in Samson's office when the text arrived.

Having stayed in the marketplace long enough to make sure the firefighters had everything under control at Taylor's, and that the growing crowd wasn't in harm's way, he'd been eager to be back where he had some chance of finding out what was going on. Whether Delilah was safe or not. Whether Stuart Lister had been located.

So he'd sent Neil Taylor home to start compiling a list of Taylor's rental properties – although he wasn't banking on that yielding anything of use, seeing as the information was probably contained in the hardware he himself was now in possession of – and had then made his way to the office building on Back Street, Taylor's PC unit under one arm, rescued plant in his least burned hand. With his singed uniform and scorched eyebrows completing the ensemble, his arrival had caused a bit of commotion and, Danny sensed, a welcome distraction for folk every bit as exasperated as himself at being so far removed from the real action. Ida had set to bandaging his hands, Nathan had found him a spare jumper of Samson's to put on in place of his scorched jacket, while Joseph took charge of the plant, giving it a temporary home in a pint glass.

But then they'd all gone back to kicking their heels. Waiting. And drinking tea.

Until the text came in.

'Delilah is at Quarry House,' Ida Capstick exclaimed, springing to her feet and knocking her mug to the floor. She didn't even blink at the mess, too busy notifying the WhatsApp group. 'We need to get up there!'

'Let's go!' On a wave of adrenaline, Danny shot up, heading for the door, reaching for his keys— 'Damn!' He came to a halt by the desk, everyone on their feet, ready to follow him.

'What's the matter?' asked Nina.

'No car. DCI Thistlethwaite has my 4x4.' Danny stood there. Feeling frustrated. Feeling useless. Wondering how long it would take him to run up to the quarry.

Arty let out a groan and slumped back in his chair. Nathan let out a few curses not normally considered appropriate for a lad of his age. Ida, meanwhile, was running up the stairs at a speed never normally associated with a Capstick. When she came back down into the office moments later, she was holding a set of keys.

'The Mini,' she announced. 'Look sharp!'

'You can drive?' blurted out Danny.

The look Ida gave him was as blistering as the fire at Taylor's. 'I grew up on a farm, lad. There's not much with an engine I can't handle.'

'There's too many of us,' said Joseph as everyone began to move again. 'Arty and I will stay here.'

Arty went to protest but Joseph laid a hand on his arm. 'They're younger and fitter, my friend – your heart, my broken wrist. We should sit this one out.'

Ida nodded. 'It's us four then,' she said to the teenagers and Danny, 'come on.'

She hustled them out of the office, into the hallway, and saw Tolpuddle, already sitting at the front door. 'Happen that'll make it five,' she said with a half-smile, herding the dog out of the door.

With the rain having finally petered out, Barry Dawson was standing in his shop doorway, inspecting the skies above, trying to decide if it was worth putting his stock back out on the wet pavement. He still hadn't come to a decision when he received the WhatsApp message giving Delilah's location, nor when the door to the Dales Detective Agency flew open and Ida Capstick appeared, tailed by Nathan Metcalfe, Nina Hussain and Tolpuddle.

She saw him. Nodded, as if his presence was pre-ordained. Then spoke.

'Grab tha mop, Barry.'

Barry needed no further encouragement. Snatching a Vileda 1-2 from the display, along with a coil of washing line, he locked the shop and hurried across to the Mini, where Ida was already revving the engine.

Arty was sulking. Slumped in a chair behind Samson's desk as the Mini pulled away.

'Sit this one out!' he muttered. 'I can't believe you actually said that. There'll be time enough for sitting things out when you're in a box six feet under.'

Joseph didn't rise to the bait, although he had to admit he was feeling a bit frustrated himself. Sick with worry about whatever was going on up at the quarry, and unable to do anything.

'And as for being fit – you seem to forget I worked nightclub doors as a bouncer on the side. I still have a tidy right hook.'

Joseph sighed. It was going to be a long wait. Although . . .

He reached into his trouser pocket and pulled out his keys. Selected the one that hadn't been used in over fifteen years, and got to his feet.

'Come on, then,' he said, walking out of the office and towards the rear porch. 'Let's see how fit you are. But if that heart of yours finally gives up the ghost, don't go blaming me.'

Arty was hurrying after him. 'What . . . where . . . how . . . ?'

Joseph opened the back door, pointed at the tarpaulin-covered shape at the end of the yard and held up a key. A key he'd kept all these years, a memory of happy days with his wife.

'The Royal Enfield?' Arty's face split into a smile and he slapped his friend on the back. 'You genius!'

'Don't go praising me until we see if I've remembered how to ride it,' muttered Joseph. 'And whether having an arm in a cast makes any difference!'

Minutes later, they were pulling out of the ginnel and heading across the marketplace in the wake of the orange Mini.

She could hear the snap and crackle of the fire now. It must have broken through the door above the cellar stairs, the heat intensifying. Panic forced her to her feet. Forced her to try jumping, her right arm stretched high to catch the window ledge but catching nothing but stone wall, while her left arm jarred against her side in a kaleidoscope of pain.

She tried again and again until she thought she would be sick.

'Stuart!' she finally called out, the smoke catching her throat, making her cough and splutter.

There'd been no word from him since he disappeared out of the window. Had he gone to get help? In the condition he was in, she doubted it.

'Stuart!' she called again.

She tilted her head towards the window, straining to hear. But heard nothing beyond the roar of the approaching flames.

30

They crested Gunnerstang Brow at considerable speed, Ida proving true to her word and more than adept behind the wheel. To their right, the quarry loomed in the distance; to their left, at the Harrisons' old place, smoke could be seen spiralling into the sky.

'The cafe's on fire!' exclaimed Nathan as they shot past the entranceway, heading for the track to Quarry House.

Ida flicked a glance to her left. And frowned. 'That GPS technology, like on Delilah's watch,' she said, addressing the teenagers in the back. 'How reliable is it?'

'Fairly good,' said Nathan. 'Although there can be some deviance—'

He was cut off by sudden braking, Ida whipping the Mini around in a tight circle, throwing her passengers about in the process.

'Bloody hell, Ida!' exclaimed Danny, as they hurtled back towards the driveway leading to the former cafe, passing a startled Joseph and Arty on the Royal Enfield. 'What's going on? We're supposed to be going the other way!'

'Fire!' she muttered. 'Happen that's been Rick Procter's calling card today.'

The Mini took the next corner in a screech of tyres, bursting onto the drive and racing towards the burning building. Laid out in a horseshoe around a yard, the main farmhouse was a wall of flames, the roof partially collapsed, the rest about to go any minute. Either side of it, the outbuildings were also on fire. And in the yard, staring at them in shock, were two men.

The men started running.

Danny was first out of the car, haring after one of them, Barry on his heels, mop at the ready. The other man darted past the Mini and down the drive, where Joseph and Arty were skidding to a stop. As Nina would attest later, for a man his age, Arty was nimble. Leaping off the bike, he clocked the man in the face with his helmet.

Meanwhile, Nathan had scrambled out of the rear of the car, Nina with him, and was running towards the burning building.

Ida ran after him, catching his arm, pulling him back. 'No, lad, no! Tha'll be killed for sure!'

'Delilah!' Nathan shouted, pointing at the flames, sparks spitting into the sky, ash falling around them. 'She's in there.'

Ida nodded, feeling her heart breaking. 'And there's nowt we can do about it. The fire brigade will be here as soon as they can.'

But when she turned to Nina, the lass was shaking her head as she looked at her mobile, tears on her face. 'There's no fire crews left in Bruncliffe. They've both gone down to Thorpdale.'

Ida looked back at the inferno. With the town volunteers occupied with the blaze at Twistleton Farm, it would mean waiting for a support fire engine. From Skipton. Forty minutes away.

'We need to do something!' said Nathan, the lad beside himself.

It was only then that Ida noticed one of their group was missing.

Tolpuddle followed his nose. At first he smelled only carbon and something else, something sweet. Staying away from the heat, he kept his concentration on the ground and the air, sniffing as he went. Out round the side of the buildings, round the back. For he had caught the scent of her. Faint but sure. Enough to lift some of the anxiety which had swamped him since his confrontation with the man. Enough to make the ache in his heart that had been there all morning feel less painful.

Oblivious to the burning grass and the hot bits of debris beneath his paws, he carried on, along the outside of the buildings. He got his reward. A shape lying on the ground. A man.

He ran over, nudged the man. Whimpered. Because the fire was hot this close to the house. But the man didn't move. So he caught hold of him and dragged him, back towards safety. And as he did so, he caught her scent again. Stronger this time, on the man's clothes. She was nearby! He lifted his head and he barked. Loudly. Several times.

The flames had reached the corridor, visibility reduced to almost nothing. And even with the open window, the air was quickly turning deadly, each inhalation more poisonous than the last. She didn't have long left.

Then she heard him. A bark, outside.

'Tolpuddle!' she shouted, her voice croaking, the smoke almost too much to bear now. She lifted her head and shouted again. 'Tolpuddle!'

Above her, through the opening, a grey head appeared. When he barked, it was the sweetest sound she'd ever heard. But then he started wriggling through the window.

He was about to jump down. Determined to rescue her when in fact he would be joining her in what would be certain death.

'Stay!' she cried, forcing her voice out of her scorched throat. 'Stay there, Tolpuddle.'

The Weimaraner looked anxious. Hearing her command. Not wanting to obey. He barked down at her. Made to jump again. Her brave dog, knowing no fear when it came to her safety.

She tried to shout once more but her voice cracked into nothing, and he bunched himself together, preparing to leap to her defence. Then two strong hands appeared, grabbing his collar.

'Tha daft bugger!' The dog was dragged, barking and protesting, away from the window. He was replaced by a face far more angular, but no less precious to see. 'Here, lass. Get this round tha waist and hurry up about it or tha's likely to be barbecued.'

A length of yellow washing line came dangling down towards her, neatly tied in a loop. Slipping it over her head, Delilah was hauled up the wall to the window, where several arms reached down to grab her and pull her out to safety.

'You found us,' she murmured as they led her to a patch

of grass and sat her down, the sweet sound of sirens in the distance.

'No lass, this one found thee.' Ida was patting Tolpuddle, who had his head resting against Delilah's shoulder.

'He's Bruncliffe's answer to GPS,' said Nathan, a relieved grin on his smoke-streaked face. 'Led us straight to you.'

'And not a moment too soon,' said Danny Bradley gravely as, with a crash that sent sparks and black smoke spiralling out of the window Delilah had just escaped from, the rest of the farmhouse roof collapsed into the building.

Frank barely had the car stopped before Samson was out of it and running, not towards Quarry House, but towards the still-burning structure that had been the Harrisons' farm.

She was safe. So was Stuart Lister. Nina had updated the WhatsApp group to let them know where they were and what had happened. But until Delilah was in his arms, he wouldn't believe it.

He ran past his Royal Enfield, past the orange Mini, a swarm of people beyond it, Ida, his father, Arty, Danny, some paramedics, a deathly still form on a stretcher being lifted into one of the ambulances . . . He went to run towards it when he heard her.

'Samson!' It was a croak not a shout.

He turned. She was there, sitting on a bed inside the other ambulance, a paramedic with her. A blanket around her shoulders, face streaked with soot, her hair singed, she was holding one arm with the other, blisters visible on her hands. Tolpuddle was sitting beside her, his head on her lap, going nowhere.

Samson didn't know how he made his legs move. Because in the relief of that moment, his limbs had turned to liquid, threatening to give way. But somehow he staggered over to her. Collapsed beside her on the bed, his eyes on hers, drinking her in.

'Jesus!' he muttered, wanting to take her in his arms and hold her tight but afraid of hurting her. 'You've got to stop doing this to me.'

'Tell me about it,' retorted the paramedic, Samson recognising him as he turned around. The same paramedic who'd taken them to hospital after the shooting at the quarry. 'For the second time in less than a month, I'm going to have to explain to A and E why I'm turning up with a bloody dog in the back!'

31

Early Saturday morning, with the sun shining in a peaceful sky, the intensive care unit of Leeds General was bathed in light. And filled with the sound of bleating.

Carol Kirby, surfacing from the deepest of sleeps, came to with a smile on her lips.

'That's it, lass! Come back to us!'

She knew the voice. Pushed harder to break through the final vestiges of darkness, and blinked her eyes open. Groggy. Disorientated. A nurse to her left, all brisk business. To her right, Clive. Holding his mobile out, a video playing across it.

'It did it!' he said. 'It worked!'

The nurse laughed. 'Seems so.'

Carol blinked again. Eyes struggling to focus on the screen. Recognising the scenery, the glorious pink of a magnificent dawn. And those sheep. Texels. Equally pink.

Mire End Farm.

'He's been playing that non-stop for the last few days,' said the nurse. 'That place must be pretty special to have brought you round.'

Carol raised her focus to Clive.

'We've missed you, lass!' he said, tears in his eyes. 'Thought as you'd gone and left us for a while there.'

She lifted a finger, what felt like a huge effort, and touched the screen. 'Home,' she mumbled.

'Aye, home.' Clive Knowles took her hand in his. 'We'll be back there soon enough. And then we're getting married. No more waiting around. Life's too short!'

He broke off on the final words, choking back emotion as Carol squeezed his hand.

Wanting to give them a bit of privacy, the nurse slipped from the room, heading for the desk at the end of the unit where her colleagues were gathered, where she told, for the first of many times, the tale of what would become known as the Pink Sheep Miracle.

Across in Bruncliffe, as morning pushed towards noon beneath what was an equally glorious summer's sky, a bright orange Mini pulled up opposite the pub on Back Street. From the doorway of the Fleece, Seth Thistlethwaite and Troy Murgatroyd watched Samson get out of the car and hurry round to the passenger's side. He opened the door and Delilah eased herself out, left arm in a cast, her hands bandaged, cuts and grazes on her face.

She was a personification of the bruised and battered state of the town.

'Welcome home, lass,' said Seth, raising his pint in her direction.

'Aye, good to see you in one piece,' Troy concurred.

Delilah managed a smile, her singed hair pulled back to reveal pale features. 'Good to be back,' she said, her voice little more than a croak.

The two men watched the pair walk towards the office building, Troy shaking his head, grim-faced despite the sunshine. 'We almost lost her this time. Bloody hell. Rick Procter.'

The landlord's succinct comment pretty much summed up how the locals were dealing with the revelations which had left Bruncliffe rocking.

'Are you up for a bit of company?' Samson asked as they walked up to the front door. He'd been shocked at how frail she looked when he'd driven over to Airedale Hospital to collect her and wasn't sure that a full-on Bruncliffe welcome was what she needed. 'Or do you want me to go ahead and tell your reception committee to bugger off?'

Delilah shook her head. 'I'm fine,' she rasped.

'You don't sound fine. You sound like Eric Bradley without his oxygen tank.'

She laughed. And then grimaced, holding a hand to her side. And he realised, yet again, how close he'd come to losing her. If it hadn't been for her smartwatch . . . If it hadn't been for Ida . . . If it hadn't been for Tolpuddle . . .

So many ifs. He was painfully aware that one day those ifs would run out. He gently drew her to him and kissed her forehead.

'Brace yourself,' he said, looking down at her with a grin as he opened the front door. 'I'm not sure who's the most excited about you being back.'

The scrabble of paws across the floor and the sharp barks of delight answered his question. Tolpuddle was already in the hallway, beating everyone else despite having all four legs wrapped in luminous green bandages. And despite limping in pain, he was trying to jump up at Delilah, his greeting holding nothing but joy.

'Oh, Tolpuddle,' she murmured, dropping to her knees and gathering him to her with her right arm, her head on his. 'How are his paws?' she asked, voice cracking as she glanced up at Samson.

'Burned but not too badly. Herriot said they should be healed in a week or so. But no running in the meantime.'

'Happen Herriot would be giving thee the same advice,' came a sharp comment from the doorway of Samson's office, Ida Capstick standing there, a crowd of faces looking over her shoulder, the vet amongst them. Then her lips relaxed into what resembled a smile. 'Good to have thee home, lass. Not least,' she added, tipping her head at Samson and Tolpuddle, 'because those two have been moping round the place the last couple of days like tups after castration!'

A shout of laughter came from the assembled group and then Will was calling out.

'Come on in, sis, you're missing the party. There's cake!'

Delilah got to her feet, Tolpuddle shadowing her, his warm flank touching her leg as she entered the office.

It certainly resembled a party. Will was standing alongside Frank Thistlethwaite and Danny Bradley, the constable in his uniform, hands bandaged, while on the other side of the room, Joseph O'Brien was with Arty, Eric, Edith and Clarissa, Herriot perched on the window ledge next to them. Nina and Nathan were busy laying out plates of food and mugs of tea on Samson's desk, which had been turned so that it spanned the room from front to back, a table added onto the end of it. And supervising it all was Lucy Metcalfe.

It was a feast more than worthy of the Peaks Patisserie

Julia Chapman

owner. Spread out across the vibrant tablecloth were small quiches, homemade sausage rolls, bite-sized tarts, mini-pizzas, a variety of sandwiches and, in the centre, a cake decorated with a Weimaraner, a smartwatch and a washing line. Samson's stomach let out a loud rumble, while Delilah glanced over at her sister-in-law and mouthed the word 'Thanks'.

'Right, folks,' said Ida, nodding at the table. 'Grab a seat. This spread won't eat itself.'

Over the scrape of chairs and the resumption of chatter, Will Metcalfe spoke up.

'Have you seen today's headlines?' he asked, holding out his mobile as Samson and Delilah sat down, Tolpuddle lying on the lino between them, two of his paws on Delilah's feet.

Samson shook his head. He'd spent the first part of the morning with Frank Thistlethwaite and Sergeant Clayton, going over what had happened on Thursday yet again, explaining how it had all come to a cataclysmic conclusion. He doubted it would be the last time he saw them in an official capacity either, given how much had been uncovered in the space of the last week.

'Look,' Will was saying, pointing at a photo on the *Craven Herald* twitter account. 'Danny's made the news!'

Emblazoned across the screen was a dramatic image of Danny, in uniform, face streaked with soot, stepping out of Taylor's, flames visible in the background. In his arms were the PC unit which had broken open the Procter case and . . .

'Is that a plant?' asked Samson.

The room burst into laughter while Danny just grinned bashfully, his grandfather, Eric, looking on in admiration.

'It's a peace lily,' said Ida, taking pity on the lad. 'Happen as we could do with a bit of peace in these parts.'

Samson couldn't have agreed more.

'Any news?' Nathan asked. 'Have they got enough to charge him?'

He didn't need to mention the name. They all knew who he meant.

'Enough and more,' said Frank Thistlethwaite from the end of the table. 'Drugs manufacturing, money laundering, human trafficking, kidnap . . . murder.'

'*Murder?*' Delilah turned to Samson, the lingering rasp in her voice making the word sound even more shocking, while the others looked stunned. 'Pete?'

He nodded. 'It seems so. That mobile phone Carol took from Pete's caravan was damning enough, not to mention the cash Bernard had ferreted away in his wardrobe. It looks like Pete was blackmailing Rick and Bernard, so Rick got rid of him.'

'How will they prove it?' asked Will, around a mouthful of quiche. 'Cos I don't see Rick making a confession any time soon.'

'We think the ketamine in Pete's lurchers might hold the key,' explained Frank. 'Sergeant Clayton had the lab run a comparison yesterday of the samples Herriot took at the time and the batch found in Nathan's locker. It's a match. And what with Delilah finding those fishing flies of Ryan's in Rick's kitchen, Rick has a lot of explaining to do.'

'I can add a bit to that,' said Danny. 'I just heard from the sarge before I arrived that Carol Kirby came round earlier this morning. Apparently Clive played some video or other of his sheep to her and that did the trick!'

Murmurs of relief swept the room, Ida dabbing discretely at her eyes with a tissue, while Will laughed.

'Them damn pink Texels,' he said. 'They'd shock anyone out of a coma.'

'Aye,' said Danny. 'But the interesting thing is that Carol was able to identify the person she saw running away from the burning caravan. It was Rick Procter.'

'Trying to get rid of evidence? Like a mobile phone containing photos?' mused Frank.

'Looks bad however you view it.'

'Poor Pete,' murmured Delilah.

'Yes, poor Pete. Especially as I don't believe he was even going to go through with the blackmail,' said Samson. 'Remember he left me a message the night before he died? He said he wanted to report a crime.'

'You think he was going to spill the beans?' asked Frank.

Samson nodded. A weight of guilt he'd never shift lying heavy across his shoulders at the thought of the poacher's demise.

'To Pete!' said Nathan, raising his mug, the others doing likewise.

'Let's hope they can make Rick pay for this,' muttered Will darkly. Like many in the town, he'd been struggling to accept that a man he'd known all his life and had considered to be a friend as well as an integral part of the community, could have been so corrupt. So ruthless. He was taking the betrayal personally.

'Even if they can't pin Pete's death on him, Rick Procter

is going down for a very long time,' said Danny. 'The stuff on that PC unit is dynamite.'

'Is that why you made the front page of the paper?' quipped Nathan.

They laughed. But Samson knew the constable was right. By rescuing Taylor's hardware from the fire, Danny had given Frank and his team a direct link to the bank accounts being used by a major organised crime network with connections across Europe. Combined with the backup Delilah had made of Taylor's original IT system, it was looking like the police would have sufficient information to bring the network down.

'Is it true Rick tried to steal a million pounds?' asked Nina, a look on her face that told Samson she was hooked on being an investigator, even after just a week in the role.

'Not tried,' said Danny. 'He actually did it. Unfortunately for him, though, we now have the details of the account he paid it into.'

'The fake rental fees,' murmured Delilah, eyebrows raised. 'He stole the money he was supposed to be laundering!'

Will whistled. 'Christ! Whoever he took it from isn't going to be happy.'

'Niko and Andrey Karamanski,' muttered Frank, shaking his head. He looked at Samson. 'Those brothers set my radar twitching as soon as I clapped eyes on them up at that Bruncliffe Manor shoot last month. The fact they were the guests of Procter and Bernard Taylor . . .' He gave an apologetic shrug. 'I should have spotted that connection when we ID'd my dead canal man and that stabbing victim as Bulgarian. If I'd done my job right, we'd have been onto

Procter sooner and things might not have escalated so badly.'

'You weren't the only one to make that mistake,' said Samson. 'I allowed my dislike of Neil Taylor to blind me to the bloody obvious.'

'Don't be so hard on yourselves,' said Will, slapping the detective on the back before looking over at Samson. 'Most of us round this table have been living with that bastard Procter all our lives and never suspected a thing. Thought the sun shone out of his backside, we did.' He shook his head in disgust. 'There's nowt to be ashamed of when it comes to what you did.'

'Hear! Hear!' said Edith Hird, not even blinking at the profanity.

'These Karamanski brothers,' asked Arty, a glint in his eye. 'Are they the forgiving sort?'

Frank Thistlethwaite let out a snort. 'Hardly.'

'Which means that instead of sunning himself in the Caribbean, Rick will spend his days watching his back,' said Danny.

It was the one consolation Samson had when he thought about the trail of destruction Rick Procter had visited on the town. While some were saying the property developer should have been left to drown in Twistleton bog, Samson knew that what was coming for Rick in prison would be far worse.

'Is that where he was heading?' asked Will. 'The Caribbean?'

Frank nodded. 'We think so. The bank account where he funnelled the money is in the British Virgin Islands and he was all set up for a quick getaway. He had ten thousand pounds in cash on him when we took him in. Which brings me to a bit of an oddity we've hit in the case.' He turned to Joseph and Arty. 'When Rick turned up at your place, did he actually go inside the building?'

'No,' said Joseph. 'The minute Tolpuddle started kicking off at the Range Rover, Rick came hurrying back and drove off.'

'That's what I thought you'd said,' continued the detective. 'So Danny and I went over to Fellside Court yesterday, because we were curious as to why Rick would have risked going somewhere so public with Delilah in his car. We discovered a safe in the manager's office, hidden behind a bookcase – there was a false passport inside. We think that's what he was going to pick up when Tolpuddle foiled his plans.'

'That and some more money, probably,' said Samson, nodding, a memory from a cold December day coming back to him and finally making sense. 'I saw Rick in that office once when Delilah and I were on a case. I was outside, looking through the window, and he didn't know I was there. He had bundles of banknotes on him. I reckon that safe you found must have been where he was storing his illicit funds.'

The comment drew a frown from Frank Thistlethwaite. 'Funny you should say that, O'Brien, because that's the oddity I mentioned. We found a ledger in the safe listing payments made to Procter for his part in the money laundering, which suggested there should have been upwards of two hundred thousand in there. But there wasn't a trace of it.'

'Could Rick have collected it earlier?'

Frank shook his head. 'If he did, then he's spent it, because we didn't see hide nor hair of it in all the searches we've carried out at his office and his home.'

'So what are you suggesting?' asked Will. 'That someone else has taken the cash?'

'Only if they knew how to crack a safe,' said Danny. 'It was locked when we got there.'

'A locked-safe mystery,' said Clarissa. 'How interesting—'

'More tea?' Edith was standing, looking around the group, teapot in hand.

Before anyone could respond, a loud knock came from the hallway and the front door opened, accompanied by the yap of a small dog. Tolpuddle lifted his head and looked towards the sound with an audible sigh.

'Sorry to interrupt.' Mrs Lister appeared in the doorway, her Westie making a beeline for Tolpuddle. 'Don't get up,' she said, as Samson went to give her his chair. 'I'm not staying. I'm just on my way to Airedale to see Stuart and wanted to thank you both in person.'

'How is he?' asked Samson. 'I called in to see him yesterday when I was over there but he was asleep.'

'On the mend. A broken leg. Again. Same one as last November. And he needs feeding up.' She gave a sombre shake of her head. 'He's been through a lot.'

It was an understatement typical of the Dales. Coming across the lettings agent snooping around the Henside Road property, Rick had rightly assumed the worst: that his network of bogus rentals and cannabis farms had been rumbled. Stuart had tried to make a run for it but had been no match for two guards with guns and a Rottweiler.

Taken to the Harrisons' old place and thrown in the cellar, his leg breaking in the process, he'd been left under no illusion about the dire straits he was in.

Samson couldn't imagine the torment of the subsequent three weeks. The pain and the terror. Alleviated only by a disembodied voice, floating down through the airbrick and carrying a promise made in Romanian, and two solitary words of English.

I help!

Grigore's intervention had been all Stuart had to cling to in his darkest hours, until that promised help finally did arrive.

'But my lad's alive and that's all that matters,' concluded Mrs Lister. And she gave a knowing smile. 'That lovely lass from the office has been in to see him and he seems right keen to get back to work.'

'You must take him some cake!' said Lucy, knife in hand, already cutting off a large corner before any protest could be made.

'Might as well take some of the rest too,' said Ida, transferring some sausage rolls, tarts and sandwiches into one of the Tupperware boxes they'd come in. 'Tha said he needs feeding!'

'Thank you,' said Mrs Lister, her head shaking in wonderment as she took the proffered food. 'That's right nice of you. He'll appreciate that.' Then she bent down and kissed Samson on the cheek before turning to take Delilah's bandaged right hand gently in hers.

'You saved him,' she said, her voice thick with emotion. 'He told me you stayed in that room despite the fire, putting yourself in peril, making sure he got out first when no one would have blamed you for leaving him there. For that, I will always be in your debt.'

Delilah was blushing, trying to shake off the gratitude, but Mrs Lister wasn't having it. She leaned forward and kissed her on the cheek as well.

'Two kisses,' she said, wiping a hand across her face where tears were visible. 'Them's the two kisses which were missing from his postcard. Thank you for believing me.'

With a final nod at Delilah, she turned and left the room, the Westie trotting behind her. The front door opened and closed in her wake.

'Don't know about anyone else,' said Will, a frog in his throat as he looked at his sister, 'but I'm right proud of you, lass.'

His statement was met with a rumble of support from the others, but Delilah shook her head.

'It's Grigore who deserves the praise,' she murmured. 'And Lady Luck. If Grigore had left a day earlier, he'd never have stumbled across Stuart and given him the hope to keep going.'

'It's certainly been a tangle of coincidences,' agreed Samson. 'Not just Grigore seeing Stuart, but the chaos at the quarry. I'm convinced that if it hadn't been for DI Warren trying to kill us up there last month, Rick would have got rid of Stuart earlier. But with such a heavy police presence across the road, he didn't dare.'

'That's pretty much what we've concluded too,' said Frank gravely. 'The fact he established the lie of Stuart's disappearance so thoroughly – texting the lad's mother, taking clothes from his flat, sending the fake postcard. It makes us think he had no intention of sparing him.'

It had all been so calculating, Rick even having had the foresight to task Ida with cleaning the flat above the Happy House, removing any evidence of his visit in the process. Samson knew he wasn't the only one around the table filled with self-reproach at having been played for a fool.

Nathan's grin lightened the atmosphere. 'So if you're saying that Aunt Delilah getting shot by Samson's old boss saved Stuart's life, then surely Mrs Lister owes her another kiss.'

'Happen as Samson'll be happy to provide the missing one,' cackled Ida.

Samson glanced at Delilah, who was smiling at him, looking like she was more than willing to take up Ida's suggestion, despite the cuts and the bruises and the bandages. And suddenly all he wanted to do was to whisk her away somewhere quiet, where it was just the two of them—

A warm weight landed on his foot beneath the table.

Just the three of them, he corrected himself, as he stooped down to pat Tolpuddle.

Arty meanwhile was shaking his head, his grin matching Nathan's. 'You can keep your kisses, lad. It's a slice of that cake I'm after!'

'Seconded!' said Will.

Lucy started cutting slices, Nathan handing them out, while Ida was pouring top-ups of tea.

'New teapot, Ida?' Samson asked, all innocence.

Delilah smothered a laugh while Ida glared at him.

'This one's made of rubber,' said Nina with a grin.

'Oh aye, tha can mock,' muttered Ida as she gently placed the teapot back on the table. 'But if it hadn't been for that first teapot needing replacing, I'd never have been here to find out what was going on with them poor lads.'

A silence fell over the table.

Thanks to Manfri, the full horrors of what Grigore and Pavel had been through had become apparent, the Gypsy relaying the efforts of Grigore to find his brother once it became clear Pavel had been tricked by a trafficking gang. Taking the huge gamble of deliberately getting himself taken by the same organisation, Grigore had ended up at Henside Road, working in the cannabis farm, before being moved to the empty cafe in the old Harrison place on Gunnerstang Brow. It was there he finally got his first tip-off about his brother, finding himself working alongside another poor soul who'd been brought over in the same shipment of labourers as Pavel. The man remembered the younger brother's flute. His haunting music.

Knowing nothing but the name of the place where his brother was being kept, Grigore had escaped. But one of the guards had seen him. Tried to stop him. Grigore had stabbed him and run. Afraid to go to the authorities because he was convinced he'd just murdered someone, he'd hid out in Quarry House, trying to get some coherent plan together so he could find his brother and rescue him. Which is when the quarry had become the focus of intense police scrutiny in the wake of the shoot-out instigated by Samson's old boss.

Grigore had fled. Taking food and clothes for the journey. Walking under the cover of darkness, he'd taken his time, stealing food where he could, only occasionally asking for directions. No real sense of his bearings, of where he'd come from. All he knew was his destination: Twistleton Farm. When he'd finally reached it, he studied the place for a few days. And then he'd broken his brother out.

'Every time I think of those boys running across that field with that damn dog chasing them . . .' Ida petered out, shuddering. Lucy laid a hand on her arm.

'What courage,' murmured Arty. 'Not sure I'd have had the stamina to go through all that for someone else.'

'Don't worry, lad. Not sure any of us would bother doing it for you, either,' wheezed Eric Bradley, laughter lifting the mood.

'What happened to the Rottweiler, Herriot?' asked Lucy. 'Did you manage to rehouse it?'

The vet nodded. 'A dog rescue charity has taken him on. They're hopeful that with some rehabilitation, he'll be able to go out to a family at some point in the future.'

'Was it the same dog the lads escaped from?' asked Samson.

'Seems so,' said Danny. 'Bit ironic, really, that the men in charge of the hellish working conditions at the cannabis farm were willing to inflict misery on their workforce, but couldn't bear to put down a dog.'

'Almost as ironic as the fact that the bog which saved the two brothers was the same bog which then brought a halt to Rick,' commented Frank.

'You couldn't make this up,' muttered Will. 'So how about Grigore? Is he going to face charges for the stabbing?'

'Not if I can help it,' came a loud voice from the doorway. Sergeant Clayton was standing there, helmet under his arm. 'There's already a lack of evidence and the victim is hardly likely to come forward and press charges. Besides, the lad's actions have been instrumental in cracking a major human-trafficking ring wide open.' He shook his head, distress blanching his normally ruddy face. 'Eight properties and counting have been raided so far. And suffice to say, if I never witness the likes of it again, I'll be glad. Men, more ghosts than human, coming out of those infernal places, quivering afraid. No passports. No money. Barely the clothes on their backs . . . I'm ashamed it took us so long to figure out what was going on in our own community.' He fell silent. Then he grunted. 'So no, there won't be charges laid against Grigore. I'm thinking it'll just be something that gets lost in translation.'

There was a murmur of approval around the room, Frank Thistlethwaite nodding in agreement.

'Bloody Procter and Taylor,' muttered Arty. 'Don't know how they slept at night.'

'Don't think I'll be sleeping much till this is sorted,' said the sergeant. 'There's some things in this line of work that never leave you. This is going to be one of them.'

'Happen tha's in need of a brew and some sustenance,' said Ida, already pouring tea and handing the sergeant a plate, offering comfort in time-honoured Capstick fashion.

'Here, have my seat.' Herriot had stood up and was moving towards the door. 'I need to get back to the surgery.'

Unlike Mrs Lister, the sergeant complied with alacrity, a plate of food piled high in front of him before the vet was even clear of the table. As he reached the doorway, Herriot glanced back shyly at Delilah.

'Are you still going to be running things as normal?' he asked. 'You know, with you being injured?'

'You mean the Speedy Date night?'

Will let out a hoot of surprise, causing Herriot to blush. 'What the hell is a good-looking lad like you doing going to that?' the farmer demanded. 'Surely women are queuing up for you!'

'I'm just . . . I thought I'd try . . .'

'Leave him alone, Will!' Lucy smiled over at the vet, who turned a deeper crimson. 'It'll make my evening seeing you there, Herriot. At least I'll be able to guarantee an exchange with someone whose idea of interesting conversation isn't boasting about how much they got for the last tup they sold!'

Herriot smiled back at her and, with cheeks still on fire, hurried out.

'That there Romeo's not the only one focused on his work,' said Sergeant Clayton, as he made short work of a couple of tarts. 'I had word from DC Green this morning about that photo of Pete Ferris she sent up. Thought you'd like to know that, thanks to that and what we've uncovered here, her team have been able to tie DI Warren to the same gang Rick was working with.'

'The Karamanski brothers?' Frank asked in disbelief. 'Warren was involved with them?'

'Yep.' Sergeant Clayton gave Samson a sympathetic glance. 'Seems you went from the frying pan straight into the fire by coming back up here after what happened in London. A mobile found on your old boss contains a phone number for a burner found in Procter's Range Rover. DC Green reckons Procter knew everything that was going on in the attempts to frame you and even had prior knowledge that a hitman had been dispatched to take care of you.' He shook his head in amazement. 'And yet you're still here. You must have more lives than Barry Dawson's bloody cat, O'Brien!'

'And be a rotten judge of character,' muttered Samson, feeling the sense of betrayal all over again.

'Present company excepted,' said Arty with a grin.

'Talking of rotten judges of character,' said Edith, 'with Bernard Taylor being involved in all of this, does anyone know what's going to happen to the estate agent's?'

Frank Thistlethwaite grimaced. 'It's a bit early to tell, but so far as the investigation is concerned, it's an integral piece of the puzzle and I know the prosecutors will be looking at the Proceeds of Crime Act to see if they can apply it. But seeing as some of the business was being run legitimately, I think it's unlikely it will all be confiscated.'

'I hope it isn't,' said Delilah. 'Nancy called in to the hospital to see me yesterday and we had a long chat. The poor woman is reeling. She said all the awful revelations about Bernard are like a second bereavement. But she's made of tough stuff. She's even talking about reopening when the police investigation is concluded, but under a different name. Apparently Julie and Stuart are both keen to be on board so I guess it will be a smaller and new-look estate agent's, but still operating.'

'That's good to hear,' said Edith.

'And what about that waste-of-space son of hers?' demanded Ida. 'Is he going to help her?'

Delilah shook her head. 'It seems Neil has lost his desire to relocate up here since someone tried to throttle him.' She stared at her brother, who gave an unrepentant shrug. 'He told Nancy he preferred to live somewhere more civilised, so he's gone back to London.'

'No loss,' muttered Ida, voicing Samson's own thoughts.

'And Twistleton Farm?' The quiet question from Joseph O'Brien was directed at Frank, but his gaze was resting on his son. 'What's going to happen to that?'

'That's more clear-cut, I'm hearing,' said Frank. 'Financed through Procter's criminal activity and used to further his ill-gotten gains, so . . .' He spread his hands wide and shrugged.

'It'll be coming up for auction?' asked Ida.

Frank nodded, sending Samson's heart thundering in his ears, hope and despair crashing over him in equal measure. By contrast, the rest of the group were celebrating the news as if the restoration of Twistleton Farm into O'Brien hands was already a given.

'Hear that, lad?' exclaimed Arty. 'You might be able to get your old home back!'

'Just in time, seeing as a little birdy told me he's coming back for good,' said Eric with a wide smile.

'Would you farm it?' Nathan asked excitedly. 'Because we could help if you did, couldn't we, Uncle Will?'

'We can have a housewarming party!' declared Clarissa.

Even Ida was looking happy at the news and what it might mean. And Delilah . . . ?

She was holding her mug to her lips, focus on her drink. A stillness to her that Samson didn't think was just fatigue. Meanwhile, across the table, Will Metcalfe was watching on with the brooding countenance Samson had come to know. And dread.

'Let's not all get ahead of ourselves,' said Joseph, calming the animated chatter. 'None of this is a done deal, and besides, Samson might have other plans.'

'Other plans?' Arty was shaking his head, grinning at

Delilah. 'What on earth could tempt him away when he has everything a man could wish for right here? Eh, lad?'

Samson nodded, tried to smile. Tried not to let the pressure overwhelm him. For how could he explain his situation in the midst of such warm acceptance from a community which hadn't always taken him to its heart? How could he explain that not only did he lack the finances to be able to buy the farm back, but that quite possibly he wasn't going to be around to live in it even if he could.

Because there was a letter in his pocket which had arrived that morning, making official all he'd been told when he was down in London. He'd been completely exonerated and invited to resume his old post with the Met, and to recommence his secondment as an undercover officer with the National Crime Agency.

How did he explain to the people around the table that if it wasn't for the woman sitting next to him, he would be off like a shot.

32

Delilah could sense Samson's torment. The idea that his childhood home might be coming back on the market, aligned with the pain of knowing it would be out of his reach. Not to mention the lure of his life back in London that, according to the email from DC Green, was beckoning . . .

Would he go?

Awash with fatigue, she found herself wishing for time alone with him. So they could sort this out once and for all.

'Right,' said Sergeant Clayton, heaving himself to his feet as though he'd read her mind. 'I hate to break up the festivities, but I'm needed back at the station. You too, Constable Bradley.'

'Do you want to take some cake with you?' asked Lucy.

The sergeant's face lit up. 'That would be just the ticket for helping me wade through the mound of paperwork these two have landed on my desk.' He gestured at Samson and Delilah, his gaze resting on her bruised face, the bandages, the cast. 'And as for you, lass,' he continued, 'next time you decide to go and have a chat with a man caught up in a cut-throat criminal organisation, at least leave a bloody note saying where you've gone.'

Delilah managed a grin. 'Next time?'

'Aye, next time. Because while some might say I'm a slow learner, after seven months of mayhem where you pair are concerned, I'm not witless enough to think it can't happen again!'

Knowing the likelihood of Samson being involved in any future investigations in the town was hanging in the balance, Delilah was saved from having to think up a reply by Frank standing too.

'I'll come with you, Sergeant,' he said. 'I've got a call with Europol this afternoon. They're keen to hear everything we have on the Karamanski brothers. Something tells me it could be an interesting conversation.'

But Arty was holding a hand out, forestalling the detective's departure. 'Before you go,' he said. 'This Proceeds of Crime Act you mentioned. Am I right in thinking it means Procter will be stripped of *everything* he owns?'

'Everything that can be shown to have been purchased or acquired as a direct result of his criminal dealings,' Frank clarified. 'Why? Are you thinking of something specific?'

'Fellside Court?' Arty's question brought a shocked silence to the room.

Frank paused, clearly debating what to say. He opted for honesty. 'There's a lot of work needs to be done by the forensic accounting team before I can answer that in detail, but if Fellside Court was funded through illicit means, then yes, it will be confiscated by the state and put up for sale.'

A gasp of dismay went up from the pensioners.

'Does that mean we'll be kicked out?'

'What'll happen to our homes?'

'I knew it! The bast—'

'Time we all left,' Edith Hird announced loudly, drowning out Arty's expletive. We can discuss the ramifications of this back at home. Delilah is just out of hospital and would no doubt appreciate a bit of peace and quiet.'

'Aye,' agreed Ida, patting Delilah's hand. 'Tha's looking right peaky lass. And I need to get my shopping done. Them Romanian lads have eaten me out of house and home. Reckon it would've cost a lot less if George had have had worms!'

The good-natured grumble sparked laughter, and Delilah felt a surge of affection for the two women and their Bruncliffe diplomacy as everyone began clearing up. Within minutes it was all done, Ida heading for the door bearing a tray of mugs and plates, Nina, Nathan and Lucy carrying similar loads behind her.

'Are you taking the Mini shopping, Ida? Planning on doing a few handbrake turns on the way?' Nathan asked, winking at Nina as they crossed the hall. She grinned back at him.

Ida gave a loud tut. 'The Mini is only on loan. And handbrake turns are only for emergencies, young man!'

Delilah watched them head up the stairs, Ida still chuntering, the teenagers openly laughing now, Lucy bringing up the rear with a smile. It was a good team, this Dales Detective Agency crew. An assortment of talent, all brought together by Samson's return. If he were to leave . . .

'Let us know if you hear owt about Fellside Court.' Arty's demand of Frank pulled Delilah's attention back to the room and onto the pensioners, who were also moving towards the door, boxes of surplus food in their hands.

'Yes, please do,' concurred Edith. 'You'll appreciate our concern.'

'Can't believe we might end up homeless!' wheezed Eric, face even greyer than normal.

'I promise I'll keep you in the loop,' said Frank.

'Thanks,' said Arty. 'And as for you, lass,' he gave Delilah a roguish smile as he gestured at Samson, 'we all know it's not the chance of getting the family farm back that's keeping this lad of ours here! We owe you for that!'

'Enough, Arty. Let's go.' Joseph shot Delilah an apologetic glance as he placed a firm hand on his friend's back and propelled him towards the door. But not before the weight of Arty's words had settled heavily on her shoulders.

In a bubble of anxious conversation, the five pensioners left the building, voices audible as they went past the window, Fellside Court and its perilous future troubling them.

'That damn bloody Procter,' muttered Danny Bradley. 'Grandfather and his pals don't deserve to be put in such a position. Worrying if their homes are at risk.'

'I've a feeling we'll be suffering the consequences of Procter's actions for a long time to come, young Danny,' said Sergeant Clayton with a weary sigh. 'Come on, let's get back to the paperwork and make sure the case against him is as watertight as can be.'

Frank made to follow them but paused in the doorway. 'No doubt we'll need to be in touch over the next few days, so if you're on the move at all, O'Brien, can you keep us posted as to your whereabouts?'

It was said casually, but there was an undercurrent beneath the official request, as if he too knew Samson was heading off. Which was possible, given Frank's connections high up in the force.

'Sure. No problem.' Samson's expression was unreadable.

The three policemen departed, leaving only Will. He leaned over, kissed Delilah on the cheek and squeezed her shoulder.

'I probably don't say this enough,' he muttered gruffly, 'but you mean the world to me and, well . . . that fire . . . when I thought . . .' He broke off, shaking his head. Then cleared his throat before resuming. 'Anyway, I know you think I'm always trying to tell you what to do, but do me a favour and take it easy over the next few days, sis, okay?' The look he gave her was of pure affection.

She nodded. Too choked to speak. Then he looked at Samson.

'Have you got a minute, O'Brien?' He gestured towards the door.

Samson followed him mutely out of the building and Delilah finally found herself alone. Apart from Tolpuddle, who'd sat up at Samson's departure and was now looking anxiously at the door.

Yet another one whose world revolved around the man.

She rubbed the Weimaraner's head and let out a long sigh, allowing the silence to settle. She needed to focus. Which meant ignoring her throbbing arm, the pounding in her temples and the weariness which was dragging at her bones. It also meant ignoring her tempestuous nature. Because this wasn't the time for being rash. This was the time for being calm and collected, a state of mind she was finding hard to achieve after the morning's whirl of emotions.

The reaction when Joseph asked about Twistleton Farm had been both heart-warming and terrifying. Folk, not all of whom had been keen to see Bruncliffe's black sheep back in town, now expressing genuine delight at the prospect of Samson staying.

It was a testimony to the man. That infuriating charm he had. The way he could make you feel like you were the most important person in his world. The way he cared. About her. About his father. Ida. Tolpuddle.

It was also an indication of how devastated they would all be if he went away again.

What should she do? Use the power she knew she had and bind him to her, to Bruncliffe, something her whole being was crying out for? Something everyone else would want, too, not least her hound? Or . . . ?

She laughed softly at her predicament. There was no way she could win in this situation. Because she wasn't the only one who loved Samson O'Brien.

From upstairs came the sound of voices, Ida and Lucy, making sure everything was shipshape before they left. It was tempting to just pop up there, take a seat at the kitchen table, lay out her troubles and get the advice of two women she respected. But she couldn't. This one she had to figure out for herself. Even if it was the most important decision of her life.

Because what she did and said when Samson came back in the room would determine their future. And it was something that this time she had to get right. Not just for her, but for all the people in this town who cared about the man who had stolen her heart.

Steeling himself for yet another brotherly warning – or worse – Samson stepped out into the street. For once there wasn't a soul around. No one looking out of the windows in the Fleece. No sign of Barry at the shop next door. It was deserted. No chance of any witnesses.

Will was already on the pavement, turning towards him, customary frown in place. 'I want a word,' he began.

'I'm all ears,' said Samson, discreetly keeping an eye on that famous right fist, which was suspiciously curled.

Then the farmer stepped forward in a sudden movement, right hand raising, a blur of motion, before the flat of his palm landed on Samson's shoulder, heavy enough to make him stagger. 'I need your hidden talents, O'Brien!' he said, cracking into a smile. 'Got the Bruncliffe Show coming up and we're short a judge for the sheep section. I've recommended you for the job.'

Samson found himself agreeing. 'Sure. No problem,' he mumbled, willing to consent to anything if it kept Will Metcalfe in this affable mood.

'Great. Knew you wouldn't mind. I'll be in touch with the details.' He paused, his gaze turning solemn. 'That's presuming you're going to be around, of course.'

Samson went to protest, but Will held up a hand.

'You've got your own life to lead, O'Brien, and, Bruncliffe Show notwithstanding, whatever you decide to do next is none of my business.' He gave a twisted smile, gesturing up at the fells in the distance and the blue sky overhead. 'Personally, I think you'd have to be mad to want to leave all this, but someone was at great pains to point out to me recently that not everyone is content to lead a life lived in one place. And I accept that. But I just want you to know that if you do get the chance to take on Twistleton and decide to run it as a working farm, Nathan was right. We'll help you in any way we can.'

Wrongfooted by such uncharacteristic support, Samson was left speechless.

'That said,' continued Will into the silence, 'I think you've probably gathered by now that if what you choose to do leads to you breaking my sister's heart in the process, it won't be just me you'll have to deal with.'

Samson nodded. Understanding the origins of the threat. And the truth of it. Seven months back in town and he'd seen plenty of evidence of the deep affection Bruncliffe folk had for Delilah.

'Right, then. Like I said, I'll be in touch.' With a final nod, Will turned and walked away.

Lifting his face to the sun, Samson stood a moment longer, aware of the letter in his pocket. Equally aware that once upon a time he'd have been on the Enfield, taking flight as soon as things became difficult. But this was different. This was Delilah.

The woman who'd changed his life. The woman he couldn't imagine living without.

There'd been no need for Will's well-intended warning. Samson was going nowhere. He reached into his pocket and pulled out the letter. Read it through one last time. And then ripped it into pieces.

He was prepared to give up everything for Delilah Metcalfe.

It was about time he told her that.

Tolpuddle let out a soft bark as Samson re-entered the office, the Weimaraner's tail wagging furiously in welcome.

'Well?' Delilah asked dryly, the dark circles under her eyes looking more pronounced, her energy clearly sapped by the welcome home. 'Did my oldest brother give you a lecture about treating me well?'

Samson shook his head, opting for a half-truth. 'He was just coercing me into judging the Bruncliffe Show,' he said, taking a seat next to her and rubbing Tolpuddle's ears.

She let out a relieved laugh. 'Thank goodness. Although that's punishment of a kind!'

He nodded. Slightly awkward now it was just the two of them. Wondering how to begin.

As usual, she beat him to it, gazing straight at him. Her chin jutting out slightly. 'Eric wasn't the only one who heard talk that you're coming home for good.'

'This bloody place,' muttered Samson. 'News travels fast.'

'Good and bad,' she said enigmatically.

'Ida told you?'

Delilah nodded. 'George is super excited, apparently. He said you'd promised him you were coming back to Twistleton.'

Samson sighed. Ran a hand over his face. 'I can explain—'

'You don't have to. In fact, I'm only raising this because I don't want you to come home . . . I mean . . . I do, but I don't . . .'

He smiled, leaning forward to hold her good hand. 'Which is it?'

She didn't laugh. A seriousness to her that made him afraid of what was coming next.

'I saw DC Green's email,' she said quietly, 'when she sent me the photo of Pete. There was a message for you attached . . . I'm sorry. I shouldn't have read it but . . . is it true? Have they offered you your old job back?'

'Yes. But I haven't accepted—'

'You should.'

He sat back. Stunned. 'Are you breaking up with me?'

Now she laughed, no more than a croak from her tired throat. 'You sound like a teenager!' She shook her head. 'No, I'm not. I want nothing more than for you to stay in Bruncliffe for the rest of our lives. But you're not me. Which is why I'm saying you should go to London. Take that position. Let's give it six months and see what happens.'

Dumbfounded, he scrabbled for words. 'What about the detective agency?' he blurted. 'How will you manage when you have your own businesses to run?'

Delilah smiled. 'We appoint Ida on a permanent basis. She's already proven her worth, solving at least two cases. And Nina has said she'd like to help out on Saturdays. If we're selective as to what we take on, we can handle it.'

'But what about us? I'll be back undercover. It won't be a matter of getting regular days off.'

'I gathered that.' She shrugged. 'We'll make it work. I quite fancy the odd trip to London. And I can always wear a disguise, if that helps.' She grinned at him.

He didn't know what to say. For he'd thought his decision was made. He was staying in Bruncliffe. And now this. She was offering him the opportunity to resume the career he loved. To see if he could have the best of both worlds. Except . . .

'I can't do that to Dad. Not again. Not when he might be facing eviction. And everyone else,' he murmured, 'they'll hate me for abandoning you.'

But Delilah was shaking her head. 'Your dad only wants what's best for you, you should know that by now. He'd hate to think you were making decisions about your future based on what may or may not happen to Fellside Court. As for the rest of them,' she shrugged again, devilment in her eyes this time, 'they won't hold it against you for long.'

'Of course they won't. Bruncliffe people don't bear grudges.' His dry tone elicited another raspy laugh. Then she squeezed his hand.

'You know I'm right,' she said softly. 'If we don't give this a go, there'll be nothing but regrets between us and what we'll have will be built on a foundation as solid as . . . as solid as bloody Twistleton Bog.'

'That sounds very wise,' he said carefully.

She snorted. 'Wisdom gained through bitter experience. It's easy to say you love someone. Showing them you do is a lot harder.'

'Is that why you kept stopping me from declaring my undying devotion?' he asked, with a wry smile.

Her nod carried a weight of painful memories. 'Neil used the word like it was common currency. It made it meaningless, especially in light of how he behaved. So I suppose that made me wary. But what I also learned from my time with him is that love doesn't work if you try to change someone into what you think they should be.'

He let that sit for a moment, taking in the significance of it, before replying. 'Is that what this is between us, then, Delilah Metcalfe? Love?'

'It seems that way.' She smiled at him. And he knew she was right. About all of it.

Epilogue

Grigore Vlaicu exited the hospital into a perfect summer's day. The sky was a soft blue, the sun was shining, and the wind was no more than a gentle kiss. But what was even better was that he felt himself again. A complete person. Not someone on the run. Not someone who'd had to use violence in order to survive.

And his brother was making good strides, flirting with the nurses, making the most of being able to take it easy, those ribs of his getting a chance to recover.

The police had said they would be free to go once the investigating officers had finished interviewing them. But Grigore found he was in no rush to head home to Romania. Ida had agreed to let him stay with her and George as long as he wanted, and Grigore was enjoying his time there. He was even getting used to the weird concoction she called tea. Of course, he'd made sure his mother knew they were safe. She'd been crying down the phone in relief and had then insisted on having a conversation with Ida, Manfri serving as translator.

A very practical lady, was his mother's verdict on Grigore's hostess.

Grigore smiled at the thought of how similar they were. Both so forthright. Both so courageous. The gods had been looking down on him and Pavel the day they'd staggered into the barn at Croft Cottage. And he had to conclude that in his short time in Bruncliffe, while he'd experienced the worst of humanity in the evil that was Rick Procter, he'd also seen the very best in the community that bound the people of that special place.

He walked up the path towards the car park, George's old-fashioned mobile in his hand. Manfri had texted him to say that Ida hadn't been able to come and pick him up but had sent someone else to give him a lift back to Croft Cottage instead. He was hoping it wasn't George on the Little Grey tractor, when he heard his name being called.

'Grigore!'

He turned into the sun to see who it was, blinded for a moment. As he blinked away the brightness, he saw her. Blonde hair shimmering like a halo, that beautiful face of hers illuminated with a smile. She waved. Something in her hand.

He hurried towards her, aware of the stupid grin on his lips. Then he saw what she was carrying. A Serbian–Romanian dictionary.

She was speaking. Pointing at a car by the kerb. Gesturing for him to get in. A picnic basket on the back seat.

Grigore had no idea where they were going. Or what his angel was saying. But he would have followed Ana Stoyanovic to the ends of the earth.

Acknowledgements

So, number eight in the Dales Detective series is done and dusted – hard to believe when it feels like only yesterday I sat down to plot the first one! It's been a blast to write and, as always, I have some very special people to thank for helping to get it across the line. I owe each of you some of Kamal Hussain's amazing samosas from Rice N Spice . . .

Getting first credits are Viorel and Julie Fulea. With a storyline too serious to be trivialised, I turned to Viorel and Julie to ensure I had portrayed the world of Grigore and Pavel accurately and sensitively. Thanks to their help, I hope I have brought life to these young men with a semblance of authenticity, but must point out that any mistakes in the depiction of Romania or Romanian culture should be laid entirely at my door.

Readers will know by now that a lot of my research is done while I'm out running or on a bike, picking the brains of whichever person happens to be unfortunate enough to be accompanying me. There were several instances of this during the writing of *Date with Evil*. David Dewhirst has always patiently answered my questions on the flora and fauna of the Dales (quite often deliberately asked at the bottom of a steep climb . . .) and so finally gets recognition, while Catherine Speakman yet again proved happy to share her extensive veterinary knowledge. Thanks, both!

Likewise, on an early-morning run, local lass Jacky Hickson was able to corroborate my use of the word 'baulks' without even breaking stride, and Mark Stickland agreed to a specific running route just so I could get him to balance precariously on a chair in a dilapidated barn, in order to gauge the height needed for a particular plotline. He's a keeper.

Date with Evil

Two further birds were killed with one stone when my sister Claire not only pulled out all the stops yet again to give the manuscript a read-through before submission, but was also a great sounding board on the topic of financial shenanigans and shell companies. An expertise gained from study, not experience, I hasten to add!

As always, the people who work in the wings deserve huge recognition. So a heartfelt thanks to the wonderful Vicki and the editing team at Pan Mac – Charlotte, Fraser and Natalie – who made sure that the entire process was joyful and informative, and finished to a deadline that wasn't even their own. Thanks also to Hannah for approaching publicity with such enthusiasm, and to the rest of the Pan Mac crew who have thrown their energy behind the series.

Across the channel, the lovely Camille and her La Bête Noire colleagues have ensured that the phenomenal success of *Les Détectives du Yorkshire* is far from waning. Meanwhile, Oli and Alexandra at AM Heath have brought even more countries to the Bruncliffe party – for that I can only say *danke*, *grazie*, *bedankt*, *tak*, *tack*!

Finally, a much overdue mention for narrator extraordinaire, Elizabeth Bower, who breathes life into the audio version of the books and brings a sensitivity to her reading that makes Bruncliffe even more of a special place. I particularly want to thank her for highlighting the issues surrounding the terminology we choose to use to discuss suicide, and the negative legacy terms like 'committed' still carry. It's a joy to work with someone so dedicated and compassionate.

So that's it. All done. Oh, apart from Mark – although after eight books, he should know by now he has my undying gratitude!

The complete
Dales Detective series

'A classic whodunit set in the spectacular landscape of the Yorkshire Dales, written with affection for the area and its people'

Cath Staincliffe